FEMMES FATAL

Homicide sleuths have long followed the unofficial motto: *"Cherchez la femme*—find the woman, and you'll solve the crime!"

Now, though, the women in violent crimes are ever more likely to *be* the killers. Rage burns in women, who are now committing record rates of murder. Hardened street hustlers, fresh-faced teens, bored housewives, and grandmotherly types—all have killed, for reasons of greed, lust, and hate . . . or for no sane reason at all.

True Detective's ace crime reporters draw on their exclusive sources inside law enforcement to detail the authentic true stories of women who kill:
—MARY GRIECO, who finally got the attention of her couch potato husband by shooting him in the head!
—VALERIE SWANSON, who teamed with her young stud lover to carry out the hideous hacking death of her returned Gulf War veteran husband!
—MARY LOUISE EASLON, sexually enslaved to her cousin, joined him in slaying the churchgoing lady friend who spurned their offer of a kinky threesome!

And two dozen more!

D1225655

BOOK YOUR PLACE ON OUR WEBSITE AND MAKE THE READING CONNECTION!

We've created a customized website just for our very special readers, where you can get the inside scoop on everything that's going on with Zebra, Pinnacle and Kensington books.

When you come online, you'll have the exciting opportunity to:

- View covers of upcoming books
- Read sample chapters
- Learn about our future publishing schedule (listed by publication month *and author*)
- Find out when your favorite authors will be visiting a city near you
- Search for and order backlist books from our online catalog
- Check out author bios and background information
- Send e-mail to your favorite authors
- Meet the Kensington staff online
- Join us in weekly chats with authors, readers and other guests
- Get writing guidelines
- AND MUCH MORE!

**Visit our website at
http://www.pinnaclebooks.com**

FROM THE FILES OF
TRUE DETECTIVE **MAGAZINE:**

KILLER
BABES

Edited by
David Jacobs

PINNACLE BOOKS
Kensington Publishing Corp.
http://www.pinnaclebooks.com

Some names have been changed to protect the privacy of individuals connected to these stories.

PINNACLE BOOKS are published by

Kensington Publishing Corp.
850 Third Avenue
New York, NY 10022

Pinnacle and the P logo Reg. U.S. Pat. & TM Off.

First Pinnacle Printing: February, 2000
10 9 8 7 6 5 4 3 2 1

Printed in the United States of America

CONTENTS

"SEXY BRIDE'S HONEYMOON OF HORRORS"
  by Don Lasseter   7

"TINA KILLED MOM TO WINE, DINE, AND
GET BACK HER EX-BEAU!"
  by Steven Barry   24

"SURGEON CAUGHT A BULLET BETWEEN HIS EYES!"
  by Charles W. Sasser   42

"KISSING COUSINS KILLED FOR KINKY THRILLS!"
  by Pat Burton   55

"TWISTED TRIO'S RX FOR MURDER: WITCHCRAFT"
  by Richard Devon   69

"BLOODY WELCOME FOR THE RETURNING SAILOR"
  by John Griggs   86

"HE GAVE THEM A LIFT—THEY SLIT HIS THROAT!"
  by Brad Cochran   99

"SPURNED SEDUCTRESS SNUFFED THE
THREE-TIMING ROMEO!"
  by Don Lasseter   112

"RUTHLESS LOVERS' BLOODY VALENTINE TO ELVIE"
  by Jake Crew   126

"DRUGSTORE COWBOYS THROTTLED THE RUNAWAY"
  by Lynne Bliss   139

"PIZZA MAN BECAME A HUMAN JIGSAW PUZZLE!"
  by Duke Foxx   154

"TULSA'S MAN-HATING TEEN LEFT HER DATE
FLOATING IN A POND!"
  by Charles W. Sasser   168

"LETHAL LESBIANS MATRICIDE PLOT"
  by Michael Sasser   181

"WHO HACKED CHARLIE'S HEAD OFF?"
by Brian Kerrigan   193

"PREGNANT CAME THE TEEN SLASHER!"
by Steven Barry   206

"CALIFORNIA'S GREEDY COUPLE SCARED THEIR
VICTIM TO DEATH!"
by Don Lasseter   220

"DIVORCE WAS NOT ENOUGH FOR THE BLONDE
BOMBSHELL!"
by Bill G. Cox   236

"THE SUSAN SMITH CASE: A NATION MOURNS
TWO 'SMALL SACRIFICES' "
by Richard Devon   253

" 'THELMA & LOUISE' RAN DOWN THEIR GAL PAL
OVER & OVER!"
by Charles W. Sasser   279

"DEADLY TEEN LOVERS IN THE MESQUITE
FLATS CAMPGROUND"
by Russell P. Kimball   291

"NEW JERSEY GAL PALS' PREY WAS BAILED
OUT & BUMPED OFF!"
by Barry Bowe   309

"TULSA'S LADY MACBETH COULDN'T
WASH AWAY HER CRIME!"
by Charles W. Sasser   324

"TWO GREEDY BLONDES BLUDGEONED BILLY"
by John Griggs   338

"TEXAS'S MURDER BY 'PROPHET' "
by Turk Ryder   352

"FLORIDA'S NOTORIOUS COUCH POTATO CASE:
WAS IT MURDER OR SUICIDE?"
by Julie Malear   365

"NORTH CAROLINA HOMICIDE PUZZLE: DID A
BLACK WIDOW CLAIM THREE LIVES?"
by Chris Kelly   390

"SEXY BRIDE'S HONEYMOON OF HORRORS"

by Don Lasseter

Still groggy from sleeping late on Sunday morning, December 1, 1991, John Popovich saw the red Corvette pull up in front of his house for the second time.

Earlier that morning, at about 9:15, he had been awakened by a loud knock on his front door. A little cranky about the intrusion, Popovich had pulled aside his bedroom window blind, glanced outside at the sporty red car, grunted drowsily, and pulled the covers back over his head. He didn't know anyone who drove a Corvette with Texas plates. Must be for my roommate, he thought, and he curled up and went back to sleep.

Now, a little after noon, Popovich stood at his front door and watched as the Corvette screeched to a halt at the curb. An exotic young woman, dressed in formfitting pants, black gloves, a loose white blouse, and dark glasses, scrambled from the driver's seat and hurried toward him. Popovich did know her, but he had never seen her drive a red Corvette. She was trembling, crying, and "all shook up."

"I've been raped," she sobbed, and proceeded to tell Popovich the most grisly, horrifying sequence of events he had ever heard, conjuring ghastly mental images more dreadful than his worst nightmares.

Omaima Nelson had previously visited John Popovich several times at his home in Costa Mesa, California. He knew her as "Ishta." During the hot summer months she had been a guest at a few of his outdoor barbecues. Popovich had also occasionally noticed the curvaceous 23-year-old woman enjoying the music and dancing at a local bar. That was before her recent marriage.

"My husband just raped me and cut me," Omaima wept. "Can you help me?" She accepted Popovich's offer of a cigarette, and removed a black glove, along with her dark glasses. Popovich saw that the bare hand was marked with cuts and scrapes, some covered with plastic bandages. Whimpering, Omaima described how her husband had bound her to the bed and forced her to have repeated "kinky" sex.

Popovich would later repeat for police the beginning of Omaima's story: "She said her husband tied her up . . . that he had been drinking, and, I guess, doing drugs. He was having sex, and forcing her to have oral sex. There was physical abuse. . . . He was cutting her."

The wounds, Omaima told Popovich, might require some first aid. She would show him.

While Popovich watched in astonishment, Omaima lifted her blouse, pulled aside the top of her bra, and revealed two parallel scratches, over two inches long, oozing small amounts of blood on her left breast. Then, without any hint of inhibition, Omaima began to unbutton her tight black pants to show him even more.

"She pulled her pants down," Popovich would subsequently recall, "but I could already see the cut on her thigh. It was kind of visible through the vents on the side of her pants, little pieces of cloth like little Xs."

Standing before him in her underwear, Omaima Nelson displayed her various wounds. Her wrists, Popovich thought, "had signs of being tied up." The wounds even extended to a toe that bled when she removed the gauze bandage.

The circumstances and injuries notwithstanding, Omaima wasn't bad to look at. With her olive complexion, shoulder-length brown hair, and voluptuous five-foot-one figure, Omaima frequently caught the attention of men's wandering eyes. Her high cheekbones, wide mouth with sensuously full lips, and smoldering brown eyes gave her an exotic kind of sex appeal.

Born near Cairo, Egypt, on August 19, 1968, Omaima brought to mind the mysteries of Nefertiti or the eroticism of veiled dancers. She had recently been employed as a model.

John Popovich knew some of her background, but not all of it.

As a young child, Omaima Aref lived in a squatter's section of Cairo known as the "city of the dead," so named because of its proximity to cemeteries. She was one of eight children in the family, five of them half siblings. She had been sexually abused and painfully circumcised, without the use of anesthesia, when she was six years old.

Omaima was raped the first time at the age of 10 and again at 18. In Moslem culture, she later confided, her loss of virginity would create serious problems if she married. A future husband's discovery of her violated purity could result in harsh punishment for her and shameful dishonor for her whole family. She feared that it might even result in her being killed.

So when Omaima, at age 18, met a young American, she married him and moved to the United States on November 26, 1986, to escape her hopeless future in her native land.

Omaima's marriage soon floundered, and she struggled with a series of unsatisfactory relationships before being divorced in 1990. Omaima found work in Southern California as a nanny and as a department store model. In the fall of 1991, in the Costa Mesa tavern she frequented to dance and listen to music, she met William Nelson, a brawny 230-pound six-footer who, at age 56, was 33 years her senior.

"It was really nice," Omaima told her friends. "He was a gentleman." Bill would open the door for her and take her out to dinner. "I was in love. I was looking for someone who was kind and nice and wouldn't beat up on me and [would] give me love . . . love I never [found] before."

Nice as he was, William Nelson was also an ex-convict. Before he met Omaima, he had served four years in a federal prison on drug trafficking and tax-evasion charges. Upon his release, he had resettled in Costa Mesa.

Nelson took the beautiful young Egyptian to Phoenix, Arizona, and married her on the first day of November 1991. They spent their honeymoon driving cross-country, through Arkansas and Texas, where Bill acquired the sporty red Corvette. Now, after four short weeks of marriage, something was terribly wrong.

The words that spilled from Omaima Nelson's mouth brought John Popovich back to reality, and nearly sent him into shock. The horrifying litany, as she put her clothes back on, was interrupted by another knock at the door. Popovich whispered to Omaima to remain calm and not to worry. He cautiously opened the door just a crack, peered out, and was relieved to see only a friendly neighbor woman. Before letting her in, he cautioned Omaima.

It would be better not to tell the neighbor what had happened, Popovich whispered. "She goes to church and she's a real peaceful person. I don't want to scare her. Let's just say that you got in a brawl with your old man or some girl." Omaima understood, and when the neighbor entered, Omaima explained that the cuts on her hands were a result of a domestic dispute. The kindly visitor offered to clean, treat, and bandage the wounds.

Mulling over Omaima's request for help, Popovich finally decided what he must do. After telling Omaima that he would assist her, he made an excuse to go to the store first. The visiting neighbor would give him a ride, and Omaima agreed to wait in the house.

Popovich left with his neighbor. From the first public telephone he saw, the distressed young man telephoned the Costa Mesa Police Department.

The sanctuary Omaima sought with Popovich was not her only plea for help that morning. When Popovich hadn't responded to her earlier knocking, she had driven the Corvette a few miles away to the home of an ex-boyfriend, George Faustino, with whom she had lived at various times during the five years they knew each other. At 10:30 A.M., while crying hysterically, she related to him the same hideous chain of events she subsequently related to Popovich.

Faustino couldn't picture Omaima's new husband raping her. He had met Bill Nelson in mid-November when Omaima and Nelson arrived in the red Corvette to pay back an old debt, a $250 loan Faustino had made to Omaima. Nelson, Faustino thought, was obviously much older than his attractive bride, but he seemed like a nice enough guy. And he knew very well that Omaima was not ordinarily resistant to sex.

Just as she would with John Popovich, Omaima stripped to her underwear to show the wounds to her ex-lover while she begged for him to help her. Faustino still felt friendly toward Omaima, but he just didn't want to be involved. It would be better if she left, he told her. In tears, she returned to Popovich's house, and shocked him with the revolting narrative.

Popovich had no choice but to notify the police.

At 2:05 P.M. Officer Danny Hogue, of the Costa Mesa Police Department, arrived at Popovich's house to question Omaima Nelson. A former member of the homicide squad, Hogue was a veteran interviewer. Omaima, even though startled at finding the police suddenly involved, answered his questions calmly. She told Hogue that her husband, Bill Nelson, was away on a business trip in Florida. She didn't know exactly where he was staying in Florida or when he would return.

Because of the ghastly nature of the report by Popovich, Officer Hogue asked Omaima's permission to search the Corvette. She did not object, and oddly volunteered that he would find no "coke," even though, she said, she had "done" some approximately 20 minutes earlier. A subsequent blood test revealed no trace of cocaine.

The car, registered to William Nelson and bearing a Texas license plate, was not locked. While Omaima asked what was going on, and complained that someone "was trying to set her up," the officer looked inside and found a plastic trash bag. He had to suppress the urge to gag when he saw what it contained:

bloody meat and internal organs. He couldn't tell if they were animal or human.

While a backup officer remained with Omaima and the Corvette, Officer Hogue drove the short distance to the address listed on the car registration for William Nelson. At the upstairs apartment, there was no answer to his knock, so he forced his way in. He noted that the inside front doorknob was blood-stained. Full cardboard boxes near the entryway and tied plastic trash bags in other rooms gave the appearance that someone had packed to move out. In the bedroom, Hogue saw an open clothes hamper at the foot of the bed that contained a blood-soaked sheet that was still wet. A large butcher knife lay in the kitchen sink.

As a veteran of combat in Vietnam and of innumerable homicide scenes, Officer Hogue was not rattled by the sight of blood. He secured the premises and radioed headquarters to advise the watch commander of the suspicious circumstance.

Detective Bob Phillips was enjoying his leisurely Sunday afternoon by running an antique miniature train, part of his extensive collection of rare toys. A native of Costa Mesa, and a 13-year veteran of the police department, Phillips had worked a four-year stint in narcotics until his recent transfer to homicide. He was anticipating his first assignment as lead investigator, and when he answered the phone at 3 P.M., he had it. Phillips's Thanksgiving weekend was over, and he was on his way to pick up another detective.

Frank Rudisill's phone rang, interrupting a backyard barbecue, and he learned that his friend and carpool partner, Bob Phillips, would pick him up. Rudisill was excited because he, too, had transferred from the narc squad, and this would be his first investigation with the new team. So far, though, it was just a "possible" homicide.

During their ride to the scene, Phillips, with remarkable prescience, remarked to Rudisill, "I've got a feeling this is going to be a house of horrors."

A third member of the team was brought out of a lazy Sunday nap by her ringing phone. Lynda Giesler would lend valuable experience to the job at hand, having been hired 30 years earlier by the Costa Mesa Police Department as one of the first female detectives in the state.

After a short stop at the Popovich home, Detectives Phillips and Giesler obtained Omaima Nelson's agreement to be interviewed at the police station.

In a well-lighted room, seated in a comfortable upholstered chair, Omaima faced Giesler and Phillips across a circular oak table. Haltingly, in a soft, trembling voice, she began a disjointed, rambling story that was virtually impossible to follow.

Omaima repeated that her husband was out of town. With tears starting to stream down her face again, she stated that Nelson had raped her on Thanksgiving Day. She made allusions to strange dreams in which she wondered, "Where's Bill?" and "I don't have Bill's phone number." She vaguely hinted that Nelson had also raped two other girls not long after he had been released from prison, the previous March. The girls were missing, she thought, and their passports were in Bill's possession.

Answering questions between sobs, Omaima said that Nelson had forced her to pose for "thousands" of risque photographs.

Because she was again wearing the black gloves, Detective Phillips asked Omaima to remove them. She explained that she had sustained the obvious injuries during a fight with an unknown woman in a bar in nearby Santa Ana. She voluntarily stood up and began to disrobe to show the investigators her other wounds. Detective Giesler listed them, while Phillips gallantly turned his back. Giesler thought it was peculiar that woman claiming to have been brutally raped was so immodest.

Completely denying any knowledge of the bags in the Corvette, Omaima claimed that she had given a guy a ride to the Laundromat. Maybe he had left the bags in the car.

Adding more details to the events of Thanksgiving Day, Omaima said that before her husband raped her, she and Bill had spent the day with his friends in Riverside. Then, a little later in the interview, she changed her mind, saying that they had eaten dinner at home.

Something just wasn't adding up for Detective Phillips. He entertained the thought that perhaps the missing ex-convict, Bill Nelson, had set up a big scam to disappear. Phillips made a mental note to pursue that angle if Nelson wasn't found soon. Meanwhile, Phillips needed to fill out the paperwork for a warrant to search the apartment, so he released Omaima to be transported to Hoag Memorial Hospital, where she was given a routine rape examination.

At the hospital, Laurie Crutchfield, a criminalist with the Orange County Sheriff's Department, used a rape kit to test Omaima for possible evidence of sexual assault. Dr. Brian Grade also examined her. The subsequent report stated that no semen was found in Omaima's body cavities.

The various wounds on Omaima, Dr. Grade concluded, were old enough that scabbing and preliminary infection had started.

Detective Phillips confronted John Popovich to hear the details of what the Egyptian woman had told him. Still shaken, the witness described to Phillips how Omaima had arrived at his house, cried about being raped, and stripped to show him her injuries. "Then she asked me if she could trust me with her life." When Popovich asked what she meant, Omaima had given him a stunning reply.

"She told me that she had killed her husband," Popovich divulged. "I asked her how, what happened? She said she was tied up on the bed while he was raping her and cutting her, but she broke loose with her right hand and reached over and grabbed the lamp and smacked her husband over the head with it." According to Popovich, Omaima said that when Nelson fell over unconscious, she grabbed "the tool" he had used to cut her and stabbed him. She had demonstrated it to Popovich with a wild slashing motion, which he reenacted for the investigator.

Popovich still felt stunned and sickened as he revealed the next part of Omaima's story to Detective Phillips. "She said that she chopped him up in pieces and cut off his head and she wanted me to dispose of it. She said that she had washed the blood off the body parts, wrapped them in newspaper, and put them in plastic bags and left them in the apartment. She wanted me to go over there, you know, and do some cleaning."

Omaima had offered Popovich $75,000 and two motorcycles, he disclosed, if he would agree to help clean up the apartment and dispose of her husband's remains.

Continuing with Omaima's revelations, Popovich said, "She told me she took the body parts to the bathroom to clean them up and wash off the blood in the bathtub. She washed the parts so they would be drained of blood so they wouldn't drip any-where." He had agreed to help her, Popovich told Phillips, just to stall for time until he could call the police.

The horror of Popovich's story climaxed with a final com-ment. "She told me that when I disposed of the head, to make sure I crushed it, with the dentures, so there wouldn't be any trace of who it was."

Detectives Giesler and Jack Archer later talked to George Faustino, the ex-boyfriend who had rejected Omaima's request for help.

"Yeah," he reluctantly told them, making it clear that he didn't like cops, "she told me she killed her husband. She said she was tied, beaten, and raped, and she hit him over the head with a lamp. He was in pieces."

Faustino had seen some cuts on Omaima, but wasn't sure he believed her story. He just wanted Omaima out of there. When she left, he walked to the Corvette with her. He saw some credit cards, in Bill Nelson's name, on the passenger seat of the car.

Back at police headquarters, Omaima denied to Detectives Phillips and Giesler that she had killed her husband. Instead, she claimed, she had received a telephone call. Someone had yelled into the phone, "Well, bitch, you got what you wanted! Look in the trash bag. Why don't you check in the kitchen? You want some hamburger?" She had looked, Omaima said, had seen the grisly remains, and had rushed over to Popovich's house for help. She thought maybe the bloody mess was someone her husband had killed.

"He's chopped up women before," Omaima asserted. Then

she reverted to more accounts of sexual abuse, whimpering that Nelson had made her watch pornographic videotapes, and that she had been a "beautiful model" before Nelson "cut her everywhere and made her ugly." Omaima kept wanting to know if she was going to the "gas chair."

"Do you live with your husband at the apartment?" Detective Phillips asked.

"I haven't been there for nearly two weeks," Omaima responded, explaining that Nelson had been in and out of town and he didn't want her to occupy the apartment while he was gone. But "a number of people" had keys to his place.

Detective Phillips used an old investigative gambit. "How do you explain the fact that someone saw you there very recently?"

"It must have been the chick who looks kind of like me. She lives in the complex," Omaima quickly shot back. Finally, saying that she "wondered" if the body parts had been the remains of her husband, Omaima said she wanted to talk to a psychiatrist. The detectives concluded the interview at 10 o'clock that night.

On Monday afternoon, December 2, Detective Phillips, Giesler, and Archer, armed with a search warrant, entered the apartment rented to Bill Nelson. They were accompanied by Bruce John Radomski, a civilian evidence technician employed by the Costa Mesa Police Department.

The homicide team "rookie," Frank Rudisill, had been delegated the unpleasant task of digging through the huge trash bin outside, which was packed to the rim with garbage and Thanksgiving debris. "You want to be a homicide detective, don't you?" Phillips asked, grinning. "Well, this is an important part of the job."

Inside, within minutes, the investigators began making grisly discoveries. They opened one of the plastic bags and found human legs severed at the knee. Various other body parts were wrapped in newspaper and stuffed into another plastic bag. One contained human male genitals. From a cardboard box near the entryway, Detective Giesler removed a newspaper-wrapped bundle and began to peel away the layers of paper. She recoiled in horror at the sight of a pair of severed hands, with the left ring finger hacked off, lying in the loathsome bundle. It would later be revealed that the hands had been cooked in oil, apparently to destroy the fingerprints.

Radomski was curious about the neatly made bed, wondering where the bloody sheets had come from. He lifted the heavy mattress, turned it over, and was appalled to find that the entire underside was drenched in blood. Someone had removed a bloody wet sheet, turned over the heavy fluid-soaked mattress, and carefully made up the bed.

Several boots were standing at strange locations around the room. Radomski found, when he moved them, that each had been placed to cover a bloodstain.

Meanwhile, fighting the disgusting odors, Rudisill dug through the trash in the bin and found a pile of still frozen, unused boxes of peas, corn, frozen dinners, and other food, obviously removed from a freezer. It hit him all at once, and he raced up the stairs to tell his colleagues that something big was in that freezer.

Slowly, in awful anticipation, the detectives swung open the freezer door. An innocuous blue plastic tray, filled with foil-wrapped packages, was all they saw. Detective Archer lifted out the largest foil package and began to unwrap it. He cringed in horror when he peeled back the last layer.

Shrunken, sightless eyes gazed at him from a grinning skull. Some of the skin had been boiled away, and the jaws were blackened and charred from being partially cooked. The head had been scalped. The hairy flap of skin that had been sliced off was found in another package.

In another location, Detective Giesler found a portable ice chest, and when she lifted the top, the stench of blood assaulted her nostrils. In the cold room, steam began rising from the soaked clothing and rags stuffed into the chest, cloth that had apparently been used to mop up the gore.

Meticulous searching of the apartment also turned up passports for two young women. In the bedroom, Randomski found a portfolio of color photographs of a smiling Omaima Nelson. In some, she wore nothing but white panties and a bra; in others, she was completely nude. Detective Archer found a steam iron, bent and bloodstained, which he carefully inserted into an evidence bag.

In a most unusual departure from normal procedure, the pathologist, Dr. Ronald Katsuyama, was brought to the crime scene to begin an autopsy examination. He would later have the body parts transported to his lab, where he would spread the remains on a stainless steel table for a macabre reassembly for identification. The body parts proved to be all that was left of the missing William Nelson.

Omaima Nelson, still in custody, was arrested at 5:55 P.M., on suspicion of murder.

Detective Phillips and his team then began the long process of interviewing prospective witnesses. The resident of a neighboring apartment said that he had last seen Bill Nelson in front of the building at a little after noon on Thanksgiving Day. He had seen Omaima on Sunday, December 1, while he was washing his car. She had arrived in the Corvette, parked near the trash bin, and disappeared into the apartment. Moments later, she reappeared carrying a rectangular trash bag that she had started to throw into the bin, but she apparently changed her mind.

Another neighbor had overheard "chopping noises," and was bothered by Nelson's garbage disposal running most of the night. The information was no surprise to the detectives, since they had disassembled the plumbing and found traces of human flesh in the disposal. Remarkably, there had been no odor in the apartment, and the first stench came from the opened drain trap below the sink.

After the sensational case hit the newspapers, one more acquaintance of Omaima Nelson came forward. Orville Whittaker, who had known Omaima since 1989, reported that she had been with him in his bedroom in November 1990. He said, "Well, she wanted to have sex with me, and so we went upstairs to the bedroom, and she says, 'Let me tie your hands. Don't worry, I'm not going to hurt you or anything.' " Whittaker added that Omaima used two of his neckties to bind his wrists to the bedpost.

"After she got my hands tied, she pulled a gun out and she put it to my face and says she wanted for me to give her money. I thought she was kidding. I really did. You know, I [was] laughing." He told her to put the gun away, Whittaker said, "because, you know, something could happen." But Omaima refused, and demanded money.

"I finally got one hand free from the left side," Whittaker continued, "and then I got up and got my other hand free, and I pushed her back against the dresser. I took the gun away, and told her to get the heck out. She left and I kept her gun."

"What were you both wearing?"

"She was in her panties, and I was wearing shorts."

Asked about their prior relationship, Whittaker stated that Omaima had lived with him for three or four months. Shortly after she left him, he was furious because he received a department store bill for $1,600. When he checked, he found that his credit card for that particular store was missing.

Detective Phillips tracked down the women whose passports were found in Bill Nelson's apartment. Contrary to Omaima's suggestion that both women were missing, they were alive and well. They explained that their passports had been stolen in New York in May 1990. They didn't know, nor had they ever heard of, Bill or Omaima Nelson. How the documents came into the possession of Bill Nelson would never be solved.

A Texas attorney, who had represented Bill Nelson in the case that sent him to prison, disclosed that Bill and Omaima had visited him in Laredo in early November. "She said she was from a wealthy family and she spoke French and English and sixteen dialects of Arabic."

William Nelson's record indicated that he had been a military pilot, who later transported by plane narcotics and stolen electronics across the Mexico-Texas border. His plane had been shot down twice by Mexican authorities. Detectives also discovered that Nelson had been previously married. His estranged wife had filed for divorce while Nelson was in prison, but it had never been finalized. The marriage to Omaima, then, was not a legal one.

Meanwhile, Omaima Nelson asked to talk to a psychiatrist. She ultimately spoke to two of them. One psychiatrist learned of even more depravity related to the death of William Nelson. In a later report of the psychiatrist's findings, the doctor stated that Omaima's husband was sexually assaulting her in their Costa Mesa home on November 30, 1991, when she reached for a pair of scissors, stabbed him, and then "freaked out." She followed up the stabbing by beating him with a steam iron until he was dead.

Before Omaima started to mutilate Nelson's body, the psychiatrist said, she put on red lipstick, a red hat, and red high-heeled shoes. She explained that she was fascinated with the color of her husband's blood and wore red to make her butchery into a kind of ritual. She worked at her savage task all night long.

Detective Phillips thought he had heard everything, but when he heard the next part of the doctor's report, even he was shocked. Omaima Nelson had admitted to the psychiatrist that she ate part of Bill Nelson's ribs after cooking them in barbecue sauce! The psychiatrist quoted Omaima's words: "I did his ribs just like in a restaurant." Sitting at the kitchen table, she reportedly said to herself, "It's so sweet, it's so delicious. . . . I like mine tender." The doctor added that Omaima later denied the cannibalism.

In his diagnosis of Omaima Nelson, the psychiatrist stated, "I believe she was psychotic." He asserted that in his 20 years in practice, he had never seen anything so bizarre.

Another psychiatrist also concluded that Omaima was psychotic. The suspect had told the doctor that she hacked off Nelson's genitals, and stuffed them in his mouth along with his left ring finger. Omaima allegedly said she removed the finger because [Nelson] "always came home and instead of kissing me hello, he would take his finger and shove it in [me]. . . . I hated that so much. It hurt, and it hurt my feelings so much. Why couldn't he just be nice?" If Omaima's story was true, she had rearranged the victim's body parts before wrapping them in newspaper and foil.

Deputy District Attorney Randy Pawloski, of the Orange County District Attorney's Office, drew the assignment of prosecuting Omaima Nelson. The trial started on December 3, 1992, one year after her arrest.

Deputy Public Defender Tom Mooney decided to use the psychiatric testimony to prove that Omaima Nelson was a battered woman who had simply defended herself.

In Prosecutor Pawloski's opening statement, he told the jury that this would be the "ghastliest" story they would ever hear. "In the next few weeks you're going to hear a Rod Serling *Night Gallery* type of thing." He disputed the self-defense theory, arguing that it was William Nelson who was tied to the bed and stabbed, not Omaima. William was then clubbed into unconsciousness with an iron and dismembered, Pawloski informed the horrified jurors. "The evidence will show that we got a predator, we got evil, we got a mean person who goes from guy to guy."

Omaima's wounds, he figured, had occurred during her wild frenzy of chopping Bill Nelson's body apart.

When Defense Attorney Tom Mooney addressed the jury, he said that Omaima was the victim of a domineering man, who had attacked her several times. She finally lashed back in self-defense, Mooney proclaimed. "She was reacting to years of abuse by other people. . . . She was out of it at the time and didn't know what she was doing. Mrs. Nelson is, and was that night, psychotic. Omaima will testify and tell the true story of what happened that night," Mooney promised.

On December 9, a tearful Omaima Nelson took the stand and admitted to killing and dismembering her husband, but she claimed she had done it to stop his continual abuse. He had raped her on Thanksgiving Day, she testified. Then he knocked her to the floor, ordered her to strip, and tied her up naked on the bed. When she couldn't stop crying, she said, he cut her breast with a knife and got on top of her. To protect herself, she grabbed a pair of scissors and started stabbing him. She then found the iron. "I hit him," she testified. "I breaked [sic] the iron."

During her two days on the stand, Omaima also told jurors that because of the painful mutilating circumcision she had endured at age six, she had never been able to enjoy sex. (During the trial, a local newspaper carried a story reporting that female circumcision of infants—excision of the clitoris and surrounding tissue, without the benefit of anesthesia—is still a common practice in some African countries.)

On cross-examination, Prosecutor Pawloski got Omaima to admit that she had told a boyfriend that she had been hoping to make a lot of money, maybe $50,000, so she could return to Egypt and start a business. He also showed her a photograph of herself taken one day after she claimed that Nelson had beaten her savagely. The photo revealed no bruises or injuries. Finally, with a touch of sarcasm, Pawloski said that investigators had not yet found all of the "meat" of Bill Nelson.

"We're missing about one hundred and thirty pounds of Bill," Pawloski growled. He then spun toward Omaima. "You know where he might have gone?" inquired Pawloski.

In his closing argument, Pawloski pointed out that the remains of Bill Nelson's legs, chopped off at the knees, were bruised around the ankles, indicating that he had been bound during a struggle just before death. The headboard to the bed had also been broken, Pawloski said, showing that Nelson had struggled mightily for his life.

Omaima Nelson was a "predator," the prosecutor insisted, who killed Bill Nelson so that she could flee with his money, credit cards, and the new red Corvette.

Defense Attorney Mooney reiterated that Omaima was "an ill woman," who was certainly not guilty of premeditated murder.

Following six days of deliberation, the eight-woman, four-man jury filed solemnly back into the box and handed the verdict forms to the bailiff, who gave them to the court clerk. Reading the verdict aloud, the clerk announced that to the charge of first-degree murder, Omaima Nelson was not guilty.

A murmur rippled through the court before the clerk came to the second form. To the charge of second-degree murder, Omaima Nelson was guilty. She was also found guilty of assaulting Orville Whittaker in November 1990.

In the hallway, afterward, jurors spoke of the horrors they had heard. One said, "The whole thing was very gruesome. I lost sleep thinking about it. . . ." But they decided that there was inadequate evidence of premeditation to support a first-degree murder conviction.

Detective Bob Phillips was quoted as saying, "Omaima Nelson is the most bizarre and sick individual I've ever had the occasion to meet. No one needs to look to the Dahmers of Milwaukee or the Hannibal Lecters of the screen. A new predator had emerged, named Omaima."

On March 12, 1992, Orange County Superior Court Judge Robert Fitzgerald sentenced Omaima Aref Nelson to the maximum possible prison term, 27 years to life. She will not be eligible for parole until well into the 21st century.

"TINA KILLED MOM TO WINE, DINE, AND GET BACK HER EX-BEAU!"

by Steven Barry

When Carol Jean Burris missed work on Friday, April 20, 1990, two of her co-workers were very surprised. It was totally out of character for Carol not to show up at work or phone to explain why.

At age 42, Carol was an attractive, divorced mother of a 20-year-old daughter who lived with her father in Clayton, Delaware. Carol had a boyfriend, but preferred to live alone in her home on the 300 block of Lafayette Avenue in the Oak Valley section of Deptford, New Jersey. Carol went to work early each weekday morning at the Association for Retarded Citizens complex in nearby Woodbury, where she was employed as an accountant. It was her routine to return home each afternoon around five o'clock

But now, Carol had not shown up for work and her colleagues were worried. When she still failed to arrive for work the following Monday morning, the two co-workers were quite concerned. They telephoned her home, but got no answer. That afternoon, they decided to drive to Carol's home to investigate.

"We stayed outside the house for over an hour," one of the co-workers would later explain, "and we saw [one of] Carol's [relatives], who'd also come over to check on Carol. But she didn't have a key and we couldn't get in.

"We walked around the house for a while and were ready to start back to the office, when we noticed Carol's car approaching. We started waving, but the car kept going.

"It stopped at the corner and I kept watching, and I could see the driver's eyes looking at me in the rearview mirror. It looked like Carol. I waved and called Carol's name, but she didn't wave back. Then she made a right turn and started driving away.

"We just stared at each other. We couldn't understand why Carol would try to turn away from us."

The co-workers jumped into their car and started following Carol's car. They honked their horn repeatedly. Instead of pulling over, however, the other car sped up and led them on a high-speed chase through the streets of the residential neighborhood, at a time when school buses were dropping off students.

"I had no idea what was going on," said the co-worker who was driving. "I gave up the chase after she started driving recklessly. I didn't want to risk a collision or hitting any of the kids."

So the co-workers headed back to their office, asking each other, "What's up with her?" all the way back.

But nothing was up with their friend. As they would soon learn, Carol Burris was already dead. It was impossible for her to have been driving her car at the time they saw it. But somebody was. The question was—who?

A couple of hours later, around dusk, Carol's relative phoned the Deptford Police Department. "I haven't seen [Carol] for the last five days," she told the dispatcher, "and I'm worried about her."

Detective George Kelly responded to the complaint. He knocked on the front door of Carol's home. When no one answered, he walked around to the back and spotted the broken pane of a window opening into the recreation room. The pane was about nine inches square and appeared to be too small for anyone to reach through.

Detective Kelly carefully removed several shards of glass,

which were still wedged into the window frame, then reached his hand through it and unlatched the window. Moments later, he was inside the house.

"Mrs. Burris!" he called out.

No one answered.

There were no sounds coming from the television, radio, or stereo, so Kelly looked for other signs of life. On a kitchen counter, he saw three empty Michelob bottles sitting neatly in a cardboard six-pack carrier and another empty beer bottle close to the carrier. One beer cap was on the counter, another on the floor in front of the refrigerator.

"Mrs. Burris!" Kelly called again.

Again, no answer came.

Kelly didn't know what to expect as he walked toward the hallway. It was getting dark, so he flicked on the lights. Pausing at the end of the hallway, he thought he heard a noise coming from the bathroom, some sort of whimpering. He approached the bathroom door and glanced inside.

"It was the woman's dog," Detective Kelly would later explain, "hiding behind the toilet. It was shaking."

The detective's search ended in the master bedroom. There, he found Carol Burris's body on the floor. Several plastic trash bags had been placed over her, and a carpet mat was underneath her head. From the look of things, she'd been dead for a few days.

Then the lawman saw Carol's black pocketbook lying on the bed, wide open. It looked as if someone had rummaged through its contents.

Detective Kelly called headquarters and requested a computer search for armed burglars.

As night descended over the otherwise peaceful neighborhood, Carol Burris's home was transformed into a crime scene. Yellow tape was stretched around the perimeter of the property to preserve the scene until the homicide detectives and medical examiners arrived.

Detective Kelly contacted Carol Burris's relative to break the bad news to her. Afterward, he asked her what kind of car the victim had owned. The woman told him it was a 1985 Chevrolet Caprice. Since there was no such car parked outside, the detective concluded that it must have been stolen. He therefore had an alert transmitted over the police radio network, advising police departments throughout the state to be on the lookout for the stolen vehicle.

Detective Kelly then asked Carol Burris's relative for the names of the victim's friends, acquaintances, and family members. On that list were Carol's boyfriend, her ex-husband, her daughter, Tina, and Tina's boyfriend, Tom Drake. Since more than 85 percent of all homicide victims are killed by someone they know, these people are immediately viewed as the first suspects. They are interviewed one by one until such time as they are either eliminated or placed on the list of prime suspects. That was how the investigators regarded these individuals in the Carol Burris probe.

When some of the investigators from the Gloucester County Prosecutor's Office began to arrive, Detective Kelly started interviewing the neighbors who'd spilled outside their homes to see what was going on. One of the neighbors told him that he'd seen the victim's daughter, Tina, several times during the past few days, coming and going in Carol's car. The detective decided to take a ride to Tina's boyfriend's house, which was only four blocks away, to see if Tina was there and to find out if she could shed any light on the investigation.

Parked at the curb in front of the boyfriend's home was a 1985 Caprice.

Detective Kelly knocked on the front door and found both the boyfriend, Tom Drake, and Tina Burris inside.

"Is that your mother's car outside?" Kelly asked Tina.

"No," she replied, "it belongs to my girlfriend."

He asked her to step outside with him. From his car, he radioed the police dispatcher.

"I need you to look up a tag number for me," he told the

dispatcher. "440 U6X." Then he waited in silence with Tina Burris.

A few moments later, the police dispatcher's voice crackled on the line. "That vehicle is registered to Carol Jean Burris," the dispatcher said.

"Did you hear the lookup?" Detective Kelly asked Tina.

"Yes, I did," she replied, "but it's my girlfriend's car. I swear. It must be a mistake."

Detective Kelly transported Tina Burris to the police station to sort out the mistake. There, she kept insisting that the car belonged to her girlfriend. Detective Kelly left her alone for the time being and interviewed Tina's boyfriend.

Tom Drake said that he'd dated Tina off and on for a couple of years. During that time, they'd lived together for a while, and they'd even been engaged. But just last week, on Tuesday night, he'd broken off the relationship. Tina must have called him from Delaware a dozen times that night to try to talk him out of it, but Tom held fast to his decision.

Then, two nights later, the young man told the investigator, Tina called and said she was pregnant. She wanted to patch things up between them and suggested a romantic getaway. He agreed.

Tina picked up Tom the next night—Thursday, April 19—and they drove to the Deptford Mall. She bought him two pairs of shorts and a pair of silk pajamas for their fling, then treated him to dinner at a Chinese restaurant. She paid for everything with her mother's charge card. The next day, Tina drove Tom to Cherry Hill to the Inn of the Dove, a posh motel reputed to be an ideal spot for intimate trysts.

"On the way there," Tom told the detective, "Tina said she's just gotten a job at a bank, thanks to her girlfriend, the same one who loaned her the car. She was going to pay her mother back for the weekend by borrowing money from her girlfriend—she said five hundred dollars—and would pay her girlfriend back when she started working at the new job."

"How did she act?"

"She seemed normal," Tom replied. "She didn't act strange in any way. She was just like any other day. At one point, she even said, 'I feel lucky.' "

After they checked into the motel, Tina changed into some sexy lingerie and they engaged in sex several times before they checked out the next day.

Later, the detective would contact Tina's girlfriend and ask if she'd loaned her car to Tina Burris.

"I don't own a car," the girlfriend said.

"Did she ask to borrow any money from you?"

"Not this past Sunday," the girlfriend replied, "but last Sunday, Easter Sunday, she called me and asked if she could borrow a couple of dollars. She said she needed it to drive back to Delaware.

"To be truthful, I only had three dollars to my name. My husband added two dollars and told me to give her five."

"Did you recently help her get a job?" the sleuth asked.

"Once I did arrange for her to work at a collection agency," the girlfriend replied, "but that was last year. Three of us started working the same day, but Tina and I quit the first day when our ride changed her mind about working there."

To Detective Kelly, it was obvious that Tina Burris was lying. Nevertheless, she seemed too timid and shy to be a killer, and she had no history of criminal behavior.

"I know Tina better than anybody," a family member would tell the investigators, "and she doesn't have a violent bone in her body. Tina and Carol did everything together. They went everywhere together. They used to dress alike. They used to wear their hair alike. They were companions."

Assuming that Tina Burris hadn't killed her mother, then who was she trying to protect?

By then, Sergeant Joe Szolack and Investigators Richard Burke, Bob Rowand, John Robinson and Angelo Alvarado—all from the county prosecutor's office—had arrived at Carol Burris's house and were waiting to get started. Shortly after midnight, Detective Jeff Wright led them inside. They started in the kitchen by processing the beer bottles for fingerprints. From there, they moved to an unoccupied bedroom.

On top of the dresser, Detective Wright found two sales receipts: one from a shoe store and another from Victoria's Secret. Both stores were located in the Deptford Mall, and both purchases had been made with Carol Burris's American Express card. The purchases were dated April 19.

Although the victim's body had been found on the floor of the master bedroom, it looked to the investigators as if she'd been killed in another part of the house, then dragged into the bedroom. Pursuing that premise, they discovered several faint spots on the wall in the hallway, another large spot on the floor, and what looked like a trail leading from the hallway to the bedroom, all of which appeared to have been cleaned recently, yet still had reddish tints to them.

In addition, the sleuths found a bullet hole in one of the walls in the hallway. It was an entrance hole. On the living-room side of the wall, they found the exit hole. And in the bookcase next to the piano, they found a .38-caliber slug that had come to a rest on top of a stack of five hardcover books.

Dr. Claus Speth, the county medical examiner, arrived and removed the plastic bags which had been placed on top of the body. Carol Burris's corpse was fully clothed in a skirt and blouse, a blazer, nylons, and shoes.

To Detective Wright, if the victim wasn't dead, he would have thought that she'd just gotten home from work. Since Carol hadn't gone to work on Friday, he theorized that she had been killed sometime after work on Thursday, April 19. The prior discovery of the sales slips in the other bedroom made it appear as if she'd stopped at the mall on her way home from work.

The medical examiner pronounced Carol Burris dead. Then he found a few strands of hair in her right hand and one .38-caliber slug in the breast pocket of her blouse. The hair was bagged for testing. The bullet, which appeared to have passed through her body and then found its way into the pocket, was later packaged with the previously found bullet. Both were sent to the state police crime lab for ballistics testing.

The investigators failed to find any signs of additional shots being fired. Apparently, the killer had fired two bullets, and that was it.

Detective Wright examined the contents of the black pocketbook that was lying on the bed in the master bedroom. Inside were several of the victim's personal belongings, but no cash and no credit cards.

During the autopsy, the medical examiner would remove the victim's outer clothing and learn that, when she was killed, Carol Burris had also been wearing a slip, panties and a bra, and a garter belt. He would identify a single entrance wound in her back, near the upper right shoulder, just to the right of the spine.

"The bullet severed the spinal cord," he would later explain, "paralyzing her immediately from that point down. It then went through her body . . . through the esophagus . . . through the windpipe . . . through the atrium of the heart . . . causing a massive amount of blood to pool on the deceased's face . . . causing her, virtually, to drown in her own blood.

"Blood smears on the face, the condition of the body, and the path of the bullet indicate that death was not immediate. She probably experienced a period of consciousness before she died. Based on the number of breaths that would be required to inhale the amount of blood that was found in the lungs, she survived anywhere from one to three minutes."

The ME placed the time of death at approximately four days prior to the discovery of the body—April 19—which was consistent with what had already been established in the investigation. In addition, he observed that the victim's left leg had been broken postmortem, probably when the killer dragged Carol's body from the hallway to the bedroom.

On his way to the Deptford police station, Detective Wright stopped at Tom Drake's house to inspect Carol Burris's car. In the trunk, he found a number of shopping bags. One bag was from Victoria's Secret and contained pantyhose and a pair of black high heels, size $8^1/_2$B. He also found a white cardboard box with ROMANTIC GETAWAY printed on its side. Inside the box were three containers of body oil, a vibrator, a smaller box marked NIGHT MOVES, two pieces of white lingerie, a black and green negligee, a can of whipped cream marked FOR LOVERS ONLY, and two crystal candleholders.

A second bag contained new sneakers and jeans and a top, along with an American Express receipt dated April 22. A third bag held a white bathrobe with an Inn of the Dove insignia on the breast, a curling iron, and two forks, spoons, dishes, and bowls.

In the glove compartment, Detective Wright found Carol Burris's checkbook, Social Security card, driver's license, and check-cashing cards. Inside the checkbook, on the back of an envelope, was a handwritten "list to do" dated April 20, the day after Carol Burris was murdered.

To the detective, it was looking more and more as though Tina Burris had murdered her own mother.

Wright met Tina for the first time at the police station a little while later. She was 5 feet 6 inches tall and a thin 110 pounds. Her hair was long and wavy and her eyes were big and dark. She looked pale and frightened and told him that she'd moved out of her mother's house in January and now lived with her father and stepmother in Delaware.

Detective Wright asked her if he could examine her pocketbook.

Tina consented.

Inside the silver-studded black bag, the detective found a set of car keys for her mother's Caprice and a 1990 appointment book. In an inside pocket of the appointment book, handwritten on a pink slip of paper, were the directions to the Inn of the Dove, the motel's phone number, a price quote of $174.90. To Detective Wright, the handwriting appeared to match the hand-written list he'd previously found in the glove compartment of the Caprice. There was also an American Express Optima card issued to Carol Burris.

"How did you get your mother's credit card?" the sleuth asked.

"I took it when I moved out in January," Tina replied.

Detective Wright picked up the card and looked at it. He compared the numbers with the credit card slips he'd found in the unoccupied bedroom at Carol Burris's house and in her car. They didn't match. Apparently, Tina was telling the truth about the card.

Wright examined the credit card itself once more, then threw it on the table.

"This wasn't issued until March," he said, "two months *after* you moved out." He stared into the young woman's eyes. "How do you explain that?"

Tina Burris looked down, averting her gaze.

"Do you understand that your mother's been murdered and you're being considered as a suspect?" the investigator asked her.

Tina started crying. She said yes, she knew her mother had been murdered. What's more, she knew who did it.

"Who?" Wright asked.

Tina hesitated at first. Then she started to speak.

"Anthony Cruz picked me up at my house in Delaware last Thursday afternoon," Tina said, beginning her first statement about how her mother was killed. "Right before we left, I asked him to get an Easter basket from my stepmother's bedroom— she'd made it for Tom. But instead of getting the basket, he went into the closet and took my stepmother's gun.

"He drove me to my mother's house. We went around back and he broke a small window and squeezed through the opening. When my mother came home, I got into a big argument with her. After a while, he got angry because of the way my mother was treating me."

Tina said that one thing led to another, and Cruz wound up taking out the gun and shooting her mother.

It was now the middle of the night, but it was no time to stop. Detective Bill McGough placed a telephone call to Clayton, Delaware, and woke Tina's stepmother out of a sound sleep. The detective informed her that Tina was a suspect in the shooting death of her natural mother, a crime that had just been discovered. He then asked the woman if she owned a handgun.

She said yes—she was a prison guard in Delaware and owned a .38-caliber revolver.

"Would you see if it's still there?" the detective asked.

While the detective held the line, the woman opened her bedroom closet. She saw that the Smith & Wesson was inside the closet, then returned to the phone.

"It's in its usual place," she told the detective.

"Did you look to see if any rounds were missing?"

"It didn't look like it had been moved," she replied, "so I didn't bother to look."

"Could you please look again?"

She went back to the closet, opened the gun, and glanced inside.

"All the bullets are in there," she told the detective.

After hanging up, she explained the substance of the phone call to her husband. For the next two hours, sleep was impossible for either one of them. Finally, he said he wanted to see the gun for himself.

"When he opened it," the woman would later explain, "all the bullets came out and we saw that two bullets had been spent. He screamed and threw the gun.

"When we regained our emotions, we called [Detective] McGough."

Gloucester County detectives were then dispatched to Delaware to retrieve the weapon, which would be sent to the state police crime lab to see if it was the murder weapon. When the detectives brought Anthony Cruz in for questioning, they asked him about his relationship to Tina Burris.

"She's just a friend," the suspect replied. "We went to high school together."

The sleuths asked him to describe the events that transpired between him and Tina Burris on and around April 19.

"Last Wednesday," Cruz began, "I drove down to Delaware and took Tina to a mall in Dover. When we were leaving the mall, she said she wanted to mix sleeping pills in her mother's drink. She said her mother usually drank a glass of soda when she got home from work."

"Did she tell you why she wanted to drug her mother?"

"She wanted to put her to sleep and take her credit cards."

"Why?"

"She said she was pregnant," Cruz continued, "and Tom had just broken up with her and she wanted to get back together with him. She wanted to take him to some motel. She said this plan just had to work."

"Do you think she meant it?"

"No," Cruz replied. "I started staying, 'Yeah, Tina—right!' "

"Anyway, she asked me to pick her up the next day, early, and drive her to her mother's house. She said she wanted to go out dancing with Tom.

"I picked her up around two o'clock . . ."

"The next afternoon?" the detective inquired, for clarification. "Thursday, April the nineteenth?"

"Right," Cruz replied. "I picked her up and drove her to her mother's house. We got there around four o'clock. She told me to park out front, then she asked me to follow her to the back of the house."

"Then what happened?" the investigator asked

"She tried the back door," Cruz said, "but couldn't get in. I felt like a burglar and kept saying, 'Let's get out of here.' But she said, 'Wait, wait.' And then she got down on her back and began kicking a window with both her feet.

"After two tries it broke and she began removing some of the glass. Then she eased in, feet first, and twisted her way through an opening that was so small I thought only a cat could squeeze through it.

"She told me to come inside, but I said no. Then I started walking home and that's all I know. I swear."

Detective Wright believed Cruz.

The next time the detective sat down with Tina Burris, he asked her if she was pregnant.

She said she wasn't.

"Last week," the detective asked her, "did you tell your boyfriend you were pregnant?"

Tina hesitated, then replied, "I thought I was, but it was a mistake. I just missed my period and got it later."

"Aside from the time we just discussed, did you, at any other time, tell Tom Drake that you were pregnant?"

Tina hung her head.

"A couple of times," she responded.

"Did you kill your mother?"

"I don't remember," Tina replied, and she paused before saying, "but something did happen." Another pause. "I didn't mean to hurt her. I love her so much . . . I swear. But I just don't remember what happened. I didn't think anything happened the whole weekend. It was so weird. I kept thinking I'd better call an ambulance, but it didn't seem real."

"Did you ever call an ambulance?" the lawman asked.

"I don't know what I was thinking," Tina continued. "I don't know why I didn't call an ambulance, but I didn't."

"Why did you drag your mother's body from the hallway into the bedroom?"

"I don't remember doing that, but I do remember taking off my sweatshirt, because it was all bloody, and throwing it on the floor."

"Do you remember using your mother's credit card at the Inn of the Dove?"

"I don't even remember going to the Inn of the Dove!"

"Is this your handwriting?" the detective asked, placing in front of her the "to do" list he'd found in the glove compartment of her mother's car.

"It looks like mine," Tina admitted, "but I don't remember filling it out."

At this point, Detective Wright felt certain that Tina Burris had murdered her mother, but his evidence was circumstantial. Although Tina was now admitting that she knew something had happened to her mother, she wouldn't outrightly confess to killing her. She still blamed Anthony Cruz. Nevertheless, a decision was made to arrest Tina Burris. She was remanded to the Gloucester County Jail. Pending arraignment, her bail was set at $250,000.

At the arraignment three days later, Judge Isaac Serata told the prosecution that its case barely met its burden to show cause. Still, he charged Tina Burris with nine criminal offenses, including murder, burglary, and unlawful possession of a handgun. However, acting upon her request for a bail reduction, he lowered her bond to $100,000, full cash, which she failed to post.

More than two years passed. Between the time of her arrest and the beginning of her trial, Tina spent 783 days in jail. Part of the extended delay resulted from awaiting the outcome of a jury selection issue that had been raised by the defendant in another case, but which might prove applicable to this one, as well. The delay was increased because Tina, overwrought with depression, tried to commit suicide in her jail cell in November 1990.

A year after that failed suicide attempt, in November 1991, Tina sent a three-page handwritten letter to Judge John Wallace, requesting a bail reduction. In part, it read: "Getting ready for my trial is the most important thing to me. I need to prepare in a much better atmosphere. I can't possibly be at my best going to trial from jail. My nerves are a mess. I have no time to myself at all to think clearly, and my physical condition isn't as good as it would be if I were living under better conditions. I'm asking you to please have mercy on me and give me the chance I need for the most important thing I could ever prepare for."

Judge Wallace turned down the request.

By the time the trial began, the investigators had tightened the case against Tina Burris considerably. Trying to enhance her motive, they ran an extensive background check.

"Tina and Carol were so close," said the relative who'd found the body, "but after the divorce, everything changed. Tina resented not having her father. She used to say to me, 'Why can't things be the way they used to be?'

"She started staying out late at night and her grades dropped. She had to go to summer school to graduate from high school.

"Then she couldn't hold down a steady job. She worked for two or three months, then quit. And she started writing bad checks. It got so bad, Carol put Tina out.

"When Carol put Tina out, she lived with her father for a while, then she moved in with Tom. When that didn't work, back with her father.

"At that point, I wrote Carol a letter and asked her: 'Please take Tina back.'

"So Carol and Tina signed an agreement that Tina could move back in as long as she got a job and didn't open a checking account. But that didn't work out, either. Carol put Tina out for good in January and changed all the locks, and Tina moved back in with her father."

By this point, the investigators had pretty much concluded that Tina had broken into her mother's home around 4 P.M. on April 19. When her mother came home from work, mother and daughter got into an argument, Tina pulled out the .38—which had since tested positive as the gun that fired both bullets—and shot her mother.

Working with fraud investigation units from American Express and Carol Burris's local bank, and two telephone companies, the investigators followed a trail of credit card slips, bank checks, and phone calls, which filled in what occurred after the shooting.

On the night of April 19, less than an hour after Carol Burris was shot and killed, telephone records listed a call to the Inn of the Dove. Shortly after the call, Carol Burris's American Express card was used to charge $260.50 worth of lingerie from Victoria's Secret, a few articles of clothing from another store, and dinner at a Chinese restaurant. Telephone records indicated that a two-hour phone call to Tina's boyfriend was placed shortly before midnight. The same American Express card had a charge for a room at the Inn of the Dove the following day.

In between and afterward, the card was used three other times for more than $600 in charges. Each charge slip was signed *Carol Burris*.

Carol Burris's MasterCard was also used for several purchases between the time Carol was murdered and within minutes of when her body was discovered four days later. By then, her credit cards had run up $1,100 in purchases.

Upon a second search of Carol Burris's car, two weeks after the discovery of her body, Detective Wright found in the ashtray the American Express card and MasterCard which had been used to make the purchases.

In addition, two checks had been written on the victim's checking account, one for $10, the other for $5. Both checks were made out to and endorsed by Tina Burris. They were dated April 20 and 21, one day and two days after the victim was killed.

In his opening remarks on Monday, June 15, 1992, Larry Magid, the county's first assistant prosecutor, described the murder as premeditated. If Tina Burris was convicted, he was planning to seek the death penalty.

Jeff Wintner, Tina's public defender, told the jury, "You will be examining a tragedy . . . Tina Burris went shopping and to the Inn of the Dove because she suffered from a histrionic personality disorder and she wanted desperately for everything to be okay." He added that the disorder also caused amnesia, which prevented her from recalling many of the details.

"As a child, he continued, 'she learned how to please her parents by being pretty, by performing. But after the divorce, her mother began to reestablish her own social life. Kristina was no longer the most important person in her mother's life.

"At some point [on the day Carol Burris was shot], Tina was made aware of the fact that Anthony Cruz had stolen her stepmother's gun. She knew it was wrong. She knew he could not have it. So she took it from him and placed it in the waistband of her jeans.

"When she met her mother, they engaged in an argument. Her mother called Tina's boyfriend a bum. Tina called her mother's boyfriend a bum and an alcoholic. Her mother turned to walk away and Tina grabbed the gun because she wanted to get her mother's attention.

"She said, 'Listen to me. You never listen to me.'

"The gun went off. It struck and killed her mother."

The crux of the trial boiled down to how Tina would come across on the witness stand. On June 25, she was sworn in and testified for four hours.

"'Do you remember saying Anthony [Cruz] climbed through your window and shot your mother?" Prosecutor Magid asked her on cross-examination.

"Yes, I do," Tina replied, "but it was a lie. I needed her to listen to me. I pulled out the gun to show her. It went off accidentally and it hit my mother. It was the last thing I wanted to happen.

"I heard a ringing in my ears and I watched her fall down. I just froze. I heard her say, 'Tina.'

"I said, 'Mom! Mom, get up!' But she wasn't moving or anything. I wouldn't accept it. It was too horrible to believe. I didn't want her to be dead. I wanted her to be alive.."

The prosecutor made his closing argument the next day.

"This is the gun that Kristina Burris says accidentally went off," Magid said, showing the silver-plated Smith & Wesson .38 to the jury. "It's a double-action handgun. Cocking and pulling the trigger at the same time requires thirteen pounds of pressure."

He then pulled the trigger, his face grimacing to show the effort required. "There is only one way for this gun to go off accidentally," he continued. "It requires two acts. She had to pull the hammer back first." He cocked the hammer. "Then she had to pull the trigger. But only three pounds of pressure is required to squeeze the trigger if the hammer is already pulled back." Magid then squeezed the trigger easily.

"But if the shooting was an accident," he asked the jury, "why did she have the hammer cocked? And why did she shoot her mother in the back?

"She said she doesn't recall what happened. But during statements given to the police, she said she remembers touching her mother's arm and wiping off the gun and putting it back at her father's home.

"She was pressured. She'd lost Tom Drake again, and she was going to do anything to get him back—except work. She was going to steal her mother's credit cards. Maybe she didn't mean to kill her mother. But we only have circumstantial evidence to [prove that]."

The jury deliberated for six hours on Thursday, July 2. They found Tina Burris guilty of murder, unlawful possession of a weapon with intent to use it unlawfully, and credit card fraud. One juror recommended leniency in regard to her sentencing.

In August, Judge Wallace sentenced Tina to serve at least 30 years in prison before becoming eligible for parole.

Tina Burris is currently serving her term at the Edna Mahan Correctional Facility in Clinton, New Jersey, and actively appealing several aspects of her case.

In December 1992, she requested an immediate, early release, citing a need to get out of prison to receive psychiatric counseling to treat her personality disorder.

"It's a nonissue," the prosecutor said at this time. "She got a mandatory sentence."

Six months later, in May 1993, Judge Joseph Lisa denied the request, calling the sentence fair and reasonable.

"SURGEON CAUGHT A BULLET BETWEEN HIS EYES!"

by Charles W. Sasser

Happy families, Tolstoy once observed, are all alike, while every unhappy family is unhappy in its own way. Homicide investigators in Tulsa, Oklahoma, had the opportunity to reflect upon that piece of wisdom beginning late on the cold night of January 22, 1993. At approximately 10:30 P.M., Tulsa 911 dispatchers received a frantic telephone call from a woman who sobbingly identified herself as Barbara Bell.

"Oh, my God! This is a nightmare!" shrieked the voice. "Help me! Help me! He is not awake. He's breathing. What do I do? Send me an ambulance."

The woman could then be heard wailing, "Don't die! Don't die!"

Emergency services—fire rescuers, an ambulance, and the police—sped to the house on East 66th Street on Tulsa's exclusive south side. Patrol Corporal Paul Eskridge, along with Patrol Officers Connie Evans and Kim York, were among the first uniformed arrivals.

Eskridge observed that the garage door to the large natural rock-and-wood house hung open. New cars sat parked in the drive. Lights inside the garage glared brightly upon the scene of tragedy, as though exposing it for all the neighbors to see.

A petite woman with short stylish auburn hair crouched on the garage landing leading into the house. In her lap, she cradled the handsome head of a well-dressed middle-aged man who appeared to be unconscious. Blood throbbed from an ugly bullet hole almost directly in the center of his forehead. Both man and woman were spattered with bright blood.

"Things like this don't happen to people like me," the woman sobbed.

That plaintive phrase launched Tulsa detectives, led by veteran Homicide Sergeant Wayne Allen, into a probe that seemed designed to prove the old adage that money cannot always buy happiness.

Even as 51-year-old Dr. David Lloyd Bell was trundled to St. Francis Hospital in critical condition, detectives took their first steps toward reconstructing the events that led up to the bloody scene.

From the thoroughly civilized and genteel front the Bells presented, an observer would conclude that they lived a storybook life. Dr. Bell was a highly successful, "more than brilliant" orthopedic surgeon and a full partner in the largest orthopedic practice in Tulsa. He and his wife, 46-year-old Barbara Lynn Bell, headed the ideal American family. Together they resided in the ideal house in the best part of the city. They were active in civic affairs such as the Tulsa Opera and the Tulsa Mental Health Association.

Over the next several days, police questioned the Bells' friends and relatives, trying to determine exactly what happened that tragic night. What happened to turn the lights off for the brilliant surgeon and his attractive wife?

One of Dr. Bell's associates remembered the surgeon as being "carefree and happy" in recent months. Bell, he said, was a private person who liked to study and work with his computer. "His mind was into medicine, and that's where he functioned day and night. His ego was as strong as any physicians you'll know. He had a very high self-esteem about his abilities in this specialty of medicine. . . . Money was important to him, but his ego was more important than money. Money was the way you kept score. He was more interested in how you make money."

Other friends told authorities that David Bell left the running of his home, the rearing of the children, and other domestic affairs almost exclusively to his wife, Barbara, while he immersed himself in his medical career, his computer, and his yard work.

Detectives learned that the Bells went out for dinner with Carl and Freda Heinz early on the Friday evening of the violence in the garage. During dinner, Carl Heinz would tell police, David Bell seemed rather "uncommunicative" with his wife over two upcoming trips she proposed, but otherwise, everything appeared normal.

The two congenial couples returned to the Bell home after dinner. It was about 9 P.M. The Bells' teenage children were not at home. The men returned to Dr. Bell's computer room to talk. Shortly thereafter, Bell received a page.

Heinz told authorities that Bell "said he had to go to the hospital for something minor. He usually didn't drink when he was on call."

The Heinzes left the Bell residence: Dr. Bell presumably departed for St. Francis.

Slightly more than an hour later, police swarmed into the Bells' bloodstained garage in response to Barbara Bell's plea for help. Patrol Officer Kim York said she first saw Mrs. Bell in her kitchen rushing from a telephone back to the garage.

"Help me," the tearful socialite begged.

"There was a male lying in the garage," Officer York recounted. "[Mrs. Bell] was trying to clean his mouth out. He was breathing."

Officer York said she "picked up" Mrs. Bell, who weighed only 99 pounds, and escorted her outside so emergency crews could get to the fallen man.

"[My husband] told me he had to go to the hospital," Barbara Bell subsequently explained, according to Officer Connie Evans. "I was very tired and was going to bed. I was going to call David at the hospital and ask him to wait up until [our son] came home. I called two hospitals and a pager company and couldn't find him."

Investigators questioned switchboard operators at nearby St. Francis Hospital. The on-duty operator remembered one call for Dr. Bell. It came in at 9:29 P.M. that Friday from "a lady asking him to call home."

Minutes later, the St. Francis emergency room secretary received a similar call, this one from a woman who identified herself as Mrs. Bell. She asked for Dr. Bell.

"I told her he wasn't there," the secretary said in statements to police. "She said that he must be in surgery, so I transferred her up there. She called back and I put her on hold as I paged Dr. Bell on the overhead. He wasn't there. When I looked down, the light wasn't flashing. She had hung up."

Then who, police wondered, paged Dr. Bell at home at 9 P.M. and asked him to come to the hospital. Or *was* he paged to the hospital—and if not to there, then to where?

Dr. Marvin Rawls was one of the surgeons who worked on the critically wounded Bell at the St. Francis emergency room, trying to save his colleague's life. Bell died at 12:23 A.M. without regaining consciousness and without reviving enough to tell police what happened. Less than four hours after Bell's death, Rawls and a group of the Bells' friends met with the new widow to console her.

"I told her the children were fine and the house was secured," Rawls told reporters. "She asked, 'Where's Silkie?' At first I didn't know what she meant. She told me it was her dog."

Rawls admitted the inappropriateness of the question may have been due to shock. He described Barbara Bell as "zombielike. She seemed catatonic. She stared into space."

On Sunday, when Dr. Rawls and friends met at the Bell residence to help the widow work out funeral arrangements, Barbara

Bell seemed to have recovered. She remarked, "I have no re-morse. I've done nothing wrong. It wasn't an accident. It was a mistake."

A man with a bullet hole between his eyes was a mistake?

Sergeant Allen and his sleuths continued to probe the dark depths of the puzzle, asking countless questions. To their sur-prise, they learned that both David and Barbara Bell had engaged in an odd game of hiding funds from each other. Bank records indicated that in October 1992, Barbara moved $100,000 from one account to another. David apparently had his own secret bank account containing $66,000.

In looking for a motive, Tulsa County assistant district attor-neys Sam Cox and Jay Holtzhouser homed in on the couple's finances. They admitted that they were suspicious over the fact that David Bell's death left his widow with a financial windfall of $6 million—including $2.5 million in assets and $3.5 million in insurance.

"A lot of money," murmured one police investigator.

Police then learned that each partner in the marriage may have been plagued with emotional problems. One of Dr. Bell's rela-tives would later testify that he and David grew up in a "dys-functional family" and had been estranged from each other for 21 years. When the relative learned of Bell's death, he said he wasn't too surprised. His first reaction was, "That just fits our family. I think my father killed my mother."

As for Barbara Bell, records indicated that she took antide-pressant drugs, headache medication, and a sleep aid. Her attor-ney quickly asserted that "the allegation Mrs. Bell thrives on preferential treatment, has a litany of lawsuits, and runs off bill collectors with a burglar alarm is utterly unsubstantiated and flies directly in the face of the financial condition of the Bell family. . . . [Mrs. Bell] categorically denies that she ever said she is the 'Leona Helmsley of Tulsa.' "

The so-called "Hotel Queen" Leona Helmsley was a self-described "rich bitch" who was convicted and sentenced to prison for tax fraud in late 1992.

"The most spurious allegation," Barbara's attorney continued, "is that [Mrs. Bell] has obtained indirectly over five million dollars as a result of David's death. The truth, of course, is that his death cost her about five million dollars . . . and can be documented by agreements reflecting the entire proceeds from insurance premiums have gone directly to her children, not her."

Apparently, Tulsa sleuths acknowledged as they built on the case file, the on-its-face storybook family had courted disaster for years. The Bell marriage, they learned, rested on rocky soil. It existed in a kind of darkness similar to the cold night that finally claimed David Bell's life.

"They didn't have a marriage in the true sense," Barbara's friend Freda Heinz would subsequently testify. "They lived like brother and sister. They were like friends. They had no sexual relationship for twelve years. . . . [Barbara Bell] asked [David] to go to Masters and Johnson [famed sex therapists]. He always refused. That's what I would expect. He was very concerned someone in the medical community would know what his private life was really like."

Heinz testified that Barbara had confided in her 10 years before that she was very unhappy in her marriage and had contemplated divorce. But then the unhappy woman changed her mind.

"I'm not going to do this to my children," Barbara had decided. "I don't want them to come from a broken home. He doesn't beat me, and he doesn't lie to me, and I'm going to make the best of it."

Five years later, Heinz asked Barbara how much longer she intended to stay with her unresponsive husband.

"She said not until the kids were out of school, would she even consider [divorce. . . . Barbara] was dramatic and very, very outspoken. She could rant and rave, and I always thought her bark was ferocious, but that's where it ended. They didn't have a lot of communication. It was not a close-knit relationship. They never touched each other or showed any affection at all."

Detectives discovered that David Bell had likewise considered divorce.

"My wife and I never do things together anymore," David once complained to a friend, and then he openly admitted that the only thing that kept him with Barbara was money. It would cost him $1 million to leave his wife, he calculated. Apparently, for him, it was better to stay with his wife and keep his money than to leave her and lose part of his wealth, which he held so dear.

As far as police could determine, neither partner knew the other had seriously contemplated divorce, at least not on that fateful January night when David Bell fell mortally wounded. And David, police learned, had also kept another, more devastating, secret from his wife.

"There is no evidence to show that [Barbara Bell] had any knowledge if Bell was preparing to divorce her," announced Barbara's attorney. He then added that Barbara had no knowledge that her husband was having an affair at the time of his death.

But if Barbara Bell knew nothing about the affair, almost everyone else in the Bells' social circle did.

The Bells' accountant told authorities that he found out about the doctor's extramarital relationship in the autumn of 1992, about the time it began, but he did not tell Barbara. A friend of David's at the gym where he worked out would later testify that David told her on January 11 that he was having an affair with a nurse. Dr. Marvin Rawls related how he had heard the rumor but had not passed it on. A plastic surgeon recalled that David said he was "very much in love" with a nurse.

Barbara Bell had apparently learned of the affair two days after her husband's violent death. A friend of hers explained it to police: "She ran up to me. She was crying. She said, 'David was having an affair?' It was more of a question than a statement. She was in disbelief."

Sergeant Allen, along with Detective Tim Bracken and other

probers, picked up the mystery girlfriend's trail. They learned not only of deceit in the Bell household, but also fear.

"David had to hide [the affair] from Barbara," a Bell friend opined. "He was afraid of her."

On the day before he was shot, Dr. Bell reportedly confided to another surgeon that his wife threatened to kill him if he ever left her. That notwithstanding, he still said he intended to divorce Barbara, money or not, in order to be with his lover.

"He was very up," the surgeon-friend commented. "He didn't think his wife knew anything specific about the affair. I told him to be careful."

On Friday, a mere seven hours away from the bloody scene in the garage, Dr. Bell told still-another surgeon-friend that he was "in great fear of being killed" by his wife.

"You're joking!" the friend had responded with amazement.

"No, she means it," Bell had replied.

"If you have any guns in the house," the friend advised, "you'd better get rid of them."

The friend then recounted how Bell planned to leave his wife when she was out of town. He would live with a security system and file a restraining or protective order to keep Barbara away from his office.

"This was not the type of family situation that existed on *Father Knows Best* or *The Brady Bunch*," Barbara Bell's attorney conceded. "These people had an unusual relationship. . . . [David Bell] was having an affair with a young nurse whom he was quite enamored of. He thought he loved her but was having difficulties making a decision. Over the months, he was in the process of having to choose between the other woman and his wife. He feared [his wife] would extract a heavy financial blow."

Questions remained. Was the shooting an accident, a tragic mistake—or was it premeditated, cold-blooded murder?

Six million dollars was a lot of motive. So was an unfaithful husband.

When located, Dr. Bell's love interest proved to be a twice-divorced brunette with two young children. Medical assistant Pam

Albright would later testify about her relationship with David Bell.

"He said his wife had told him that if he ever left her, she would kill him. He told me money was the only thing that kept him there. . . . Money was real important to him, as was I. . . . Money was who he was—how he wanted to express himself, how much money he had and how much he could make. I kept trying to make him understand why I needed to see beyond money."

She said Bell told her she was his first affair.

"I didn't believe him initially. He was well liked, attractive, and had been unhappily married for all those years. After I got to know him, it was really obvious he wasn't lying."

"Did you love Dr. Bell?" ADA Sam Cox would ask her at the trial.

"I did."

"Did he love you?"

"He did."

Pam Albright in her official statement finally disclosed where David Bell went after being paged at home on Friday evening. She testified that Bell had had himself paged as an excuse to leave home and visit her. She said Bell telephoned her for the last time from his car phone about 25 minutes before his fatal encounter with a killer in the garage of his own home.

Detectives said there were apparently only two people inside the Bell residence on that fateful night: David Bell and his wife Barbara. As detectives pursued their investigation, Barbara Bell reportedly expressed conflicting sentiments to friends which heightened police suspicion of her.

The shooting, she told friends, according to the recorded statements, "was not an accident. An accident is when you walk into the bright sunshine and lightning strikes a tree and it falls on you. That's an accident. This was a mistake. He made a mistake. Any idiot knows you don't run toward a gun."

Crucial questions centered around the "half-cocked" 9mm Browning semiautomatic pistol that Detective Bart Dean recovered lying on a kitchen table the night of the shooting. Dean said the weapon's magazine was fully loaded with 10 rounds, with a spent shell casing still in the chamber. Normally, a semiautomatic ejected a spent round after it was fired.

Richard Raska, the police department's weapons expert, subjected the weapon to various tests. The pistol had four safety mechanisms, he said, each of which must be released before the weapon could be fired. He soon concluded that the fatal bullet had been fired from that gun.

The presence of the shell casing in the gun's chamber could indicate, he said, that someone had grabbed the gun's slide as it was fired, thereby preventing ejection.

Did David Bell grab the gun while it was in the hands of his assailant?

Autopsy reports revealed that the fatal shot was fired at Bell from no closer than one inch and no farther than three feet. Certainly it had been within the victim's reach, prompting Barbara Bell's attorney to contend that Bell may have caused his own death by grabbing the gun and causing it to fire.

"It could have been *his* finger on the trigger," the attorney suggested.

Police Corporal Paul Eskridge reported that Barbara Bell appeared overwrought and in tears the night of the tragedy. She uttered "rambling statements," the officer said.

"She said she had shot her husband. It was an accident, is what she said. . . . She said she was unfamiliar with firearms but believed the pistol to be unloaded when she went to a garage landing to scare her husband. When he pulled up . . . he tried to grab the gun."

"[Barbara Bell] clearly believed the gun was unloaded," her attorney added. "All she had to hang on to was that he didn't lie to her. She went and got a gun to make this noncommunicative husband talk to her. . . . Barbara Bell made a tragic mistake. She is not a criminal."

Officers Kim York and Connie Evans remained with Barbara Bell at police headquarters up into the wee hours of the morning of the shooting awaiting news of the wounded doctor's condition.

"[Barbara Bell] made a call to someone," Officer York recounted. "They told her that her husband was dead. She was upset. She seemed to be a little confused. She said that he couldn't be dead. She said, 'Things like this don't happen to people like me.' She kept saying that she didn't do anything wrong—all she did was point a gun at him to scare him."

At 4 A.M., Officer Evans asked Mrs. Bell to change her clothes since the blood-spattered apparel she wore would be needed as evidence.

"She took off the wedding ring and threw it at us," Evans said. "I tried to give it back to her. . . . She wouldn't take it back."

During nearly six hours of questioning following the slaying, Mrs. Bell shed some light into the darkness that had hovered over her marriage for so many years. In her statements to the Tulsa policewomen, the anguished slaying suspect gave her account of the night's events.

"She kept repeating her story over and over again," Officer York would later testify in court.

Barbara Bell told the officers that although her husband said he'd been paged by the hospital, she knew he was lying. She went to the closet in the master bedroom and retrieved a gun, the 9mm semiautomatic pistol. She pulled the safety and lay the gun on the washing machine as she waited for her husband to return. She got impatient and called him at the hospital, but while he was being paged, she heard him approach.

As he came into the garage, she met him. She demanded to know where he was. He said he was at the hospital.

"No, you weren't," she told him.

"I must have been in the back room," he countered.

"No," she said, "you weren't."

He then told her that he was out "driving around." She leveled the gun at him.

"I'm going to blow your head off," Barbara Bell told her husband.

David Bell grabbed for the gun.

"She couldn't understand [why he did that]," Officer York later testified, "since he knew it was loaded."

The gun discharged. The bullet penetrated the doctor's forehead just above the brow.

Law enforcers stretched the probe into the week after the slaying as they strove to determine whether the crime was truly accidental, and as such manslaughter, or premeditated, and therefore murder.

On January 28, 1993, after reviewing evidence and statements in the high-profile case, Tulsa County DA David Moss said he thought there was "malice aforethought" and charged Barbara Bell with first-degree murder, which could carry a death penalty.

ADA Sam Cook, who, along with assistant prosecutor, Jay Holtzhouser, would handle the case, pointed out that he felt Barbara Bell had two motivations for shooting her husband.

"She knew of an affair her husband was having and [that] he intended to divorce her, and because of the monetary gain she would receive. . . . Nobody else pulled that trigger. Barbara Bell pulled that trigger."

It was simply a "domestic dispute gone bad," added Police Sergeant Wayne Allen.

In September 1993, the news media spread the darkness of the Bells' unhappy and ultimately disastrous marriage all over the front pages and the airwaves during a two-week trial that attracted huge crowds of spectators.

"There is a hypocrisy so pervasive—a desire to satiate puritanical beliefs by watching the painful mishaps inflicted upon others, " said Barbara Bell's attorney. "When those suffering are high up in the social and economic echelons, it draws a public clamor like a moth to a flame."

The defense's strategy to prove the slaying accidental failed. On September 30, 1993, a Tulsa district court jury found Barbara

Lynn Bell guilty of the lesser-included offense of second-degree murder. On November 3, 1993, Judge Clifford Hopper sentenced her to serve a term in the Oklahoma State Penitentiary.

"KISSING COUSINS KILLED FOR KINKY THRILLS!"

by Pat Burton

A lonely road at night. An overturned car.

The Oklahoma highway patrol officer pulled his patrol unit over onto the Johnsongrass and cut the engine. The vehicle's lazily circling dome light swept its beams across the dying leaves of a stand of oaks and turned the chrome of a vehicle that was lying upside down in a shallow ditch alternating shades of red and blue.

Patrol Officer Michael Manning was the first law officer at the scene of the one-car accident at the intersection of Mobil and Baseline Roads northeast of Velma, Oklahoma. It was just past midnight on Saturday, September 5, 1992. The long Labor Day weekend stretched ahead, and Manning suppressed a sigh as he got out to work the first in the rash of accidents he and his fellow troopers expected would occur during the next 72 hours. As accidents go, this one didn't amount to much.

The red 1990 Chevrolet Cavalier, flipped over on its top, hadn't sustained much visible damage. There were no skid marks, and it looked to Manning as though the compact car, which had been traveling no faster than 20 or 25 miles per hour, had been driven partway up a sloping embankment before it turned over. The trooper, who was experienced in viewing highway carnage, was almost certain that the wreck had not been serious enough to injure anyone. The lucky driver had apparently walked, or been driven, away.

Officer Manning cast the beam of his flashlight inside the overturned vehicle and saw the scattered contents of a woman's handbag. There was no sign of blood, but the officer was disturbed by the presence of the handbag. In Manning's experience, no woman leaves her purse without good cause. Was an injured female wandering, dazed and disoriented, somewhere in the darkness of the surrounding countryside? The trooper was groping for the purse, hoping to establish the identity of its owner, when he was interrupted by the beam of approaching headlights.

A 1929 Model A pickup pulled up behind Manning's patrol car, and a man and a woman got out. The woman, a slender dishwater blonde who looked to be around 40 years old, told Manning that she was looking for her kids who were late coming home from a ball game. The worried woman peered at the wrecked automobile and seemed relieved that it did not contain the mangled bodies of her youngsters. As she returned to the ancient pickup, her male companion blurted out, "That looks like Kay's car!"

The man appeared much younger than the faded blonde. He was tall with dark curly hair and a drooping mustache. He identified himself as Thomas Nooner and introduced the woman as his cousin, Mary Easlon. Nooner told the trooper that he boarded with the Easlons who lived less than two miles away. He said that a friend named Kay Busey had visited the Easlon home earlier that night. She had left around 11:30 P.M., driving away in a Chevrolet Cavalier identical to the one that was lying upside down in the ditch.

Manning was still talking to Thomas Nooner and Mary Easlon when Stephens County deputy Donnie Foraker arrived at the scene. Foraker, attired in the cowboy boots and the wide-brimmed white hat much favored by southwestern lawmen, had been notified because the accident occurred on a rural road.

Together, Foraker and Manning examined the contents of the

handbag and determined that the Chevy Cavalier did indeed belong to one Verna Kay Busey, a resident of nearby Elmore City, known to her friends as Kay. The photo on Busey's driver's license depicted a smiling woman with brownish-blond hair, who weighed 120 pounds and was 5 feet 2 inches tall. In Busey's wallet, along with the driver's license and various credit cards, the officers found a $100 bill and a couple of one-dollar bills.

A further search of the overturned vehicle yielded a wrinkled blouse and a bra. Both articles of clothing had obviously been worn since they were last laundered, but neither garment was bloodstained or torn.

When Deputy Foraker later contacted the Busey family, he learned that Kay Busey had not been seen since she left her home around 8:30 Friday evening to visit a friend, Mary Louise Easlon, who lived in the country. A family member told Foraker that Mary had just called to tell them she saw Kay's wrecked and abandoned car. Mary, who had been the missing woman's best friend since high school, wanted to know if Kay had made it home.

The relative reported that the 37-year-old wife and mother had not returned home, nor had she called to tell them that she had been involved in an automobile accident.

For a long moment, family members and the lawmen silently reflected on the possible whereabouts of Verna Kay Busey. Had she, while walking to a telephone, suffered a delayed reaction to an injury sustained when her car overturned? Was she lying comatose somewhere along the road? No one wanted to voice the chilling possibility that the pretty young woman had unwisely relied on the kindness of a passing stranger.

There was yet another possibility that the experienced investigator was hesitant to voice to the worried family.

Verna Kay Busey could have staged her own disappearance.

All lawmen are fully aware of one statistical fact that is hard for concerned relatives to accept. It is that a surprisingly large percentage of missing adults disappear of their own volition. Though Stephens County authorities would do everything in their power to locate the missing woman, none of them would be unduly surprised if Verna Kay Busey turned up alive and well.

Nonetheless, after a check of area hospitals proved fruitless, Deputy Foraker and Stephens County sheriff Ron Hunter coordinated a full-scale search to begin at daybreak.

The area of south central Oklahoma that surrounds Velma and Elmore City is oil country. Towering drilling rigs were etching their stark outlines against the pink canvas of dawn as the first searchers gathered in the semidarkness. As the sun rose higher in the sky, local officials and highway patrolmen were joined by more than 200 volunteers. While Busey's family waited anxiously by their phone, searchers scoured the eastern section of Stephens County, parting the tall grass that had grown up around rusting oil field equipment, and peering into the deep pools of shadow cast by vast oil storage tanks. The sun was down and darkness had once again enveloped the countryside when word spread through the ranks of exhausted searchers that a body had been found.

A searcher on Lake Fuqua Road, eight miles from where Busey's car was found wrecked and abandoned, had sighted the crumpled corpse of a white female lying in shallow water beneath a bridge.

The dawn-to-dark search had ended.

Deputy Foraker was the first lawman to arrive at the bridge. His trained eyes immediately recorded vivid details of the scene. The body, later positively identified as that of Verna Kay Busey, was bare from the waist up. Clad in sodden blue jeans, unzipped to reveal white panties, the corpse bore little resemblance to the attractive woman who had smiled up at him from the photo on her driver's license. Rigor mortis had passed, and the body was relaxing into decomposition. The deputy was appalled to see that a deep laceration on the woman's upper left scalp was already infested with maggots.

It was readily apparent that Kay Busey had been shot four times with what appeared to have been a large-caliber gun. An enormous bullet wound gaped under her left arm and another in her upper abdomen. Two jagged holes in her sodden jeans indicated that she had been shot once in each thigh. The position of her body indicated a fall from the bridge, but the medical examiner would later determine that Busey was already dead when she was thrown from the overhead structure. Despite the partial nudity of her corpse, the subsequent postmortem would produce no evidence that Busey had been sexually assaulted.

With the discovery of the body, there was no longer any question as to whether the pretty young wife and mother had voluntarily disappeared. The missing person case had now become a homicide investigation.

To lawmen, the first phases of a murder investigation can be compared to a choreographed ritual. Each person involved knows their role and the proper time to perform their part of the routine. First, the area must be sealed. The first officer on the scene cordons off the restricted area to protect the crime scene from alteration. He, or she, then makes immediate radio contact with a superior or the investigator who will handle the case. Upon the arrival of the homicide team, the body is photographed and the surrounding area is examined for any physical evidence the killer or killers may have left. The medical examiner officially confirms that the victim is, in fact, dead and examines the corpse for probable cause of death. Only after these steps have been taken can the body be searched and moved.

While all that was going on, Deputy Foraker, assigned as lead investigator in the case, pondered what he knew of Kay Busey's last hours of life.

Less than an hour before her car was discovered, the victim had been in the company of a lifelong friend. Busey's car had been wrecked—and Busey quite probably murdered—less than two miles from the safety of that friend's home.

This fact reminded Foraker of another disconcerting statistic: violent death is most often inflicted by those closest to the victim. To lawmen, one of death's ironies is that grief-stricken friends and family members are automatic suspects in a murder case.

Was it possible that a relative had staged the car accident to make it appear that the young wife never made it home after her evening out? Was Kay Busey's marriage a happy one? Aware that women usually confide any marital problems to their best friends, the investigators had another talk with Mary Louise Easlon.

Easlon told the sleuths that Kay Busey, who had been maid of honor at Easlon's own wedding, was a Christian woman who had been happily married for 19 years. According to Easlon, Busey was acting in the role of church counselor when she visited the Easlon home on Friday.

"I was having some troubles," Easlon told the investigators. "I called Kay and asked her to come over and talk." Easlon then added, "Kay was the best friend anybody could have had."

The officials pondered the woman's last statement.

According to Michael Manning, the highway patrol officer who had talked with Easlon at the accident site, Easlon "didn't seem too terribly upset" at the sight of her friend's wrecked car.

Deputy Foraker remembered that one of the victim's close relatives had voiced much the same sentiment. While speaking of the telephone conversation he had with Easlon right after Busey's disappearance, the man had told investigators, "I was so upset and she wasn't. It kind of surprised me."

The sleuths also found this seeming lack of concern odd in a woman who claimed to have frequently sought the advice and counsel of her "best friend."

Officers learned that both Busey and Easlon attended the same church in nearby Duncan, Oklahoma. In 1989, the Easlon family had been honored with a much coveted annual award given in recognition of an exemplary family within the denominational faith. But Easlon's church attendance had recently become sporadic, and acquaintances said that she had turned to Kay Busey for counseling about some rather unusual problems she was encountering in her marriage.

It turned out that these marital difficulties centered around Easlon's 27-year-old first cousin Tommy Nooner. It was alleged that for the past two years the unemployed Nooner had shared the 37-year-old woman's bed while the man lawfully entitled to that privilege slept in another room of the same house.

Before talking to the odd man out in this unconventional domestic arrangement, the sleuths set out to learn all they could about the lodger who had moved into his cousin's home and allegedly redefined the term "bed and board."

A background check revealed that Thomas E. Nooner had a criminal record that went back to 1984 when he was convicted for grand larceny in Stephens County. In 1987, Nooner had been convicted twice for second-degree burglary in Carter County and in 1988 was convicted for carrying weapons, drugs, and alcohol into the Okfuskee County Jail.

On Sunday, September 6, officers visited the Easlon residence for an in-depth talk with Mary Easlon and Tommy Nooner. Questioned separately, they each gave identical accounts of their activities on the night of Kay Busey's visit. According to their story, the three were together all evening except for a period of about 30 minutes in which Easlon went to a nearby store to get some soft drinks. Shortly after Easlon's return from the store, Nooner walked Busey out to her little red car and watched her drive away.

Questioning others in the Easlon household, the officers learned that on the night of Busey's disappearance, one family member had been visiting relatives who lived next door. "Mary called and asked me to stay over there," the man explained. "She didn't want me to come home because Thomas had had a few drinks and was upset about the death of his grandfather. Mary said that a good friend was coming over to counsel with him."

The man went on to tell investigators that he had heard, at approximately 11:30 P.M., four shots comings from a direction some distance from the Easlon house. "I didn't think nothing about it," he said. "I figured Tommy was shooting at some varmint."

After quietly discussing the significance of the neighbor's statement about hearing four shots (at that point it was not public knowledge that the victim had suffered four gunshot wounds), the officers obtained the homeowner's consent to search the premises.

While Deputy Foraker looked through the Easlon house, Doug Perkins, a criminalist with the Oklahoma State Bureau of Investigation (OSBI), checked the vehicles parked outside. After obtaining a consent to search from the vehicle's registered owner, Perkins centered his attention on a 1970 Toyota Corona Mark II station wagon. There was visible evidence that the vehicle had recently been wiped down, and Perkins found what looked like traces of blood on the rear carpet.

Inside the house, Deputy Foraker found a bag of reloaded .45-caliber ACP ammunition and a box of .45-caliber UMC full-metal jacket ammunition. Nooner, who admitted that he often used a .45-caliber handgun for target practice on the Easlon property, did not produce the weapon he practiced with, and Foraker did not find such a handgun in his search of the residence.

On Tuesday, September 8, Foraker's investigation went into high gear with the simultaneous arrival of two reports from the Oklahoma State Bureau of Investigation.

Ron Jones, OSBI ballistics expert, advised that a bullet removed from the victim had been identified as a .230-grain, .45-caliber, full-metal jacket bullet. This positive identification gave added significance to the ammunition seen in the Easlon home.

OSBI Criminalist Perkins reported that stains he found on the carpet and elsewhere in the Toyota station wagon, reacted positively to luminol, a chemical that causes any area where blood has been to light up with a fluorescent gleam. The driver's side rear-seat cushion had an approximately 14-inch-long streak near the junction of the seatback and the cushion. Further, a swipe was observed on the passenger rear door that was consistent with the streak on the cushion. Both streaks exhibited the characteristic cleaning patterns of a wetted towel or a sponge.

More significant to the success of the investigation, the blood was found to be consistent with Type A, the blood type of the murder victim!

By now, the investigators were reasonably certain that the Toyota station wagon had been used to transport Kay Busey's corpse from the car accident scene to the location where it was found. They felt it likely that Tommy Nooner had murdered Busey and that Mary Easlon—if not actively involved in the killing—had assisted Nooner in concealing evidence of the crime.

In the continued search for evidence, the sleuths turned up unsavory tales indicating that Nooner fancied himself a ladies' man and had a tendency toward sexual aggression. According to one woman, his sexual enslavement of his first cousin had so inflated Tommy's ego that he found it difficult—if not impossible—to tolerate rejection. Another woman claimed that on August 29, after he failed to seduce her, Nooner had demanded sex from her under threat of force. The woman alleged that Nooner threatened to cut her with a knife if she did not yield to his demands.

While these tales did not offer the hard evidence the prosecutor would need, they did offer some insight into a possible motive for the slaying. Had Tommy Nooner suffered sexual rejection from Kay Busey on that fateful night? Had he murdered her in retaliation for the intolerable blow to his macho self-image?

Or, had the murder followed a different scenario? Perhaps Mary Easlon, returning from her short trip to the store, surprised her virile young lover making amorous advances to her attractive friend? Could the scene have triggered a jealous rage in which Easlon fired the fatal shots?

The investigators put these conjectures on hold while they interviewed a male witness who claimed to have seen a case for a handgun in the 1929 Model A pickup Nooner sometimes drove. Another witness said that just days before the murder, he saws a large-caliber handgun under the dashboard of Nooner's Toyota station wagon.

Convinced that the murder weapon was hidden somewhere on the Easlon property, officials obtained a search warrant granting them authority to make a more thorough search of the premises. Even if they did not find a gun, they had probable cause to arrest Nooner on a charge of feloniously possessing a firearm after former conviction of a felony.

On Saturday, September 12, Stephens County authorities and Oklahoma Highway Patrol troopers left Duncan, the county seat of Stephens County, and drove 25 miles northeast to the Easlon home near the small community of Tussey. Their search of the home yielded a bag of UMC brand .45-caliber full-metal jacket ammunition, some spent bullets, and, in the bedroom shared by Nooner and Easlon, some photographs of a .45-caliber Colt Gold Cup semiautomatic handgun.

Nooner and Easlon were nowhere to be found.

"The lovebirds flew the coop," a family member informed the officers. He said that Tommy and Mary had packed suitcases and departed the previous day to stay with relatives in Moore, Oklahoma.

Late on Sunday night, a Moore police detective contacted Stephens County sheriff Ron Hunter and advised him that a Moore resident named Louise Layne wanted to make a statement relating to the Busey murder case. Hunter, who recognized the name as that of the relative with whom the two suspects were allegedly staying, immediately dispatched investigators to Moore, which is located just south of Oklahoma City.

Waiting at the Moore police station was a middle-aged woman whose face reflected the stress of internal conflict: fear versus family loyalty. She feared that her guilty knowledge might pose a threat to her own safety. Anxious to disassociate herself from involvement in a crime, Louise Layne told the officers that the two suspects had "just showed up" at her house on Saturday and asked to stay the weekend.

"Thomas said that him and Mary had been getting death threats," Layne said. "He told me that they were both under suspicion and had to be back in Stephens County on Monday for more questioning." Layne also said that "Mary seemed upset and just talked mostly to Thomas, but when they both told me they had nothing to do with the killing, I felt okay about the visit."

Then, on Sunday afternoon, while Mary secluded herself in a bedroom, Layne and Nooner left the house to rent some videos. On the trip to the video store, Nooner surprised Layne by asking her if she thought Mary might be "twigging out" on him. Shocked by the unexpected question, the woman realized that her uninvited guest was afraid that his companion would confess to the murder!

To Layne's further dismay, Nooner then admitted shooting Verna Kay Busey after the two got into an argument outside the Easlon house. "Thomas said that Mrs. Busey threatened to take Mary's two kids away from her because 'she wasn't a good Christian' and because her and Tommy were sleeping together right in the house," Layne told the officers.

"Thomas told me that he fired his forty-five caliber pistol in the air 'to get her attention,' and then forced her to drive down to the end of the road. Busey thought he wanted to rape her, so she took off her blouse and bra and told him to 'just go ahead and do it.' "

In Nooner's account of the crime—as retold by Layne—he then hit Busey in the face with his gun and told her that he had no intention of raping her.

In the somewhat garbled story related by Layne, Busey was driving the car when it turned over. "Tommy said she slowed down to about twenty-five and deliberately drove toward the ditch." After the car turned over, the two got out and started to struggle. "Tommy said that the next thing he knew, he'd emptied the gun on her." Layne ended her statement by saying that Easlon had helped Nooner move the body and get rid of the gun.

The murder weapon, Nooner assured Layne, would never be found. He claimed to have taken the gun apart and melted down the barrel.

Shortly after midnight on September 14, a contingent of officers surrounded the house in Moore where Tommy Nooner and Mary Easlon were sleeping. The pair offered no resistance when placed under arrest. Nooner was charged with first-degree murder, and Easlon was charged with accessory to murder after the fact.

Faced with the evidence against him, Nooner admitted to shooting Verna Kay Busey but—with a surprising display of gallantry—insisted that Easlon was not, in any way, involved in the killing. He said that after the shooting, his mistress was in a state of panic and that he had forced her to help him put the body in the car and drive to Lake Fuqua Road, where he "dumped it off the bridge."

Nooner explained that he was drunk on the night of the murder. "When I drink, sometimes I laugh and joke around, but sometimes I have a harder time dealing with things," the ex-con told the officers. He added that, "Me and Mary were fighting that night because I wanted her to ask Kay to come over so the three of us could have sex."

Nooner went on to say that he eventually persuaded his girlfriend to call Busey. "Mary asked her to come over to the house. But not for sex—she was just coming over to talk," Nooner said.

The ex-con claimed that the shooting was an accident but could offer no rational explanation as to how the victim had "accidentally" been shot four times. He adamantly insisted that he had forced Mary Easlon to help him cover up the crime.

Stephens County prosecutors would not accept Nooner's claim that Easlon was innocent of involvement in the killing. "How could she subject her best friend to a man like you?" was a question Assistant District Attorney Brent Russell would later ask Nooner in court.

The prosecutors had little doubt hat Tommy Nooner was what psychologists call "a high dominance" individual; after all, the unemployed ex-con had moved into an "exemplary" Christian home and made that home's churchgoing wife and mother his willing bed partner. But District Attorney Gene Christian believed that the sexually enthralled woman should be held accountable for her actions. DA Christian was certain that Mary's need to please her lover outweighed any concern she may have had for her friend's safety. In short, without Mary's complicity in the murder, Kay Busey might still be alive.

Under questioning, Mary Easlon confirmed her lover's claim that he was intoxicated during Busey's visit. "Tommy was out of control and waving his gun around. At one point I hid the gun but went and got it when he threatened to beat me."

The sad-faced blonde admitted to feeling jealous when Nooner wanted Busey to join them in three-way sex. The green-eyed monster resurfaced when she was sent to the store "so Tommy could be alone with Kay." Easlon said that when she returned from her errand, she told her friend, "You need to go home."

Easlon confessed to slipping outside and watching distrust-fully as Nooner and Busey stood talking beside Busey's car. "But when Tommy yelled, 'Are you going back in the house, or am I going to start blasting?', I went inside and started praying that God wouldn't let anything happen to Kay."

Easlon learned that her prayer had gone unanswered when, some minutes later after the couple had driven away, she heard the distant echo of gunfire.

Easlon described her state of mind when Nooner returned to her house immediately after the shooting. "I kept crying, but Tommy said, 'Shut up and let me think.' He told me where to go and what to do."

The two suspects were placed in the Stephens County Jail to await trial. While incarcerated, Easlon, her passion for Nooner unabated, attempted to "kite" a note to her lover. Housed in a cell adjacent to Easlon was a woman named Jane Adams, who intercepted the rolled-up note as it was passed from cell to cell through the air vents. After reading the note, Adams, who is currently serving five years on a drug charge in the Oklahoma Department of Corrections Facility at Mangum, turned it over to her jailers.

The note read in part, "They let your mom come back and visit me today. I told her you didn't mean to do it." Easlon wrote in some detail about how Nooner had shot and killed Busey, then described how she had helped him get rid of the body and dispose of evidence. Prosecutors felt that Easlon's missive was virtually a written confession.

The long cold winter in jail must have given Tommy Nooner ample time to reflect on death by lethal injection. Shortly after the new year, he instructed his attorney to negotiate a plea. On January 14, 1993, Thomas E. Nooner stood before District Judge Joe Enos and pled guilty to first-degree murder. A condition of Nooner's plea bargain was that he would testify against his cousin in her upcoming trial.

Judge Enos sentenced Nooner to life without possibility of parole for first-degree murder. When the killer pleaded guilty to feloniously possessing a firearm after former conviction of felony, the judge imposed an additional sentence of 10 years to be served consecutively with the life sentence.

On Monday, January 25, 1993, Mary Louise Easlon entered a not-guilty plea to the charge of accessory to murder after the fact.

Insisting that she had participated under duress, Easlon said, "I knew I had done something I shouldn't have done. Kay was dead and I was a part of it." Admitting that she helped load Busey's corpse into the Toyota and drive to Lake Fuqua Road, Easlon testified that she and Nooner dumped the body and hurried home where they haphazardly cleaned the blood from the station wagon. Then, under the pretext of looking for her children, the two got in the Model A pickup and drove to where Oklahoma highway patrol officer Michael Manning was examining Busey's overturned car.

It took the jury just 90 minutes to find Mary Louise Easlon guilty of helping her cousin conceal the murder and attempted rape of her best friend.

Associate District Judge Joe Enos followed the jury's recommendation and sentenced Easlon to 30 years in prison. The judge said his only regret was that he was not allowed to sentence Easlon over and above 30 years, since he believed the evidence showed that she was involved much earlier than she stated.

"TWISTED TRIO'S RX FOR MURDER: WITCHCRAFT"

by Richard Devon

The call was the kind the North Myrtle Beach, South Carolina, Police Department received all the time during the summer months. Some family member had not heard from a vacationer, and the caller wanted police to check on the relative who could not be contacted as expected.

The caller, who identified herself as a Mrs. Smith in Laurinburg, North Carolina, said she had been unable to get her husband on the telephone after repeated attempts. He was supposed to be at the couple's vacation mobile home, but her efforts to call him had been unsuccessful, and she was afraid something had happened to him.

Communications technician Dot Sorra explained that in order for North Myrtle Beach Police to respond to such a request it would have to be made through a police information network (PIN) request from another police jurisdiction.

Later on the afternoon of July 17, 1989, the required official request from Laurinburg came through. The petition concerned one Harold Dean Smith, 49, who had left his home the previous Friday for a fishing trip to the South Carolina coast. Smith was supposed to be staying in a family vacation home at Cherry

Grove, a beautiful area on South Carolina's Grand Strand, which stretches some 40 miles between Georgetown and Little River.

Patrolman Asa Bailey took the call from the dispatcher and drove to a trailer park at Cherry Grove. The blue Chevrolet pickup truck Bailey had been told to look for was found parked in front of a neat mobile home. Bailey knocked on the door but received no answer. He then walked around, peering in through the trailer's narrow windows. From what little he could see, everything appeared to be in order. At the back door, Bailey knocked again but still got no response from inside the trailer.

After walking around the trailer and seeing nothing out of place, Bailey went back to the front door and knocked again. As he did so, he noticed that the door near the doorknob was scraped and dented with what appeared to be pry marks. He tried the door, It was unlocked.

Opening the door and calling out, the patrolman walked into the small living room. Adjacent to it was a clean, compact kitchen. The place was neatly kept. If someone had battered and pried his way through the front door to make an illegal entry, he certainly had taken care not to muss things up, Bailey thought.

As Bailey walked down the narrow hallway, he came to a bedroom on his left. Glancing through its door, Bailey did a double take. There, half on and half off the bloodstained bed, was the body of a man dressed only in undershorts. The man seemed to be lying facedown on the bed before he fell or was dragged off and left nearly standing on his head. Bailey could only see the back of the dead man's head, under which was a large bloody stain on the carpet.

After quickly searching the rest of the mobile home and discovering no one or anything else out of the ordinary, Bailey returned to his vehicle and asked communications technician Sorra to send a supervisor and a detective.

It was shortly after 2 P.M. when other officers began to congregate at the scene. Among them were Chief of Detectives Walt Floyd and Detective Don Repec.

After a cursory inspection of the crime scene, investigators found nothing to provide identification of the victim. Copious amounts of blood marked the bedroom. Large bloodstains blotted the bedclothing and the floor under the victim's head. Blood also spattered the wall and the shade of a bedside lamp. The stains on the wall and lampshade looked to professional eyes like drops shed in the backswing of a bloody weapon.

Before any effort was made to gather possible evidence, Detective Repec photographed the undisturbed bedroom and its contents. Then he moved into the kitchen area and photographed a number of items, including a liquor bottle, a couple of empty beer cans, and a trash can that contained several items. With the video of the scene complete, detectives began a meticulous search for evidence.

When the victim's body was moved and turned over, it became obvious that the cause of death was a horrific beating. In fact, the battering had been so fierce that one eye socket had been crushed and the eyeball itself knocked out of the victim's head.

Other than the beaten victim in the bloody bedroom, investigators found no clue to what might have occurred. Although there were pry marks on the front door, there was no evidence of the type of rummaging and ransacking that usually accompanies home robberies.

After realizing there would be no quick or easy solution to the crime, investigators began to dust for fingerprints. Interestingly enough, there weren't any on the most likely surfaces. The mobile home had apparently been thoroughly wiped down. Neither could sleuths find any weapon that might have inflicted so much blunt damage.

While the crime scene search was continuing, the phone rang. Detective Floyd answered and found himself talking with Rebecca Smith, the woman who had contacted police earlier that day.

As gently as he could, Floyd explained that police had found a dead man in the residence, but he had not been identified yet.

The battered corpse could have been that of the missing Harold Dean Smith. Then again, it could have been someone else. Floyd did not explain to the anxious woman that it might not be possible to recognize the dead man's face, even if they had a picture of it, since someone had nearly destroyed it.

Later that afternoon, members of Smith's family arrived from North Carolina, among them his wife. Although no positive identification of the deceased had been made at the time, investigators felt certain the man at the crime scene was Harold Dean Smith. He fit the physical description police had been provided, his truck was still parked outside, and clothes scattered on the floor appeared to have been casually tossed aside as if the man had undressed and gone to bed.

Detective Floyd met with the wife and her relatives, one of whom agreed to go to the residence and identify the body. Rebecca Smith related that her husband had left Laurinburg on Friday after work and joined other family members who had been vacationing at North Myrtle Beach. These relatives had returned to Laurinburg on Sunday night.

Rebecca Smith told Detective Floyd that she had spoken with her husband by phone on Sunday night at the request of a family member who wanted him to bring something back from the beach for her. Later, a second relative had also called to say she had left a silk blouse at the vacation spot and wanted it returned. The widow said she had planned to pass this information along to her husband by phone on Monday morning.

On Monday morning, Rebecca Smith said, she began trying to contact her husband by phone again but was unable to get him. She knew her husband's habits, the woman insisted, he should have been in the vacation home when she called. After repeated attempts failed, she called the police to ask them to check on her husband.

When he interviewed Rebecca Smith, who was obviously upset, Detective Floyd did something that surprised himself. He asked the woman to write out her own statement describing events as she knew them. Floyd would later say that, in his 17 years of police work, he had never done such a thing before. In her own handwriting, the shaken widow gave Floyd the following statement:

"I am married to Harold Dean Smith and have been for fourteen years. My family has a trailer at Cherry Grove. Harold came to the beach Friday, where my sister and her family were already there on vacation. He told me if the fish were biting he'd be home Tuesday, if not, he'd be home Monday.

"I called him between the hours of ten-thirty and eleven forty-five P.M. Sunday night. He said he had met three men from Alexandria, Virginia, or West Virginia, and that they had been shark fishing and were going back Monday. I believe he said one man's name was Jim. Monday I called at eight A.M. to tell him to bring a blouse home, my sister's. When I didn't get an answer, I began to worry. I called all day today and then I called the police department. I contacted first the North Myrtle Beach and then the Scotland County Sheriff's Department."

Investigators immediately set out to locate three men from Virginia, who might be able to offer some information on the activities of Harold Smith between the time he had talked to his wife on Sunday and when his body was located on Tuesday afternoon.

Meanwhile, as the search for clues continued, detectives discovered that someone had used the toilet in the bathroom but had failed to flush it. Probers took a sample of the urine still in the toilet bowl. It would later be determined that the sample contained cocaine residue.

Outside the residence, investigators turned their attention to the victim's pickup truck. They found a cooler, which held two spoiling fish in liquid presumed to be from melted ice. Another cooler held a six-pack of beer standing in a few inches of water that had undoubtedly once been ice.

With the preliminary crime scene work completed, Harold Dean Smith's body was removed to the Myrtle Beach Regional Hospital, where Dr. Edward L. Proctor, Jr., would conduct an autopsy.

The pathologist's report noted that the victim was 5 feet 8

inches tall and weighed 175 pounds. Aside from the head wounds that had caused his death, Smith had been in good health for a 49-year-old man.

Dr. Proctor said the victim had died from blows to the head caused by "a rounded object which had been delivered with considerable force." The autopsy surgeon compared a crowbar and a piece of lead pipe to the wounds and said that something like either object could have been used to inflict the fatal injuries. There was also a strong likelihood the weapon had been a baseball bat. Dr. Proctor determined that at least two blows—probably three—had been struck, one of which destroyed the socket of the right eye. He said the skull had been "cracked like an eggshell." There were no defensive wounds on the victim's powerful arms or hands, indicating that Smith had been asleep when he was attacked, or that he had known and trusted his attacker and was taken completely by surprise.

Dr. Proctor said there was very little deterioration of the victim's body, left as it was in an air-conditioned space. Taking into consideration all the information at hand, he judged that death had occurred about 2 A.M. on July 17, which would have been some 36 hours before the body was discovered.

Detectives went to the pier where Harold Smith was known to fish. Probers learned that Dean had three visitors. Perhaps they were the group Smith had mentioned to his wife as potential fishing partners. The threesome sought by police were described as middle-aged men who had been traveling together in a light-green Chevrolet with Virginia plates. Detective Floyd told reporters that these men were not suspects, but that he hoped they could provide information about Dean's last day.

In due course, the vacationing fisherman were located, but they provided no useful information. Their conversation with Dean had centered on fishing gear, new methods, and the usual fish tales. The polite, friendly Smith would not strike anyone as a likely candidate to be murdered, the Virginians agreed.

In looking into Harold Smith's background and habits, investigators determined that he had never been involved in drugs.

Obviously, someone who did use drugs had been at the crime scene, since the urine specimen taken from the toilet revealed cocaine.

After interviewing family members, detectives learned that it was not the victim's habit to sleep in the mobile home's bedroom. His usual choice of a resting place was a comfortable couch in the den area.

Had the victim taken home some female companion that Sunday night? sleuths wondered. That was highly unlikely, detectives were told by those who knew Smith well. Nevertheless, this angle was not immediately ruled out as a possibility.

Upon questioning Rebecca Smith, detectives learned that her husband probably had as much as $1,000 in cash on him when he left for his fishing trip. He had just received a hefty bonus from his employer, the Owens-Corning glass manufacturers, the widow said. Also missing was a good wristwatch and a horseshoe-shaped ring set with diamonds.

Neither the victim's widow nor other family members could offer investigators any information that would provide them with a suspect in the case.

Dean's next-door neighbor at the vacation spot told detectives that she had seen Harold Smith late Sunday afternoon. The woman said she was never introduced to the victim and had never spoken to him, but she did see Smith pull up in his pickup truck and clean it out at twilight that day. Other than that, the neighbor said, she had not been aware of any activity around the neighboring residence until police showed up on Tuesday afternoon.

"Not that I would have been able to hear people coming and going over there, anyway," the woman told police. "My trailer has this central air-conditioning system that runs constantly this time of year, and it's real loud."

The North Myrtle Beach police force has few homicides to deal with. Their citizens are mostly busy taking care of the vacationers, and the latter are interested in the sun, sand, fun, and games. It had been four years since the last murder.

With no leads into the murder of Harold Smith in and around
North Myrtle Beach, investigators turned their attention to Laurinburg, across the state line in North Carolina's Scotland County.
There, they were ably assisted by Major Don Saperelli and Detective Paul Lemmond, of the Scotland County Sheriff's Department.

As the North Carolina probers began their work, the investigation took a gothic turn. The detectives found themselves delving into such matters as devil worship, witchcraft, blackmail,
and some damned unusual family relationships.

Initially, these matters were obscured as lawmen heard a litany
of praise for the victim. At the plant where Harold Smith worked,
investigators were told he was well-liked and a hard worker,
frequently working through lunch breaks and volunteering to
work overtime. Friends pointed out as an indication of his family
devotion that Smith routinely turned over his entire paycheck to
his wife, who gave him back $50 a week for spending money.
Smith had spread the news, however, that he was looking forward to leaving his routine world for the fishing trip that led to
his death. Fishing was a pleasure Smith had enjoyed with his
three stepsons, his friends told investigators. This time, however,
he was going fishing alone, Smith had said, because all the boys
were employed full-time and could not join him.

"He was so happy," one female co-worker told police. "All
he talked about was going to the beach and catching twenty-three
fish at one time."

Another female co-worker said, "It's hard to believe something like this could happen. We live in the same neighborhood
and everyone's upset. My mother can't even sleep at night."

Smith had worked at the Corning plant since 1973 and was
considered "low-key" by his supervisor, who revealed that
Smith earned $37,000 a year, considerably more than his base
salary, because he worked so much overtime.

"He enjoyed his work and wouldn't trade his job for anything," the supervisor and friend added. "I've never heard anyone say a bad word about him."

Investigators were also told that Smith got along well with his three stepsons, and that they had enjoyed going on fishing trips and to the mountains on vacations. The youngest of the stepsons had been only a toddler when Smith married Rebecca. Smith had raised them "as if they were his own flesh and blood," according to those who knew the family.

A co-worker of Smith's at the plant, however, said he heard that everything was not well domestically with the family, and, curious, he had spoken to Smith about it.

"Now, I was a real good friend, and if he had wanted me to know something he would have told me," the co-worker told police. "He said, 'Don't pay attention to what people say—my home life is my life. Whatever problems we have, we can work them out.'"

The friend could offer no information about the problems in the Smith household, but as investigators delved further, the basis of the problems seemed to have been Rebecca Smith's interest in other men.

As detectives searched for a motive, they learned that there was not a great deal of life insurance on the victim—something over $50,000, most of which came from an employment benefits package. There was no indication that Rebecca, who was beneficiary on the insurance, had been involved in any way with its purchase.

As detectives began to look into the possibility that either the widow or the stepsons were involved in Smith's murder, they learned that Rebecca had recently visited a local woman who claimed to be a witch capable of casting spells and putting hexes on people. Rebecca denied any such contact, but the rumors that reached official ears were strongly worded.

Detectives also learned that Rebecca Smith was known to have been consorting with at least two men over several years.

One of Rebecca's supposed lovers was Thad Cason, a workman who lived with Charles Gainey, a relative of Rebecca's. Rebecca had arranged for the young man to live with Cason.

"I came home one day and she had just moved him in on

me," Cason told detectives. This didn't particularly please Cason, he admitted.

When Cason was first interviewed by investigators, he denied any knowledge of Smith's murder and could offer no motive for it. However, when told that detectives knew about his affair with Rebecca Smith and that this made him a suspect, the sturdily built workman quickly changed his tune.

Cason said he first met Rebecca some 20 years earlier, long before she married Harold Smith. At that time, she was married to the father of her three sons and told Cason her husband was in the habit of beating her up. It wasn't long after this that Cason and Rebecca began to have an affair, which lasted about two months, Cason said, before she moved out of state. Over the next 20 years, Cason said, he was married and divorced—four times, to be exact.

Then, some three years before Harold Smith was killed, Cason ran into Rebecca at a store. She was 20 years older but still attractive to him, and exciting memories of that earlier time rekindled his interest.

"I started talking trash to her," Cason said.

She didn't put him off, and it wasn't long before they were in bed together again. That affair lasted two years.

Their liaisons were usually in his house, Cason said. He recalled for detectives that on one occasion Rebecca showed up at the house with her son Brian and Brian's girlfriend, and while he and Rebecca were in bed together, Brian took photographs of them.

"Did she have somebody make pictures of you and her more than once?" Cason was asked.

"Nope, that was the only time."

"So you and she had stopped your affair when Harold was killed?" a detective inquired.

"Yeah, I had quit seeing her and she was running around with Billy McGee."

"Who is Billy McGee?"

"He's a thief, and he's Becky's boyfriend now."

Cason was asked if the affair had ended on his account or Rebecca's.

"I ended it, because of what she asked me to do."

"And what was that?" Cason was asked.

"Well, one afternoon she was at my house on the couch and she asks me if I would do something for her for five thousand dollars. I said, what you want me to do for five thousand dollars, and she said, 'Kill Harold.' I told her I don't get into that, and then she asked me if I knew somebody who would do it. I told her, hell no."

Cason said he had no knowledge of who killed Harold Smith, but he knew that Billy McGee had been in prison more than once for theft. Cason didn't think McGee had the gall to do a killing, but he probably knew somebody from prison who would.

The investigators learned that Rebecca's relative, Charles Gainey, had moved out of Cason's house after Harold Smith was killed and moved in with Rebecca Smith.

In the course of investigating Gainey, detectives learned that the boy had some weird affiliations and was involved in devil worship.

To put it mildly, the case was taking on some unusual aspects. Investigators learned that Gainey had been working as a dishwasher at the motel which employed Rebecca Smith, who had not returned to work after her husband was murdered. The motel owner said Rebecca had called in sick several days before the murder, but he had not seen or talked to her since her husband's funeral. Detectives then sought out Gainey at his place of employment.

When Gainey was first interviewed by investigators, he denied any knowledge of Harold Smith's murder. However, the youth was extremely nervous and, as investigators pressed him, he unraveled his first version of events on the night the murder took place at Cherry Grove.

Gainey said that on that weekend, Brian Locklear, one of Rebecca's sons from a previous marriage, came by Cason's house and picked Gainey up. When the two got to Rebecca's house, she was there with Billy McGee. Rebecca said they were going to take Brian to the beach so he could go fishing with Harold.

The four of them took the car of another of Rebecca's sons who was working at the time. Brian drove. Gainey said that as they were traveling to the beach, they hit some kind of animal.

"I knew something bad was going to happen after that," Gainey said, although he didn't know what the bad thing was until later.

"Do you know who killed Harold Smith?" Gainey was asked.

"It was Billy Ray McGee," he answered.

Gainey told investigators that he wanted them to take him back to North Myrtle Beach because he feared for his life if he remained in Laurinburg. He said McGee had warned him not to talk to them about events at Cherry Grove. In subsequent statements, however, the nervous youth would say it was Rebecca Smith who killed her husband and who warned him not to talk to the police about it.

Continuing with his story, Gainey said, when they arrived at the beach, they stopped at a fishing pier for a short time and then drove to the mobile-home park. Rebecca had told Brian to leave the lights off when he drove up and not to park in front of Harold's trailer.

"She told me and Billy to lie down in the backseat so Harold wouldn't know she had a carload of people with her," Gainey said.

With Gainey and Billy hidden in the backseat, Brian and Rebecca went inside the trailer's screened porch and knocked on the front door. A light came on, and Harold came to the door to let them in. At the time, Gainey said he didn't understand why Rebecca was holding a baseball bat.

Rebecca and Brian were inside the house for a few minutes when Brian came back out to the car and said Rebecca wanted them to go back to the pier and get a soft drink. Gainey said they were gone about 10 minutes. When they returned, Rebecca came out of the house saying, "I did it, I did it. He's dead."

All three of them then entered the trailer. Gainey was ordered to go down the hall and "look at what Becky had done." Harold was making gurgling noises, so Brian took the baseball bat and hit his stepfather with it again "to finish him off."

Gainey then described how Brian Locklear used hand lotion to help him remove the victim's horseshoe ring from his finger, and Rebecca went around the house wiping things down so there would be no fingerprints left.

As they were leaving, the witness said, Billy McGee smashed the door with the baseball bat, saying that would lead police to think it had happened after a break-in.

Upon returning to Laurinburg, Rebecca instructed Gainey and Brian to take the horseshoe ring to the root doctor as payment for her previous efforts to kill Harold by witchcraft. Gainey told detectives that, at the root doctor's instructions, he and Brian returned home to fetch a pair of Harold's pants. They put these into a cake pan along with some sulphur and red onions, then burned the whole mess. This, Gainey told investigators, was the root doctor's "medicine" to keep the police off Rebecca's trail.

Investigators paid a visit to the root doctor, who naturally denied knowing anything about the diamond horseshoe ring or any efforts to put a death spell on Harold Smith.

On August 8, 1989, Rebecca Smith and Billy Ray McGee were arrested and charged with the murder of Harold Dean Smith. Gainey was charged as an accessory, as was Brian Locklear, one of the stepsons who had been brought up so kindly by the victim.

With information provided by Gainey, lawmen located a baseball bat that had been tossed off a bridge over the Waccamaw River. The State Law Enforcement Division (SLED) analysts detected bloodstains on the object. They also discovered, embedded in the bat's grain, paint that was later matched to the paint on the door at the murder scene. There was not enough blood, however, to get a match with the victim's blood.

Shortly after her arrest, Rebecca Smith gave police a statement in which she laid the blame for the murder on Billy McGee. She admitted making the trip to Cherry Grove but said it was

McGee who had actually bashed her husband's head with the baseball bat.

Brian Locklear also told investigators that it was McGee who had murdered his stepfather, but McGee denied the slaying, at first saying he knew nothing about Smith's murder. However, when he learned that the other members of the foursome had rolled over on him, McGee came up with his own version of events at Cherry Grove.

McGee, whose life had revolved around prisons, said he met Rebecca sometime before his last jail stay. Without expounding too much on the subject, he said Rebecca "sort of took to" him and they began having an affair.

Then, when he was returned to the slammer two years before Harold Smith was killed, Rebecca began coming to visit him, each time bringing him spending money in amounts of $15 to $30. She kept to this routine until McGee was released from prison again.

McGee said Rebecca began giving him money to buy cocaine before his last trip to jail. He had not known Harold Smith personally, McGee said, but had threatened to tell the man about his affair with Rebecca. On one occasion, the suspect said, he actually called Smith to discuss some pistols and old coins that Rebecca had given him to swap for cocaine.

In their prison visits, Rebecca had talked about getting rid of Harold so she could be with McGee when he got out. She told him she had been going to a root doctor to put a spell on Harold. This was either to make Harold sick or kill him, Rebecca had told her imprisoned boyfriend. After he got out of jail, McGee said, he went with Rebecca at least 20 times to see the root doctor.

Billy McGee's statement backed up, at least in part, what Charles Gainey had said about getting rid of the baseball bat and Harold Smith's billfold. He not only led lawmen to the same spot on the Waccamaw River where they had recovered the baseball bat, he pointed out a creek over the state line in North Carolina where he said Smith's billfold and Rebecca's bloody shoes had been thrown. A search for these other two items, however, was not successful.

About the murder itself, McGee said that on that Sunday, he spent some 12 hours painting a house and reached the Smith residence sometime after 10:30 P.M. Being tired, he lay down on the foot of Rebecca's bed for a nap. She awakened him, McGee said, and they smoked a joint and snorted cocaine before heading out to the beach.

McGee maintained that he had originally been told that the purpose of going to Cherry Grove was for Brian Locklear to bring his stepfather some marijuana. However, McGee said, he had no personal knowledge of Harold Smith's using any kind of drugs. McGee also said that, when they arrived at Cherry Grove and stopped at the pier, Rebecca tried to get him and Gainey to stay there while she and Brian went to the mobile home where Harold was. McGee said he refused and they argued, a matter Gainey had alluded to in his statement. On previous occasions, McGee said, Rebecca had left him standing by the road as long as three hours while she went looking for cocaine.

McGee insisted he never went into the bedroom where Harold Smith was, but he did say that at one point, he heard Harold calling for Rebecca to help him. After they left the crime scene, they went only a short distance when Brian handed McGee the bloody baseball bat to be tossed into the river.

McGee, contradicting Gainey, said Brian was the one who had banged the door with the bat as they were getting ready to leave. But McGee also said, as Gainey had, that it was Rebecca who had wiped down the items in the mobile home. McGee said the only thing he wiped off was the handle of the screen door. Other than that, he had touched nothing in the mobile home and wasn't worried about fingerprints.

In early 1990, all four suspects—Billy McGee, Rebecca Smith, Brian Locklear, and Charles Gainey—were indicted on various charges by a Horry County grand jury in connection with Harold Smith's murder. Assistant Solicitor Ralph Wilson said he would seek the death penalty against Rebecca Smith.

The trial was initially scheduled to begin in September 1990, but Circuit Judge Dan Laney ruled that two attorneys who had been appointed to the case did not have the experience to handle a death penalty case. Although the two attorneys had considerable experience arguing appeals of death penalty cases before the Supreme Court, neither had ever gone to court to actually try a death penalty case.

"If we had tried the case, the Supreme Court would have turned it over in a minute," said one of the two attorneys of the ruling.

Finally, in December 1990, some 17 months after her husband's murder, Rebecca Smith went on trial for her life in the Horry County Courthouse in Conway. Gainey, McGee, and Locklear all agreed to enter pleas in connection with the case.

The trial lasted nine days, with the most damning testimony coming from McGee, Gainey, and Cason. The defendant took the stand in her own behalf and admitted she was an accessory in the case, having been there when McGee actually beat her husband to death with the baseball bat, but she denied having anything else to do with the murder.

Brian Locklear continued to maintain that Billy McGee had done the deed, but when McGee's turn on the stand came, he recalled that Locklear, on the way back to Laurinburg after the murder, said to him, "Billy you can be my daddy now."

The jury deliberated for nine hours before returning a guilty verdict. The death penalty was handed down in less than half that time.

Death penalty cases are automatically appealed in South Carolina, and in December 1992, the South Carolina Supreme Court ordered a new trial for Rebecca Smith, maintained that allowing information about her cocaine use in the trial was prejudicial.

In the meantime, Billy McGee and Brian Locklear had begun serving 35-year sentences for their part in the crime. Charles Gainey, who was sentenced to 15 years, was already out on parole.

Testimony in Rebecca Smith's retrial in February 1994 was virtually the same as in the first trial, with one exception. Now, Brian Locklear took the stand to say it was *he* who had beaten his stepfather to death with the baseball bat and that his mother had nothing to do with it.

Under cross-examination by Solicitor Wilson, now the chief prosecutor for the circuit court, Locklear admitted he was bisexual and had tested HIV-positive.

"You have nothing to lose, do you?" Wilson asked of the man whose latent disease was a virtual death sentence.

Again, the jury found Rebecca Smith guilty of first-degree murder, but the jury declined to give her the death penalty. She was sentenced to life imprisonment, but told the press that she was going to appeal this verdict, insisting that she was only guilty of being an accessory in her husband's murder because she just happened to be there when it happened.

At this writing, Rebecca Smith is serving her sentence in the South Carolina corrections system.

"BLOODY WELCOME FOR THE RETURNING SAILOR"

by John Griggs

It was 1:12 A.M. on April 4, 1991, a busy Thursday morning for the Virginia Beach, Virginia, police dispatcher who took the call. The woman on the line was sobbing, her shrill words at times impossible to make out. She told the dispatcher that her husband had been murdered in their home. He was lying on the floor, she said.

"I went out to the store to get some medicine for myself," the caller volunteered. When she returned, she said, she discovered the body.

"Was there anyone else at the house when you left?" The dispatcher asked.

"My husband," the woman replied.

"Anyone else?"

"No."

Calls to 911 automatically show the dispatcher the caller's address. The address that came up on the dispatcher's computer terminal screen was in the 800 block of Dryden Street in the Chimney Hill subdivision, a middle-class neighborhood miles away from the oceanfront area. The dispatcher typed that address into his computer and sent emergency workers and a patrol car to the scene.

One minute later, at 1:13 A.M., workers from a nearby rescue squad headquarters were at the house, which sat on the end of a quiet cul-de-sac. The wife, a petite woman wearing glasses and with her brown hair bobbed to her shoulders, led the rescuers through the house to the bedroom she had shared with her husband. There they found a man lying on his stomach on the floor in a spreading pool of blood from several apparent stab wounds in his chest, neck, and stomach. The emergency workers couldn't find any vital signs, and the man was pronounced dead on the scene.

The woman identified the victim as her husband, Richard D. Swanson, 32.

By now, uniformed officers had arrived on the scene. The wife led them to her daughter's bedroom. The child was away at Girl Scout camp, she explained. The woman said she believed her husband's killer had entered and left the house through a window that was still raised in the daughter's room.

The officers cordoned off the crime scene. They immediately began to shoot photos and videotape and to search for other evidence.

A few minutes later, Detective Paul C. Yoakam, a veteran investigator for Virginia Beach police, arrived at the scene. Tall and thin, Yoakam is an easygoing, pleasant man with thinning light-brown hair and a mustache. His large wide-set eyes stare out from behind glasses, taking in minute details that others might miss.

The victim's wife was not at a neighbor's house. Officers had begun a door-to-door canvass of the neighborhood where the Swansons had lived for eight years, searching for any clues that might lead them to the killer.

The wife had already produced a portrait of the victim for uniformed officers, who provided Detective Yoakam with details. Richard Swanson, a sailor in the U.S. Navy, had just returned home a week earlier from a seven-month stint in the Persian Gulf War. He'd sailed in onboard the aircraft carrier *John F. Kennedy*, where he was a chief petty officer in the carrier's supply department. Originally from Menominee, Michigan, Swanson had been on the *Kennedy* since 1989, with frequent duty tours at sea.

All agreed that Swanson was a clean-living, 15-year Navy veteran who read a lot. He didn't philander, didn't gamble, didn't do drugs or anything else that might have made someone want him dead. But a quick look at his body, with its numerous stab wounds, showed someone had wanted him dead very badly—they made sure they got the job done.

Like thousands of other sailors returning to the Virginia Beach area, Swanson had enjoyed a hero's homecoming. While such homecomings were common across the country in the spring of 1991, the celebration was especially poignant around Virginia Beach. The city is part of Hampton Roads, a sprawling five-city metropolis. The jewel of that metropolis is Norfolk, the country's largest naval port.

A neighboring couple said a cheerful Swanson had come to their house a couple of days before to borrow some WD-40. They had greeted him saying, "Welcome home, warrior!"

Another couple remembered how happy Swanson's young daughter had been to see him. The previous Friday, they'd seen him walking the girl to her school bus in the rain. He gave her the umbrella they had shared, and the Navy man ran back to his house in the rain, not seeming to mind.

Swanson had brought his daughter several presents, neighbors said. One was a T-shirt that said, "Who do you love on the *Kennedy?*" with her father's name printed underneath.

As Swanson and his fellow sailors had settled back into domestic life, they realized that, although they may have left a war behind, a different kind of war was still raging in the streets of Hampton Roads, which was reeling from the crime wave that rolled across the rest of the country, as well.

The day before Swanson was killed, the body of another Navy man had been found at a Hampton Roads construction site. Police believed that the man fell victim to "pickup robbers," who offered him a ride, then robbed and killed him.

The public didn't take crimes against their war heroes lightly. As Detective Yoakam studied the Swanson crime scene in the warm spring night, he must have realized this would be a sensitive case with crushing public pressure.

A few minutes later, Yoakam talked to the victim's wife. She had wrapped a blanket over her clothes and was crying. Yoakam noticed she was clutching a bloodstained purse.

The interviews with the neighbors had produced an interesting tidbit: the victim's wife apparently had a boyfriend. They'd seen the man visiting her for about two years, always while her husband was away. He rode a black 10-speed mountain bike and always entered with his own key, the neighbors said. One neighbor said she had actually thought about telling Swanson of the apparent boyfriend but didn't think it was any of her business. She'd hoped things would get better, she said.

Neighbors told probers that they hadn't heard the Swansons arguing since the sailor's return, and there were no other signs of trouble or strain.

Detective Yoakam asked the victim's wife about her alleged boyfriend. She denied having one and said nobody had been visiting her. As the sleuth pressed her on the issue, the wife got mad and dashed inside a neighbor's house, saying she had to use the bathroom. When she came out of the bathroom, she threw a blanket she had with her onto the sofa and lingered as if she didn't want to go back outside with Yoakam.

A few minutes later, however, she did emerge. Detective Yoakam persuaded her to come down to headquarters and answer a few questions. The detective treaded cautiously. Plenty of people play around on their mates, and few want to admit it. The last thing a homicide detective wants to do is go after the wrong suspect, especially if that person is the grieving widow of a returning warrior.

As the investigator cleared the scene, he ordered the body sent off for autopsy. Pathologists would find that the Navy man had been stabbed 65 times—in the face, throat, neck, stomach, and both sides of his torso.

Meanwhile, other officers had discovered the boyfriend's name from neighbors. A records check showed the man had been convicted four times of petty larceny and had done time at least twice. He'd also been arrested for grand larceny, breaking and entering, contributing to the delinquency of a minor, refusing to identify himself, giving false identification to police, failing to complete community service, and failing to show for trials. His driver's license had been suspended after numerous arrests for drunken driving, reckless driving, and disregarding traffic signs. Hence, the 10-speed bike that neighbors saw him using. He'd also been arrested several times for driving without a license.

Officers set out to find the man as Detective Yoakam began his interview with the victim's wife. The minutes were ticking toward Thursday's daybreak.

Valerie Otero Swanson, 32, worked as a nurse's aide. She and her husband had been married 11 years, she told Yoakam.

Swanson held firm to her story. She'd gone out to get a bottle of cold medicine and returned to find her husband slain, she said. She produced a computerized receipt for her medicine that showed the date and time she had gotten it from a nearby supermarket. She was almost too eager to present that receipt. And Yoakam saw that the time of the receipt was a few minutes after the 911 call had come in.

The investigator was still moving cautiously. Anybody can make an honest mistake, especially a shocked widow.

But still, there were questions. . . .

The sleuth pressed the victim's wife. She amended her story, now saying she *was* there when her husband was killed, but a stranger had done it.

The uniformed officers had told Yoakam that there was a layer of undisturbed dust on top of the dresser in the girl's bedroom. The wife had told officers that the killer had apparently entered and exited through that room, moving the dresser. But, checking the damp dirt outside the bedroom window, the officers had found no signs of footprints.

The detective pressed Valerie Swanson further.

Suddenly, Valerie changed her story again, admitting not only that she had a boyfriend but that *he* was the one who had killed her husband. She, however, was not involved, she said.

Why, if she was a nurse's aide, didn't she administer first aid to her husband? the investigator asked.

Swanson explained that she did check her husband's left wrist for a pulse.

Did she get blood on her fingers? the detective asked.

Swanson said she didn't.

The detective reminded Valerie that her husband's left hand had been coated with blood. Valerie then said it was the right wrist she had checked. Yoakam reminded Valerie that her husband's right hand had been folded under his chest.

Seeing that she had painted herself into a corner, Swanson told Yoakam that she *was* involved in the slaying. She and her boyfriend had come up with the plan in March, she said, shortly before Richard returned home.

Whose idea was it to kill him? Yoakam asked.

Valerie said Richard got so angry at her that it was her idea. She wanted some excitement in her life, and all her husband wanted to do was read. She and her boyfriend had been living together in her home for about two months prior to Richard's return. They had been lovers for about five-and-a-half months, she claimed. They'd met in a Virginia Beach bar. Yoakam would later find out that Valerie and her beau met in the bar about three years before, not five-and-a-half months.

Valerie's boyfriend had moved out on March 27. Richard sailed in the next day.

The plan to kill Richard Swanson had been set for April 1. That night, Valerie left her bedroom window open while she and her husband went to the Heartbreak Café nightclub.

Valerie's boyfriend was supposed to climb in the window and ambush Richard. But the Navy man decided to return home early from the club. Noticing that the window was unlocked, he locked it.

A couple of nights later, Valerie and her boyfriend tried again.

This time, Swanson gave her boyfriend a key with which to enter the house. She and Richard had gone back to the Heartbreak Café and returned home about 10:30 P.M. on Wednesday. Valerie read for a while and went to sleep.

Early Thursday, Richard was awakened by a noise. He got up, saying he was going to another room to watch TV. As he opened the bedroom door, Valerie's boyfriend struck.

Valerie, who'd gotten up to go to the bathroom, watched the killing from there, less than 10 feet away. Richard cried out his wife's name, and she screamed, "Oh, my God!"

Her boyfriend was stabbing the victim so fast, Valerie couldn't even see the knife, she said. She thought her boyfriend was using his fists. Richard fought back to no avail.

With his last words, Richard begged his wife for help. In a state of panic, Valerie sat in the bathroom and cried. The boyfriend, covered with blood, finished his grim task and went to a hallway bathroom to clean up.

Valerie came out of her own bathroom to hear the last breaths of her husband. She told Detective Yoakam she never thought the murder would "become a reality." She'd had second thoughts about the plot and was praying her husband would die of natural causes, she said.

With the interview over, Yoakam, who jotted down Valerie Swanson's statement, charged her with first-degree murder and conspiracy. She was placed in the Virginia Beach Jail under $75,000 bond.

Up until he charged her, Yoakam had been careful to let the woman know she was free to go whenever she wanted to. Under that condition, Yoakam knew, her statement would be considered voluntary and could be used against her in court. The detective did not read her her rights because he did not want to scare her into silence.

Valerie Swanson, however, would soon change her story again.

Meanwhile, officers continued with their search for her boyfriend. By now, they had a physical description and were hunting a man matching that description who was seen riding a black mountain bike.

As the hours ticked past daybreak on Thursday, uniformed officers found a man matching the boyfriend's description riding a black mountain bike near the Swanson home. They stopped the man, and he confirmed that he was Valerie's boyfriend—24-year-old Alan John Marcotte, a part-time dishwasher who'd bounced from job to job. He had woken up thirsty, he said, and had been headed for a 7-Eleven to get a Dr Pepper Big Gulp. The short suspect with thick glasses never got his soda.

The officers persuaded Marcotte to ride down to headquarters with them. There, Marcotte gave Detective Shawn W. Hoffman a statement. Hoffman, a husky young detective with longish brown hair, was helping Yoakam on the chase.

Marcotte told Hoffman that he and Valerie had planned to kill her husband because he was always "bitching at her about this and that." Marcotte corroborated what his girlfriend had said about the planning. He said Richard had opened the bedroom door after he heard Marcotte in the hallway.

"When Richard Swanson opened the bedroom door, that's when I started using the knife on him," Marcotte said. "I hit him about fifteen times or more in the stomach, and then I went for the throat."

After the slaying, Marcotte washed his hands and smoked a cigarette. He told his girlfriend, "You wanted the job, and it is done."

Marcotte blamed the killing on his lover.

"It was Valerie Swanson's idea to kill Richard Swanson," Marcotte said. "I know it was wrong. I'm sorry for it. I feel upset for doing it to another person."

Detective Hoffman charged Marcotte with first-degree murder and conspiracy. The defendant was placed in jail without bond. Like his lover, he, too, would later alter his story.

With the charges taken care of, Hoffman consulted with Yoakam and got a warrant to search Marcotte's rented room, a few miles away from the Swanson home. When he arrived there, Hoffman found a small room with a single bed and dresser.

In the dresser drawer, Detective Hoffman found a dark-blue T-shirt and black stone-washed jeans, both bloodstained. He also found the apparent murder weapon: a hunting knife with blood and what appeared to be human flesh on it.

Hoffman collected a pair of bloodstained black tennis shoes from the room as well. From a wall, he took down an 8-by-10 color photo of Marcotte, Valerie Swanson, and Swanson's daughter. Investigators would later find they had posed for that shot at a local mall the afternoon before the killing.

In a Dumpster outside, Detective Hoffman found several blood-spattered towels. He sent all the bloodstained items off for laboratory analysis. Tests later revealed that the knife was in fact the murder weapon, and the blood on it and on the clothing, shoes, and towels was all Richard Swanson's.

So, the sleuths mused, Valerie Swanson and Alan Marcotte had bungled their murder plot.

While Valerie Swanson had told Detective Yoakam that it had been her idea to kill her husband, her lawyer implied at her first court appearances that she would change her tune.

David Moyer, a tall, mustachioed former prosecutor, disputed Marcotte's claim that his client had been the instigator.

"It's like pancakes: No matter how you mix the batter, they always come out with two sides," Moyer told a reporter. "Our defense will be that Marcotte acted on his own that night."

After a later hearing, Deputy Commonwealth's Attorney Karen Lindenmann told a reporter, "To some extent, this is the case of people pointing fingers at each other now that they are in trouble. Love can be schizophrenic, I guess."

Marcotte had told a reporter a few days after the slaying that he really loved Valerie Swanson and would like to marry her upon his release from prison. In that interview, the garrulous defendant also said, "I lost count after fifteen stabs. I wanted to see how long it would take until he stopped moving."

Marcotte told the reporter that he'd killed Richard Swanson

because he'd returned to the home to retrieve some health insurance forms and the Navy man had confronted him.

After the killing, he said, "I didn't have any trouble sleeping. I just wasn't thinking about it. I put it on the back burner."

Marcotte told the reporter that the victim knew he and Valerie were friends but never realized they were lovers.

As Detective Yoakam tied up loose ends in the case in the months after the arrests, it was clear that this saga of love and lies would yield more than a few courtroom surprises and revelations as the two ex-lovers pointed accusatory fingers at each other.

On September 16, 1991, Alan Marcotte, apparently realizing the heavy evidence stacked against him, pleaded guilty to first-degree murder and conspiracy in Virginia Beach Circuit Court. The defendant said little. Sentencing was set for December 16.

Marcotte's lawyer, Paul E. Sutton, had said before the hearing that his client would testify against Valerie Swanson if asked.

Lindenmann, the assistant prosecutor, said of Marcotte and Swanson, "At this point, I think he's realized he has to look out for number one. And I expect his love for her may have waned a bit in recent months."

Outside the courtroom, Prosecutor Lindenmann told a reporter that she would interview Marcotte before Valerie Swanson's trial, but she didn't believe his testimony would be essential to the case.

At the sentencing hearing, Marcotte claimed that Swanson had promised him a four-wheel-drive pickup truck as payment for killing her husband. The defendant's relatives testified that Swanson had a hold on Marcotte and that he loved her obsessively.

However, Judge Kenneth N. Whitehurst wasn't swayed by the testimony.

"I cannot have sympathy for what you did," he told Marcotte. "What you did was cold, calculated, cold-blooded murder."

Judge Whitehurst heaped a maximum life term plus 10 years on the defendant. Marcotte, his hair closely shaved to his head, showed no emotion. He will be eligible for parole in 2006, when he is 39.

Valerie Swanson's trial began January 28, 1992, in Virginia Beach Circuit Court. Lindenmann would be prosecuting the case with her boss, Robert J. "Bob" Humphreys. Humphreys would be pursuing the death penalty.

Humphreys and Swanson's attorney, Moyer, were old friends. They'd worked together years earlier as assistant prosecutors in Norfolk. Humphreys, 41, had been a prosecutor for 18 years, winning election as head of his office in 1989.

He and Moyer, though, would leave their friendship at the courtroom door each day as they battled it out in the Swanson trial. Moyer made it clear from the start that he would try to put the blame on Alan Marcotte alone, portraying his client as the victim of blackmail and threats from her lover in the months before the killing.

"Mr. Marcotte was a jailbird. He was a bad character," Moyer told the seven-woman, five-man jury in his opening argument. "Why she ever got involved with him, I'll never know. It was a mistake."

Valerie Swanson, free on $75,000 bond, wept and wrung her hands as her attorney urged the jury to see that she, too, was a victim.

In his opening statement, Prosecutor Humphreys maintained that it was Swanson who helped set up the murder plan.

"The defendant and her lover could not tolerate the presence of her husband," the prosecutor told the jury. "Rather than talk to a divorce attorney, the decision was made to do away with Richard Swanson."

Detective Yoakam was Humphreys' key witness the next day, testifying for more than two hours from the notes he took as Valerie Swanson made her confession. He coolly stood up to Moyer's battering cross-examination.

The next day, Wednesday, Valerie Swanson took the stand. She told the jury that she had only lived with Marcotte because he had refused to leave her home. She feared he was a member of a street gang, she said, and he had raped her numerous times.

They had broken up in 1989 after her husband caught them together, she said, but Marcotte became obsessed with her.

"He [Marcotte] beat me. He set my hair on fire. He used a bullwhip on me once," Swanson testified. And she had loved her husband, she maintained.

Prosecutor Humphreys blasted her testimony for more than two hours on cross-examination, asking her repeatedly why she hadn't reported the alleged abuse to the police. Humphreys accused Swanson of lying to protect Marcotte when she gave Yoakam three different versions of what happened on the murder night. The prosecutor had a bailiff bring in Marcotte, whom Humphreys had waiting in an adjacent holding cell.

Marcotte, wearing a blue jacket and tie, walked into the courtroom and stared at his ex-lover. That was enough. Humphreys did not put him on the stand.

In later testimony, Swanson admitted that she suspected Marcotte was going to kill her husband the day it happened. She had even told her husband about it, she said, but he made light of it.

"Didn't it occur to you to call police about a murder that was about to take place?" Prosecutor Humphreys asked.

"My husband didn't believe it," Swanson answered.

"But you did," the prosecutor said. You're a big girl. You know how to dial 911, don't you?"

"I listened to my husband," Swanson replied.

"Are you saying that by listening to your husband, you cost him his life?" Humphreys asked.

He didn't get an answer.

A few minutes later, the prosecutor finished his brutal cross-examination, leaving the defendant visibly shaken.

"You said you loved your husband," the prosecutor said. "Apparently the night he died, you didn't love him enough to help police catch his killer."

The jury got the case at noon on Friday. They came back four hours later with their verdict: guilty of first-degree murder and conspiracy. They gave Swanson a maximum sentence of life plus ten years.

The jury's decision stunned the defendant's family. Cries of "She didn't do it!" rang out in the courtroom as bailiffs led Valerie Swanson away.

The jury foreman told a reporter the vote had been 10 to 2 for conviction at the start of deliberations. The two dissenting jurors were the only ones who had given any credence to Swanson's tales of abuse.

Swanson will be eligible for parole in 2007, when she's 48. She and Marcotte had apparently ended their affair with their fingers pointing at each other. If they do decide to rekindle the flame, the Virginia Department of Corrections will see to it that the affair doesn't get past the letter-writing stage.

Detective Yoakam, honored by Humphreys's office for his diligence on the case, continues his work at the Virginia Beach Police Department.

"HE GAVE THEM A LIFT— THEY SLIT HIS THROAT!"

by Brad Cochran

The biblical parable tells of the Good Samaritan who stopped to help a badly beaten robbery victim in ancient Jericho after two other persons had ignored his plight and passed by. The Samaritan gave the injured man medical aid and took him to an inn, where he even paid for his lodging.

It's an inspiring story, but in the violent society of America today, it doesn't always work out that way. More often than not, the roles of the principals in the Good Samaritan tale are tragically reversed. . . .

The city of Amarillo in the Texas Panhandle is a long, long way from ancient Jericho, both in time and space. On the night of Thursday, April 26, 1990, two passersby discovered a man slumped over in the front seat of a pickup. He appeared to be dead, and the witnesses didn't linger there.

One of them called the 911 emergency line from the nearest telephone and reported the unsettling discovery. The call was logged at 10:06 P.M. There was some confusion regarding the location of the vehicle, resulting in the responding patrol officers going to the wrong street, but that was cleared up soon enough with a second call from the individual who had called before.

The first officer to reach the scene was Patrolman Bill

Leonard, who found the pickup in the middle of 49th Avenue, near Maverick Street, a seldom-used roadway that is some distance from mainstream traffic. The lawman immediately saw that the man inside the pickup was bloody and lifeless. He reported what he saw to the police dispatcher, and minutes later, he was joined at the scene by Sergeant Jim Burgess. An ambulance was dispatched to the site, as well as a justice of the peace, who serves as a coroner in Texas. The Potter-Randall Counties Special Crimes Unit (SCU), which investigates crimes in that two-county area, was also notified to get rolling.

When the SCU detectives and evidence technicians arrived, a spring thunderstorm was brewing in the southwestern sky. Lightning flashed frequently and thunder rumbled in the distance. Rain was imminent, and if it came, the investigators feared, it would wipe out fingerprints and other evidence.

Quickly, a call was placed for a wrecker. After photographs were taken of the truck and body at the scene, the pickup with the dead man still inside was towed to the county garage located across town.

Before the downpour began, the investigators managed to photograph and follow a trail of blood spots leading from the right front passenger door of the pickup across the street to a nearby alley. There, the trail played out in a weed-covered vacant lot. It was presumed that the blood trail was left by the killer, who had obviously fled across that vacant lot.

A butterfly knife, an illegal weapon with a two-edged blade, was discovered on the pavement beneath the right front door before the pickup was moved. Bloody fingerprints could be seen on it.

At the county garage, after the body was removed, SCU evidence expert Greg Soltis began processing the four-door 1990 Ford pickup. He observed that the violence of the attack on the man was literally written in blood inside. Blood spurts had struck the ceiling of the cab and soaked the front seat and floorboard. In the backseat, the investigators discovered a green jacket that was drenched with blood. The technician saw that blood had even splashed onto the inside of the rear windshield.

Soltis and the others noticed something else before the dead man was loaded into an ambulance. The victim's left hand bore what appeared to be defensive wounds; in fact, one finger had almost been severed, probably when the victim grabbed at the deadly knife blade that claimed his life.

In stark contrast, his right hand was free of blood, and there was a clean spot in the midst of the blood on the front seat, as though the man's hand might have been held down there at the time of the vicious assault.

A cursory examination showed that the man had suffered at least three deep wounds in the throat area; his throat had been slashed from left to right. The slashing indicated that the knife wielder had been in the backseat.

"The killer must have grabbed him and yanked his head back before cutting his throat," one of the detectives observed.

The victim's shirt was pulled out over his hip pocket. Technician Soltis observed what appeared to be bloody streaks on the hip pocket, possibly left by the killer's fingers as he jerked the victim's wallet out after knifing the victim.

On the outside surface of the pickup, the technician found bloody fingerprints on the right front door. If those prints proved to be good enough to "read," the killer might well have left his identity written in blood, the sleuths hoped.

Brown paper bags were placed on the slain man's hands to preserve any possible trace evidence. Scrapings were taken from the bloodstains for later lab analysis. All the interior areas of the truck were photographed carefully, with close-up shots made of the bloody fingerprints.

The expert technical work would prove to be a major factor in solving the heinous murder.

A check with the dispatcher on the license number of the pickup produced the name of the owner. The vehicle was registered to 66-year-old Robert Doyle Laminack, who lived at an Amarillo address.

As they got their probe under way, the detectives—including Sergeant Sandy Morris, who was assistant coordinator of the crime unit and the lead investigator in the slaying—first talked to the victim's relatives. From his family members, the sleuths were able to reconstruct his last movements before his violent death.

The sleuths learned that Laminack was a well-respected Amarillo businessman and owner of a flooring company, which was located in the 4800 block of South Western—not far from where the victim had been found in his pickup. He and his wife had dropped by the business on Thursday evening and found their daughter working late. The mother had not wanted the younger woman to stay there alone. Laminack offered to stay while his wife went home, saying he would follow before too long.

Later, around 9:15 P.M., Laminack went outside to his truck for a minute when he was approached by a young couple asking for help. His daughter was working in a back room when he came back inside.

"He came in and asked if I was close to being through," the tearful young woman told the sleuths. "He said two kids needed a ride. He said he was taking them to the Salvation Army. He said the girl was sick."

The woman said she felt some apprehension about her dad accompanying two strangers and volunteered to go with him. But he told her he would be all right.

As Laminack drove away at the wheel of his pickup, turning east onto 49th Street, the woman looked out the window and saw another man sitting in the backseat. Someone else—she thought it was a girl—was in the front seat.

She couldn't give much of a description of either stranger because she had not gotten a good look at them as the pickup drove away.

The victim's family said that was like him to help out even strangers if he thought they needed help. He was always helping someone, a Good Samaritan in every sense of the word.

The detectives quickly concluded that robbery was the motive for the vicious, frenzied knife attack on Laminack. The businessman was not believed to have been carrying a large sum of money, but his wallet and cash were gone.

In reconstructing the crime, the sleuths figured that the attack on the unsuspecting pickup driver started almost immediately after he turned off busy Western Street into the less traveled and darkened block near the intersection of Maverick Street. The man in the rear seat must have grabbed Laminack and jerked him backward. Then the girl riding in the front joined the struggle, the detectives' theorized, and tried to help subdue the victim. She probably grasped the victim's right hand and held it down, which would explain the clear spot amid the bloodstains on the front seat. She either held his hand down with both her hands or else she sat on it, because no blood was found on Laminack's right hand.

If it happened that way, the girl's clothing would have become extremely bloody from the gushing knife wounds. The officers surmised that she had been wearing the blood-saturated green jacket left behind in the rear seat of the pickup.

It had not yet started raining at the time of the assault, but when the officers first saw the pickup, they noticed from the position of the wipers on the front windshield that they must have been turned on.

"The wipers might have been turned on accidentally when the driver was yanked back," one of the investigators speculated.

The ignition was off. A search of the area for possible clues failed to turn up either the keys or the victim's wallet. The investigators observed that the neighborhood was dark, except for an occasional streetlight's illumination.

The small stores in a strip along the block where the pickup and body were discovered were daytime businesses that were closed at this time of night. The only other nearby building was an apartment complex, the back of which faced 49th Avenue. It was doubtful that anyone in the complex had seen or heard anything when the slaying occurred.

Noting that busy Interstate Highway 27 was only a couple of

blocks south of the crime scene, the sleuths speculated that the couple who got a ride with Laminack could be transients who had been hitchhiking. If that was the case, though, why hadn't they dumped the body and taken the pickup—unless perhaps because it was so bloodstained.

Or maybe they left the vehicle because they lived somewhere in the area. The SCU detectives canvassed the apartment buildings within a radius of several blocks seeking witnesses who might have noticed something.

On Friday, the investigators were contacted by a young woman who had heard the news about the violent murder and said she had some information.

Giving her name as Patricia Jenkins, she said she thought that the two individuals who had gotten a ride with Laminack had approached her a short time earlier on that Thursday night, asking for a ride to the Salvation Army. She had turned down their request.

The witness told the sleuths that after she left a nightclub located in the same block as Laminack's flooring company, she was approached by a young woman trying to get a ride. It was about 9 P.M. when the woman reached out to block Jenkins from closing the door of her van. The long-haired stranger appeared to be both anxious and angry, said the witness.

"She couldn't understand why I wouldn't give her a ride and why I expected them to sleep in the street," Jenkins related. "I finally just told her, 'I am not giving you a ride!' And I grabbed the door and shut it."

The witness recalled that the aggressive woman was accompanied by a teenage boy, but she had not gotten a good look at him.

Patricia Jenkins volunteered to undergo hypnosis in an attempt to draw out from her subconscious descriptions of the pair. During that procedure, she was able to furnish a detailed description of the woman, from which a police composite sketch was made for distribution to the news media.

As they continued the probe, the investigators questioned

Judy Massengale, a resident of an apartment building located not far from the murder scene. She provided the first tangible lead to the possible identities of the suspects.

The nervous 20-year-old woman told the investigators that the girl and her male companion matched the descriptions of a couple who had previously been staying with her. She said that the girl, who worked as a topless dancer, had moved in with her on April 6, and the boy arrived three days later.

But on Thursday, April 26, said Massengale, the couple was evicted from the apartment at her request to the manager. The pair left the apartment about 8 P.M., saying they would try to find shelter at the local Salvation Army.

Massengale overheard the couple talking about "going to the Boulevard, getting someone to go with them to a motel room and taking their money." From what the witness could hear, the girl suggested that her boyfriend could hide behind the motel door, knock the person on the head, and take his money.

The "Boulevard" is an old street in the northeast part of the city along which U.S. Route 66 used to run. It is lined with cheap motels, bars, and strip joints. It is often frequented by prostitutes, which would have made picking up an unsuspecting "john" an easy thing, the detectives realized.

It was apparent to the investigators that the couple had robbery or worse in mind when they left Massengale's apartment after being evicted by the manager.

But, to Massengale's distress, they returned around 9:45 P.M. She noticed that the boy's hand was cut badly. "He said he jumped over a fence and cut his hand," the witness told the investigators. "Both of them had blood pretty much on them."

Earlier, the girl had left the apartment wearing a jacket, but she did not have it on when she returned, Massengale recalled.

"Her shirt was soaked with blood, especially in the back," the witness said. "He was worried about his hand, and she was acting kind of crazy. She kept running back and forth to the bathroom and out again and kept saying she wanted the blood off her back."

Finally, the couple left Massengale's apartment to go to a hospital to get medical attention for the boy's hand, which was bleeding badly and would require stitches. When they came back again, Massengale said, they stayed only long enough to pick up their suitcases. Then they left with a friend who'd offered to give them a ride.

She gave the couple's names as Kristie Lynn Nystrom and Brent Ray Brewer, who were, she believed, both in their late teens. She remembered that the girl said they were going to Kansas, but Brewer had mentioned going to Dallas.

As the sleuths sought more information about the mysterious couple, another witness came forward. He turned out to be the man who had given the couple a ride to the local bus station after they left the apartment. He gave his name as Bob Landon.

Landon said he'd been present when the blood-covered couple returned to Massengale's apartment. He said he walked out on a balcony to talk to Brewer.

He quoted Brewer as telling him, "You'd better not tell nobody . . . I just stabbed a man."

Later, Landon said, Kristie told him that the stabbing victim had begged for Brewer not to kill him.

"She told me what happened," Landon told the detectives. "The guy—the gentleman—pleaded and begged Brent not to kill him. She said that the guy told Brent, 'Boy, please don't kill me! Boy, please don't kill me!' "

Landon's story also shed some light on why the pickup windshield wipers had been on before the rain actually started that night. Kristie told him that the knife victim turned on the wipers, pushed on the horn, and stepped on the gas pedal as he was being stabbed and slashed.

The girl showed Landon a wallet and set of keys, which she said had been taken from the stabbing victim.

Brewer received a severe cut on his hand as he struggled with the victim and knifed him, Landon told the sleuths. Landon said he gave them a ride they asked for to the bus station to get rid of them because he was afraid.

Lieutenant Ed Smith, the coordinator of the SCU, released the composite drawing of the girl to the newspaper and TV stations.

"We initially thought the suspects may have been transients," Smith said. "But we determined they were locals."

The SCU investigators issued a statewide bulletin for the two suspects wanted for questioning in the murder of Robert Laminack.

From various witnesses and other sources, the probers were able to develop descriptions of the pair. Brent Brewer was described as 19 years old, about 5 feet 9 inches tall, weighing about 195 pounds, with long hair and a thin mustache. According to the witnesses, the young man wore a flannel shirt and a pair of blue jeans.

Kristie Nystrom was said to be 21 years old, about 5 feet 4 inches tall, weighing 130 pounds, having long blond hair and several tattoos. When last seen, she was not wearing any makeup and was dressed in a checkered shirt and blue jeans.

The two were described as possibly armed and dangerous.

At the bus station, the investigators failed to come up with any leads as to the possible destination of the couple, though a clerk thought he remembered such a pair.

"But a lot of people come through here," the clerk said.

The bulletin for the two was extended to Kansas and other nearby states. And since Brewer had spoken of going to the Dallas area, officers there were alerted, too.

On Monday, May 7, around midnight, the investigators received an anonymous call saying that the suspects might be found at an address in Red Oak, in Ellis County, about 16 miles south of Dallas. After the tip was relayed to the Red Oak officers, a force composed of members of the Red Oak Police Department, Ellis County Sheriff's Department, and several Texas Rangers converged on the location.

At 4:30 A.M. the law enforcement team surrounded a trailer house and arrested Brewer and Nystrom on capital-murder warrants issued by a district judge in Amarillo. The pair offered no resistance.

The suspects were booked into the Ellis County Jail. Two Randall County deputies returned the suspects to Amarillo on May 8, 1990. When the pair was arraigned in Amarillo before State District Judge David Gleason, Kristie Nystrom broke into sobs. The girl held Brewer's hand and rested her head on his shoulder.

Bond was set at $250,000 for each defendant.

The bloody fingerprints from the victim's pickup, along with blood samples from the victim and the suspects, the knife with the bloody fingerprints on the handle, the bloody jacket and other evidence were sent to the FBI laboratory for analysis.

Later, the detectives took photos of the suspects, along with mugshots of other individuals, to the bus station. There, an employee identified Brewer and Nystrom as the couple who left from the terminal on the night of the murder.

The trial of Brent Brewer began on Tuesday, May 28, 1991, in the 47th State District Court in Randall County, in the county seat of Canyon, 17 miles south of Amarillo.

Witnesses for the state included the victim's family; Judy Massengale, the woman in whose apartment Brewer and Nystrom had stayed; Bob Landon, the man who gave the suspects a ride to the bus station; and a series of officers and evidence experts who investigated the case.

During the testimony of Patricia Jenkins, the nightclub patron who said that a long-haired blonde and a teenage boy had tried to get her to give them a ride a short time before the slaying of Laminack, Kristie Nystrom was brought into the courtroom to be viewed by the witness.

Jenkins identified her as the girl who asked for the lift to the Salvation Army. She was unable to identify Brewer as the boy who was with Nystrom.

The jury of eight men and five women—including one alternate juror—were also shown videos of the crime scene, the blood spatters leading from the pickup, and the blood spatters and stains inside the vehicle laying bare the violence of the knife attack. Graphic photos of the slaying victim were displayed to the jury, as well.

The jury panel was told that the stains on the inside back window were caused by blood spurting from the victim when Brent Brewer grabbed him from behind, yanked back his head and stabbed and slashed his throat from left to right.

The pathologist who performed the autopsy testified that Laminack died from savage stab wounds to the carotid artery and the jugular vein in the neck. He testified that death probably occurred about two minutes after the wounds were inflicted.

The medical expert also told the jury that the defense wound that almost severed a finger on the victim's left hand was suffered when he grabbed the two-edge knife blade and pulled it away from himself. The stab wounds were consistent with Laminack having been attacked from behind, the pathologist said.

The doctor went on to explain that the lack of any blood on Laminack's right hand indicated that it might have been held down on the seat while another person was attacking him. The prosecution theory was that Kristie Nystrom had grabbed the victim's hand, perhaps even sat on it, to keep him from fighting off Brent Brewer, her companion.

The state sought to cinch its strong case against Brewer with testimony from FBI agents and lab experts on the blood and fingerprint evidence prepared by SCU evidence investigator Greg Soltis. The FBI experts testified that the bloody fingerprints found inside and outside the victim's pickup truck matched those of Brewer and his companion, Nystrom. They also identified the bloody prints on the murder weapon as Brewer's.

Blood on the girl's discarded jacket, which had been found in the backseat, was also identified as Laminack's. The trail of blood spots on the pavement leading from the front of the pickup to an alley was identified as Brewer's blood, which had dripped from his own hand wound.

Scrapings of blood taken from inside the truck were identified as Laminack's and Brewer's blood, the FBI agents testified. The positive blood identifications had been made through serology and DNA analysis.

After the state finished its presentation of evidence and the defense elected to call no witnesses, the final arguments to the jury began.

The defense attorney tried to convince the jury that Brewer sustained the cut on his own hand when he tried to stop Nystrom from stabbing Laminack, and that Brewer's fingerprints were on the handle of the knife because of a second effort to take the weapon away from the girl.

"Brent Brewer was in the wrong place with the wrong person," the lawyer maintained.

In their turn, the prosecutors argued that the evidence against Brewer was "overwhelming."

"From the instant they left the apartment house until they got on the bus, their intent was to do exactly what they did," the assistant prosecutor told the jury.

The defense attorney objected to the prosecutor's use of the word "they," since, he said, there was no other person on trial except Brewer.

"Counsel is right," the state's attorney replied. "Mr. Laminack got in his way. The knife contained Brewer's prints, his blood, and the blood he drew—the life he drew from Mr. Laminack."

The prosecutor declared that Brewer attacked Laminack "like a vulture" after riding with him only a little more than a block.

Said the assistant prosecutor: "Remember Robert Laminack being asked by this defendant to commit an act of goodwill—to take this sick girl to the Salvation Army—and despite his daughter's protests, he did it. His payback was the blood that drained into his shirt."

The district attorney told the jury, "Brewer knew what to say to get the confidence of a good man. Then he stretches him out in his pickup and stabs him repeatedly as he begs for his life."

The jury left the courtroom at 3:43 P.M. on Thursday, May 30, 1991, to begin their deliberations. The panel came back about 5 P.M. with their verdict: They found Brent Brewer guilty of capital murder—a conviction that would carry either a life prison sentence or death by lethal injection.

The punishment phase began the next day before the same jury, which would decide Brewer's final fate.

On Saturday, June 1, the jury deliberated for three hours. They returned a verdict mandating the death penalty for the convicted killer.

When Brewer arrived at death row in the state prison at Huntsville during the first week of June 1991, he had the distinction of becoming the 1,000th inmate in the history of the Texas prison system to be assigned a cell on death row.

He joined 340 men and 4 women awaiting lethal injection.

On Thursday, August 27, 1992, Kristie Nystrom entered a plea of guilty to capital murder in Robert Laminack's death in exchange for a life term in prison. The state waived its right to have a jury trial and to seek the death penalty, explained a prosecutor, because, "We think the evidence shows that she participated in the robbery-slaying. But as far as the actual wielding of the weapon, we don't think the evidence showed that."

The 24-year-old woman's defense attorney told reporters that a jury might have found Nystrom innocent, "but the stakes were so high that you can't really afford to take many chances."

And yet, a Good Samaritan in all his innocence had taken a chance on that terrible night in April 1990—and lost his life.

"SPURNED SEDUCTRESS SNUFFED THE THREE-TIMING ROMEO!"

by Don Lasseter

Detective Bob Russell, of California's Orange County Sheriff's Department, had just finished wolfing down a sandwich with some of his homicide detail pals at their favorite feeding trough when his car phone buzzed. The voice of Sergeant Jim Sidebotham, his boss, ended Russell's leisurely lunch.

"We've got a shooting over in Lake Forest. A female subject called 911, hysterical, and said her ex-boyfriend broke in, got violent, and she shot him.

"Probably going to be an easy case," the sergeant remarked. "Smoking gun. Self-defense. Go over and take a look."

The "easy case" would tax Russell's considerable skills for the next four months.

With his partner, Detective Rudy Garcia, Russell drove past a man-made lake surrounded by luxury dwellings, each with private boat docks, wound along a silvery eucalyptus grove, and arrived at the home on Owens Lake Circle at 12:44 P.M. It was Thursday, May 28, 1992.

Russell was well qualified for his assignment as lead investigator on the case. He'd been tracking killers since July 1985, after completing five years with the fugitive warrants, narcotics, and arson squads. Russell had been a latecomer to police work. He joined the U.S. Marine Corps at age 19 and served three years at the nearby Tustin Air Base as a helicopter crew chief. After several years in the civilian aerospace industry, Russell became a reserve cop at age 33, and one year later took the test to become a regular. The cutoff age to join the force was 35. Russell was accepted two days before his 35th birthday. Now, he was a seasoned 21-year veteran.

The two detectives quickly spotted the shooting scene, a large home where two black-and-white patrol cars sat at the curb. Russell observed an attractive, petite woman with long blond hair sitting in the backseat of one of the cars, dabbing at her eyes with a handkerchief.

Still outside, Deputy Marcus Patrick Carter of the Orange County Sheriff's Department briefed the detectives. He had been dispatched by 911 at 11:55 A.M., from a nearby location, and had arrived exactly one minute later, followed shortly by Deputy Brian Scanlon and the emergency medical technicians.

Deputy Carter pointed to the woman in the backseat of his car and told the investigators that she had identified herself as Linda Phillips. She had been standing outside, sobbing, when the officers arrived. "I shot him in the head," she blurted out. "He's upstairs."

The two deputies had raced up the stairway, into a master bedroom, and had seen the body of a man.

"The victim was lying on the floor, partially on his right side, partially on his back," Deputy Scanlon reported. "He was not in a fully seated position, but not in a lying-down position, either. It was kind of like a teetering effect." His head, which was blood-covered, was propped up against a closet door, the deputy noted, about "knee-high."

"The victim was definitely not breathing at the time," Deputy Scanlon said. "The emergency medics worked feverishly to revive the man but finally declared him dead." Unfortunately, in their efforts to save his life, they had moved the body and a few of the items around it.

"When we first went up there," Scanlon said, "there was a wicker breakfast tray straddling his body, around the midsection. It was like the guy had it around his lap, and had pulled it up toward his stomach." The tray was "turned around," with its top facing toward the bed," Scanlon added.

In an effort to preserve as much of the original scene as possible, Deputy Scanlon had marked the carpet with a pen to indicate the location of two live rounds of .38-caliber ammunition. He had feared that they would be inadvertently kicked away by the paramedics—which is exactly what did happen.

Before entering the house to continue the investigation, Russell chatted briefly with Linda Phillips, who still sat crying in the patrol car. He asked her to sign a form giving permission to search the home. She tearfully agreed.

Upstairs, in the master bedroom, Russell and Garcia scanned the death scene. The body of a man whom Phillips identified as Ricardo Ornelas was lying flat on his back on the tan carpet, his face a blood-caked mess. He was dressed in blue trousers, the tattered remains of a long-sleeved dress shirt, and black shoes. The front of his shirt was torn away and his T-shirt was cut open to allow the paramedics to place EKG pads on his chest. One of the bullets had knocked out four of his teeth.

Streaks of crimson trailed down the white closet door a few feet away, where the victim had initially been discovered, propped in grotesque repose. A white wicker chair lay on its side near the body.

Stepping over to the California king-sized bed, Russell noticed a couple of blood spots in the center of the rumpled black comforter. The cover had not been moved, the deputies told him. Curious, both Detectives Garcia and Russell leaned over the bed, trying to figure out how a victim could have been shot twice while standing so that he bled onto the center of the bed. It didn't seem to work. Russell entered a notation in his brown covered notebook.

On the floor at the foot of the bed, partially protruding from under the black comforter, Russell saw a Smith & Wesson .38-

caliber revolver with a four-inch barrel and wood grips. One of the evidence technicians carefully placed it in a paper evidence bag.

After examining the room for a few more minutes, Detective Russell wanted to talk to Linda Phillips. He had her transported to the local office of the Orange County Sheriff's Department and seated in an interview room. Russell began questioning her, with a videocamera recording the session at 2:22 P.M.

Still weeping, Phillips told Russell that she and the victim, Ricardo Ornelas, had been dating about one year, and that she had been his secretary at a nuclear power plant in Irvine before she left the company. They had broken up in February, she sniffled. But Ricardo had called her twice that morning, begging to have lunch with her. She had refused. Then, about noon, he forced his way into the house, came up to the bedroom where she was, and they had argued.

Having heard stories of lovers' disputes hundreds of times, as a patrol cop and later as an investigator, Russell had no reason to doubt Phillips's emotional account of the confrontation. He listened carefully as she tearfully continued.

Ricardo had been angry, she said. Her voice trembled as she told Russell that Ricardo had pulled out a gun and yelled, "I'm going to kill you first, and then myself!" She was terribly frightened, she recalled, but hoped that she wouldn't be killed when Ricardo put the weapon down and sat on a couch next to the bed. She grabbed the gun, to prevent him from pointing it at her again. But then, there was a "terrible accident."

In fear of her life, Phillips continued, she must have been shaking, because when she picked the gun up, it fired. "I didn't see any blood," she said.

Ricardo stood up and cried out, "Linda!" as he lunged toward her. In terror that he was going to attack her, she fired again, and he fell to the floor. Panic-stricken, Phillips then called 911.

Before the interview was over, Phillips told Russell that she had been fired from her job because she was absent with an infection. She was distraught about it, because she thought she had been infected, by Ricardo, with a serious kidney disease. She explained that she had nearly died from it.

Just to be sure that he clearly understood the sequence of events in the shooting, Detective Russell took Linda Phillips back to her house and asked her to reenact the entire incident. In front of a video camera again, she complied with his request. Then she was transported to a relative's house, because she said she didn't want to spend the night in the bedroom where Ornelas had died.

Back at the house on Owens Circle, Detective Russell observed while criminalist Lori Crutchfield bagged a spent bullet recovered from the bedding. Forensic specialist Will Prothero took over 50 photographs of the body and the interior of the house. The exterior was examined, as well, and no evidence of forced entry was discovered. Technician Tanya Vermeulen examined the bloodstains in the room and made careful measurements of each spatter and pool.

Under the couch in the same room, the investigators discovered and collected a stack of papers, including traffic citations, all bearing the name Marshall Cochrane. Linda later acknowledge that she knew him, and recalled that he had moved into her residence on May 3, but had stayed only one week. She had no idea where he could be found.

Detective Russell learned that Phillips shared her house with six men, but none of them could shed any light on the probe.

It had been a long, exhausting day, but Russell had one more task to perform: the notification of nearest kin. When Ornelas's relatives had calmed down, they told Russell that the victim was a respected supervisor at the power plant, where he worked since getting his masters in nuclear engineering from UCLA in 1976. Russell also learned that Ornelas had recently left his family to live with his ex-maid.

The weary investigator finally headed home at midnight.

On Friday morning, Detective Russell wanted to satisfy his curiosity about the gun Linda Phillips had used to shoot Ricardo Ornelas. First, he keyed the serial number into the Automated Firearms System (AFS) and learned that the weapon was not stolen. Then he ran the name Ricardo Ornelas and discovered that the victim did not have a gun registered to him. A quick telephone call to the tracing center of the Federal Bureau of Alcohol, Tobacco, and Firearms (ATF) didn't help much. They were only able to tell Russell that the revolver had been manufactured 50 years earlier and had been shipped to the U.S. Navy on December 10, 1942. It was, they told him, "too old to conduct further history tracing."

If he had been willing to accept Linda Phillips story before, Russell was now entertaining serious doubts. The victim's family had emphatically stated that Ornelas disliked guns, had never owned a gun, and wouldn't have had a gun around him. And the death weapon could not be traced to him. It just didn't add up that Ornelas had brought the weapon to Linda Phillips's house.

At 9:15 on Friday morning, Detective Russell attended the autopsy. He heard Dr. Joseph Halka report that the victim had been shot twice—once in the back of the head, and once in the mouth. The bullet that struck him in the mouth knocked out four teeth, ripped open veins and arteries, and caused his lungs to fill up with blood. The damage caused by the other bullet was equally horrifying. It had partially severed the spinal cord, immediately paralyzing the victim's arms and legs. He could still breathe and speak, even after the second shot. Death was caused by exsanguination—bleeding to death. Dr. Halka said that Ornelas might have lived up to 10 minutes after the bullets hit him.

Criminalist Nathan Cross examined the .38-caliber Smith & Wesson revolver. After test-firing it, he was able to verify that an expended casing found near the bed had been fired by the weapon. The recovered slugs probably were, too, but damage to them prevented scientific proof. More important, Cross stated that whoever fired the gun had to know what they were doing, because the weapon had a peculiarity. There was a dirty spot between the cylinder and the ejector rod. This caused erratic rotation of the cylinder. Also, the hammer moved slower than normal during a "double-action pull on the trigger." It was highly improbable that someone not familiar with the gun would have been able to shoot accurately with it.

At the victim's workplace, Detective Russell heard that Ornelas had been scheduled to attend a meeting at two o'clock the previous afternoon, and he had been observed leaving the parking lot at 11:30 that morning. Russell knew that the 911 call had been received 23 minutes later, at 11:53 A.M., so he drove from Ornelas's office to the Owens Circle house, a distance of less than two miles. It took Russell 3 minutes and 31 seconds. That meant that Ornelas was at Phillips's house only about 19 minutes before he was killed.

The victim had parked his car, a late model BMW, two houses away from Linda's home. No one seemed to know why. Detective Russell had it towed to an impound lot, where it was painstakingly searched by specialists on Friday afternoon. They were specifically looking for a holster, ammunition, spent shell casings, or bullet boxes. No trace of anything associated with a gun was found in the BMW. The searchers did find, in a briefcase, an application for vision-care insurance. It was signed and dated the previous day, the same day Ornelas had been shot to death. Why, Russell wondered, would a man intent on a murder-suicide be applying for vision-care insurance? It didn't make sense.

It was time to look into the background of Linda Phillips. Russell was astonished when he read the rap sheet. Phillips had been arrested several times for writing bogus checks, for forgery, and for fraud. She had served time in Frontera women's prison on the fraud charge and was on probation until 1994. Included in the record sheet were no less than 25 aliases that she had used, along with eight Social Security numbers. Phillips had been arrested up and down California's coastline, from Santa Barbara to San Diego. Russell learned that when Phillips claimed to have been absent from her job due to an "infection," an incident for which she was fired, she had really been in the Santa Barbara jail for a week.

Phillips had listed three different birthdates. Russell hadn't believed the one she'd given him, even though she did look about

35. Phillips was blessed with features that made her seem age-less—unblemished skin, bright eyes, and a stunning figure. If her five-foot-four frame had been enhanced with a little cosmetic surgery, no one could tell for sure. Certainly not the detective.

Later that day, however, Russell learned that Phillips had a twin brother. They were born in 1942—which was 50 years ago. By some strange coincidence, Linda Phillips was the exact same vintage as the gun that killed Ornelas!

On Monday, June 1, Detective Russell confronted Phillips again. He didn't reveal what he knew about her criminal history. He simply wanted to know if she was positive that Ornelas had brought the gun to her house. There were strong indications, Russell suggested, that Ricardo had never had a gun in his possession. Even so, Phillips steadfastly insisted that Ornelas had forced his way in while holding the pistol. Furthermore, she added, he "was always talking about suicide." She gave Russell the names of some of her friends who might be able to confirm her statements.

During the next week, Detective Russell interviewed Phillips's current housemates, several former housemates, and her friends, as well as acquaintances of the victim's. No one recalled any suicidal tendencies ever displayed by Ornelas. On the contrary, most of them said he was "very low-key, nonviolent, and jovial," especially when he'd had a few drinks.

But one of Phillips's ex-roomies, a former Israeli policeman, dropped a comment that confirmed to the sleuth that he was on the right track. Phillips had made an unusual request the previous month. She had asked the ex-housemate if he could help her acquire a gun.

"How did she approach you?" the investigator asked.

"One day I came home from work, and I found her little boy going through the stuff in my room. I told Linda to keep him out of there because I had a gun in my room." It wasn't true, though, the ex-cop told Russell. He had said it just to prevent the child from entering his room again. Not long after that, he recalled, Phillips had approached him and asked if he could get a gun for her "to protect herself in case anyone broke in." She wanted to pay $50 for it, and didn't care if it was stolen or not. He'd made some excuse about not being able to find one, and dropped the subject.

Phillips had told Detective Russell that a man who had taken care of her landscaping and gardens for several years had been trying to date her for a long time. But his version was quite different. Nah, he shrugged, he had never tried to date her. She had approached him a few times, but he had declined. She seemed upset and jealous that her boyfriend, Ornelas, wouldn't leave his wife.

Each time Russell returned to his office, he found messages waiting for him that Linda Phillips had called. When he reached her, she always wanted to know if there was anything new on the case, and she often passed along more negative stories about Ricardo Ornelas. Yet none of her new information could be verified.

There was now no doubt in Detective Russell's mind that Linda Phillips had murdered Ricardo Ornelas. He figured that she was furious with the victim for throwing her over and replacing her with a younger woman, with whom he had moved in after refusing to sacrifice his marriage for Linda. She had invited him over, perhaps coerced him, and when he was sitting on the bed, she shot him to death. But Russell was well aware that his scenario was only a theory, and there was certainly not enough evidence to haul Phillips into court. He would just have to keep plugging away and hope for a break.

In his travels on other cases, Detective Russell found excuses to make detours to question various people who knew Linda Phillips. He stopped in Carson City and Reno, Nevada, and Colima, a small town in Northern California. A few morsels of promising information turned up, but nothing substantial enough to put handcuffs on his suspect.

Three months rolled by. Russell kept hoping to locate Marshall Cochrane, whose name had been on the papers found under Phillips's couch. A check of his criminal records revealed an outstanding arrest warrant on Cochrane for passing bad checks. His crimes were remarkably similar to those committed by Linda Phillips.

The break came in early September, over three months after the shooting. A former friend of the suspect's, who wanted to remain anonymous, telephoned Detective Russell with the news that Marshall Cochrane had called and asked for Phillips's phone number. The informant recalled the brief conversation for the sleuth . . .

"Haven't you heard?" the former friend asked Cochrane.

"Heard what?" growled the fugitive.

"Linda shot somebody."

"Who?"

"Her ex-boyfriend. He broke into the house."

"Did she use the gun I got her?"

"No. I think her boyfriend brought the gun."

But Marshall Cochrane couldn't be convinced that Phillips hadn't used the gun he had obtained for her. He seemed "all shook up" about Phillips's trouble, the informant said. Cochrane had agreed to call again in a few days.

Detective Russell could barely conceal his excitement. He asked the informant to get Marshall Cochrane's telephone number. Two days later, the sleuth learned that Cochrane was in Tampa, Florida, in a halfway house for released convicts.

Marshall Cochrane sounded as if he was dumbfounded when he answered a call from Detective Russell asking about Cochrane's relationship with Linda Phillips. The investigator pointed out that, considering the outstanding warrant, Cochrane would probably want to cooperate. In mid-September, Russell flew to Tampa with the warrant in his pocket. He met Cochrane at the Embassy Suites Hotel in Tampa.

Eye to eye with the fugitive, and making it clear that he would accept no nonsense, Russell asked if Cochrane had provided Linda Phillips with a gun.

Recognizing that Detective Russell meant business, Cochrane

groaned, grunted, and finally confessed, "I bought Linda a gun, for her self-protection before I left."

"Where did you get it?"

"From a guy in Santa Ana." Cochrane was referring to the largest city in the Orange County, where Russell's office was located.

"When?" the sleuth asked.

Cochrane remembered that he had acquired the revolver the week prior to May 10. Phillips had driven him to Santa Ana to the house of a drug dealer, where Cochrane had done business before. The dealer gave them directions to another location, and followed in his own car. In a squalid section of town, where gangs congregate and anything illegal is for sale, Cochrane offered the seller $200 for the gun. That wasn't enough, so Phillips threw in a VCR to complete the deal. But no ammunition was included.

A couple of weeks after that, Cochrane divulged, he again accompanied Phillips to Santa Ana, this time to a gun store. She remained in the car while he went inside and bought a box of .38-caliber bullets.

"Is this the gun?" Russell asked, flashing a full-color photo of the Smith & Wesson .38.

"Yeah, that's it," Cochrane mumbled.

Two days later, Detective Russell flew back to California, accompanied by Marshall Cochrane.

In Russell's office, Cochrane dialed Linda Phillips's telephone number, while the detective listened in on an extension. Cochrane asked Phillips several questions, but she was noncommittal about the gun and the death of Ornelas.

Just when it appeared that the whole effort had been wasted, Russell's phone rang. It was Linda Phillips herself. Only 20 minutes had elapsed since her conversation with Cochrane had ended. She wanted to meet the detective to explain something to him.

At 6:45 that evening, Wednesday, September 22, in the South County sheriff's substation close to Lake Forest, Linda Phillips sat twisting in a swivel chair. She gave Detective Russell a flirtatious smile, hesitated, and then said that she had not been completely honest about the gun.

After halting the discussion long enough to read Phillips her Miranda rights, which she waived, Russell listened. Phillips now admitted that the .38 belonged to her. The true story, she coquettishly revealed, was that Ornelas had forced his way into the house and threatened her while yelling that he was going to commit suicide. He was always whining about killing himself. She decided to call his bluff, so she put the revolver down on the couch, insinuating that if he wanted to kill himself, there was the gun.

She was surprised, she said, when he picked the weapon up and aimed it at her. They struggled for it and the gun fell to the floor. She managed to get her hands on it, and just when she picked it up, it fired, hitting him in the back of the head. But he apparently wasn't badly wounded, because it enraged him, and he lunged at her. Her hands were shaking so badly that she pulled the trigger again. That's when he fell to the floor.

At 9:07 P.M., Detective Russell told Linda Phillips that she was under arrest for the murder of Ricardo Ornelas.

"What do you mean?" she howled. "You can't be serious!"

He had never been more serious, Russell told her. He stepped out of the room for a moment, and when he returned he noticed that her purse was standing open. A metal detector verified that she had no weapon on her, so Russell led her to his car to transport her to the Orange County Jail in Santa Ana.

After carefully logging the time and odometer reading, a precaution all male officers take at both ends of a trip when transporting female prisoners, Russell headed the car north, toward the Interstate 5 freeway. The suspect, sitting in the front seat with him, was behaving oddly, so Russell kept glancing at her. Luckily, he spotted some clear plastic protruding from beneath her long gray skirt. He grabbed it; it was a plastic bag containing 97 sleeping pills.

Twenty minutes later, while they sped along the freeway, Phillips suddenly grabbed at a door handle, as if she planned to jump from the vehicle. After restraining her, Russell simply informed her that she could ride in the front with him if she behaved, or she could ride in the rear seat cage. There were no more incidents during the trip, but Russell kept the overhead light on as a precaution so that he could watch her hands.

While waiting for the trial, Detective Russell found more acquaintances of the suspect's who described her vituperative personality. A marine corporal said, "Everything's fine if you go along with her, but if you cross her, *stand by*."

Witnesses told of her jealousy and anger when Ornelas dropped her for his maid. Phillips was furious, they said, when Ornelas left his family to move in with the new lover.

During her October 1993 murder trial, while Linda Phillips sat at the defense table wearing stylish clothing and glamorous makeup, Deputy District Attorney Ron Cafferty called 11 witnesses. Cafferty argued that the killing was premeditated, as evidenced by the advance acquisition of a gun, and it was deliberate, motivated by the defendant's anger and jealousy.

Linda Phillips's attorney, Public Defender Tim Severin, told the jury that although his client had obviously shot Ornelas, it was in self-defense, out of fear of her own life. Severin made a motion for the court to reduce the charge to second-degree murder.

Judge Everett W. Dickey sent out the jury as he considered the motion. With his wavy white hair, matching trim mustache, deep sonorous voice, and movie-star features, Dickey reminds a lot of people of film actors Ronald Colman or John Forsythe. The judge noted that if Phillips believed Ornelas was a threat to her she wouldn't have met him alone, and she certainly would not have placed a loaded weapon beside him while she fixed sandwiches.

Furthermore, the judge noted, there was nothing to support the defendant's opinion that the victim was "in an abnormal state of mind." It was not credible that the victim's employer "would have an engineer on a nuclear site whose behavior was aberrant," the judge said. And the defendant's emotional histrionics could have been faked, even when she was calling 911. That was for the jury to sort out.

The motion was denied, Dickey announced. Linda Phillips was still charged with first-degree murder.

Prosecutor Cafferty appealed to the jurors to look at the crime scene evidence. The victim, Cafferty said, had held up the wicker bed tray in a desperate and pitiful attempt to shield himself from the lethal bullets. There were no signs that he had broken into the house and no marks or injuries on Phillips's body to indicate that they had struggled. The whole scenario she'd described was physically impossible. Linda Phillips lured Ornelas there to kill him, shot him twice, and let him lie helplessly, with a damaged spinal cord that made him a quadriplegic, while he slowly and painfully bled to death.

Public Defender Severin shook his head and asked, "Did something evil and wicked happen in Linda Phillips's bedroom, or something spontaneous and tragic? What if Ricardo Ornelas had used the bed tray as a weapon, not as a shield?" After summarizing the evidence, and arguing that it proved nothing except a tragic accident, Severin appealed to the jury to find his client not guilty.

Following five days of deliberation, the jury reached a verdict that some would call a compromise. They found Linda Phillips guilty of second-degree murder, plus the use of a firearm. She didn't take the verdict mildly. Standing, she loudly berated the court, the trial, and the prosecution.

The sentencing date was pending when this report was filed. Linda Phillips asked the court to relieve Public Defender Severin from her case, in effect firing him. With Severin's concurrence, because Phillips would no longer speak to him, a new attorney was appointed.

When Linda Phillips finally stands before Judge Everett Dickey again, she faces a probable term of 20 years to life for the murder, with an additional five years tacked on for use of a firearm.

"RUTHLESS LOVERS' BLOODY VALENTINE TO ELVIE"

by Jake Crew

The deputies knew this was no routine missing-persons case as soon as they walked in the door and found traces of blood. And it just kept getting worse.

It was late on the afternoon of Friday, February 15, 1991, in Trinity, North Carolina, a small town in rural Randolph County in the central part of the state.

Elvie Rhodes's relatives had reported her missing since the day before, which was Valentine's Day. Rhodes, a 64-year-old widow, grandmother, and factory worker, lived alone on a quiet, tree-shaded dead-end street of gravel in her small frame house atop a hill. It was a home Rhodes had lived in for 30 years.

On Friday, February 15, Rhodes's relatives met deputies with the Randolph County Sheriff's Department at the Rampy Street house and let them in.

Using luminol, a chemical that causes blood traces to glow in the dark, deputies would soon find numerous bloodstains—on the living- and dining-room walls, and in the bathroom and bedroom. In the living room, the stains extended from the floor to the ceiling.

Apparently, someone had tried to clean up the blood; much of it was only visible with the luminol.

A partial dental plate, which Rhodes's relatives said belonged to her, was found beside the TV set in the living room, across from a couch. Deputies gathered a tooth and hair in the kitchen trash can.

In the bedroom, papers were spread across Rhodes's bed. The papers included life insurance documents, old paycheck stubs, medical insurance forms, old electric and telephone bills, and 1990 W2 forms.

Lieutenant Charles Flowers videotaped the ransacked house. Other deputies gathered samples of the blood, sketched the crime scene, dusted for fingerprints, and bagged and tagged what pieces of evidence they could find.

It was no question that Rhodes had met with foul play. But where was she? Her 1985 black Oldsmobile was not outside.

With the relatives' help, deputies got the license plate number of the car and put out a lookout for it.

By now, veteran sleuths Lieutenant Don Andrews and Captain Richard Hughes, who work under Sheriff Litchard Hurley, were on the scene. This promised to be one tough probe, and State Bureau of Investigation (SBI) agents would lend a hand.

One relative told the local investigators that he last saw Rhodes the day before, when they had dinner together. Rhodes had not been seen since.

The sleuths gathered what they could from the crime scene, but by early Saturday morning, they seemed to be at an impasse. No usable prints were found in the house.

Maybe it was a robbery gone haywire. In addition to Rhodes's car, her purse, jewelry, and radio had been taken. Yet other valuable items had been left behind. And the violence suggested something more personal.

A grim piece of the puzzle surfaced Saturday afternoon.

Two men were hunting for deer tracks in southwestern Randolph County. As they scanned the ground in a wooded area beside a logging road, they spotted something in a thicket of briar and honeysuckle. The men studied the object, which was partially wrapped in a flowered quilt and green garbage bags, just long enough to discern that it was a human body. That was all they needed. They hurried to the nearest phone and called the sheriff's department.

Deputies arriving minutes later found that the cold corpse had been beaten so badly, they could hardly tell if it was a man or a woman. A window drape cord was wrapped around the victim's neck. A laundry tag on the body's clothing identified the corpse as that of Elvie Rhodes.

The deputies, knowing who was working the Rhodes case, notified Captain Hughes and Lieutenant Andrews. The detectives studied the scene and had it videotaped. But aside from the body itself, there was nothing else to be gathered.

Pathologists at the state medical examiner's office in Chapel Hill soon compared the body's teeth with Elvie Rhodes's dental records and found that this was in fact her body.

Rhodes had died a gruesome death. She had been hit several times in the face and head with a blunt object. There were several cuts on her face and head. She had suffered a broken nose, broken teeth, bruises, and cuts on her arms and legs, 11 broken ribs, multiple skull and chest fractures, and several internal hemorrhages—including one on the lining of her brain.

Pathologists compared the hair and tooth found in the trash can at the crime scene with Rhodes's hair and teeth and found they were hers.

Rhodes had also been strangled with a drape cord.

In the final analysis, Rhodes had died from ligature strangulation and multiple skull and chest fractures.

As the detectives worked from their headquarters in the county seat of Asheboro on Sunday, the next important piece of the puzzle surfaced.

A citizen who'd been following news reports on the case spotted Rhodes's car behind a restaurant in Thomasville, a small city that borders Trinity. Officers dusted it for prints, finding one latent palm print that they couldn't identify. They saved it, hoping to find a magic match for it.

The detectives continued their interviews with Rhodes's

friends and associates in the week after the slaying. They visited a Thomasville woman who, the victim's relatives said, was a close friend of Rhodes. As they waited in the woman's house to talk to her, one of her relatives, 28-year-old James Edward Williams, chatted with sleuths.

Williams made statements that aroused detectives' suspicions, Lieutenant Andrews would later say.

"He had knowledge," the detective would say, apparently referring to knowledge of the crime. The sleuth declined to elaborate.

The investigators checked Williams's record. He was on parole for burglary, forgery, and other convictions. His record also included charges of assault and robbery. He had a history of substance abuse that began with his sniffing glue when he was 11.

The detectives decided to interview Williams. Williams told Lieutenant Andrews that he'd never met Rhodes, didn't know where she lived, and had never been in her car.

Working from fingerprints in Williams's prison records, scientists compared the latent palm print from the car with Williams's palm prints. SBI Agent E.R. Hicks found that Williams's left palm print matched the one on the car.

In fact, Williams lived less than a mile from where the car had been found.

Although it was good news, it was not enough to hang a murder charge on. The sleuths kept working as the weeks since the slaying stretched into months.

They found witnesses who contradicted Williams's statement that he'd never been in the victim's home. In fact, the witnesses said, Williams had often visited Rhodes's home, had talked with her on the phone, and had been out to eat with her several times.

Williams had few friends, and Rhodes had befriended him several weeks before her death, witnesses told investigators. The detectives learned that Williams had a live-in girlfriend, 29-year-old Bernice Sykes. Williams and Sykes had met when they both worked the third shift at a Thomasville factory.

Sykes, too, had a record for forgery convictions, and had

served time in prison for passing a bad check. Sleuths learned that she'd been confined from January 11 to February 7, 1991—just one week before the Rhodes slaying.

But the best information of all came from Abe Goshen, a relative of Williams's whom the detectives tracked down in Florida.

On the night of Thursday, February 14, 1991, Goshen told the sleuths, he went bowling with Williams and Sykes in High Point, North Carolina. About 11 that night, Williams and Sykes asked Goshen to drive them to Rampy Street in Trinity. Goshen did so, not asking, and not finding out, why the couple wanted to go there. Goshen dropped off the pair on the street and left. Shown a photo of Rhodes's house, Goshen said it was within 300 feet of the structure where he dropped off the couple.

The investigators had the palm print, and now they could place Williams and Sykes at the scene. It was strong stuff, but they needed more.

Lieutenant Andrews approached Williams, who allowed deputies to search his room and closet. There, the sleuths found jewelry and a radio that Rhodes's relatives later identified as belonging to her. Probers also found a black baseball bat. They checked it for prints but found none.

On March 2, another crucial piece of the puzzle surfaced. Two children found Rhodes's purse in a dried-up pond in Davidson County, which adjoins Randolph. The children brought the purse to their grandmother, who told her husband. He called Davidson deputies, who in turn called Randolph deputies.

The rectangular, multicolored pocketbook was caked with mud, but it contained drivers' licenses belonging to Elvie Rhodes and her late husband, as well as Rhodes's keys, papers, and bank deposit slips.

Adding to the significance of the find was that it was made behind the home of a relative of Sykes's, a home that Sykes had visited.

In April, the detectives studied their bulging files on the Rhodes case. It looked strong, what with the palm print, the evidence found in Williams's house, his contradictory statements to the sleuths, and the witness from Florida.

The probers' emerging theory of the case was that Williams, ordered to pay $3,600 in restitution to the victims of his forgery and burglary, was behind $500 in his payments. Rhodes wasn't rich, but Williams would have known that she got a government check each month. He would also have noticed that she wore nice clothes and jewelry. Williams must have been furious to the point of violence when he didn't find the cash he needed.

The sleuths consulted with longtime Randolph County district attorney Garland Yates and opted to charge Williams and Sykes each with first-degree murder and common-law robbery. They chose to seek a direct indictment from a Randolph County Superior County grand jury against the two suspects. By that method, Yates would have the case in the trial court and skirt the danger of losing in the probable-cause hearing in the county's lower district court.

The grand jury returned the indictments of first-degree murder and armed robbery by April 22. Williams was easy enough to find. He had violated parole on the burglary conviction and was at a prison camp in nearby Salisbury. Deputies served the warrants on him there on April 22. Williams refused to make a statement.

The same day, the investigators found Bernice Sykes in Charlotte, North Carolina, about an hour from Randolph County.

Upon her arrest, Sykes agreed to make a statement. She told investigators that she killed Rhodes as she fought with the woman and then disposed of the body. Sykes didn't mention Williams.

Hours later, local newspapers broke the story of the arrests. Detectives would not comment on whether or not the suspects made statements.

Rhodes's family told reporters that they were pleased with the arrests.

"This is the answer to our prayers," one relative said. "We all prayed someone would be caught one way or another because we were deeply hurt by [Rhodes's] death."

Quietly and behind the scenes, the investigators continued to work. On April 23, they again interviewed Sykes, who was being held without privilege of bond. The sleuths explained to Sykes that they had a palm print from Rhodes's Oldsmobile, a palm print that they knew belonged to Williams.

Sykes said that Williams was at Rhodes's house the night of the murder, but was too drunk to break up the fight between Sykes and Rhodes. He left and later returned to find Rhodes dead. He then helped Sykes clean up the crime scene and dispose of the body.

Time dragged by as Williams and Sykes cooled their heels in jail, awaiting a space on the crowded criminal docket. Then, in January 1993, with the slaying almost two years old, Sykes contacted the investigators saying that she wanted to talk.

On Tuesday, January 5, 1993, Sykes told sleuths that it was Williams, not she, who killed Elvie Rhodes. Later Sykes gave varying reasons for the change in her story. She would say that Williams told her he would "hang" if convicted of the slaying, but a jury would go easier on Sykes because she was a mother of three.

Sykes later said that Williams threatened to kill her children and family if she didn't take the rap. If she didn't say she did it and they both "went down," Williams told her, she would never walk off the prison grounds because she would be killed in prison.

Sykes said she tried to protect Williams because she loved him and didn't want to see him go back to prison. He had been in prison most of his life, and she feared he would commit suicide if given a life sentence. But she couldn't take the blame for something she didn't do in the first place.

In her statement to detectives on January 5, however, Sykes's emphasis was more on what really happened in Rhodes's home than on Sykes's reasons for changing her story. She described Williams as a sadistic, drunken killer.

The month before the slaying, Sykes told the investigators, when she was doing the prison stretch for forgery in Raleigh, she talked to Williams by phone several times. He told her about a woman they could "knock off" for a car and some cash. Williams didn't mention the woman's name because he was afraid the conversation was being recorded. Sykes had never met Rhodes. Williams talked about this plan several times over a period of a month.

By the time they got to Rampy Street on the night of February 14, 1991, Williams had consumed as much as a fifth of whiskey and several beers.

They walked by the darker side of the house. They tried in vain to get into a locked outbuilding in the backyard. Then, they got in through the house's cellar. There, Williams downed a six-pack, throwing the cans in the yard as they talked and got drunk.

Williams told Sykes that he and Rhodes had had dinner several times. But he put a knife to his chest and told Sykes, "I'll eat it now if you don't think I love you."

Sykes took the knife away from Williams, but he grabbed it back. Williams then prepared to go up to the house, telling Sykes that under no circumstances was she to leave the cellar. He told her that he didn't want Rhodes to know Sykes was out of prison.

Waiting in the cellar, Sykes could hear, during lulls in the furnace's rumbling, snatches of conversation emanating from upstairs. Then she heard a loud noise, "a great big bang." She ran out of the cellar and up to the front door. She tried to turn the knob, but it was locked.

She knocked on the door. From inside, Williams asked who it was. Sykes replied that it was she. Williams, wearing only his underwear, opened the door and pulled her in quickly.

Sykes saw Rhodes lying on a couch. Her face was beaten bloody and her eyes were swollen shut, but she was still conscious. Williams pulled Sykes close to Rhodes and said to the victim, "This is Bernice."

Williams ran his fingers down Rhodes's face and licked the blood from his fingers. He kicked the victim in the stomach and side and slapped her. He took a wooden pole from a chair in the kitchen and beat her in the face.

Elvie Rhodes begged him to stop.

"You know I'm going to kill you, don't you?" Williams taunted. "But I'm going to make love to you first."

Sykes pleaded with Williams not to rape the woman, so he didn't.

Rhodes asked permission to go to the bathroom to look at her face. Williams took her into a bathroom beside the kitchen.

"Don't you look pretty?" he mocked.

"I can't see nothing but blood," Rhodes replied.

Williams let out a "funny little laugh," Sykes later told police. He slung Rhodes from the kitchen floor of the den, beat her, and grabbed her in a wrestling choke hold. He kicked her and stomped on her chest, stomach, and throat three times, causing her to vomit blood.

Sykes later said that Williams told her, "Baby, she just won't die."

Williams told Sykes to get a cord from the venetian blinds behind the sofa. She did so, cutting the cord free. Sykes would later say that she was scared. Williams looped the cord around Rhodes's neck and pulled hard.

Finally, Rhodes was unconscious. The poor woman's ordeal in her own home had lasted about two hours.

Williams and Sykes searched the house for money and weapons. They gathered a flashlight, a purse, a radio, and some jewelry. Sykes helped Williams clean the blood off his body, then they tried to clean the house, as well.

They wrapped the body in a flowered quilt blanket and green garbage bags, loaded it into the trunk of Rhodes's car, and left the house at about 6 A.M. Williams was driving.

They drove to Thomasville. There, they went to a car wash, where Williams threw into a Dumpster a plastic bag containing the bloody paper towels they cleaned the crime scene with and the wooden chair stick that he'd used on Rhodes. Williams drove to a Thomasville fast-food restaurant, where he ordered four bacon, egg, and cheese breakfast biscuits, some hash browns, and two sodas. He ate two of the sandwiches in the parking lot before driving off.

The body was still in the trunk of the large black Oldsmobile.

Williams then drove himself and his girlfriend to his residence, where they slept until 11 A.M. When they got up, they drove the body to southwestern Randolph County and dumped it.

They drove the car back to Thomasville, and, after trying to wipe it clean of prints, they parked it at the restaurant where it was later found. Then they walked back to Williams's home.

Sykes's statement and her subsequent agreement to testify against her boyfriend would save her from a possible death sentence, although she still faced the same charges as Williams and a life term in prison.

DA Yates would later say that Sykes, with her 10th-grade education, was not smart enough to invent her final statement. Another reason to believe her, the prosecutor said, was that the victim's beating was so brutal, another woman could not have inflicted it.

Indeed, it had been a brutal slaying. Yates would seek the death penalty against James Williams. Williams's trial began in late October 1993 at the old stone courthouse in Asheboro.

North Carolina death penalty trials consist of two phases. In the first phase, attorneys present evidence as to guilt or innocence. If prosecutors secure a first-degree murder verdict from the jury, attorneys come back and argue for and against the death penalty before the same jury.

Sykes, who had yet to be tried, was the star witness against her now ex-boyfriend. The state's case went well in the first phase of the trial.

In his closing argument on Thursday, October 28, Defense Counsel Ed Bunch, who was representing Williams with Pete Oldham, argued that there was not enough evidence to prove that Williams murdered Elvie Rhodes. Williams had nothing to gain by murdering Rhodes, a family friend, the lawyer argued.

Bunch reminded jurors that Sykes had confessed to her family, to law enforcement officers, and to her own attorneys that she killed Rhodes before she changed her statement in January 1993. Bunch maintained that it was doubtful that a drunken Williams could do everything Sykes said he did. If Sykes was afraid, Bunch asked, why didn't she leave during the murder? She was sober, the lawyer said.

"She was perfectly capable of walking out the door, she was perfectly capable of stopping a fight, and she was perfectly capable of committing this murder, as she told law officers she did," Bunch said.

In his closing, DA Yates argued that none but Williams had committed the "brutal, senseless murder."

Williams went to Rhodes's Rampy Street house with the intent of stealing her car and money, Yates said.

"How are you going to rob somebody and take their car?" Yates asked. "There's only one way. You've got to kill them."

But Yates added that Sykes wasn't innocent.

"She stood there and did nothing," Yates said. "Worse, she cut the cord. She admitted that. That makes her as guilty as him."

Jurors deliberated less than 90 minutes before returning with their verdict on Friday. Williams was found guilty of first-degree murder and common-law robbery.

Williams sat quietly and expressed no emotion, as he did throughout the trial, at the jury's decision. His family cried.

Attorneys returned the following Monday to present evidence for and against the death penalty.

A psychiatrist testified for the defense that he had interviewed Williams since his arrest, and Williams said he regretted what happened to Rhodes. But Williams had told the psychiatrist that he wasn't in Rhodes's house when the murder went down.

The doctor testified that Williams said he left Rhodes's house for about 30 minutes on the night of the murder, and when he returned, Rhodes was dead. Williams was haunted by the murder, the doctor said.

"He sees her face floating in the air," the psychiatrist said. "He had very few friends. Ms. Rhodes was one of the few people who befriended him. They went out to dinner while Bernice [Sykes] was in prison."

Factors, including the defendant's attention-deficit disorder and drug abuse, led Williams to his criminal activity, which began as early as age 11, the doctor said. He said Williams was "dependent, avoidant, and self-defeating" and relied on other people to make decisions for him. When Williams acted on his own, he often did things without thinking, the doctor said, adding that Williams was a hyperactive child and failed gym class as a boy because "he sat on the bench and stared into space," a classic sign of attention disorder.

Defense attorneys said Williams was a gifted artist. They entered into evidence several drawings, handmade cards, and handkerchiefs covered with artwork that Williams had made in prison. He was a very good prisoner, doctors testified, because the system provided much-needed structure in his life.

Williams's case worker at the Piedmont Correctional Center in Salisbury testified that Williams worked his way up from dorm janitor to cook. He was enrolled in the prison's GED course and completed an alcohol rehabilitation program, she said. Williams didn't get his GED, the caseworker said, because of a lack of interest and concentration.

In closing arguments, Bunch argued that Williams was "misunderstood, misdiagnosed, and not treated" for his problem.

"We ask you to search in your heart, to consider all the mitigating circumstances, and consider the disabling effect that mental health problems can cause," Bunch said. "[Williams's] life is worth saving. We're not asking you to let him go home or go free."

But in his closing, DA Yates argued that Williams should die for the slow death that he caused Rhodes. He reminded jurors that Williams owed more than $3,000 in court payments three days before the murder.

The prosecutor said Rhodes made the mistake of telling Williams that she got a government check, and that he went to her Rampy Street house with the intention of robbing and killing her for her money. Pecuniary gain, Yates pointed out, is an aggravating factor warranting the death penalty. The other aggravating factor, Yates argued, was that Rhodes's death was "especially heinous, atrocious, and cruel."

"Sure, he [Williams] drank alcohol, but how did that in any way lessen what happened February fifteenth?" Yates asked. "How does it lessen the moral culpability? How does it lessen what he did to Ms. Rhodes, who befriended him?

"Would there be a worse homicide than someone beat around their house for two hours?"

The seven-woman, five-man jury deliberated about three hours before returning on Wednesday, November 3, 1993.

Williams, dressed in a navy blazer and gray slacks, expressed no emotion when the court clerk read the recommended sentence: death. Superior Court Judge Rick Greeson affirmed the verdict.

James Williams is currently on North Carolina's death row at Central Prison in Raleigh. By state law, he will have his choice between lethal injection and the gas chamber.

UPDATE:

On June 6, 1994, murder charges were dismissed against Bernice Sykes. She was found guilty of being a felony accessory after the fact and given a 10-year sentence.

"DRUGSTORE COWBOYS THROTTLED THE RUNAWAY"

by Lynne Bliss

Just after 10 P.M. on Monday, December 2, 1991, the El Paso County Sheriff's Office (EPSO) in Colorado Springs, Colorado, received a phone call from North Carolina. The caller, who declined to give his name, told the dispatcher that a relative in Colorado Springs had called to say that she had witnessed a murder and that the body was dumped on a mountain road. Later, the North Carolinian tried to call the family member back but was unable to get an answer. That's when he contacted the EPSO. The caller refused to give his name and phone number or the name and number of the relative in Colorado Springs. With so little information, detectives could only hope that someone else would come forward with more information.

Fortunately, five hours later, at 3 A.M. on Tuesday, the man called again. This time, he was more cooperative. He identified not only himself, but also his family member in Colorado— Melinda Stewart. Melinda had told him that she had checked herself into a local psychiatric hospital and that she now feared for her safety if she talked about the incident. In particular, Melinda feared a woman who was involved in the plot. The North Carolina man suggested that Melinda's husband, Dan, may also have been mixed up in the crime.

With this information, EPSO detective Stan Presley telephoned the hospital to check on Melinda Stewart's admission. As he feared, hospital personnel would neither confirm nor deny that Melinda Stewart was at their facility. Detective Presley called the family member in North Carolina and asked him to advise Melinda that detectives wanted to speak with her, but were being hindered by hospital rules.

During the conversation, the North Carolina man told Detective Presley that the alleged murder may have had occult overtones. Melinda had told him that a man named "Catman," who lived with her and her husband, had planned and carried out the murder. She believed the victim's name was Maggie and that her body had been dumped in the "band-aid" area of Gold Camp Road. Detective Presley wasn't familiar with that term and he hoped that Melinda would be able to give him more information.

Family members in North Carolina succeeded in arranging for Melinda to talk to law officials, but they warned detectives that Melinda was terrified. The interview was planned for 2:45 P.M. on Tuesday, December 3.

When Detective Presley first met Melinda Stewart, she appeared nervous and even disoriented. Hospital personnel told him that, on that day, she only answered to the name "Amanda."

While Melinda/Amanda appeared to be in her early 30s, she clutched the front of her sweater in a childlike manner. Hospital personnel had to assist her as she walked into the room. During the interview, Melinda/Amanda spoke rapidly in bursts of short sentences. Sometimes she would whimper instead of answering questions or give a reply totally unrelated to the inquiry. Other times, she would rock back and forth and repeat, "They will kill me, they will kill me if they know I'm talking."

With two hours of perseverance and patience, Detective Presley eventually pieced together Melinda's story. She stated that on November 30, she went out with a couple of friends, Maggie and Jill Yousef. She didn't know Maggie's last name. The threesome picked up some tequila and went up Gold Camp Road to look at the sights and to party. Then, Melinda said,

Yousef took out an elastic athletic bandage, wrapped it around Maggie's neck, and choked her to death. Melinda also said that she remembered seeing a rope or string around Maggie's neck and that Maggie wouldn't wake up.

Melinda said that Yousef was Maggie's best friend, but that she herself was afraid of Yousef. Now she feared her own husband, Daniel, as well. Melinda clutched her throat and said, "We have to find Maggie. We have to find Maggie. Maggie's cold." Detective Presley asked Melinda where Maggie was, and Melinda said she was at the "band-aid" part of Gold Camp Road. Melinda couldn't give any more description and didn't know how to get there. Then, with a far-off look in her eye, as though listening to someone only she could hear, Melinda said, "Daniel tells me to shut up." And she did. Melinda would not answer any more of Presley's questions regarding the body's location or the events that occurred that night.

The investigator tried a different tactic and asked if she knew anyone who knew where the band-aid area was. Speaking like a little girl, Melinda told him that Steve Abrahamson, her ex-boyfriend, knew. Steve liked her and wouldn't hurt her, she said. Then she gave Presley Abrahamson's work phone number.

Melinda's demeanor did not indicate a high degree of credibility, but due to the seriousness of the allegations, Detective Presley felt obliged to follow through with an investigation. Presley contacted Abrahamson and arranged to pick him up for the purpose of locating the band-aid area of Gold Camp Road.

The investigator also ran a check for the criminal histories of Melinda Stewart, Jill Yousef, Daniel Stewart, and Steve Abrahamson. All but Daniel had been arrested before.

Gold Camp Road was originally a railroad bed for the grain that ran from Colorado Springs to Cripple Creek during the gold rush days a century ago. The road twists and turns 1,000 feet above the 6,000-foot elevation of Colorado Springs, directly south of Pikes Peak. With a steep embankment on one side, this road curves up the mountain with sharp switchbacks. Breathtaking vistas of pine-covered mountains and the city stretch out below. In the summer season, tourists and hikers swarm the area.

In early winter, though, few travelers used the often snow-covered and slippery road. The area is secluded and quiet, making it a perfect location for a crime. After a couple of miles, the pavement ends at a small parking area and a gravel road traverses the backside of the mountain and then returns to Colorado Springs.

When Detective Presley and Steve Abrahamson arrived in the parking area near the end of the paved road, Abrahamson told him this was the "band-aid" area, so named because of the high rock wall that CB-radio buffs used to bounce their signals off. This technique "aids their band" and extends their range toward the Eastern plains.

Although it was almost dark, the detective inspected the site but did not find a body. The sleuth also determined that the area was inside the Colorado Springs city limits and therefore out of his jurisdiction.

When Presley returned home about 6:10 P.M., he called Sergeant Curtis Pillard, the shift commander of the Gold Hills subdivision of the Colorado Springs Police Department (CSPD). Detective Presley relayed all the information he knew about Melinda Stewart and her story of a murder. Sergeant Pillard sent Officer Derek Phillips, Canine Officer Rob Kelley and his dog Harry, and Reserve Officer Jim Leach to search the brush-covered mountainside of Gold Camp Road. Together they searched over the rugged mountainous terrain in the crisp, mountain air of early December. Snow had fallen earlier in the day but, as is typical of Colorado, the afternoon sun had melted much of it away.

The three officers had searched only a short time when they found a lightly clad figure about 15 feet down the embankment of the road. The blonde woman lay facedown in the snow and appeared to be in her mid-20s. She wore a light denim jacket, white tennis shoes, and dark-colored jeans and sweatshirt. The investigators thought it was odd that she did not have a heavy jacket on in such cold weather. In the area where the woman was found, a snowplow had passed by earlier and the driver did not see her. She easily could have been there until the first hiker of spring discovered her, and probably *would* have been, if not for the information from the man in North Carolina.

In spite of the scarcity of evidence, crime scene technicians were called in to process the scene. Like much of the Pikes Peak region, the embankment on the side consisted of decomposed granite, a grayish brown, gravellike substance that would not hold the outline of a footprint or tire tread. The snow had melted, erasing any tracks or prints it might have held. The only evidence was the woman's body, which showed the signs of her death-causing trauma. Petechia—red spots of oxygen-starved blood vessels—dotted her eyes, and bruises streaked around her neck. She had no identification, and the amateur tattoos on her fingers and above her knee gave no clue to her identity. She would be the 26th homicide in 1991 for this city of 350,000.

Soon after the discovery, the head of the homicide division assigned Detective Brian Ritz as lead detective in the effort to solve the murder. A tall man with compelling hazel eyes, Detective Ritz began his career as a patrol officer with CSPD in 1979. By 1987, he had impressed his lieutenant enough that when the lieutenant transferred to General Investigations, he asked if Ritz would like to be moved with him. Although Ritz enjoyed patrolling, he agreed to the change. In June 1990, a local civic organization honored Detective Ritz for his investigation into a suspect with many aliases who had over $1,000,000 worth of stolen airline tickets and merchandise in his vehicle. Soon after that, Ritz moved to Homicide Investigations and developed an appreciation for the challenge of working murder cases. He believed that every murdered person deserved a proper investigation, and every grieving family deserved to know what happened to their loved one.

With the discovery of a body and confirmation that the death was by homicide, Detective Ritz intensified the search for more evidence. Officers searched among the scrub brush and gray rock formations that lined Gold Camp Road. About a mile west of the crime scene, searchers found a plastic sack containing a tequila bottle, cigarettes, a lighter, and an elastic athletic bandage with two rolls of pennies taped to it.

Back at police headquarters, Detective Ritz read the transcript of the interview the sheriff's detective conducted with Melinda Stewart. To begin his own investigation, he prepared a major case investigation packet—an outline and schedule to properly manage a major crime investigation by entering the details he already knew about the case. The rest of the packet contained nearly 50 pages of fill-in forms and reminder lists of necessary research, interviews, and investigative techniques. Throughout the investigation, this book would be an organized summary of all pertinent data on the case.

At the top of the page with the list of interviewees was Jill Yousef, Maggie's supposed best friend.

Detective Ritz ran a criminal history on Yousef. Besides getting her current address, the investigator discovered that she was a bit of a "drugstore cowboy." She had a pending charge of prescription fraud against her. Metro Vice and Narcotics officers told him that Yousef was addicted to prescription medication.

Another entry on her record dated November 22, 1991, indicated that Yousef had been charged with shoplifting $358 worth of clothing from a discount store.

Based on information from Melinda Stewart, Detective Ritz prepared a probable cause affidavit and secured a warrant to arrest Jill Yousef.

In the early-morning hours of Wednesday, December 4, investigators located Yousef and brought her in for questioning.

Jill Yousef was a waitress of average height, with straggly brown hair, large blue eyes, and thin lips. Although only 29, her face belied a hard life of drugs and crime. She provided Margaret's last name—Fetty—and stated that November 30 was to be a "girl's night out" with Melinda and Maggie. Melinda's husband, Daniel, and Jill's boyfriend, James Catlin, stayed home while Jill drove over to the west side of town to pick up Maggie. Melinda sat in the backseat and Maggie sat in the front. The threesome drove to a liquor store for some tequila, then to a drug store to get a prescription filled, and then to Gold Camp Road.

They parked where they had a good view of the city lights below. Jill Yousef said she didn't drink that night, but Melinda and Maggie passed the bottle of tequila back and forth and chased it down with cola. Instead of alcohol, Jill downed four tablets of Vicodin, a painkilling prescription medication that she had purchased earlier.

Jill Yousef's accounting of the events coincided with Melinda Stewart's version with the exception of one key point. Jill stated that it was *Melinda* who pulled the bandage around Maggie's neck and strangled her. Detective Ritz asked Jill why she didn't report it to the police. Jill explained that she believed Melinda when she looked at her with "fire in her eye" and said that if Jill said anything, she would get killed the same way. In fear for her life, Jill followed Melinda's instructions to drive up the road farther so they could dump the body. Before rolling Maggie's body from the car, Melinda tore a necklace from the girl's neck. On the chain necklace hung a half-circle medallion engraved, "Best Friends." Jill Yousef wore the other half.

Afterwards, Melinda told Jill to drive to Melinda's house. Once there, Jill stated, Melinda and her husband, Daniel, would not let Jill leave for two days and prevented her from calling the police.

Their original story, should they be questioned by police, Jill said, was that the three of them went to a bar, where a soldier picked up Maggie, and they never saw her again.

Obviously, one or both of the women were lying. Detective Ritz concluded the interview and arrested Jill Yousef for first-degree murder. Later investigation would reveal that Jill had given her boyfriend, James Catlin, a ride to work on Monday, December 2, thus discounting her claim that she had been held against her will. She had also stopped by the public defender's office to discuss one of the earlier pending charges against her. In either of these situations, she could have sought refuge or gone home.

Based on the information Jill Yousef provided, Detective Ritz prepared an arrest warrant for Melinda Stewart plus a search warrant for her residence and her room at the psychiatric hospital. Soon after Melinda's arrest, her attorneys had her placed at the state mental health hospital in Pueblo, about 30 miles south of Colorado Springs.

After the interview, Ritz ran a background check on the full name of the deceased girl. He discovered that Margaret Ann Fetty and her two siblings had been placed in foster care a couple of years before. The record indicated that soon after that, Maggie ran away. When authorities found her later, they placed her in an alternative home that offered short-term care for runaways. The youths were observed there but were not under detention. Most benefited greatly from the programs provided by the facility, but some found the rules and regulations, plus the need to get along with 36 other kids, too difficult. Maggie ran away from the home in 1990 and was still listed as a runaway when her body was found on December 3, 1991. At the time of her death, Maggie had been living with friends on the west side of the city.

The coroner performed Maggie's autopsy the following day, Thursday, December 5. His findings confirmed that the cause of death was asphyxiation by strangulation and that the bruise marks on her neck were from a ligature. Maggie's blood tested positive for alcohol at .065, just over the legal limit for impairment. She did not have any needle tracks on her arms, nor were any cocaine, barbiturates, or amphetamines found in her system.

Detective Ritz and the team of investigators began broadening the circle of people to interview to include Maggie's roommates; Melinda Stewart's Colorado Springs relative; Melinda's husband, Dan; and James Catlin, the man Melinda referred to as "Catman" in her conversation with her family in North Carolina.

Maggie's roommates on the west side of town said that they didn't know where Maggie had been and it was not unusual for her to take off for several days at a time. The only information one of them could provide that might be related to Maggie's death was that Maggie and Jill Yousef had had a falling-out over a shoplifting charge a few days before. Since Maggie was still a juvenile, Jill wanted her to take the fall alone. Jill did not want to be implicated since the penalty would be more severe. There was no indication that Maggie's roommates were involved in any way in her murder, and they couldn't provide anything specific about the actual crime. Detectives dismissed them as potential suspects.

Next on the list was Eva Waring, Melinda Stewart's relative who lived in Colorado Springs. She gave the following account of her conversations with Melinda and Dan Stewart.

Melinda had called Eva the day after the murder, Sunday, December 1, and related the frightening account of Saturday night's events. Melinda feared that she would get blamed for the murder. On Monday, Eva tried to call Melinda at home to see if she was all right. Daniel told her that Melinda had checked into the local psychiatric hospital. When Eva questioned him about Melinda's claims of witnessing a murder, Daniel downplayed it and told Eva that he had destroyed the clothes that Melinda wore that night. He said that if everyone kept quiet, everything would be okay.

The information given by Jill Yousef and Eva Waring implicated Daniel Stewart in the brutal crime. The investigators had enough information to charge him with being an accessory to murder, but they wanted to hear his side of the story.

Detective Charles Lucht, a member of the investigative team, interviewed Daniel Stewart first. The suspect denied prior knowledge of Maggie Fetty's murder. He stated that he and Melinda, Jill Yousef, James Catlin, Lyle Beckman, and others were partying that night. He said that Jill called Maggie, and then Jill and Melinda left the house about eight o'clock. He claimed that he didn't know where or why.

He also related that Jill was supposed to spend Thanksgiving with Melinda, James Catlin, and him. Instead, Jill went over to Maggie's because Maggie could get drugs for her. Jill would forge prescriptions for Vicodin and then send Maggie into a drug store to get them filled.

Jill got drunk on alcohol and stoned on her favorite prescription that day, so Daniel Stewart and James Catlin drove over to Maggie's to bring Jill back home. Jill didn't stay long; she hitch-hiked back to Maggie's. That made the three of them angry, particularly since Catlin tried to get Jill to quit abusing Vicodin.

In an effort to spread the blame, Daniel Stewart further stated that James Catlin also knew that Melinda and Jill had killed Maggie.

In spite of Daniel's denials, Detective Ritz charged him with accessory to murder and had him taken to jail at the El Paso County Criminal Justice Center.

In her earlier conversation with Detective Presley, Melinda Stewart implicated Catlin in the crime. Now Daniel was saying the same thing.

Detective Ritz had Catlin brought in for an interview. At first, Catlin denied any involvement or knowledge. All he could recall is that Jill made a phone call to Maggie to see if she wanted to party. When Ritz confronted Catlin with Daniel's accusation, Catlin changed his story. His resolve to remain uninvolved weak-ened. He said that he had seen a "thuggy cult movie" where coins wrapped in scarves were used to strangle people. He said that Melinda and Jill were going to a rough bar that night and wanted something for protection. So he improvised the movie's technique, using pennies and an elastic athletic bandage, and demonstrated how to use it. He also finally admitted to knowing afterwards that Maggie had been killed. Detective Ritz arrested Catlin as an accessory to murder.

Also present at the party on the night Maggie Fetty died was another friend of the foursome—Lyle Beckman. Detective Ritz hoped he would give them additional information on what tran-spired in the hours before Melinda Stewart, Jill Yousef, and Mag-gie Fetty drove to Gold Camp Road.

Beckman provided the investigators with a lot of missing pieces. At the party on that fateful Saturday night, he overheard all four suspects—Melinda and Daniel Stewart, Jill Yousef, and James Catlin—talk about how to kill Maggie. Beckman did not participate in the conversation, but he was sure that the discussion involved something more than self-defense in bars. Catlin and Daniel Stewart actively discussed the precautions that Melinda and Jill would have to take. He saw Catlin bring out an elastic athletic bandage and show how it could be used to strangle someone. It seemed to Detective Ritz that Daniel Stewart and Catlin were not as innocent as they wanted to appear. If Stewart and Catlin knew about the plan ahead of time, Ritz would be able to raise the charges to first-degree murder.

In an interview on December 20, Catlin admitted that all four of them had participated in the planning of Maggie Fetty's death, although he thought Jill Yousef may have been too stoned to realize what was happening. He also admitted to lending Jill his compact car and providing her with the car keys. He recalled that Daniel told Melinda to be sure no one was around, and he gave her a knife just in case she needed it. Melinda also advised Jill to wear dark clothes so they couldn't be easily seen.

Catlin was arrested on January 6, and charged with first-degree murder.

Eventually, Daniel Stewart did admit to knowing about the murder after it happened. He said Melinda came home that night and said, "The Clown had hurt someone." He went on to explain that Melinda had multiple personalities and that "The Clown" was one of them. He also said that there was a necklace on his dresser that night, a chain with a "Best Friends" half-circle medallion on it. Daniel also admitted to cutting up the tennis shoes and destroying the fringed jacket that Melinda wore that night.

After sorting through the array of conflicting stories, accusations, and denials, Detective Ritz presented the district attorney with the case in early February 1992. They would go to trial accusing all four friends of first-degree murder. Jill Yousef and Melinda Stewart were also charged with conspiracy and two counts of a crime of violence.

As the Rocky Mountain winter gave way to spring and the trial dates neared, Melinda Stewart became more and more anxious. When prosecutors approached her with a plea bargain, she accepted. She pled guilty to second-degree murder and accepted a 48-year prison term in exchange for prosecutors' dropping their pursuit of first-degree murder charges against her. She would also be called as a witness during the trials of Jill Yousef and Daniel Stewart.

Prosecutors believed that Melinda's decision might have been based on her inability to prove insanity. Although she was being held at the state's mental hospital in Pueblo, Colorado, her veneer of multiple personalities had cracks. Melinda's other personas only appeared when she thought other people were watching and never when she was being watched without knowing it. To maintain a consistent facade against the almost certain barrage of professional mental health experts was more than Melinda wanted to handle.

Once Melinda entered her guilty plea, she provided inconsistent details of the killing. At one point, she stated that she wrapped the athletic bandage around Maggie's neck and pulled on one end while Jill pulled on the other. Another time, she said that she alone pulled the strap around Maggie's neck.

A week later, the DA offered James Catlin the same plea-bargain arrangement—second-degree murder plus testimony against Jill Yousef and Daniel Stewart. He accepted and was sentenced to 30 years in prison, with possible parole in 10 years.

Jill Yousef and Daniel Stewart steadfastly maintained their innocence. Yousef went to trial in January 1993. Melinda Stewart's testimony at that trial included accusations that Maggie Fetty was the victim of a satanic cult killing. Other times Melinda said Maggie was killed because she was a "bad influence" on Jill. She said that Daniel and Catlin believed that Jill would be able to stay away from drugs if she stayed away from Maggie.

During Catlin's testimony at Jill Yousef's trial, he recanted a previous statement on the witness stand and said that Melinda made the phone call to lure Maggie out that night. The prosecutor showed him his statement to police in which he indicated that Jill made the phone call to get Maggie out, but Catlin still stuck to his new story.

Catlin wasn't the only one with surprise testimony at Jill

Yousef's trial. During his half day on the witness stand, Lyle Beckman stated that the day after the killing, he heard Jill say, "I wish I didn't do this." He was reminded that at the preliminary hearing, he had testified that it was Melinda Stewart who had made that statement. When asked to explain, Beckman said that Melinda made the statement in the morning and Jill made it later that afternoon.

Jill Yousef's version of events was consistent from the start. That night on Gold Camp Road, she said, the three of them were laughing and having a good time. Maggie got a little drunk and silly. "Amanda told her just to relax, to put her head backward . . . and it would relax her," Yousef said. Yousef was looking out over the city when she felt Maggie touch her. She looked over and saw that "Amanda had that [bandage] wrapped around her. I told Amanda to stop, and she wouldn't stop."

Detective Ritz asked Yousef why she didn't go to the police. She explained that she had considered it but thought that if she just kept taking her pills, it would all go away. She also believed that she would not be able to convince the police that she had nothing to do with it. Police, she said, are "higher" people; she always thought of herself as "real low."

Jill Yousef's defense counsel maintained throughout that Maggie Fetty was her best friend. She had no motive to kill her. Not even the shoplifting incident was important enough to kill for, she said.

The jury deliberated eight hours before finding Jill Yousef innocent of first-degree murder and conspiracy but guilty of being an accessory after the fact. She was sentenced to six years in prison.

The lingering question of motive still remained, and the real reason that these four participated in Maggie Fetty's murder may never be known. On one occasion, Melinda accused Maggie of flirting with her husband. Or perhaps, as Melinda suggested, Jill would be able to stay off drugs if it weren't for Maggie. But if Jill were determined enough, she would find someone else to get drugs for her.

Others speculated that Maggie was a nuisance to the two couples, a fifth wheel to the foursome. The local newspaper ran a companion article about the death of three local runaway teens, including Margaret Fetty. The director of the children's division at the Colorado Mental Health Institute in Denver was quoted as saying, "When kids run, they become incredibly vulnerable to the dark side of our society because they become so damn needy. You have a kid on the street [who is] hungry, cold, and unconnected. Who's the most likely person for them to run into? Roaming, disconnected adults on the street." In retrospect, this seems like an apt description of Maggie Fetty.

The last defendant, Daniel Stewart, went to trial in early November 1993. In spite of his protestations of innocence, the overwhelming testimony of his coconspirators sealed his fate. Additionally, jurors saw a letter that Stewart had written to his wife in October 1992. It stated in part, "Baby, I don't think I am innocent. In fact, I know I am going down, but I just want to get it down as low as possible, okay?" Later in the letter, he added, "I didn't mean to imply I'm innocent. We both know the truth." The jury found Stewart guilty of first-degree murder.

With the last of the four defendants convicted, the investigators turned their attention to Maggie Fetty's last resting place. Prosecutors who visited the gravesite were surprised to see that only a single plastic flower marked the plot. She had been buried a week after her death in the pauper's section of the city cemetery. The local newspaper got hold of the story and also noted the fact that no family or friends on behalf of Maggie attended the three-and-a-half-day trial of Daniel Stewart. Soon after that story's publication, community compassion surged and more than 100 offers of markers and money poured into the DA's office.

Finally, on a snowy day almost two years after her death, Margaret Ann Fetty received a fitting burial. A few of her relatives were there, as well as the investigators on the case and representatives from the DA's office. They all watched as a local monument company set a donated headstone in place. After Assistant District Attorney Rob Jones gave a brief eulogy, relatives gathered at the gravesite. They spoke of how much Maggie liked cats and said that she had wanted to be a beautician. She always said "toodles" instead of "good-bye."

On December 3, two years to the day after police officials found Margaret Fetty's body, the judge sentenced Daniel Stewart to life in prison without parole.

"PIZZA MAN BECAME A HUMAN JIGSAW PUZZLE!"

by Duke Foxx

A junkman spotted the first of the body parts one autumn morning in 1992 along Philadelphia's waterfront. It was 7:40 A.M., and the sun was still low in the sky as he was making his rounds near the northern end of Delaware Avenue, in the Port Richmond section of the city. This is a desolate area where people are in the habit of illegally dumping their trash.

For much of its length, Delaware Avenue winds back and forth, following the serpentine banks of the Delaware River. But here, it is straight as an arrow, and a massive power plant stands between it and the river. Beams of sunlight were streaming around the sides of the power plant and over its roof, creating a dramatic contrast of lights and darks. And there, scattered along the curb, half in brilliant sunlight, half in dark shadows, were several large trash bags.

Other than the junkman, the area was deserted.

He stopped to rummage through the bags. The date was Friday, November 13—an unlucky Friday the 13th. The junkman was bending over the bags, searching for anything of value. Suddenly he found something he'd seen only in his worst nightmares. He stopped at once and summoned the Philadelphia Police Department.

Lieutenant Joe Witte (pronounced "witty") of the homicide unit was among the first of the detectives to arrive at the scene. In a city in which 400 homicides per year is the norm, not much surprises a seasoned detective like Joe Witte. But this case would turn out to be one of those rare ones that packed several unexpected wallops even for him.

"What happened?" the lieutenant asked the junkman.

"I picked up that bag," the junkman replied, pointing to one of the green plastic bags, "and an arm came out."

"It was the victim's left arm," Lieutenant Witte would later explain.

To the lieutenant, the arm looked fresh, as if it had recently been severed from the rest of its body. It appeared to have come from a mature white male.

"There were several bags in the same general area," the lieutenant would later report, "within a twenty-to-thirty-foot radius."

Next to another trash bag was a bloodstained blanket.

"Then we found another bag with the right arm."

A few minutes later, inside another bag, the detectives found a black waist-length jacket. It was bloodstained.

"Then we found the bags with the severed head and the upper torso," Lieutenant Witte continued. The victim's upper torso was still clothed in a short-sleeved pullover shirt. The head had been battered with some sort of blunt instrument, and the victim's left eye was missing.

"It looked like he was cut up with a hacksaw. Clean cuts. All the way through."

But other than where the head and arms had been sawed away from the upper torso, and where the head had been bludgeoned, the lieutenant observed no other marks, no bullet wounds. And that was it, which made this worse than most "dump jobs"— cases in which a victim is murdered in one place and the body is dumped somewhere else, miles away from the evidence. In most dump jobs, at least the investigators have an entire body to work with. But here, there were no legs, no pelvis, and no lower torso.

Where was the rest of the body?

The detectives fanned out, away from the trash bags, looking for more plastic bags, for the body's lower extremities. A few minutes passed. Newspaper reporters and TV crews began arriving. Then . . .

"Hey, Lieutenant," one of the other detectives yelled, "over here!"

The lieutenant walked halfway down the block to a nearby field. A detective standing in a patch of weeds was pointing toward the ground, to a .38-caliber semiautomatic pistol. Carefully poking a pencil through the trigger mechanism, the lieutenant picked up the gun. It was loaded with three rounds.

"Is that the murder weapon?" one reporter asked.

"At this point," Witte answered, "we don't know if it's related or not."

The detectives scoured the area for hours, but they failed to find the rest of the victim's body.

"What we did is," Lieutenant Witte would subsequently explain, "we picked up all the trash that was in the area, went back to headquarters, and started going through it and cataloguing it. At the same time, the body parts were taken to the medical examiner's office, and the head was photographed separately."

At the morgue, it was determined that some "twenty-odd blows to the skull" had been the cause of death. The time of death was placed within 24 hours of the junkman's discovery.

"From the looks of it," an assistant medical examiner told Witte, "the victim was dismembered while he was still alive. And because of the strength that would have been required to saw through the neck and arms swiftly, while the victim was still alive, it's highly likely that two people were required to dismember him," one to hold the victim, the other to do the cutting.

At noon, the junkman's grisly discovery was the lead story on the televised newscasts throughout the city.

What no one knew, except for the killers, was that the story had started some 30 hours earlier, at 1 A.M. on Thursday. That was when Eleftherios Eleftheriou had closed his pizzeria for the night. Called Pandela's Pizza, it was located in the 200 block of Allegheny Avenue, in West Kensington, about three miles from where the body parts were discovered.

For the previous four years, Eleftheriou, a 50-year-old Greek immigrant, had been partners in the pizza shop with one of his relatives. Eleftheriou was a short man with graying temples and a heavy accent. He lived a few miles to the north of the pizza shop, in the Oxford Circle section of Northeast Philadelphia, with his wife and two children.

Around 2 A.M., his family called the partner. Armed robbery was a definite occupational hazard in the pizzeria business, and his family members were frantic. What had happened to Eleftherios?

The partner assured them that Eleftherios had closed the pizza shop at 1 A.M., as usual, got into his 1987 Hyundai, and drove away, apparently on his way home. But he never got there.

Several fitful hours passed. When morning dawned and Eleftheriou still hadn't come home, his family went to the police station.

"He was reported missing to Northeast detectives," Lieutenant Witte explained. "However, the missing-persons criteria with the police department is to make out a report. We don't actively look for a male or female over the age of eighteen who has no history of mental problems unless there's a sign of foul play. If there had been any sign of a struggle—some blood or something like that—we would have acted. Otherwise, what we do is take a report and file it in the computer. And that was done.

"So his wife hired a private investigator. The private investigator notified all of his credit card companies and learned that one of his credit cards had been used on Thursday night."

Nearly 18 hours after Eleftheriou disappeared, his credit card purchased $115.45 worth of children's clothing at a shopping center on Aramingo Avenue, which was between the pizza shop and where the body was discovered, but much closer to the latter.

Had Eleftheriou used it? Or someone else?

Eleftheriou's family printed a thousand missing-person fliers and posted them in the vicinity of the pizza shop. Then, early that afternoon . . .

"I believe [a relative of Eleftheriou] is a police officer," Lieutenant Witte explained, "and she had seen the noon news that body parts had been found in the same general area where her [relative's] pizza shop was located. She called and said, 'It's possible it's my [relative].' Then she came down and viewed the photos and said it was her [relative]."

Six hours after the body was discovered, an identification was made. The victim *was* Eleftherios Eleftheriou.

But who killed him? And where was his car?

"We had no suspects at this point—at all," Lieutenant Witte explained. "So we put out a more aggressive message on police radio, looking for the car—it was being broadcast almost every half hour—with the license number and description of the car."

But the late afternoon and early-evening hours passed without any further developments.

At 7:40 P.M., uniformed officers Timmy Simpson and Rich Fegley were cruising the general area in a 24th District patrol car, looking for the missing Hyundai. They were members of the 24-Tom-One Squad, an anticrime team.

"A homicide detective had stopped by and given us the license number and description of the vehicle," Officer Simpson would recall. "We're driving along and we look to the right and see this vehicle—and it's on fire.

"We must have just missed whoever set it off because the fire was just getting started. But within about thirty seconds, it's really flaming. Windows are popping. Paint's peeling off. The whole car's just melting right in front of our eyes.

"Then it starts rolling—eastbound on Clearfield Street." The flaming car was a 1987 Hyundai.

"It was a stick shift," Officer Simpson continued. "Whoever set it on fire left it in gear and apparently threw a firebomb inside. And the fire melts the wires and starts the starter and the starter's dragging it down the street.

"The fire's really hot and we can't get very close to it—to

stop the car—and it just keeps rolling for about sixty feet. Finally, Rich Fegley threw a board under the wheels and stopped it just before it ran into a warehouse."

But the car was still burning. So Officer Simpson called the fire department. Since it was the same year and make as Eleftheriou's missing car, he checked the tags. When the tag numbers matched, he notified his supervisor, who called the homicide unit.

"The firemen put it out," Lieutenant Witte explained. "The fire had forced the trunk open and they found two severed legs, still clothed in jeans—[the killers] had cut right through the clothing—and the lower torso. The parts were within the metal frame of what probably had been a suitcase. It had melted inside the trunk.

"Medical examiner's personnel came and examined the body parts. They found the fly open on the jeans and they found that the torso was missing the genitalia."

So 12 hours after the upper half of the body was discovered, the lieutenant now had the lower half. But he returned to headquarters with no idea who killed Eleftherios Eleftheriou.

"By the time we started our paperwork," Witte continued, "it was after the eleven o'clock news. We were going to start backtracking on the trash the next day, but then we get a phone call from a woman who lives on Richmond Street.

"This woman tells us she knows about the body parts that were found. She believes that the person was killed in her apartment. The people that she believes did it are in her apartment now and they won't let her back in. And there was also an elderly man there at this time, who was a relative of hers."

The caller said she was at a friend's house, not far from her apartment.

Lieutenant Witte instructed the woman to go to the intersection of Richmond Street and Allegheny Avenue, just a few blocks away. Detectives would meet her there.

After the lieutenant hung up, he dispatched a pair of detectives to pick up the woman. Then he went back to the evidence they had recovered from the waterfront.

"When she gave her name and address," Witte explained, "I thought I remembered seeing it when I was going through the trash earlier. I went back through the trash and found a phone bill in her name and I thought to myself, This looks like a good tip."

The caller's name was Myrtle Martin and she met the detectives at Richmond and Allegheny. She rented an apartment in the 3100 block of Richmond Street, in the Port Richmond section, two miles from the pizza shop and a mile from where the junkman had discovered Eleftheriou's body parts. The neighborhood is predominantly blue-collar.

Richmond Street sits in the shadows of Interstate 95, which is elevated at that point. The street is just a block away from the interstate and parallel to it. A set of trolley tracks runs down the middle of Richmond Street and three-story brick rowhouses line both sides. Most of the homes have been renovated and are tidy-looking, and some have been converted into business establishments.

Myrtle Martin had been away for a few days, to the mountains. When she returned to her home a few hours earlier, she was rested and relaxed from her short vacation. But her composure changed as soon as she stepped inside her front door.

To begin with, a large portion of her living-room carpet was missing—right in the middle of the room. For another thing, two friends were staying with her and one of them was acting peculiar.

Her friends were Billy Gribble and Kelley O'Donnell. They were boyfriend and girlfriend. He was 28 years old, short and balding, with sandy-colored hair, a goatee, and mustache. She was 25, short and skinny.

Kelley O'Donnell's face was drawn in the emaciated manner common to many crack-cocaine users. Indeed, both she and Gribble were known to be drug addicts. Eighteen months earlier, they'd had a daughter who was born with a crack addiction. Due to the baby's addiction, they never brought the baby home from the hospital. Instead, they gave her up to foster care. Altogether, Kelley O'Donnell had six children. All were living in foster homes.

Three months earlier, Gribble and O'Donnell had shown up in the neighborhood for the first time, which was when Myrtle Martin first met them. A bar across the street from her apartment had previously gone out of business and was vacant. Gribble and O'Donnell approached the landlord with a proposal to open a video store and arcade. When they said they'd take care of the renovations, the landlord was agreeable.

But the couple had no intentions of opening a business. Instead, they threw a couple of mattresses on the floor and turned it into a flophouse. It took two months for the landlord to catch on to the fact that the couple was living there illegally. When he did, he kicked them out.

"I have a heart of gold," Martin told the detectives. "I don't want to see anybody else in the street. And they had no place to go."

So Gribble and O'Donnell carried their mattresses across the street to Martin's apartment and moved right in. They stayed there for several weeks without paying rent.

"I never actually invited them to stay," Martin told the sleuths. "But once they were inside, I couldn't kick them out.

"Kelley told me they'd leave by January. She seemed to be, like, the boss. More than him. If she said jump, he did. He was, like, an easygoing guy.

"But today, when I got home, she was acting funny."

"How so?" one of the detectives asked Martin.

"She said, 'I need to sit down and talk with you,' " Martin replied. "She said, 'Something happened. We committed a murder.' "

When the detectives asked Martin for more details, she told them that someone had been killed right in the middle of her living room—her carpet had been cut up and thrown away because it was bloodstained—and the victim had been cut up in her basement. So when she saw the 11 o'clock news about the body parts being found a mile away, she put two and two together and phoned the police.

"Who set the car on fire?" one of the detectives asked Martin.

"I don't know anything about that."

At this point, the detectives believed that Billy Gribble and Kelley O'Donnell were involved in the murder of Eleftherios Eleftheriou. But they weren't sure whether or not Myrtle Martin herself had played a role in the killing. So they took her into custody and transported her to headquarters—called the Round-house due to its circular structure.

"I then went up to Richmond and Allegheny," Lieutenant Witte explained, "and called for a stakeout, which is our SWAT team. A decision was made at that time to force our way into the house—because of the possibility of a barricade-type situation and the safety of the elderly relative that was in the house at that time.

"Our SWAT team broke down the front door very quickly—because of the possibility of their taking the man hostage. But he was sitting there, unharmed, in the living room. The girl was also found in the living room and the gentleman was in the bedroom—they offered no resistance.

"We found a bloodstain on the living-room floor and there were signs in the basement—blood and spatterings—that looked like the body was cut up in the basement.

"Detectives then transported them to the homicide unit.

"We were doing the scene in the basement—forensics people and detectives. It had been a big old house at one time, but they'd cut it up and redone some of the plumbing. Some of the old sewer pipes had been cut off and were still imbedded in the concrete. One of our female detectives was nosing around, looking into these pipes, and she noticed a pencil case."

It was a zipper-type bag, the kind children use for school. It was plastic and black and white in color.

"So she pulls the pencil case out," the lieutenant continued, "and opens it. And the left eye and the penis are inside the case."

Lieutenant Witte returned to the Roundhouse. The homicide unit is on the second floor of the Roundhouse. It's a large rectangular room with desks and file cabinets everywhere. The long exterior wall is a series of windows. Small interrogation rooms line the long interior wall. Square see-through mirrors are near the top of each door.

Detective Mike Gross was interviewing Bill Gribble in one of the interrogation rooms. Detective Dennis Dusak was questioning Kelley O'Donnell in another. Lieutenant Witte and Assistant District Attorney Dave Webb were walking from window to window, trying to oversee both interviews.

"What happened?" Detective Gross asked Gribble.

"I came home from a bar," Gribble told the detective, "and I saw him all over Kelley. I freaked out. I grabbed a hammer and hit him over the head.

"Later, I dropped the body into the basement and I got my saw and I started to cut him up."

"What about Kelley?" the detective asked.

Gribble said his girlfriend had nothing to do with it.

At the same time, Detective Dusak was asking Kelley O'Donnell the same types of questions.

"I borrowed ten dollars from him at his pizza shop," O'Donnell began.

"Who do you mean by him?" the detective clarified.

"The pizza man."

"When did you borrow the ten dollars?"

"Around eleven o'clock on Wednesday night," O'Donnell responded, "and he asked me what I was doing later. I said nothing. He asked me for a date and I said sure. Later, I took him home with me."

"That would be sometime after closing time," the detective said.

"Right," O'Donnell replied—which would have placed the time shortly after 1 A.M. on Thursday. "He came to my apartment for sex, but he got killed instead."

"Who killed him?" Detective Dusak asked her.

"I did."

"How?"

"I beat him in the head with a hammer."

"Billy didn't help you?" the detective asked.

"No. He was sleeping at the time."

"Why did you kill him?" Dusak asked.

"I don't know. I just got carried away."

"How did you get rid of the body?"

"With a saw," O'Donnell answered. "It took a while to cut it up—about an hour and a half, two hours. But Billy had nothing to do with it. I did it myself. He had no knowledge of what was going on."

"How did you get rid of the body?"

"I put the body in a bunch of different trash bags. After Billy woke up, I told him what happened. He drove me down to Delaware Avenue and I dumped the bags while he kept driving. Later, Billy set fire to his car."

"Why did you cut off the penis?"

"To get back at him from before."

"Why?" the detective asked her. "What happened before?"

"One time," O'Donnell said, "he [masturbated] in front of me."

"What did you do with the penis after you cut it off?"

"I put it in a black-and-white pencil case."

"Why?"

"Because it's plastic and it doesn't leak all over," O'Donnell replied. "I was going to send it to my father—just to bust his balls."

When the detectives finished their interviews, they met with the lieutenant and the assistant district attorney to compare notes.

"What do you think?" the prosecutor asked.

"It looks like they're trying to cover for each other," Lieutenant Witte suggested.

Everyone agreed. To the lawmen, it appeared as if Kelley O'Donnell had lured Eleftherios Eleftheriou back to her apartment on the pretense of having sex, but all along she and her boyfriend had planned to rob and kill the pizza man.

Bill Gribble and Kelley O'Donnell were arrested. They were charged with murder, robbery, abuse of a corpse, theft, receiving stolen property, unauthorized use of a vehicle, arson, and risking a catastrophe. They were denied bail, but Myrtle Martin was released—eight hours after being taken into custody.

"That was a scary scene," she told a reporter afterward. "But then I told them my alibi. I told them where I was.

"Now I'm going to try to pull my life back together. I'm not functioning right. But I don't think I'll ever let anyone else use my apartment. I don't want to come home to another scene like this."

Seven months passed.

On June 30, 1993, Billy Gribble and Kelley O'Donnell sat before Judge Paul Ribner in Courtroom 4 on the second floor of Philadelphia's City Hall. They had both opted for a nonjury trial. In their case, Judge Ribner would be acting as both judge and jury.

Both defendants stuck pretty much to the stories they'd told the detectives earlier. Each was claiming sole responsibility for the victim's murder—Gribble's scenario was short and sketchy. O'Donnell's more detailed.

"I beat him with a hammer," she told the judge, "and took him down the basement. Then I sawed him up with a hacksaw."

Tom Perricone, the assistant district attorney who was prosecuting the case, maintained that both defendants had acted in concert. He said that O'Donnell had lured Eleftherios Eleftheriou back to her apartment on the pretense of having sex with him. Then she and her boyfriend murdered him, robbed him, and dismembered him.

"They both beat him," Prosecutor Perricone told the judge. "They both cut up his body."

It didn't take long for Judge Ribner to convict both defendants of first-degree murder. All that was left was the penalty phase.

When Gribble took the witness stand, he begged for his life. In testimony that was interrupted several times because Gribble broke down and cried, he told the judge that he first started using drugs at age 14 and had been addicted ever since.

"I was higher than you can imagine," Gribble told the judge.

"I didn't mean to do that. I wasn't like that. I remember hitting him with the hammer, but I don't know how many times. Maybe five.

"I don't remember cutting up the body. I remember walking in the door. I remember seeing him on the couch with Kelley. And we had a fight."

Gribble's lawyer asked the judge for leniency for his client, citing the fact that he had no prior criminal record.

"Had it not been for the drugs," the lawyer contended, "the killing would not have occurred."

But Prosecutor Perricone disagreed. He said that Gribble was trying to hide behind his addiction, trying to use his drug problems as an excuse for killing Eleftheriou.

"Mr. Gribble," Perricone told the judge, "knew exactly what he was doing when he killed the victim."

As he awaited Judge Ribner's decision, Gribble sat at the defense table, squeezing O'Donnell's hand with one hand and covering his eyes with the other.

"Your crime was savage," Judge Ribner said to Gribble, "and the horrible nature of the killing far outweighs any mitigating factors."

When the judge told him that he was being sentenced to death by lethal injection, Gribble cried once more.

But O'Donnell's fate would not be decided until the next day. Judge Ribner wanted prison doctors to examine her and verify that the sedatives and other medications that were being prescribed for her would not interfere with her ability to participate in court.

A day later, July 1, 1993, Judge Ribner sentenced O'Donnell to death by lethal injection.

Nearly a year passed since Judge Ribner's decisions and lawyers were filing posttrial motions on their clients' behalf ever since. One such hearing took place on May 4, 1994.

On that date, Gribble and O'Donnell were brought to the second floor of City Hall—O'Donnell having put on considerable weight in the interim.

They laughed out loud as sheriff's deputies led them down the long hallway toward Courtroom 4. When they saw a camera flash in their direction, they began mugging.

"Say cheese!" O'Donnell shouted.

"Look at the birdie," Gribble said.

And they both laughed out loud.

A few steps later, Gribble snarled his best prison stare as he came face-to-face with the undaunted photographer. A moment later, the codefendants entered the courtroom.

For better than an hour, the defense lawyers presented arguments to try to sway the judge's earlier decisions, and the prosecutor parried their thrusts. This is an ongoing process in murder trials, in which the verdicts are usually upheld. At that time, the appeals process begins.

While the posttrial process runs its course, Billy Gribble and Kelley O'Donnell are biding their time in the Pennsylvania penal system—Gribble at the Western State Penitentiary near Pittsburgh, O'Donnell at the woman's prison in Muncie.

"TULSA'S MAN-HATING TEEN LEFT HER DATE FLOATING IN A POND!"

by Charles W. Sasser

The dating game and the search for meaningful relationships is ordinarily fraught with emotional risks, and when individuals of different cultural backgrounds are thrown into the mix, those risks can become complicated by the divergent perceptions of the persons involved. What few people expect, however, is that the risks might take on another aspect—the kind that actually imperils life and limb and leads to violence—and murder. That was what Yosef Akhisar, a 27-year-old exchange student from Turkey, learned on the night of Saturday, September 12, 1992, in South Tulsa, Oklahoma.

"That day was the worst day I can remember," Akhisar remarked to the Tulsa police officer who responded to his plea for help in the Villa Fontana apartment complex on the 7600 block of East 49th Street. The young man was bleeding, but he would survive. A bullet had grazed the side of his skull.

While he was being patched up at the hospital, he told the officers how he'd met a lovely girl that day near his apartment building. The Villa Fontana is one of a number of sprawling complexes in a South Tulsa area populated by Arabs and other Middle Easterners. Akhisar's new female acquaintance had introduced herself as "Shontoy" and asked him to take her for a spin in his new sports car.

Afterwards, they arranged to meet that night. At about 8 P.M., Shontoy showed up with another younger girl who, she said, was her sister Margie.

In the course of a short evening of drinking wine and beer, Akhisar apparently learned little about his new companions, other than that Shontoy's true name might be Heather and that she was studying to be a masseuse. She offered to give him a back massage.

"I was suspicious," Akhisar told the police. "I had just met them. I thought they might be there to rob me."

Nonetheless, a man's hormones are often stronger than his common sense. Margie remained in the living room while Shontoy and Yosef made their way to the bedroom. Yosef removed his shirt and lay facedown on the bed. Shontoy placed a pillow over his head and began to massage him.

The massage ended abruptly with an unexpected shock—an explosion and a brilliant flash of light.

"I jumped up and Shontoy said, 'What happened?' And I said, 'What happened?' I thought the other girl had harmed my TV," Yosef Akhisar told the officers.

Then, he said, Shontoy and Margie quickly fled out the front door. Finally realizing that he had been shot, Akhisar hurriedly telephoned EMSA—the Tulsa paramedics. The police soon determined that the pretty girl who called herself Shontoy-Heather had apparently pressed a .22-caliber pistol against the pillow over Akhisar's head and squeezed the trigger.

"If the bullet had gone an inch more toward the center of his head, we would have had a murder," remarked Detective Verna Wilson, a nine-year veteran of the Tulsa Police Department and an experienced homicide investigator. "It looks like she intended to kill the victim and then rob him—although she never demanded money or anything before the shot. Whatever the motive, it's obvious she intended to kill him."

The cops immediately broadcast APBs (All-Points Bulletins)

describing the shooting suspect as a white female named Shontoy or Heather in her late teens or early twenties, with long, reddish-brown hair, dark eyes, and a tallish, slender build, accompanied by a younger, shorter white female called Margie.

"Consider armed and dangerous," the APBs concluded.

Shontoy might be gorgeous on the outside, one lawman noted, but on the inside, she must be like a block of ice.

Detective Wilson gathered the available evidence at the crime scene and canvassed other nearby apartment dwellers for possible witnesses. She found none. Although the plainclothes officer checked out the apartments for the next few days, asking the occupants questions, she found no one to provide her a lead on the mystery girls. Likewise, computer suspect readouts turned up no clues as to who Shontoy or Heather might be, or where she was hiding.

A week passed. Although a few potential suspects did emerge, named as either matching the suspect's description or bearing the same or a similar name, none of them panned out.

Major American cities in the 20th century are so plagued with crime that their overtaxed police forces must often sacrifice the investigation of lesser crimes to tackle the more serious ones. That is a hard, bare fact. A shooting in which no one is killed—like the case of Yosef Akhisar, for example—must often be shifted to the back burner to make time for a shooting in which someone is killed. During the latter months of 1992 and into 1993, Tulsa would be suffering nearly one homicide a week for the police to investigate.

The police must therefore be forgiven for not placing heavy emphasis on the investigation of an adult missing person, whose roommate reported him missing on Sunday, September 20, 1992. After all, most missing persons turn up again within a few days. Besides, the missing man, a Saudi Arabian exchange student named Ahmed Al-Dawood, was 20 years old and apparently able to look after himself adequately. It wasn't as though he were a child who could have become lost or abducted, or a senile elder who might have wandered off.

A quick, routine probe into the missing youth's life and background, however, soon revealed that this disappearance was no routine matter, after all. Missing since Thursday, September 17, Al-Dawood had for the past eight months been studying at the Tulsa English Institute. His roommate, also a Saudi exchange student, insisted that Al-Dawood would never have gone off without informing someone of his destination. The dark-complexioned, thinly built missing youth was ordinarily punctual, thoughtful, and routine in his habits. And in spite of his having traveled halfway around the world to study in the United States, he was not so very worldly.

"Ahmed was a very, very, very naive person," his roommate told the police. "You couldn't possibly believe how naive he was."

Al-Dawood's red 1988 Trans-Am was also apparently missing. His friends knew only that they had seen him around the apartment complex where he lived on South 106th East Place on Thursday during the day—and had not seen him since. One friend remembered that Al-Dawood had mentioned he might be going camping over the weekend with a girl named "Misty."

"Who is this Misty? Where does she live?" the investigators asked.

No one knew.

Detective Bob Jackson said that considering the unusual circumstances surrounding the exchange student's disappearance, sleuths were assigned to conduct a thorough investigation. While they failed to come up with anyone named "Misty," they did come up with information that Al-Dawood might have been easy prey for other women.

"In Saudi Arabia," Al-Dawood's roommate said, "men do not go out with girls if they are not married. In Saudi Arabia, unmarried men do not date."

But when in Rome—or in this case, the USA, the land of liberty . . .

About three weeks before his disappearance, Al-Dawood reportedly met two girls in the parking lot of his apartment complex. A witness had seen the young man talking to the girls, who'd been standing outside the open window of his Trans-Am.

"I thought they were street girls," the witness, an East Indian student, told the police. "They didn't live with their parents and were always hanging around places."

Al-Dawood apparently saw a lot of the two girls after their first meeting. In fact, he saw so much of them, the probers learned, that the situation led to friction with Al-Dawood's roommate.

"They called the apartment at all hours of the day or night," the roommate complained. "It got so bad, I told Ahmed he was going to have to move out if it continued. I told him to stay away from the girls. They were trouble. They kept asking him to drive them places and buy food and things for them."

The roommate said he knew the girls only as "Rose Mary" and "Margie." He described Rose Mary as a white female about 18 or 19 years old, rather tall and slender, with long, reddish-brown hair, dark eyes, and a pretty face and figure. Margie was shorter, younger—possibly a juvenile runaway.

"Rose Mary said she loved Ahmed," Al-Dawood's roommate told the probers. "It was so funny to me that she told him from the very first meeting that she loved him. I believe she didn't really love or even like him. She only wanted his money."

The police concluded in their reports that Ahmed Al-Dawood's disappearance might somehow be mixed up with one or all of these girls—Misty, Rose Mary, and Margie. There were no clues leading anywhere else except to the girls. Detective Jackson and his colleagues launched a citywide search for them.

"Misty called for Ahmed on Sunday [September 20, the day Al-Dawood was reported missing, and three days after his actual disappearance]," said the missing youth's roommate. "When I told her he wasn't here, she hung up."

During the next few days, Detective Jackson said, the police learned that young women matching the descriptions of Rose Mary and Margie frequented various apartment-complex swimming pools in South Tulsa and had apparently lived on and off with various other Arab men. "Misty" seemed not to have existed at all, outside of that one phone call to Al-Dawood's roommate, leading the sleuths to speculate that Misty may have been Rose Mary's alias.

Five days passed and Al-Dawood still failed to reappear. In the meantime, Sergeant Wayne Allen and Detective Verna Wilson of the homicide division took an interest in the case, primarily because of Wilson's investigation in the Yosef Akhisar shooting of September 12. Quite logically, Wilson pointed out how "Heather," the gun-wielding woman who shot Akhisar, resembled "Rose Mary" and how, in both instances, the older female had a younger, shorter sidekick called "Margie." Heather and Margie apparently sought out Arab men in South Tulsa; so did Rose Mary and Margie. And although Al-Dawood's apartment on East Place was situated approximately two miles away from the Villa Fontana where Akhisar was shot, the police had nevertheless tracked Rose and Margie back to the same Villa Fontana area.

Detective Wilson spread word among South Tulsa detectives and patrolmen that she herself wanted to question Rose Mary and Margie when and if they were found.

The detectives' first break came shortly afterward. On Tuesday night, September 22—10 days after the Akhisar shooting—the police received an urgent phone call from Ahmed Al-Dawood's worried roommate.

"I've just located Ahmed's car," he exclaimed. "I saw who was driving it. It was not Ahmed."

Southside patrol officers Bob Randolph, Ed Buckspann and Misti Painter met the roommate, who directed them through the autumn night to an apartment on East 49th Street, less than two blocks from where Yosef Akhisar had been shot in the middle of his massage. There, in the parking lot, sat a red 1988 Trans-Am, which the roommate declared was Ahmed Al-Dawood's.

"I saw Rose Mary and Margie driving it," the roommate said, and then pointed out the apartment into which he saw the girls enter.

Evening-shift homicide detective Tom Campbell joined the uniformed "Green Shirts." Minutes later, the team of lawmen surprised two teenage girls inside their apartment. The pair identified themselves as 17-year-old Rose Mary Miller and 15-year-old Margie Barnes, who was indeed a juvenile runaway. Because both girls were juveniles, the police were prohibited by law from questioning them about Al-Dawood's car or anything else, outside the presence of an attorney or guardian. The officers informed the girls of their rights and then transported them downtown to the main police station, where their guardians could be contacted.

Crime scene search experts stayed behind to secure and inspect the girls' apartment and to go over Al-Dawood's Trans-Am with the proverbial fine-toothed comb, seeking blood, hair, weapons, or any other clues that might help explain the young man's disappearance. The searches turned up little of value. Ahmed Al-Dawood remained missing—and the police still had no idea where he might be.

During the drive to the police station and later, the officers observed that 15-year-old Margie Barnes was growing noticeably nervous. With several cops around her, she uttered spontaneous comments that drew the officers' attention and further shrouded the two juveniles in suspicion.

"I know where Dawood is," Margie allegedly murmured, "but I don't want to get in trouble. Will I get in trouble if I just know about him?"

Then, after reportedly mentioning that she knew about the shooting of Yosef Akhisar and intimating that Rose Mary was also "Heather," Margie clammed up. At least temporarily, she did. Besides, the police couldn't let her rattle on without an attorney or guardian present and take the chance of the case being compromised in the event of further legal action.

At 1 A.M., as Wednesday, September 23, began, Detective Tom Campbell telephoned Detective Verna Wilson at home.

"We have the girls you want downtown," he said. "They were

driving Al-Dawood's car. I suspect Al-Dawood is dead somewhere."

Being jarred out of bed in the middle of the night began a long and busy 24-hour stretch for Detective Wilson. For the rest of the night, throughout Wednesday, and into Wednesday night, she found herself working with Sergeant Wayne Allen, Creek County undersheriff Mark Ihrig, and Sapulpa detective Bruce Duncan in attempting to unravel a bizarre and cold-blooded tale of a young woman who "just didn't like men," as Detective Bob Jackson put it. "Apparently, she had a bad experience with a man in the past," he said.

The investigators said that it was Margie Barnes who pointed them in the right direction. The runaway began blurting out her side of the previous few weeks' events almost the instant her guardian arrived at police headquarters. She began by claiming that Rose Mary was a "pathological liar and thief, and someone with the capacity to shoot another human being." In fact, she said, it was Rose Mary who'd begun September's bloody rampage by shooting Yosef Akhisar on the 12th.

"Why?" one of the detectives asked Margie. "Robbery?"

"Naw!" the juvenile replied. "Somebody told us he was a narcotics undercover policeman."

The bloodletting continued five days later, Margie continued, with the death of Ahmed Al-Dawood. The runaway described how Rose Mary took her to a remote "pond on a gravel and dirt road" somewhere south of Sapulpa, a Tulsa suburb, and showed her Al-Dawood's body floating in the pond.

"She never actually told me she [killed Al-Dawood]," Margie later testified. "She just said it was her responsibility to take care of the body."

Rose Mary Miller defended herself in subsequent statements and testimony by countering that it was really Margie Barnes, not Rose Mary herself, who shot Yosef Akhisar.

"I'm not a dangerous person," Rose Mary declared in a news conference later. "I've never hurt anyone in my life. Never. Never."

She also appeared to be quite upset over having been dubbed a "man-hater."

"How can you be a man-hater when you have a boyfriend?" she demanded. "I never saw that man [Akhisar] before. Besides, I never hang around the old ones."

Yosef Akhisar was 27 years old.

"I don't understand it," Rose Mary continued. "I never told them I loved them. That's crazy!"

The sun rose bright over Tulsa that Wednesday, September 23. Police helicopters took to the air, and ground police swept the rural countryside south of Sapulpa, searching for the pond described by Margie Barnes. The rolling Oklahoma hills were jeweled with ponds sparkling in the September sunshine. Margie could not remember which pond was the correct one.

At Tulsa homicide headquarters, Sergeant Allen and Detective Wilson took another crack at Rose Mary Miller, who reportedly kept changing her mind about what happened to Al-Dawood.

"He's dead all right," she allegedly responded to their questioning. "But I didn't do it. My [relative], Diane Brannigan, did it."

In her videotaped statements, Rose Mary described how she took Al-Dawood to a "secret place" [the pond], where they met Diane. Diane was going to sell Al-Dawood some cocaine. Rose left the two alone there together. She returned somewhat later to find Al-Dawood dead and Diane wiping her gun with a napkin.

Rose Mary said that Diane Brannigan shot the young man because "he owed her some money. People like that don't deserve chances. Me and Ahmed were best friends. He was the nicest one of all the Iranians [sic] that I know."

Following up on this information, Detectives Allen and Wilson, assisted by Undersheriff Ihrig and Detective Duncan, traced Diane Brannigan to a nondescript residence between Sapulpa and Bristow in rural Creek County. There, the drama became even more convoluted.

Confronted by the police, Diane Brannigan loudly proclaimed

her innocence. Instead of arresting Diane, the officers arrested her father, Gary Brannigan, for covering up the murder after the fact in an effort to protect Rose Mary Miller. The charge was subsequently dismissed after he agreed to testify.

According to Gary Brannigan's testimony and that of other witnesses, Rose had been a "throwaway" child, tossed into the streets on her own when she was about 14 years old. Rose Mary spent her time running with a "wild crowd" in Tulsa.

"Rose Mary Miller," said the lawyer appointed to represent her, "was forced to go out on the street to find acceptance and love."

For a short time, the teenager lived with an Iranian man who supposedly abused her. According to official statements and transcripts, Rose Mary went to Gary Brannigan in August and asked to borrow a gun. He gave her a .22-caliber revolver.

"She said she had a problem in Tulsa with some Iranians or something," Brannigan testified. "I advised her to protect herself."

On Monday, September 21, less than a month after Rose Mary obtained her gun for "protection," she appeared at the Brannigan residence, driving a red 1988 Trans-Am, later identified as belonging to Ahmed Al-Dawood. She told the Brannigans that she had shot a Saudi Arabian.

"How's he doing?" one of her relatives asked.

"I don't know—and I don't want to know," she allegedly replied.

Rose Mary returned Brannigan's pistol, saying that she no longer needed it. Police said that Brannigan filed out the inside of the barrel to prevent its being ballistically linked to any shooting. On the other hand, Brannigan himself asserted that he filed out the barrel to enable the weapon to fire "shot" shells for killing snakes.

"I guess it was bad timing on my part," he said.

His statements effectively turned the accusing finger away from Diane Brannigan and back again to Rose Mary Miller. Sergeant Allen and Detective Wilson again confronted the teenager. This time, after laying out one more tentative story, she reportedly settled on an account that she stuck with and eventually repeated in court.

In her later testimony, Rose Mary described how she met and used Arabian men. In exchange for feminine favors, she enticed them to do and buy things for her. Even her relative, Gary Brannigan, she said, counseled her to "stay with those Arabians and drain them of every bit of money I could."

And so, Ahmed Al-Dawood had the misfortune to meet Rose Mary Miller.

The teenager told of how she and Al-Dawood drove to the Creek County pond on the evening of Thursday, September 17, the day he disappeared, to "talk over Ahmed's problems." Al-Dawood was supposedly nervous about the trip, because the pond was isolated in the timber and he was afraid of "lions, tigers, and bears."

"That should have been his least worry," one lawman remarked drily. "He had the most dangerous thing of all in the car with him. . . ."

Rose Mary testified she tucked the .22 pistol inside her shorts. At the pond, surrounded by the mild night, the couple lay for a long time on a foam rubber mattress they'd brought with them. Ahmed told Rose Mary how much he cared for her.

Suddenly, however, according to the teenager, Ahmed's demeanor changed.

"It was like he wasn't Ahmed," she said. "He was tripping like he was out of his mind. He had a knife in his hand and had it at my throat."

Rose Mary said she killed Ahmed Al-Dawood because he raped her. Twice. He tied her hands with his belt and raped her, she declared.

"You couldn't possibly understand how it feels," she later told a Creek County jury. "Especially when it's by your friend. He hurt me more than I could ever hurt him. He took away my trust. He took away my faith. He took away my dreams. He took away my freedom. How many girls would he have done this to if I hadn't stopped him?"

She testified that Ahmed untied her hands after he raped her.

"I killed him in spite of myself," she said. "I thought maybe I was just dreaming. He was my friend. Friends don't do that to friends."

She said she shot Ahmed twice in the face—first one shot, and then a second when he continued to move. She said she was afraid he would throw his knife at her.

Afterwards, frightened, she sought out her relative, Gary Brannigan, for advice. She said that he told her to drag the body into the woods and hide it, and never tell anyone about it. On his part, he would fix the murder weapon so that it could never be tied to the slaying.

Rose Mary tried to drag the body into the woods, she said, but found it too heavy to move. Instead, she rolled it down the sloping pond bank into the water. She kept Ahmed's car. She also kept her memories of that night.

"I was having dreams, talking in my sleep," she said. "I was seeing him. It was like he was haunting me."

Near 9 P.M. on that Wednesday of Rose Mary's arrest, Detective Wilson, Sergeant Allen, and the Creek County authorities stood on the high bank of a remote farm pond south of Sapulpa where the Tulsa teenager calmly pointed out the body of Ahmed Al-Dawood bobbing gently in the dark water. He resembled a partly submerged log.

By daybreak, the detectives had removed the body and collected a foam rubber mattress, sheets, pillow, clothing, and other items to be used as evidence.

Two days later, Tulsa County District Attorney David Moss reviewed the evidence and charged Rose Mary Miller with shooting Yosef Akhisar with intent to kill. That same day in Creek County, she was charged with the first-degree murder of Ahmed Al-Dawood. No motives for the crimes were listed in the felony warrants. She "just didn't like men" was the only motive the police would postulate.

Creek County assistant DA Max Cook found it preposterous that Rose could claim she killed the Arab because he attacked her. He scoffed at the accused teen's allegations that Al-Dawood removed his belt, tied her hands, took down his pants and removed her shorts, put on a condom, and then raped the girl—twice—all while holding a knife on her.

"If I was you-all," Rose Mary Miller commented almost exactly a year later, when the murder case finally came to trial, "all I know is, I wouldn't believe me."

The jury didn't. On Monday, September 21, 1993, Rose Mary Miller, now 18, found herself convicted of first-degree murder and sentenced to serve the remainder of her life in prison. She had already been found guilty of shooting Yosef Akhisar and was sentenced to 25 years in prison for that crime.

"I have to serve eight flat years for the other [shooting] charge," the pretty convicted killer said in a posttrial news conference. "I'll have to serve fifteen years of the life sentence. I'll be about forty when I get out."

She giggled. "I just laugh a lot," she said. "Maybe it's just immatureness or something."

Rose Mary "Heather" Miller, the girl who, according to the police, "just didn't like men," is currently serving her sentence in the Oklahoma State Penitentiary for women.

"LETHAL LESBIANS' MATRICIDE PLOT"

by Michael Sasser

On March 20, 1991, at 5:30 A.M., a northwest Miami resident contacted the Metro-Dade County Police Department.

"I've found a body in a car," the man said, "and she is definitely dead."

A uniformed team was dispatched immediately, and a detective was requested to follow up. That responsibility fell upon Detective William Saladrigas, a veteran of almost a dozen years with one of the busiest departments in the country.

Saladrigas drove across town to the address of the complaint on Northwest 157th Street, just west of 22nd Avenue, in the Miami suburb of Carol City. The low-income residential area was once the picture of suburban bliss. Recent changes, though, had turned it into a crime center, spurred by the free-flow of narcotics in Dade County.

Detective Saladrigas parked at the scene, on the north side of Bunche Park. He remembered when the park was a place for kids to organize a pickup ball game. Now, though, those same kids were likely to retaliate for a loss by shooting the winners, the detective mused to himself.

As Saladrigas pulled up, a uniformed police team was speaking to a man beside an old Dodge four-door. The Dodge was parked on the side of the road beside the park, across the street from a church. Saladrigas peered inside the car. In the front seat the sleuth saw the bloody naked body of a black woman. Blood was spilled and spattered all over the car's interior.

The caller had been right in telling dispatch that the woman was, indeed, very dead.

Detective Saladrigas approached the two officers and the civilian and asked what they knew.

"I just happened to be walking by here early this morning," the man said. "I thought it was strange that this car was just sitting here. So I walked close enough to look inside and I saw her there. I called 911."

"Was there anyone else on the street at that time?" Detective Saladrigas asked.

"No one that I noticed," the man replied.

Saladrigas requested a crime scene team to process the car and sectioned off the area with yellow tape. Then, careful not to sacrifice any possible clues, he took a closer look inside the car.

The dead woman had several obvious gunshot wounds to her face and head. The viciousness of the crime wasn't the only striking thing about it. Various items in the car, including the stereo, would normally have been stolen, had the woman been a robbery victim. Then, there was the fact that the woman was nude. Usually a victim's nakedness indicated a sexual assault. In this case, there was so much blood that only the coroner could say for sure. The detective could not, however, see any signs of a struggle. If the woman was raped, he thought, it had to have been postmortem, or else it had occurred elsewhere. Saladrigas knew that the forensic teams were going to be very busy in this case.

Still careful not to disturb anything, Detective Saladrigas dug the car's registration from the glove compartment. The car was registered to Annie Williams, 46, with a Carol City address. The detective figured that the dead woman was probably in her mid-40s—and, thus, was probably Annie Williams.

The crime scene team arrived and started processing the car. Saladrigas wanted the interior untouched until it could be examined thoroughly at headquarters. The technician concentrated on the exterior of the car.

Detective Saladrigas dispatched a few probers to canvass the area for possible witnesses. Meanwhile, he walked around the vehicle looking for any discharged bullet casings. There were none.

Shortly afterward, the canvassing detectives returned with a man who said he had some information that might help in the investigation.

"I was in this area early this morning," the man said. "Between one and two in the morning, I saw this vehicle pull up and park here. I saw someone get out of this car and walk across the street to where another car was. The person got inside the other car and drove it away."

"What did this person look like?" Saladrigas asked. "Was it a man or a woman?"

An odd expression cross the man's face. "I couldn't tell if it was a man or a woman. It was strange." The man could give no better description of the individual.

"How about the other car?" Saladrigas asked.

"It was a white, late-model Mustang-like car," the man said. "Someone else must have been in it driving, because the person who got in did so on the passenger side and the car drove away immediately." The man never saw the driver of the white car and had not noticed the license plate number.

Still, his statement threw some light on the crime.

Saladrigas inferred that the victim had probably been killed elsewhere, and that there was more than one person involved. Barring any other witnesses, two avenues for investigation were open. The sleuths could milk the physical evidence for every minute clue they could come up with, and they could focus on the victim's identity and interview her friends and relatives.

Metro-Dade detectives met to formulate an investigation plan, and Detective Saladrigas chose to visit the victim's next of kin.

The victim's registered address was a home just miles north of where her body was found. Detective Saladrigas and his partner, Detective Sal Garafalo, drove to the well-kept suburban home.

As they walked up to the house, Saladrigas noted the two cars parked outside on the carport. Both were covered with fallen leaves, and lawn residue had collected along and under the tires. Neither of the vehicles appeared to have been driven recently.

Saladrigas knocked repeatedly on the door of the house, but there was no answer. Could the victim possibly have lived in this expensive home by herself? It was unlikely. Still, the detectives figured that the neighbors would know something about Annie Williams, so they walked toward the neighbors to the north.

As they passed the north end of the Williams home, something caught Saladrigas's eye. Beside the sidewall, out of place in the dry Florida March weather, was a puddle. Saladrigas knelt down to inspect the puddle more closely. It was soap-foamy water with just a hint of pale red making it murky. A pipe revealed that this was the washing machine outlet, so it was obvious to the sleuth that someone had been home to wash something in the past several hours.

Next door, Saladrigas and Garafalo found a neighbor at home. The detectives identified themselves and informed the neighbor that they were seeking information on Annie Williams, Saladrigas described the homicide victim.

"That sounds like Annie," the neighbor said.

"Does Annie live alone?" Saladrigas asked.

"No," the neighbor replied. "She lives with her daughter, Cassandra, and an elderly relative. That woman is probably home, but she can't hear very well. She probably couldn't hear you knocking."

"Cassandra isn't home?" Saladrigas asked.

"No," the neighbor responded. "She drives a white Mustang and I don't see it anywhere."

Detective Saladrigas asked the neighbor to describe the Williams family. According to the woman, the Williamses were decent, churchgoing folks. Annie worked at a cleaner in Hollywood and Cassandra was a student at nearby Florida Memorial College. The neighbor's description was of a happy widow living with her studious daughter, and it made Saladrigas more angry at the savage waste of Annie Williams's life.

As they were speaking, a white Mustang suddenly pulled into the driveway of the Williams home. Saladrigas and Garafalo excused themselves from the neighbor and walked over to the car.

The driver of the car stepped out. She was a young woman with a blank expression on her face. Someone in a large T-shirt and baseball cap got out of the other door. Saladrigas concentrated on the girl, and instinctively assumed the other individual was the girl's boyfriend.

Detective Saladrigas identified himself.

"I'm Cassandra Williams," the young woman said.

Saladrigas said that they needed to ask Cassandra some questions about her mother. It was his policy, when making next-of-kin notices, to ask all his questions before informing the individual of the death so the detective could get whatever information he sought before the relative became an emotional mess.

"Could you tell me the last time you saw your mother?" Saladrigas asked.

"Yesterday morning," Williams replied. "She left for work and when I went to bed she wasn't home yet. That's not unusual because she usually goes over to her boyfriend's house for the evening after work. She didn't come home last night at all."

"Is that out of the ordinary?" Saladrigas asked.

"Yes, it is," Williams answered. "She's usually home by midnight."

Cassandra Williams, 19, said in a steady voice that she was single and a college student at Florida Memorial College.

Saladrigas wanted to ask Williams more questions—in private—and asked her if he could come inside. Williams agreed.

"Your boyfriend can wait outside with Detective Garafalo," Saladrigas said. The girl said nothing and they went inside.

Inside the house, Williams gave Detective Saladrigas the name of her mother's boyfriend. The detective asked the girl if her mother had enemies, or if she had had any fights or arguments lately.

"No, nothing like that," Williams said. She told Saladrigas that her father was dead and that both she and her mother were very active in a Liberty City Baptist church.

Something bothered Saladrigas as he interviewed Cassandra Williams. He had offered no information about the woman's death yet Cassandra Williams had not once asked why Saladrigas was asking these questions. It was the first time in his career that Saladrigas was not asked about the relative in question. In fact, Cassandra Williams acted as calmly as if they'd been chatting for half an hour about the weather.

Saladrigas made little notes about the girl's behavior but was not terribly concerned. He'd sized the younger Williams up as a happy, healthy college girl.

"Cassandra, I have to tell you something," Saladrigas said. He went on to tell her about Annie Williams's death, and the fact that it was a homicide.

Cassandra Williams put her head down and pouted into her hands. Just seconds later she lifted her head. Her eyes were dry.

"What do I do to make arrangements for my mother?" Williams asked.

Cops know that everyone reacts differently to trauma, and Williams's stoic reaction was not really abnormal. Still, Saladrigas made a note of it, then told Williams what the process would be with the body.

When they had finished speaking, Detective Saladrigas took Cassandra Williams back outside. It was then that the detective noticed the other individual was not Williams's boyfriend—was not, in fact, a boy at all. It was a young woman, and Saladrigas offered his apology for the inadvertent mistake.

Cassandra Williams introduced the other girl as Valarie

Rhodes, 19, her best friend. Neither girl seemed to mind the detective's mistake. As the two young women stood side by side, Saladrigas noticed that both girls wore wedding rings. Saladrigas thought this was strange because both girls had mentioned that they were single.

Before leaving the home, Saladrigas casually asked about the puddle beside the house.

"Oh, we washed some new red linens last night and they bled out," Williams explained. "And the dye just ran out of the washer."

Later in the day, Cassandra Williams confirmed that the victim was her mother, Annie Williams.

That night, no leads developed on the case. Detective Saladrigas was deeply disturbed at the violent breakup of what he saw as a decent family mired in an indecent world. Still, though, something nagged at Saladrigas that night. And it would not go away.

The next morning, Detective Saladrigas received the results of Annie Williams's autopsy.

"Cause of death was multiple gunshot wounds to the head and face," the medical examiner said. "They've identified the murder weapon as a thirty-eight. There was no sign of sexual abuse. However, there were marks from where a ring was pulled from her finger."

Knowing that Annie Williams had not been raped altered Saladrigas's perception of the crime. All of a sudden, he was sorely lacking a motive. Fortunately, Saladrigas had at least one witness.

The detective contacted the neighbor who had seen a suspicious car near the murder scene. Saladrigas drove the witness toward Carol City and told him to point out any car that looked like the one he had seen leaving the church beside Bunche Park, the day of the murder.

As Saladrigas was driving down the street on which Cassandra Williams lived, the man saw the young woman's white Mustang parked there.

"That looks like it!" the man said. "The white car looks like the one I saw."

Saladrigas returned to the police station and had the witness give a recorded statement.

Detectives had a solid piece of corroborative evidence. But Saladrigas did not—could not—believe that young, churchgoing Cassandra Williams was in any way responsible or involved in her mother's murder.

Later that day, March 21, Detective Saladrigas located Owen Kelly, the late Annie Williams's boyfriend. The man agreed to accompany the detectives back to the police station.

In an interview room, Kelly turned out to be a polite and cooperative witness. He answered the questions willingly. He told detectives that Williams had been at his house two nights before, but had left as usual late in the evening. Theirs had been a long relationship.

"I met Annie at the church we both attend," Kelly said. "We developed a good relationship and began to date steadily."

Kelly's answers came through a veil of tears. Cassandra Williams may have been a stoic, but Owen Kelly was the model mourner. Saladrigas could see the grief wracking the man's body.

According to Kelly, there was no one who held a grudge against Annie Williams. She had no enemies, no angry ex-boyfriends. She was not the type of person to incite anger or violence.

"Is there anything that Annie had been worried about, concerned with, or afraid of lately?" Saladrigas asked.

Owen Kelly took a long time before saying anything about this question. When he did respond, it was with shame and pain.

"I don't know whether I should say anything about this or not," Kelly said. Saladrigas assured him that anything Kelly knew might be of great help.

"Annie was very upset about something of late," Kelly said. "She found a note in Cassandra's room. It was from Cassandra's best friend, Valarie Rhodes. Annie showed me the note, and it was obvious that . . . that Valarie and Cassandra were . . . were having sex."

"They're lesbians?" Saladrigas asked.

"If that's what you call it," Kelly replied, obviously uncomfortable. "Annie told me this a week or so ago. She was very upset. She had suspected such a thing long before, when Valarie was living with them. But Annie couldn't believe it, even though she threw Valarie out of the house.

"A week or so ago, Annie said that she was going to confront Cassandra with the letter. Either Cassandra had to drop her relationship completely with Valarie, forever, or Annie was going to tell the people in the church, friends and family, everything that she knew was going on. Annie was not going to put up with anything like that."

A sudden stark realization washed over Detective Saladrigas. The little notes he'd made now started to add up: the white Mustang and the androgynous person getting out of Annie's car, Cassandra's reaction, the wedding rings—even, perhaps, the red-hued water beside the Williams house. It all began to add up. Now, there was a possible motive to link all of the evidence. Detective Saladrigas silently chastised himself for being blinded by the image of the young girls and the family home.

Saladrigas exploded from his chair, leaving Detective Garafalo to take Owen Kelly's statement. Saladrigas found his commanding officer.

"She was murdered by these two girls," Saladrigas told the officer. "I'm going back over there."

Saladrigas formulated his plan as he drove back to Carol City. He found the house filled with the victim's friends and relatives. Saladrigas asked Cassandra Williams and Valarie Rhodes to go to the police station with him so they could be eliminated from the investigation. They agreed.

Detective Mike Santos was left behind with instructions to wait for a call from Saladrigas for the go-ahead to search the house.

In the car, Saladrigas told the women that he wanted to fingerprint them to prove they weren't involved in the crime. He told them it was standard procedure.

There was silence. One minute passed.

"You know, both of our prints will be on that car," Valarie said. "We rode in it often enough."

"Well, there were some bloody prints on the car," Saladrigas said. "Those are the ones we want to eliminate your prints from."

More silence.

"Actually, they might be ours," Valarie said. "Annie had her period last week. Cassandra and I washed Annie's sheets and linens and we might have gotten Annie's blood on our hands."

Detective Saladrigas said that the prints he referred to were not single, blood-dampened prints, but many blood-drenched prints all over the vehicle.

"I doubt that will come up," Saladrigas said. But he had a strong conviction that the prints would indeed come up.

At the police station, both women consented to have the house, their possessions and the Mustang searched. When presented with the choice, they also signed a rights waiver and agreed to give a statement.

Detective Saladrigas had Detective Santos begin searching the house, then went to interview Cassandra Williams. Saladrigas was immediately confrontational with her, forcing his positive image of the women out of mind.

Under pressure, Cassandra Williams caved in like a house of cards.

"Okay, okay, we did it!" Williams exclaimed.

Williams related that her mother had confronted her with Valarie's letter. She told Valarie and they decided that something had to be done.

"We'd been talking about it for a while—maybe six months," Williams pouted.

Williams said that they'd talked about killing her mother so they could be together and use Annie Williams's $25,000 life insurance policy to start a new life. Williams said that her mother suspected the women's relationship long before the note had surfaced.

Williams said that on the night of March 19, her mother came home from Owen Kelly's place and went to bed. Valarie, who'd been hiding in Cassandra's closet, walked up to the sleeping Annie Williams and shot her several times.

"I couldn't watch it," Williams said. Nor did she help Valarie drag the body out to the car. After that, they drove in two cars to Bunche Park, left Annie's car, and went home in the Mustang.

Detectives recorded Williams's entire statement and Saladrigas contacted Mike Santos for a review of the house inspection.

"The house is loaded with blood traces," Santos said. "On the master bedroom's mattress—under new sheets, the headboard, baseboard, the floor, in the washer and dryer. There's a path of blood through the house. That puddle outside has almost dried, but there are blood traces there, as well."

All the physical evidence corroborated Cassandra Williams's confession. Both women were arrested and charged with first-degree murder.

In the following week, the investigation continued. Detectives found Florida Memorial students who said that both women had talked about killing "some woman" and had even offered a couple of young men $2,000 to kill someone for them. The talk of the killing went back six months.

One student came forward and said she was storing some luggage for Valarie Rhodes.

"She came by on the 20th to put something in one suitcase," the student said.

Inside the suitcase was a .38 that was positively identified as the murder weapon.

Forensic experts also confirmed that it was Annie Williams's blood all over the house, and the fingerprints of Valarie Rhodes on the victim's car.

Investigators found interesting things in the house, as well. Two rolls of used film were developed, revealing pictures of both women and others around Florida Memorial. Some of the shots were of Cassandra Williams in erotic poses.

Also in the house was a note signed by Cassandra Williams, dated February 14, 1991. In it, Williams took full responsibility for drawing Rhodes into the conspiracy and murder plot. It was the final piece of evidence in the case.

There was really no way to counter the prosecution's case against Williams and Rhodes. Both agreed to plead guilty to first-degree murder and weapons charges in exchange for the state not seeking the death penalty.

Williams and Rhodes are both now serving life sentences in the Florida prison system and are ineligible for parole for at least 25 years.

"WHO HACKED CHARLIE'S HEAD OFF?"

by Brian Kerrigan

The two Marines driving south on Interstate 15 in North San Diego County, California, early that Sunday morning, blinked sleepily in the grayish-yellow light. It was about 5:30 A.M. on November 3, 1991, and they were between Temecula and Camp Pendleton, not far from Bonsall, when they spotted something on the highway just south of Gopher Canyon Road, near the Old Castle Road turnoff that leads to Valley Center.

On the shoulder of the freeway lay what looked like a sleeping bag. It was a curious enough sight to arouse their interest, causing the Marine on the passenger side to snap upright and his buddy, the driver, to jump on the brakes. Even before the car came to a full stop, the passenger slipped out of his seat and headed for the black bag. His comrade was right behind him an instant later.

As the two Marines looked at the sleeping bag in the murky morning light, they realized that it was bloodstained, and then they saw the top of a man's head sticking out of it. The closer they looked, the more they could see of matted blood and flesh.

Quickly, the Marines raced back to their car, threw it in reverse and backed up about a quarter-mile where they found a roadside police emergency call box. They notified the California Highway Patrol (CHP) about their grisly discovery, and the information was immediately relayed to the San Diego County Sheriff's Office in Vista.

The sun rising in the east cast shadows down Gopher Canyon and through those shadows came fast-moving police vehicles. Out of them emerged law enforcement officers who assembled at the site off Interstate 15, a few miles south of Camino Del Cielo, in Bonsall. There, among the dark clumps of pygmy mesquite that lined the freeway, was the sleeping bag containing the mutilated body of a human being. The North County crime-fighters saw at once that they were facing a particularly brutal homicide case.

Who was the victim? Was the body male or female? Those questions would have to be answered by an examination of the remains and an autopsy.

How the body had come to be at the side of the freeway off Gopher Canyon Road, the police could only surmise. They theorized that the brutal killer had callously hurled the body out of a car, letting it lie where it fell.

If the Marines hadn't found the body when they did, the forensic pathologist noted, there wouldn't have been much of anything left. Animals had already devoured some parts of the corpse, which was missing most of its limbs.

Laboratory technicians, homicide sleuths, and identification agents fanned out and went over the body site and surroundings by the square centimeter. No identification was found with the remains or in the sleeping bag. A search of the area failed to turn up anything. Meanwhile, an ambulance transported the victim to the police morgue in Vista.

From its days as an avocado and strawberry capital, Vista has evolved into a hodgepodge of elegant homes and narrow, twisting macadam roads, barely out of reach from the sea-blown scents of San Diego. Set seven miles inland, the city has a reputation of being a "climatic wonderland" because for 340 days out of the year, the sun shines down upon the residential area, surrounded by high vegetation, wildflowers, rabbits, and an assortment of birds, coyotes, and an occasional mountain lion. At the time the dismembered body was discovered, more than 70,000 residents lived within Vista's 18-square-mile "semirural" radius.

Since the prompt identification of the body was of paramount importance, an immediate autopsy was performed.

"There's not enough for me to go with," the Vista medical examiner told investigators.

"What do you mean?" one of them asked.

"I mean, there are more parts of the body out there somewhere, and I need them to conduct a full autopsy."

"Can you tell us the sex of the victim?"

"A male—but that's all I can tell you."

With only minimal parts of the unidentified body—the head and torso—lying in a box in the morgue, police teams returned to Gopher Canyon Road and combed the entire area again, looking for the rest of the dismembered victim. Inch by inch, they searched the rocky soil of the Southern California roadside. Curious travelers, on their way to work in the beach cities, slowed down to see what all the hubbub was about. Soon the traffic on the freeway had backed up for five miles.

"I think whoever killed him dumped part of the body here, then drove further on down the highway and tossed the rest of the body out in a separate trash bag," one veteran sleuth speculated.

Meanwhile, after the ground search was suspended with the fall of darkness, Fallbrook police borrowed a helicopter from the March Air Force Base. The whirlybird was rigged to take infrared photos with special cameras developed during the Vietnam War. These cameras can detect the differences in the amount of heat expelled from the soil and heat given off by a decomposing body.

The chopper flew low over the desert growth using the special camera to scan the precipices and clumped cacti below. All the effort accomplished, however, was to send wild animals scurrying to their hidey-holes.

Just as it looked for a while as if the investigators had struck out, they ran into a change of luck.

It happened on the following Monday, November 4, as two border patrol agents were cruising an area about two miles from Gopher Canyon Road, looking for illegal aliens who might have entered the United States from Mexico. Their green-and-white four-wheel-drive vehicle bounced over the brush-dotted, rugged terrain abutting Interstate 15 near State Route 76, off Pala Road. Suddenly, the two agents felt their wheels go over something lumpy. They got out to investigate.

They discovered that they had run over a tattered green trash bag. To their astonishment, the officers could see parts of a human body sticking out. The flesh had apparently been devoured by wild animals, and what remained was so decomposed that a putrid stench filled the air. Not wishing to disturb any clues in the immediate vicinity, the border agents radioed the Fallbrook sheriff's office.

Later, when the sheriff viewed the body parts, he immediately remembered the bulletin his office had received about the body parts found in the Vista area. He quickly summoned a team of Fallbrook homicide officers to the scene of the macabre discovery, along with the county coroner. The officers carefully fanned out and examined the entire area surrounding the body. Their efforts went for naught, however. On conferring with the coroner, the sleuths became convinced that they would find little evidence at the scene.

The decomposing body parts were placed in a plastic leak-proof carryall and transported to the morgue in Vista. There, they would eventually be matched with the rest of the body found near Gopher Canyon Road earlier.

An examination of the decapitated head disclosed that several of the victim's front teeth were missing. They had apparently been knocked out by a blow in the face that split the upper and lower lip and caused blood and vomit to accumulate in the victim's mouth.

After cleaning the remains and examining them with new,

high-tech methods, the pathologist was able to reconstruct the body to a certain extent. There was nothing to suggest that the limbs had come from more than one body. A bulge in part of a pelvic (hip girdle) bone showed that it was male. The unfortunate victim had been dead for about a week. In life he was about 30 years old, stood approximately 6 feet 3 inches, and weighed 210 pounds. From the quantity of body fat he was able to recover, the pathologist determined that the victim was probably stoutly built.

Making an identification was another matter. The pathologist discovered that the fingerprints had been deliberately destroyed. Also, a tattoo from the victim's upper torso had been intentionally marred, obviously so that the victim could not be identified.

A check of missing-persons records both in San Diego County and Riverside County revealed no subject whose description fit the dismembered man.

As soon as the discovery was given media attention, several persons contacted police headquarters offering information about a missing loved one or relative. None of this information provided any leads to the identity of the mysterious corpse, however.

Other concerned citizens offered information they believed might be helpful in solving the grisly puzzle. One man told the police that while he was driving home northbound to San Marcos from Orange County, where he worked the dog shift, he glanced across the highway and saw a car on the southbound side. It was parked near the Old Castle cutoff that leads to Lilic. He noticed what appeared to be a slight man with the lid of his car trunk open. At the time, he thought the driver might have gotten a flat tire. As he recalled, it was about 3 A.M. on October 28 or 29. The body was discovered on November 3. The coroner estimated that it had lain there three to five days.

It had been too dark to get a description of the other driver or the make of the vehicle, the witness said. He did think about cutting across the grassy center divider to lend the stranded driver a hand, but then he had second thoughts and continued on his way.

"You're probably very lucky you didn't stop," one officer told the man.

Then a woman in neighboring Riverside County reported that her husband had been missing for three weeks. She partly identified a composite sketch of the body made by a police artist. When she was shown tattered scraps of the victim's pants found near the body parts, however, she said her husband possessed no clothes similar to those brown trousers.

More than a dozen sheriffs and their deputies combed the sun-seared, rocky terrain from Pala Road, where the second bag of body parts was found, clear on down to Gopher Canyon Road, the site of the initial discovery. They were searching for the murder weapon, believed to be a .38-caliber handgun. This was more or less an educated guess on the part of the investigators, since the gunshot wound to the decapitated head could not possibly reveal the exact dimension of the messenger of death.

Meanwhile, a construction worker gave the Vista police some relevant information. He said that he had been driving in Gopher Canyon on his way to his job in Hemet on the Monday before the discovery of the body and he passed within a short distance of the arroyo.

"I don't know what it was that made me look off to the side," he said, "but I did, and I saw a dog or coyote struggling with the trash bag. I thought some inconsiderate litterbug had tossed trash out on the highway, so I drove on."

An old married couple from Temecula visited the morgue to look at the drawing of the reconstructed body. They said that it might be their son, who had been missing for four months. He had gone to deposit $5,000 in the bank and was never heard from again. However, the police sketch showed that the victim had a tattoo on his right arm, proving that he couldn't be the couple's son.

Time and time again, it appeared that the dismembered victim was about to be identified, but one possibility after another went up in smoke.

The investigation pushed on. Every agency from Fallbrook to

North County pooled information on the grisly case, but no one came up with any tangible results.

Where had the body come from? Where was the victim's identification? Had he been slain for money? Revenge? Had he been involved in a love triangle? Was he the victim of an insanely jealous suitor? An insurance scam? Was a relative involved? A stranger, perhaps? The investigators were determined to find the answers to these questions.

A few days later, Oceanside authorities received a report of a Dodge pickup found abandoned in a field. Fast-moving police found that it bore a tag issued to an Escondido resident. They checked its tires against a police photograph of the tracks found on the shoulder of the highway near Gopher Canyon Road, where the first body parts were found. The results of checking out the report were disappointing.

Vital hours slipped by with no information forthcoming on the officers' queries, while the inhabitants of Vista continued to be gripped by suspense and foreboding. Whose dismembered body was lying in the morgue, anyway?

Meanwhile, the separate body parts matched partly through the scientific technique involving DNA. Deoxyribonucleic acid—DNA for short—is the chemical that carries the genetic code found in the nucleus of each living cell. It is, in essence, the stuff of genes, which are contained in human chromosomes and determine the personal characteristics of each individual human being. The DNA process is considered to be highly accurate.

With the help of the DNA process, the bloody body parts dumped in two separate locations in the desertlands of Southern California did not wind up remaining unidentified for a long time.

The forensic experts also found two intact fingerprints on a dismembered hand found in the second bag. The analysis showed that the prints matched those on record for a Siskiyou County convict named Charles Yearwood, alias Charles Lee Beabout. The hand was therefore his—as were the entire remains.

Probers soon learned that Beabout had an estranged wife in Yreka, in Northern California, near the Oregon-California border. When they contacted her, she said that she had neither seen nor heard from Charles for several years. That is, not until a few weeks earlier, when he wrote to her from an address on Stanley Drive in La Mesa.

The woman said that her efforts to contact Charles at that address to serve him with divorce papers proved fruitless. That course having failed, she published a legal notice in San Diego-area newspapers. Still, he failed to get in touch with her.

The investigators searched for anyone who even remotely knew Beabout and eventually tracked down his former attorney.

"I always liked the man," the lawyer told the sleuths. "A little strange, even weird. But a nice guy."

"What do you mean—strange?" Sergeant Manny Castillo of La Mesa's homicide unit asked the attorney.

"Anyone who demands a jury trial on a case involving buying alcohol after two A.M. has got to be a little unusual," the lawyer answered.

Then he went on to explain that Beabout had been arrested in May 1990 for buying beer after hours—a simple misdemeanor charge. At his arraignment, Charles Beabout startled the court by demanding a jury trial. The judge tried to talk him out of it, but Beabout insisted, even going to great lengths to hire an attorney. The trial lasted a full week and ended in a mistrial.

Further checking into Charles Beabout's background turned up one associate who described the 30-year-old man as a leech. Another person called him lazy. Others used words like "worthless" and "finagler" to describe the late Charles Lee Beabout.

Slowly, methodically, the police built a complete dossier on the victim. Court records in Beabout's former hometown showed that he'd been a frequent visitor to the local jailhouse over the past nine years. His crimes ranged from battery and disorderly conduct to public drunkenness and a more serious charge—the attempted murder of his wife. Each trial resulted in a legal slap on the wrist and his promise to straighten up.

But the lure of easy money can be overpowering. Thus, Beabout burglarized a neighbor's house—and wound up being caught. He was convicted and sentenced to a two-year term in the California Men's Colony under the names Charles Yearwood. Paroled in 1985, he landed right back in jail on a battery charge. Beabout wasn't out very long when he was arrested for brandishing a dangerous weapon in public. He'd been out on probation when he got himself murdered.

Not long after the news media had described the crime as "virtually unsolvable," La Mesa police chief Robert Soto, who headed the sheriff's team, instructed his probers to get a search warrant and check out the Stanley Drive address where Beabout's attorney said that Beabout had been living.

The woman who answered the door on the afternoon of Wednesday, November 6, 1991, was about 26 years old and somewhat beefy. Her hair was disheveled and her clothes rumpled, suggesting that she had been sleeping in them and had just then awakened to answer the doorbell. She introduced herself as Cindy Ann Oakley. After seesawing back and forth with the detectives, she finally admitted that she was a former lover of Charles Beabout's. She told them that she hadn't seen Charlie for over a week.

"I could just feel in my bones that something was wrong," one of the officers who talked to Oakley would later say. He described the living quarters as a two-car garage that had been converted into a two-bedroom apartment. The woman hadn't even bothered to clean up some blood that was splattered around the makeshift dwelling.

Within an hour, technicians were collecting evidence and snapping pictures in both color and black and white, while La Mesa homicide officers were questioning Cindy Oakley about the matted blood found in the apartment and the murder of Charles Beabout.

Sleuths had the two cars that belonged to Beabout and Oakley towed to the La Mesa police impound lot, where the technicians gave them a thorough going-over. No traces of blood were found in either vehicle. The investigators later determined that Beabout's killer had used a rental car to dispose of his remains.

After finding blood in the apartment and other evidence link-ing Cindy Oakley to the crime, the sleuths advised her of her Constitutional rights. Then they handcuffed her and escorted her to the La Mesa sheriff's station, where they interrogated her at length. Later that night, she was booked into the county jail, charged with suspicion of murder.

"I don't know why they had a falling-out," Sergeant Castillo told a group of reporters. "Obviously, she got tired of him, felt they were incompatible."

However, the cataloguing of evidence and the painstaking grind were far from over. Now began the tedious work of build-ing a solid case against the suspect for the district attorney's office. Law enforcement officers began quizzing friends and neighbors of both the suspect and the victim, hoping to build up enough evidence to convict the accused woman. Before the trial began, they had gathered quite a bit of information on the "moody" Cindy Ann Oakley.

From a neighbor of hers, sleuths learned that Oakley had moved into the downstairs unit in April 1990, with a man she'd called her business partner. Another neighbor said that Beabout moved in eight months later. They described Beabout as being mentally impaired and Oakley as being loud and surly.

"I really didn't know them," the landlady of the apartment complex told the investigators. "I had no trouble with her. She was moody. One day she would say hello, the next day she would snub you. All I know is, they paid their rent on time."

After a few fruitless inquiries, the homicide sleuths turned up a woman who was willing to talk openly on the condition of anonymity. She described Oakley as a "weirdo" and "fruitcake" and related how she'd gotten into several scrapes with Oakley over the past year. The woman described Oakley as one of those thoughtless neighbors who blasted the television and stereo at all hours of the day and night. The witness added, "I called the cops on her several times because her dog barked all night and kept me awake."

The woman said that the bickering came to a head in the past

July when Oakley threatened her with the warning, "I'll blow your damn head off with my shotgun!" Beyond that, the woman said, Oakley had repeatedly threatened members of her family. Eventually, the witness said, she was forced to get a restraining order against her belligerent neighbor.

Meanwhile, some of the official information on Cindy Oakley proved to be somewhat conflicting. A supervisor with the county's Department of Social Services told the sleuths that Oakley was actively involved with a program in which clients find their own homemakers to provide care for them. The supervisor described Oakley as one of her most conscientious workers.

According to the supervisor, Oakley was currently on the county payroll for services extended to a mentally disabled client. When the sleuths asked if that client was Charles Beabout, the supervisor said that the information would have to remain confidential, unless a court order instructed her to turn over her records.

At her arraignment, Cindy Oakley did not come across as the robust, snarling, aggressive woman described by her neighbors. Quite to the contrary, she appeared as an almost pitiable creature, sobbing hysterically when Public Defender Bill Youmans entered a not-guilty plea on her behalf in Judge Judith F. Hayes's courtroom. Youmans told the court that his client had been crying all morning.

"Her demeanor is one of remorse, Judge," Defense Attorney Youmans said. "She seems very concerned about what occurred. From a personal perspective . . . she seems to be somewhat miscast in the role of being a murderess."

In his turn, Deputy District Attorney August Meyer said that the arresting detectives were prepared to testify that the accused had treated her arrest almost casually, and that this drastic change of behavior was only a masquerade to impress the court. He asked that Oakley be held over on a charge of one count of murder. Judge Hayes set bail at $1 million and scheduled a preliminary hearing for December 19, 1991.

The victim's distraught relatives and close friends were there. They were shocked, grieved, and puzzled by the murder. They had no answers as to why the La Mesa woman would kill Charles Beabout.

The preliminary hearing was short and sweet. The trial began on Monday, September 21, 1992, in San Diego Superior Court before a seven-woman, five-man jury.

The opening statements by Deputy District Attorney Meyer and Public Defender Youmans proved to be gripping elements in an already dramatic case. No one present in the chock-filled courtroom was disappointed by the performance of either the defense or the prosecution. While the prosecutor portrayed the defendant as a woman who killed her boyfriend because he was a mooching bum, the public defender argued that the fatal shot was accidentally fired during a fierce struggle for the gun during a lover's quarrel.

At stake was whether Oakley was to be convicted of murder, for which she could face a term of 30 years to life in the woman's prison at Fontana, or of the lesser crime of manslaughter.

Throughout the trial, the big-city newspapers gave the case considerable attention, although they complied with the defense's unusual wishes that Oakley's photograph not be published. Aside from that, they pulled out all the stops with front-page, eye-catching headlines.

On September 24, 1992, Cindy Ann Oakley took the stand. She testified that her boyfriend had become despondent over the last several days, making her afraid that he was going to kill her and then commit suicide. She said she feared for her life and as a result, she borrowed a .38-caliber pistol.

"I hid it under the bed for protection," Oakley told the jurors.

But, she said, Charlie found the gun and threatened to kill them both. They struggled, the gun went off, the slug striking Charlie in the head, killing him instantly.

"I didn't tell anybody," Oakley testified, "because I didn't think anyone would believe me." She said she drank and drank until she got drunk the next day, and then she decided "to hide what had happened."

Dabbing at her tears with a handkerchief, the blue-eyed blonde told the jury that she'd once been madly in love with Charlie Beabout. But then that love turned into dread, disdain, and finally hate.

Having killed her lover, Oakley went on, she was confronted with the problem all killers sooner or later must face—how to get rid of the body. Since the dead man was too heavy to lift into the trunk of the car, she explained, "I decided to do things different. I guess that's when I decided to cut him into pieces."

"Why did you take his fingerprints and identifying tattoo off?" "Defense Attorney Youmans asked her.

"So that he couldn't be identified," the defendant replied. "I was afraid that if anyone figured out who he was, they would know who I was."

Under cross-examination, Oakley readily admitted that the relationship between her and her live-in lover began to disintegrate as Charlie became increasingly jealous and possessive. They fought constantly over his failure to finish his education and get a job to help with the bills.

As their squabbles became more frequent, Oakley told the jury, Beabout became more violent toward her and threatened to kill her and commit suicide. Convinced that he was emotionally unstable, she ordered him out of the house. He got a gun, they fought, and it went off.

On Tuesday, October 6, after considering all the evidence, the jury brought back their verdict. They found Cindy Ann Oakley guilty of the first-degree murder of her boyfriend, Charles Lee Beabout. UPDATE: *Cindy Ann Oakley was sentenced to a prison term of 25 years to life.*

"PREGNANT CAME THE TEEN SLASHER!"

by Steven Barry

Just 20 minutes before she was murdered, Laurie Show stood in front of the bathroom mirror styling her hair with a curling iron. It was 6:45 A.M., and the 16-year-old sophomore was getting ready for school. At the same time, her mother was on her way out the front door.

A day earlier, December 19, 1991, her mother had gotten a phone call at work. The female caller identified herself as Laurie's guidance counselor and said that Laurie had gotten into some trouble at school.

"Could you meet me at school tomorrow morning at seven o'clock to talk about it?" the caller had asked.

Laurie's mother agreed to the meeting and, that night, she told Laurie about the call and scolded her for her bad behavior.

Shortly before 7 A.M. the next morning, a Friday, Laurie's mother arrived at her daughter's high school to wait for the guidance counselor. But something strange was going on. Laurie's guidance counselor was on medical leave.

Laurie's mother waited until 7:11; then, uneasy about the turn of events, she decided to leave.

"That's not like me to be impatient," she would say later.

"Normally, I would have waited longer, but something told me, 'No, go home.' "

Home was a second-floor condominium in East Lampeter Township on the eastern outskirts of Lancaster, Pennsylvania. This was Amish country, complete with horses and buggies and towns with names like Paradise, Bird-in-Hand, and Intercourse. The Shows' was a stylish two-story brick complex on Black Oak Drive. The mother and her only child lived there by themselves.

A month shy of 17, Laurie was 5 feet 9 inches tall and attractive, with light-brown hair and sparkling eyes. She played softball and swam. She read *Seventeen,* shopped for cosmetics with her friends at the mall, and wanted to be a model. She often dressed up for children's birthday parties in a homemade teddy bear costume. She was friendly, popular, and generous.

"She'd give you anything," a friend recalled later. "The last time I was with her, I pointed out a Giants baseball cap that I liked. It cost eighteen dollars."

"You like that?" Laurie had asked the friend, and she'd bought it for him on the spot.

At school, Laurie had worked in the resource department. She helped students who had learning problems. After school, she worked at a women's clothing store at East Towne Mall. At home, social gatherings with friends were the norm—nothing wild and crazy, just friendly chats and football games and movies on TV. Neither alcohol nor drugs were allowed, and cigarettes had to be smoked outside.

"Most of her friends were pretty laid-back," the friend continued. "I'll tell you one thing, honestly, you couldn't find one person you could walk up to who'd ever say, 'I hate Laurie Show.' "

On that point, Laurie's friend was wrong—dead wrong.

Laurie's school bus stopped every morning at 7:22. She should have been gone, and the apartment should have been empty when her mother returned home at 7:25. As her mother was getting out of her car, a neighbor approached her.

"Is something wrong?" the neighbor asked.

"Why?" Laurie's mother asked.

"I heard a loud ruckus upstairs awhile ago," the neighbor said.

"I walked up the steps," Laurie's mother would later recall, "put my keys in, and opened the door. The lights were still on, and I looked in the kitchen. There was no disarray. Then I looked in the bathroom and saw her curling iron was still on, which was strange because Laurie was so fire-conscious.

"I turned to go into Laurie's room and I saw some brown spots on the floor," she continued.

"I looked up to my right and Laurie was lying on the floor on her back, with her arms moving. I didn't take it all in at first. She was trying to make sounds. I screamed to my neighbor to call 911, then I saw the rope around her neck and I got a paring knife from the kitchen. I bent down on my knees beside Laurie and put two fingers under the rope. I cut it off and she breathed deeply. She moaned.

"I thought the rope was the only problem. But when I cut it, I could see her throat was cut—and there was blood."

She cradled Laurie in her arms to try to keep the wound together. But Laurie's throat had been slashed from the Adam's apple all the way through to her spine. Her windpipe and nine large blood vessels had been severed. In addition, Laurie had been stabbed three times in the back and once in the thigh. One of her lungs had been punctured and she'd suffered more than 20 defense-type wounds to her fingers and hands. She had already lost a great deal of blood, and there was no way to stop the bleeding.

"Honey, I'm sorry," the mother told Laurie, desperately trying to comfort the injured teen. "You didn't do anything wrong at school. It was a setup. I love you, honey, and your father loves you. God will take care of you."

"I love you," Laurie whispered. "I love you."

"Who did this to you?" the mother asked.

"Michelle did it," were Laurie Show's last words. "Michelle. Michelle."

"Laurie's mother knew Michelle. For the past six months,

Lisa Michelle Lambert had been waging a vendetta against Laurie.

A newspaper reporter would later describe Michelle Lambert as having "pure porcelain skin and champagne hair that caressed her shoulders like a silk scarf, [and she] wore contact lenses to make her brown eyes blue." She was 19 years old and pretty, 5 feet 6 inches tall.

An honor-roll student during her early years of school, Michelle was the oldest child in a tight-knit, religious family. But when she reached the 10th grade, she rebelled against the strict discipline at home.

"It just seemed like she wanted more independence," a family member would later explain. "She always stayed very family-minded, but she wanted to run with kids we were afraid of. Finally, she left home and moved in with her boyfriend, but it was an abusive relationship.

"Honestly, we thought she was going to end up dead if she didn't get out of there. We wanted her to come back home."

Lambert's boyfriend was Lawrence Yunkin, a tall 20-year-old with long blond hair that he sometimes wore in a ponytail. Yunkin had grown up in a rented home on an Amish farm. He had been taught right from wrong.

Lambert had met Yunkin two summers earlier at a swimming pool where he was a lifeguard. She called him "my Adonis." After his graduation, Yunkin got a job in a wood mill and rented his own place. Lambert moved in with him. To make ends meet, she quit school and got a job as a waitress.

"He and Michelle were inseparable," a friend recalled. "It was like a fatal attraction. He'd do anything for Michelle. I met them when they were already a couple, and I was told, 'Don't ever try to break them up.'"

Six months earlier, during June 1991, Lambert and Yunkin had met Laurie Show for the first time at a party. A week later, the couple had a bitter quarrel. Despite the fact that he was still living with Lambert, Yunkin started dating Laurie.

"They went shopping together," Laurie's mother recalled,

"and they went to Laurie's grandmom's to swim. They had their pictures taken together in a dollar booth at the mall. I thought he was okay, but he came across as a vulnerable, insecure person."

Lawrence Yunkin dated Laurie for one week. During that time, their relationship became sexual. At the end of that week, Lambert phoned Laurie's house and spoke to Laurie's mother.

"Laurie stole my boyfriend," Lambert screamed into the phone, "and I'm pregnant!"

"I went outside," Laurie's mother continued, "and I told Lawrence he needed to do something about this now—talk to Michelle, talk to her parents. But Laurie didn't need to be involved in this. He listened and he left, and I just thought, 'Well, that's it. He'll go back to Michelle and they won't bother Laurie anymore.'

"But that's not the way it turned out."

Lambert became livid with jealousy.

"There's no doubt that Michelle loved Lawrence," a friend would say later. "There was nothing more important to her. To Laurie, Lawrence was just a fling. But to Michelle, Lawrence was her whole life."

Lambert soon found out that Laurie worked at the mall, and she started paying visits to harass her.

"I swear," Lambert warned her rival, "if you slept with him, or did anything with him, I'll kill you."

"Michelle called her a whore," Laurie's mother recalled, "right in front of her customers. And she called the house at all hours of the night. If you didn't answer, she'd let it ring incessantly. If you did, she'd scream obscenities.

"I told Laurie, 'Don't worry, Michelle will stop. She'll get tired of this.' "

But it didn't stop. The harassment escalated.

Over the July 4 weekend, Lambert was visiting friends, sitting at a picnic table. The conversation got around to ways of killing someone.

"Everybody agreed that slicing someone's throat would be

the quickest, easiest way, speaking theoretically," one of the friends in attendance that day recalled later.

A few weeks later, Lambert and the same friend went to the mall to get some fudge.

"You hate Laurie as much as I do," Lambert said to the friend. "So why don't we do something about it?"

Lambert suggested inventing a story about a fraternity party. They would invite Laurie to go, then they would kidnap her and take her into downtown Lancaster. They would tie her to a telephone pole and strip her naked, cut her hair and beat her. Maybe more . . .

"I swear to God," Lambert told her friend, "I'm going to slit her throat. And if you don't go through with this, I'm going to kill you."

A few days later, Lambert, Yunkin, and three friends drove to Laurie's home. Two of the friends knocked on the front door.

"But I told Laurie to stay inside," one of the friends later admitted, "with the door locked. The whole thing was ridiculous. I told Michelle her mother wouldn't let Laurie out."

One night a month later, Lambert took matters into her own hands. She assaulted Laurie for the first time. It happened at the East Towne Mall while Laurie was standing outside waiting for her mother to pick her up after work.

"Michelle pushed Laurie against the wall and almost broke her wrist," a witness to the incident recalled. "And Michelle told Laurie she was going to kill her."

Another assault took place three months later, on the night of November 22, also at the mall.

"Michelle spotted Laurie," a witness explained, "and she got out of Lawrence's car. Then Michelle went up to Laurie and started screaming and cursing. She hit her once or twice. She called her a bitch, a liar, 'whoring Laurie.' She hit Laurie's head against the cab of my truck." And she knocked Laurie to the ground.

"You ruined my life!" Lambert screamed. "And you ruined my baby's life!"

"I'm sorry," Laurie said.

"There's nothing you can do or say," Lambert yelled back. "You've ruined my life. I don't know when or where, but I swear I'm going to kill you. I have friends who'll take care of you."

The police were called and charges were filed against Michelle Lambert. But it was a simple assault. It went on the back burner and no action was taken. In less than a month, it would be too late.

Two dozen local police officers, county detectives, and state troopers began responding to the emergency call on the morning of December 20. Officer Robin Weaver of the East Lampeter Township Police Department (ELTPD) was one of the first lawmen to arrive. He found Laurie's mother sitting at the dining-room table, crying her eyes out. Her jeans and white sweater were spotted with blood. A neighbor was standing at her side trying to console her.

"Michelle did it!" Laurie's mother yelled as soon as she saw the policeman.

When Officer Weaver looked in the bedroom, he saw Laurie Show lying on the floor with large pools of blood on both sides of her neck. He also observed several clumps of blood-soaked hair, which had been scattered across the bedroom floor.

Six paramedics arrived shortly thereafter, but they were too late.

Police Chief Jacob Glick and Detective Ron Savage, both from the ELTPD, were among the next to arrive.

"It was probably the most brutal thing I've seen in twenty years of law enforcement," the chief told reporters later that morning. Detective Savage agreed.

In short order, forensic technicians started arriving and videotaping the crime scene. Then came the coroners and an assistant district attorney. By then, the detectives were interviewing neighbors.

"The front door slammed," one neighbor told Detective Savage, estimating the time around 7 A.M. "In a matter of two or three seconds, I heard a thump on the floor in the bedroom. Then five or six minutes later, I saw two people of almost the same height and build leave the building."

The neighbor said both suspects had been wearing hooded sweatshirts. One was described as a pregnant white female, around 18, about 5 feet 7 inches tall, with blond hair and brown eyes.

"We don't know for a fact that Michelle Lambert was at the residence this morning," the chief told the media, "but we're trying to contact her because of the problems these two have had."

At that very moment, police officers were speeding toward the rented mobile home that Michelle Lambert and Lawrence Yunkin shared on Pequea Boulevard in nearby Martic Forge.

By then, one of the investigators had located another neighbor who had seen something helpful. Around 7:15, as the neighbor was leaving for work, he noticed two young women walking away from the condominium complex toward a line of trees. They got into a Mercury Monarch with temporary tags, which fit the description of Yunkin's car, and they drove away. The driver was a male with long blond hair, described as 6 feet tall and weighing 190 pounds.

A few minutes later, when the investigators arrived at the mobile home, they were too late. Lawrence Yunkin, Michelle Lambert, and the third suspect had come and gone.

"About eight-thirty," a neighbor told sleuths, "I saw them leave, Michelle and Lawrence and another girl—it was the first time I ever saw her. When they left, they drove toward Route 324."

The investigators searched for the trio of suspects all day—to no avail. But Detective Savage knew that Lambert and Yunkin usually played pool on Friday nights at a bowling alley in Strasburg. Sometime after 9 P.M., state troopers converged on the bowling alley and took all three suspects into custody without incident. The third suspect was Tabitha "Tabby" Buck.

Buck, aged 17, was Michelle Lambert's best friend. Born in Alaska and raised in Oregon, Buck had only moved to Pennsylvania a year earlier. The quiet teen had long dark hair, and she played flute in the school's marching band.

As a deterrent to flight, it had already been decided that Lawrence Yunkin and Michelle Lambert would be booked into the Lancaster County Prison on outstanding warrants—Lambert for the November 22 assault against Laurie Show, Yunkin for failure to pay fine and costs on an old noise-ordinance violation. Lambert's bail was set at $100,000; Yunkin's was set at $265.

All three suspects were taken into separate conference rooms for questioning. Trooper John Duby drew Tabby Buck.

"You've got some nasty-looking scratches," the trooper mentioned, motioning to the suspect's face. "How'd you get them?"

"I was riding with Michelle and Lawrence this morning," Buck answered, "but he had car trouble and we stopped at McDonald's on Columbia Avenue in Lancaster. Anyway, these two Puerto Rican girls started calling Michelle and I sluts and whores, so we got into a fight with them and one of them scratched me."

The trooper didn't believe her story, but Buck stuck with it, and she continued to deny any knowledge of Laurie Show's killing. Sometime after midnight, with no evidence on which to hold her, Tabby Buck was released. A surveillance was established around her home to keep an eye on her.

At the same time, Trooper Carl Harnish had been questioning Michelle Lambert. She gave her alibi calmly. It was the same story Tabby Buck had told Trooper Duby. She did not appear to be nervous and gave no indication that she was hiding anything. The trooper persisted.

"Where did you get the rope you used to choke Laurie?" Harnish asked.

"I don't know what you're talking about," Lambert replied.

"Who cut Laurie's neck?"

Again, Lambert pleaded ignorance.

"Look," the trooper said. "This is serious business. Laurie's dead."

"Oh, my God!" Lambert yelled, suddenly turning frantic. "Are you serious? Are you serious?"

"I didn't see anything like that. I don't know what Tabby did. I didn't ask her. I didn't want to know. Tabby's my best friend and I don't want her to go to jail. I asked her what she did in there, but she said, 'Don't worry about it. It's better you don't know.' "

At this point, Lambert abandoned her alibi. Trooper Ray Solt took over the questioning, and Lambert confessed to witnessing the killing.

"Lawrence was the first guy I ever trusted," the girl began, "so when I found out he slept with Laurie, I was really mad.

"This morning, I decided to surprise her because I wanted to talk to her. But I was worried that if her mother was home, there might be trouble. So Tabby went in first. When I got there, Tabby was wrestling with Laurie in the hallway and Laurie was kicking her feet. So I grabbed her ankles, telling her to calm down. Tabby had her hand over Laurie's mouth.

"Then Laurie broke free, ran into the bedroom, and tried to grab the phone. But Tabby grabbed it away and threw it down. Laurie tried to grab a pair of scissors, but Tabby took them away from her and threw them down. Then I saw Tabby had a knife— until then, I didn't see a knife anywhere. I saw her bring it down—it flashed right in front of my face. It sort of bounced off, but Laurie was coughing. She wasn't breathing right and she kept making a whooshing sound."

The stab had punctured one of Laurie's lungs.

"I saw Tabby hit her in the head with the knife a couple of times and I kept hearing all this air whooshing. I felt like I was going to throw up, so I turned away—I can't stand the sight of blood. So I raced out the front door, pulled the hood over my head, and left."

The trooper asked about Yunkin.

"Lawrence doesn't know anything about it," Lambert said. "I didn't want him to know anything."

But at that very moment, Lawrence Yunkin was making a deal

with the prosecutor, John Kenneff. In exchange for cooperating with the investigators, he would be charged with a lesser offense than murder—provided he told the truth.

On Thursday evening, his story began, he'd driven Lambert to the mall. While he waited in the car, Lambert went into Kmart. When she returned, she had two black watchcaps and 50 feet of rope. From there, he drove to Tabby Buck's. The two girls talked for about 45 minutes—alone.

On Friday morning, Yunkin continued, he picked up Buck around 6:45, then dropped off both girls in the woods near Laurie's home. He said Lambert gave him five dollars, and he went to McDonald's at the mall to get something to eat.

The investigators would later interview the McDonald's manager. He remembered Yunkin as being one of the first customers when he unlocked the doors at 7 A.M. He said Yunkin bought hash browns and orange juice, but he kept standing up and sitting down while he ate. To him, the young man appeared nervous.

After he finished eating, Yunkin told the investigators, he went back and picked up the girls. Then he drove them to the mobile home.

"I didn't know they planned to kill Laurie," Yunkin said. "I thought they were just going to tie her up and cut her hair. It was about an hour later that I found out. Michelle was shaking, so I asked her what happened.

"Laurie accidentally got stabbed in the back when Tabby was wrestling with her," Yunkin claimed Lambert told him.

"They heard a hissing sound when they punctured her lung," he continued, "and Tabby said they should slit her throat to put her out of her misery. They both agreed on it."

He said the girls changed, and he helped them get rid of their clothing. Then they disposed of the murder weapons. He helped them concoct an alibi and rehearsed it with them.

"Why did you help her?" the prosecutor asked.

"Because I loved Michelle," Yunkin answered. "I'd do anything for her—just about."

Lawrence Yunkin then directed the investigators to the county incinerator in Convoy Township. There, inside a pink trash bag that had been hidden inside a truck, they found the watchcaps, bloody gloves and socks, and the rest of the clothing the two girls had worn when they killed Laurie Show.

Where were the rope and knife?

"We tossed the stuff in the river," Yunkin told the investigators. Then he led them to an area along the Susquehanna River a couple of miles from the mobile home. It was still night, so a search would have to wait until daylight on Saturday.

"Either Mr. Yunkin is the most stupid or most naive person on the face of the earth," the prosecutor explained later, "or he knew what Lambert and Buck were doing. But that's the hand dealt to the Commonwealth. We have no evidence that he plotted or assisted in the murder."

Scuba divers found the rope on Saturday.

On Saturday night, Lawrence Yunkin was charged with hindering apprehension. His bail was set at $1,000,000. Michelle Lambert was charged with criminal homicide and conspiracy, and Tabby Buck was arrested and charged with the same two offenses as Lambert. Both girls were denied bail.

On Sunday, the divers found the murder weapon: a butcher knife with a finely serrated blade.

Three months later, while she was awaiting trial, Michelle Lambert had a baby girl in prison. Her trial began four months later in July 1992, with the prosecutor seeking the death penalty and Michelle Lambert requesting a nonjury trial. It lasted nearly two weeks, and Michelle spent several hours on the witness stand trying to convince the judge that her part in Laurie Show's death was minimal.

Laurie had threatened to file rape charges against Yunkin, Michelle testified, so Yunkin and Buck came up with a plan "to keep Laurie's mouth shut."

Buck pretended to be Laurie's guidance counselor and lured Laurie's mother away from the house. The plan was to grab Laurie on the way to the bus stop, tie her up, and cut her hair. That morning, Yunkin had a coughing fit, so he dropped the girls off, then drove to McDonald's to get something to drink. But Buck got cold while they were waiting and decided to knock on Laurie's door to see what was keeping her.

Once inside, she said, Buck really freaked out and attacked Laurie. Blood shot all over Lambert's hands and clothing. The sight made her woozie.

"My knees went out from under me," Lambert testified, "and I fell to the floor. Laurie was crying and she was really hysterical. Tabby had the knife and she said, 'Shut up, shut up.' But Laurie kept crying.

"Laurie put up her hands, and Tabby's gloves started getting red streaks on them. Laurie's hands were bleeding, and she looked at me and said, 'Don't leave me here. Take me with you.'"

At that point, Lambert said, she tried to rescue Laurie.

"I grabbed Laurie's wrists and yelled at her to get up," Lambert said. "I jerked her really hard, and Tabby lost her balance. I started pulling Laurie toward the door, but her wrist slipped out of my hand and Tabby yelled, 'You're not going anywhere, bitch!'"

Lambert said she ran outside and bumped into Yunkin.

"I told Lawrence that Laurie was hurt," the testimony went on, "and he told me to sit on the landing. Then he raced up the stairs and ran in. Then Lawrence came flying back down the steps and said, 'I'm going to get the car.'

"Later, Lawrence told me Tabby killed Laurie. I said, 'Why didn't you stop her?' He said, 'I couldn't do nothing.'

"But," Lambert continued, "later Tabby told me, 'She's dead. Lawrence choked her because she kicked him in the nuts. After Lawrence choked her, I stabbed her in the leg and Laurie didn't move. She didn't flinch.'

"Lawrence told me I was pregnant and I was a girl, so I wouldn't get much time, but he'd get life in prison. He said, 'Cover up for me. Me and you can be together.'"

The judge didn't believe Michelle Lambert's story. On Monday, July 21, 1992, he found her guilty of first-degree murder. A day later, because of her youth and motherhood, Lambert escaped the death penalty. She was sentenced to life imprisonment with no chance for parole.

Tabby Buck, who had remained mum about her part in Laurie Show's murder, was tried in September and convicted of second-degree murder. She also received a life sentence.

At Tabby Buck's trial, one of Lawrence Yunkin's co-workers was called as a witness. He related a conversation he'd had with Yunkin two days before Laurie Show was murdered.

"I asked him if he was going to the company Christmas party," the co-worker testified. "He said no, he'd probably be in jail by that time."

"I asked him, 'What for?'

"Lawrence said, 'Murder.' "

After Buck's trial, the prosecution decided that Lawrence Yunkin had not been telling the truth. The charges against him were upgraded to third-degree murder.

On October 9, 1992, Lawrence Yunkin pleaded guilty to the new charge and was sentenced to 10 to 20 years.

"No one took Michelle seriously," Laurie's mother said after the trials. "They just did her bidding. This just proves how desperately lonely some kids are. They're so desperate for attention and approval, they'll do anything. Even commit murder."

"CALIFORNIA'S GREEDY COUPLE SCARED THEIR VICTIM TO DEATH!"

by Don Lasseter

A terrifying shriek suddenly roused a resident of Porterville, California, from deep sleep into blinking, confused consciousness. The visceral cry seemed to emanate from next door with enough volume to reach the foothills at the edge of the darkened town and echo up into the snowcapped Sierra Nevada mountains. It pierced the predawn darkness, shattering the silence of that spring morning in late April 1993.

The man sat up and listened in the darkness, but the only sound he heard was his own agitated breathing. The long silence served to settle the man's nerves. He lay back down and pondered what to do. It seemed foolish to call the police so he closed his eyes and drifted off into a troubled sleep.

A few days later, on the warm afternoon of Thursday, April 29, Karen McDonald attempted to visit her friend, Manuel Vaca, but she got no response to her knocking on his front door. It was her third try in three days, and McDonald was alarmed. On Tuesday, she had seen Manuel's boxer pup jumping at one of the small house's windows. Manuel's blue 1966 Ford Mustang was gone, so Karen figured that Manuel would be back soon.

Now, on Thursday, Manuel's car was still missing, McDonald

couldn't see the pup anywhere, and the front-window curtain appeared to have been torn down. Worried about the dog's welfare, she peered in through the window. What she saw caused her heart to lurch. In panic, she telephoned the police.

Officer Vicky Lynn Currier, in her third year with the Porterville Police Department, pulled her patrol car to a halt on South A Street at 5:15 P.M., and approached Manuel Vaca's home and looked in the window. When her eyes adjusted to the light, Currier saw a bloated human form stretched out on a bed. The victim's flesh, blackened and swollen, bulged from between strips of duct tape that circled his ankles, legs, waist, wrists, and most of his head. There was no question that the person was dead and had been for several days.

Within a short time after Officer Currier's discovery, the homicide team, lead by Detective David Brian Bouffard, arrived.

Detective Bouffard, at age 36, was also a three-year veteran of the Porterville PD, but he was no novice. He'd begun his law enforcement career in the San Francisco Bay area in 1978. Twelve years later he transferred to the peaceful, agricultural town of Porterville in the southeastern curve of the San Joaquin Valley. Ironically, it was in this rural community that he was to face one of the most disturbing homicides of his career.

Because all the doors to Manuel Vaca's house were locked, Detective Bouffard requested the help of the city fire department to force a door open.

"All the contents of the drawers were dumped onto the floor," Bouffard would report. "Things were strewn about the house. There was animal feces on the floor and dog food . . . papers strewn about the kitchen.

"And there was a dead body on the bed in the front portion of the house. His legs, calves, and knees were bound with silver-gray duct tape. His hands were bound in front of him and several wraps around his body [held] his hands down to his stomach."

The victim's face was wrapped over the eyes and mouth, leaving only a tiny gap at the nostrils. The bloated and discolored condition of the body made it impossible to immediately determine the cause of death.

Documents and photographs found in the house identified the victim as Manuel Vaca, age 42.

While Detective Bouffard examined the area around the corpse, another member of the team, Detective Paul Marshall, searched the perimeter of the house by flashlight. There were no apparent signs of forced entry, no pry marks around windows or doors, and no broken glass. Marshall discovered some footprints on the dirt driveway and photographed them with a flash camera.

Inside the house, one of the officers found the frightened boxer puppy cowering in a corner. Fortunately, it was neither hungry nor thirsty, since there was ample water in a bowl and plenty of dry dog food in a five-gallon bucket. The confused pet was turned over to an animal shelter.

Something in the kitchen sink that obviously didn't belong there caught Detective Bouffard's eye. It was an opened white plastic bag that contained cotton balls. Bouffard made a note to have the peculiar item examined by a fingerprint specialist.

Continuing the search, the team located several other pieces of potential evidence. A roll of gray duct tape was recovered from the floor. A curtain that had either fallen or been pulled down from the window over the victim's head rested on Vaca's face. The curtain was carefully packaged for closer examination in a laboratory.

One of the officers sifting through material vacuumed from the floor turned up some hairs, which would also be retained for microscopic scrutiny.

A man's wristwatch was found on the window ledge above the victim's head. Studying it closely, Bouffard thought he could see tiny spots of blood. The watch, along with bedding from under Vaca's body, was added to the growing inventory of possible evidence.

Between the mattress and box springs of the bed where the victim was found, officers pulled out a vicious-looking machete, but it would eventually be dismissed as the murder weapon because of the absence of wounds on the body. A three-foot ax handle found in the same room could not be eliminated as the murder weapon, however, since an autopsy might turn up bruises or fractures consistent with that kind of implement.

The initial investigation lasted well into the night. The body was then loaded onto a gurney and transported to the Fulare County Morgue in Visalia, 30 miles northwest of Porterville.

By the time the morning sun had cleared the Sierra Nevada peaks to the east, Detective Bouffard was still hard at work at the crime scene. Bouffard interviewed a distraught male relative of Vaca's who came to the house. The relative had last seen Vaca about one week earlier, he said. The investigator figured that that had been close to the time Vaca died.

Bouffard learned from the relative that the victim was employed part-time at a local bar and supplemented his income by working with the forestry service during fires and emergencies. The relative could think of no one who had reason to harm Vaca or of any recent conflicts at the bar. Vaca had several girlfriends. The relative knew some of their names, which he readily provided to the detective.

Next, Detective Bouffard interviewed Karen McDonald, who had discovered the body. McDonald had met Manuel Vaca three months earlier at the unemployment office and had visited him maybe 20 times. "He was trying to help me get into forestry and fire fighting," McDonald said. With Vaca's help, she took a test for the position and passed it, but she decided not to accept the job. She had come to tell Manuel of her decision when she discovered the body. McDonald told Bouffard that she hadn't seen anyone else around Vaca's house. She mentioned the missing blue Mustang, but Bouffard knew about the car and had already arranged for a BOLO (be on the lookout) to be distributed throughout the county.

Gary Walter, one of three partners who contracted with Tulare County to perform autopsies, began the postmortem on Friday morning. He noted the space through the duct tape around the victim's nostrils and wondered if it was meant to allow the victim to breathe.

Despite the body's bloating and advanced decomposition, Dr. Walter was able to conclude that there was no evidence of trauma to the skin or head. Examination of the internal organs led to some surprising revelations. "There were no gross changes of the lungs," Dr. Walter noted. Vaca had not been asphyxiated by the tape or by manual strangulation. There was no evidence of toxicological causes of death. Vaca had not been poisoned.

There were no fractures or injuries to tissue or bone. Vaca had not been beaten to death. There were no punctures or bullet wounds. Vaca had not been stabbed or shot to death. So just what had caused the death of Manuel Vaca?

Walter made a close examination of the victim's heart. In view of the absence of other causes, and "some arteriosclerotic changes of the aorta," the pathologist concluded that this victim had died of "cardiac dysrhythmia or an irregularity in the beating of the heart of unknown etiology." In simpler terms, Vaca had died of a heart attack.

Now, Detective Bouffard and his team were faced with a crucial question. Were they dealing with a murder case, or simply a bungled burglary or robbery and an accidental death? A huddle with Deputy District Attorney James Kordell of the Tulare County District Attorney's Office clarified the situation. If the death occurred as the result of a robbery, it would be first-degree murder, accidental or not. It probably wouldn't be too difficult to prove to a jury that Vaca's fatal heart attack was brought on by the person or persons who had brutally bound him with duct tape and ransacked his house.

The homicide investigation would continue.

On the same day that Dr. Walter conducted the autopsy, fingerprint specialist Richard Wesley Kinney, employed by the California Department of Justice (DOJ) under the state attorney general, arrived at Vaca's house to examine the plastic bag containing cotton balls that Detective Bouffard had found in Vaca's kitchen sink.

Omaima Nelson, 23, killed and dismembered her husband after 4 weeks of marriage.

William Nelson was 33 years older than his wife, Omaima.

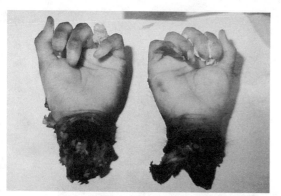

Nelson's severed hands, minus a ring finger,
were found wrapped in newspaper.

In the freezer to the right behind the orange juice
was a large package containing Nelson's head.

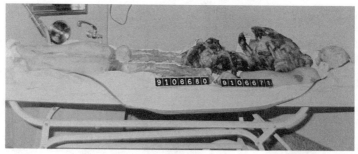

The coroner reassembled the body parts but came up short
130 pounds.

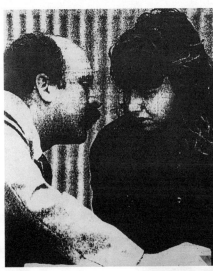

Twenty-year-old Tina Burris (right) with her attorney Jeff Wintner. Burris insisted shooting her mother was an accident.

Barbara Lynn Bell, 46, was convicted of the unpremeditated murder of her husband David, a successful surgeon.

Mary Louise Easlon (left), 37, and her first cousin and lover, Thomas E. Nooner, 27, were convicted in the death of her best friend Verna Kay Busey.

Thirty-seven-year-old wife and mother Verna Kay Busey's body was thrown from a bridge.

Rebecca Smith, reported her husband Harold missing to deflect suspicion from herself.

Harold Dean Smith, 49.

Smith was beaten to death with a baseball bat at his vacation mobile home.

Kristie Lynn Nystrom (left), 21, and Brent Ray Brewer (right), 19, killed and robbed 66-year-old Robert Laminack who had given them a ride.

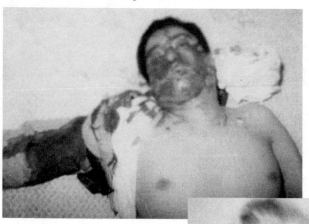

The bloody, gunshot body of Ricardo Ornelas was found in the bedroom of 50-year-old Linda Phillips, his ex-lover (right).

Elvie Rhodes, a 64-year-old widowed grandmother, was reported missing by her relatives.

 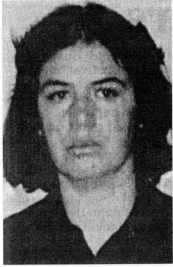

While robbing her home, James Edward Williams (left), 28, beat Rhodes to death as his girlfriend Bernice Sykes (right), 29, watched.

Crack addict Kelley O'Donnell (left), 25, lured Eleftherios
Eleftheriou to her apartment so she and William Gribble
(right), 28, could rob and kill him.

Saudi-Arabian exchange
student, Ahmed
Al-Dawood's roommate
reported him missing.

Eighteen-year-old Rose Mary Miller was convicted of fatally shooting Al-Dawood.

Cassandra Williams (left), 19, with Valerie Rhodes, 19, her college classmate, friend, lover, and partner in the murder of her mother Annie Williams.

Twenty-six-year-old Cindy Ann Oakley claimed to have acted out of self-defense in her ex-husband's murder.

A fling with another teenager's boyfriend cost Laurie Show, 16, her life.

Pregnant Michelle Lambert intended to keep her boyfriend by killing her competition.

Lambert's best friend Tabby Buck, 17, help her slit Show's throat.

Lawrence Yunkin, 20, was sentenced to 10 to 20 years for conspiring with Lambert and Buck.

Starla Rae Richmond, 23, wanted revenge for Manuel Vaca's hitting her.

James Ray Carlin, 26, and Richmond robbed and bound Vaca, leaving him to die.

Forty-two-year-old Manuel Vaca (right) dancing with Starla Richmond.

Vaca's duct tape-bound body was found in his home.

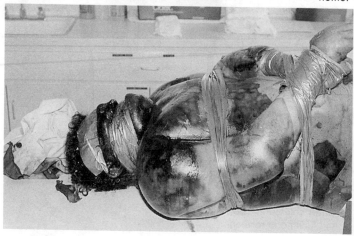

Rozanne Gailunas, 33, was stripped, bound, and shot in the head.

Joy Aylor took out contracts on her ex-husband Richmond Finley and his wife Rozanne Gailiunas.

Gary Matthews (left) and his brother Buster failed to kill Finley for Aylor.

Carol Ann Weaver (left), 37, and Glenda Lois Jones, 42, fatally beat Robbie Sue Harris, 34, before running her over.

Former cabdriver Carolyn Marie Dean, 23, killed shift dispatcher Billy Woodbridge for the money in the company safe.

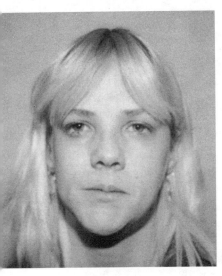

Dean's friend Pamela Sue Sayre, 31, claimed Woodbridge was alive when they left his office.

Dora Cisneros (left), 55, had honor student Joey Fischer, 18, killed when he broke up with one of her daughters.

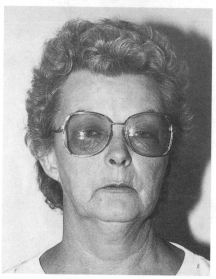

Mary Grieco (above), 48, who claimed to have a "love/hate relationship" with her husband Joseph, and their daughter Ann Grieco, 15, conspired to make it look like Joseph Grieco had committed suicide with a .32 caliber automatic handgun.

After conferring with Bouffard, Kinney carefully packaged the plastic bag and took it with him to his laboratory in Fresno. He tried simple processes with no positive results. Then he tried a process called the Rodum 6-G. "It's a dye," Kinney later explained. "You simply wash it all over the bag, and then you wash it off with the same solvent you've mixed your Rodum with. After it dries, you take it to a dark room, where you use a laser."

The Rodum produces a color that can be seen through special lenses. "The final step is to photograph the print," Kinney explained.

In the Vaca case, Kinney lifted a latent print, unseen before, from the white plastic bag. Now the challenge was to match it with someone. That would take some time.

Meanwhile, Detective Bouffard was focusing on the list of women's names with whom Vaca had been associated. The victim's relative had provided some names, and other interviews added a few more. But one name kept popping up on each list. It had a glamorous sound, like a stage name: Starla Richmond.

Several people suggested that Starla and Manuel had been romantically involved, while others thought they were just friends. But Detective Bouffard's attempts to locate the young woman proved futile. Starla Richmond had completely disappeared from Porterville.

It's over 180 miles from Oakland, on the east side of San Francisco Bay, to the Nevada border. For big-rig drivers, it's a long, slow haul involving an arduous climb from the valley floor to the dizzying heights of the Donner Pass, 7,239 feet above sea level. Driving it alone exacerbates the boredom, so, not surprisingly, drivers often pick up hitchhikers to accompany them on the trip.

On the early evening of Tuesday, May 4, 1993, truck driver Anthony Britton was a little less than halfway to Nevada from Oakland when he pulled his 18-wheeler into a service area in West Sacramento for coffee and snacks. Inside the station's minimarket, Britton noticed an attractive young woman standing with assorted baggage. She had long brown hair and dark eyes, and she stood about 5 feet 6 inches tall. She seemed nervous and frenetic.

Ordinarily, Britton avoided the women who hustled drivers at truck stops. He even kept a sign posted on the door of his truck cab that read, "No Lot Lizards," referring to rest-stop prostitutes. But this young woman seemed different and had a pretty smile.

The woman told Britton that she desperately needed a ride to get to a beloved family member who was dying. Britton welcomed the company and agreed to take her as far as Nevada.

As he started the long, grinding ascent into the Sierra Nevada, east of Sacramento, Britton began to regret his decision. "She seemed all hyped up and kept scratching herself all the time," he later lamented. "She was talking my head off."

After nearly an hour, she asked if they could stop for a few minutes to allow her to make a phone call. Britton agreed, and pulled over into a rest area.

When they got back into the truck and resumed driving, the woman began referring to a crime she'd been involved in. "She'd drift off and then she'd go back," Britton recalled. "She said she couldn't get hold of the relative she tried to call, this and that, and then she'd go back to it [the crime]."

Finally, the pretty passenger became more specific. "She told me she was involved in a murder. She said that they had gone . . . to rob this guy, and they beat him up, and he ended up dying of a heart attack." Britton also remembered the young woman admitting that she had known the victim, an "older" Latin man, and that it happened in Porterville.

Very uncomfortable with what he was hearing, Anthony Britton endured the story and the incessant chatter for nearly four more hours. At last, he reached an establishment called The Truck Inn on Exit 68 of Interstate 80, in Fernley, Nevada, where he and the woman parted company.

Moments later, at 10:15 P.M., Britton stopped at Little Sturgeon's Restaurant, where he knew that members of the Lyons County Sheriff's Office sometimes took coffee breaks. He found Deputy Patrick C. Earle, a 13-year-veteran of the force.

Britton told the officer the tale he'd heard from his female passenger. Even though she said someone helped her in the homicide, she had not revealed her coperpetrator's identity.

"How much money did she say she got from the robbery?" Deputy Earle asked.

"She said she got eighty-five dollars," Britton responded.

Deputy Earle sped to the cafe on Interstate 80 and found the young woman crouched down in a phone booth. The officer asked her for identification, but she told him that she didn't have any. She nervously told him that her name was "Donna Smith."

"She gave me a Social Security number," Earle would recall. "Several minutes later, I asked her to repeat it, and it was a different number.

"She was nervous. Her eyes were very glassy and glazed over. She was extremely agitated. She acted like she wanted to be anywhere but where she was."

Because of the truck driver's story and the woman's suspicious behavior, the officer read her the Miranda warning. He informed her that he was investigating her involvement in a homicide in California. She denied being involved in any homicide, saying that she'd heard about the crime in the papers. Deputy Earle arrested the woman anyway and took her to headquarters.

In the woman's presence, Deputy Earle contacted the Porterville Police Department. The story the truck driver heard from his passenger matched the Vaca homicide to a T, Earle was told, and the woman in his custody matched the description of the fugitive Starla Richmond. To be positive, Earle asked the California officials to send a fingerprint card for Richmond, but the suspect suddenly blurted out, "Yeah, I'm involved." She admitted that she was 23-year-old Starla Rae Richmond.

Arrangements were made to extradite Richmond back to Tulare County.

In Fresno, fingerprint expert Richard Kinney compared Richmond's prints to those lifted from the white plastic bag. He found a perfect match. Also, the strands of hair vacuumed up in Manuel Vaca's house matched samples taken from Starla Richmond's head. But since she'd had a relationship with the victim, it wasn't surprising to find evidence that she had been in his home.

Even though Richmond had been caught, the case was far from over. It was most unlikely that Richmond all by herself had subdued Vaca and bound him with duct tape. In her wild account to the truck driver, she indicated that she'd had help.

As soon as Richmond was returned to Porterville, Detective Bouffard interviewed her, with a tape recorder running. He asked her where she'd been during the week since the body was discovered. Richmond told him that she had traveled to Florida and back by hitchhiking with long-haul truckers. She was headed for Oregon, she said, when she got a ride with the driver who took her to Nevada.

Bouffard wanted to know about her relationship with Vaca. Richmond said that Vaca loved her, but that she just used him for whatever she could get. They had recently traveled together, in his blue Mustang, to Mexico.

On the subject of Vaca's death, Richmond denied any involvement. Richmond said that a relative had informed her about Vaca being found dead and all tied up, but she had nothing to do with it, she maintained.

"I think you're involved in this murder," Bouffard charged.

"I am not," Richmond defiantly insisted.

The interview was entering a second hour when Starla Richmond demanded, "What do you want?"

"You know what I want," Bouffard shot back. "I want to know who killed Manuel."

"I don't know this," Richmond replied. "You know, I really don't. I can't say that I hate Manuel. You know, it's bad. He was good to me at one time, and I do feel bad about . . ." Her voice trailed off to an inaudible whisper.

Once more, Bouffard asked the suspect to admit her complicity in the murder, and Richmond became defiant again. "I sell my [body] on the corner. I'm no murderer. I'm not no thief. I've done a lot of [stuff] in my life, but that ain't something I could do."

Richmond adamantly refused to admit her part in the killing, or to name anyone who might have been involved.

Eleven days after the discovery of Manuel Vaca's body, officers found the victim's blue 1966 Mustang parked on an abandoned farm near a quarry east of Lindsay, 12 miles from Porterville. Once more, fingerprint expert Richard Kinney and a crew of technicians swarmed over the car and its immediate surroundings, searching for anything that might point to a second suspect. Again, they found evidence that Starla Richmond had been in the car but no leads to anyone else.

With the tenacity of a pit bull, Detective Bouffard continued to search and interview, focusing on Starla Richmond's friends. It finally began paying off in August, four months after the discovery of Vaca's body. Two young women led to the name of a second suspect.

On August 10, one of the women came to the police station. In her conversation with Detective Bouffard, she mentioned that she had visited a man in the Tulare County Jail who seemed to know something about the incident with Manuel Vaca. The inmate, 26-year-old James Ray Carlin, had been arrested just three days before Vaca's body was discovered on a completely unrelated charge. The young woman told Bouffard that Carlin had instructed her to claim from sheriff's custody his personal property that he'd had with him when he was arrested.

On the chance that Carlin was connected with the murder, Detective Bouffard obtained a warrant to examine the property. It turned out to be a gold mine of evidence—literally. The items included many valuables that belonged to Manuel Vaca, including gold chains, rings, crucifixes, and a commemorative coin. Bouffard obtained verification from Vaca's relative that the items belonged to the murdered man.

A second woman from among the suspects' acquaintances revealed that one morning in late April, James Carlin had arrived at her house with gifts and money. He admitted that he had gone with Starla Richmond to Vaca's house because Vaca had allegedly struck Starla, and Starla wanted Carlin's help to even the score. According to the woman, Carlin said he choked Vaca and thought that he had killed the man.

Through an informant, Detective Bouffard learned that another Tulare County Jail inmate, Richard Hackworth, might have some information.

On August 28, in a jailhouse interview room, Bouffard made it clear to Hackworth that he would make no promises or deals for any information. The inmate, who had been locked up for over a month for receiving stolen property, tried some verbal fencing with the detective, perhaps hoping for favors in return. Finally, he decided to spit it out and hope for the best.

Hackworth said he knew a man named James Carlin, who was probably linked with the robbery and murder of Manuel Vaca.

"Where did you first learn about this?" Bouffard asked.

Squinting, with a pained look, Hackworth responded, "He [Carlin] had approached me about the robbery before he had went and done it himself."

Asked for more details, Hackworth continued: "The plan that I was told was that Starla was to go to the front door to knock on it. When the man came to the door, we [Carlin and Hackworth] was to come in the back . . . come in behind him, tie him up or, you know, do what it took to get him down and tied up to rob him. He [Vaca] was a Mexican guy that had a VCR, TVs, and lots of money. . . ." The conversation had taken place in Hackworth's dilapidated mobile home.

"Did you go along with it?"

With an even more pained expression, Hackworth whined, "I avoided it. I was out in the trailer with [a woman] and I was scared. I didn't want to go because I'd never done anything like this, and she said, 'Well, if you feel that way, then don't go.' "

"Why did he want you to help?"

"Because I had the heart or something to that effect. And it would better with two, instead of one."

"Are you talking about two people at the back door?"

"Yes, sir, and Starla at the front door."

"Are you certain that Carlin said something to you about tying someone up?"

"Yes, that we had to tie him up . . . because then the man would [have to] just sit there and let us do it."

Bouffard asked what happened next.

Hackworth said he'd seen Carlin after Vaca was attacked, and Carlin seemed to have "lots of money."

"Did you talk to him?"

"Yeah. He told me that I let him down. He told me that he got the money at the guy's house." Hackworth mentioned that the victim had been taped up.

Bouffard wanted to know more about the reference to tape. Hackworth said simply, "James said the man was taped up, that his mouth was taped shut."

Ten days later, Bouffard interviewed yet another inmate who claimed he had heard incriminating statements from James Carlin. Again armed with a tape recorder, and once more asserting to the informant that there would be no deals, Bouffard interviewed the inmate on September 8. The snitch described conversations he allegedly had with Carlin in which Carlin admitted robbing and killing Vaca.

Finally, later that week, Bouffard found a witness who was able to cast some light on a question that had been troubling the detective. Just how had Carlin and Richmond come together to commit the robbery-murder? The woman told Bouffard that she'd known Starla for six months, and one day Starla came to her asking for some help.

"She needed some muscle to help her take care of this guy who had beat her up."

"Who did you recommend?"

"James Carlin."

"Why James?"

"James is big. James could take care of himself."

The woman added that after Carlin and Richmond visited Vaca, she later heard James say that the deal "went bad" and that Vaca was "gone."

James Carlin was in jail on an unrelated charge. His time was up in September and he was released. But his freedom was short-lived. On September 10, 1993, Detective Bouffard confronted the muscular young man and arrested him for the murder and robbery of Manuel Vaca.

Deputy District Attorney James Kordell, who had advised Detective Bouffard during the investigation, began planning the prosecution of Starla Richmond and James Carlin for first-degree murder. Kordell had prosecuted 14 homicide cases among over 200 trials since he joined the Tulare County District Attorney's Office in 1981.

In his opening statement at the trial of Starla Richmond and James Carlin, which began on March 11, 1994, Prosecutor Kordell pointed out that, "Where murders are committed in hell, you don't have angels as witnesses." He was preparing the jury for the testimony of jailhouse snitches and less-than-admirable friends of the two defendants. Kordell also explained felony murder, in which the victim's death is related to a felony, such as robbery.

The two defense attorneys, Michael R. Cross for James Carlin, and Charles Rothbaum for Starla Richmond, focused their cases on the theory that neither defendant had intended to kill the victim, only to scare him and to rob him.

The jury wondered if Manuel Vaca had literally been scared to death.

Both defendants testified.

Starla Richmond, in a soft, quiet voice, said the only reason she and Carlin went to Vaca's house was "just to scare Manuel so he'd leave me alone." She admitted that they had parked in a market lot and walked across a weed-choked vacant field to Vaca's house sometime after 1 A.M. She described their arrival at the home.

"Manuel had the door open. Sometimes he kept the door open late at night because he used to sit there smoking cigarettes. The dog would go in and out once in a while. It was a warm night.

I came around the side. . . . He seen me coming up and James is coming up behind me. Manuel swung and hit at me."

All three of them went into the house, Richmond said, and Carlin began wrestling with Vaca. She recalled that Carlin was sitting on top of Vaca when Vaca stopping moving and Carlin taped him up.

"He was not resisting at all," she said. "He was unconscious."

Richmond told the jury that she went into the kitchen to give the dog some food, not knowing what Carlin was doing. When she returned to the other room, she said, "He had this pillowcase full of . . . jewelry and all kinds of stuff." They left, she whispered, in Vaca's Mustang.

Richmond's testimony lasted for hours, during which she described a dysfunctional childhood, sexual abuse, and problems with drugs.

James Carlin took the stand and admitted going to Vaca's house with Starla Richmond because, "She wanted somebody to go over there and scare him into, you know, not chasing her around in town and bothering her." He'd known Richmond for about 10 years, Carlin said.

The original plan, Carlin disclosed, included Richard Hackworth, the inmate who'd informed Detective Bouffard about Carlin. But Hackworth backed out at the last minute. So, with Richmond, Carlin drove to the Save Mart lot and walked through a field to the back of Vaca's house. "We walked up, I was following her, and he had the door open. She went up to the door, and I thought he grabbed her or hit her. I kind of went into shock, and I pushed her aside and grabbed the guy. We started wrestling around in the house. . . . It was like, uh, we was struggling around pretty strongly. The whole thing probably took about three minutes. And he just . . . he just passed out like, went limp. You know what I mean? I thought he was playing possum."

Carlin added details of the assault, then said, "I told Starla, 'Find me something to tie him up [with],' then I saw some duct tape on a stand and grabbed it." Vaca was bound with the tape, Carlin said, "to keep him from waking up and attacking us."

After they stuffed a pillowcase with stolen jewelry, Carlin took "a couple hundred dollars" and Vaca's car keys from the victim's pants pocket, and they escaped in the Mustang. He later gave Richmond $85 of the money.

In cross-examination, DA Kordell asked if the victim was able to breathe when Carlin taped him up. Carlin replied, "He was breathing. I thought he was. I mean, I could hear him breathing, kind of like gurgling . . . having a breathing problem."

"Why did you tape his mouth shut?"

"So that he wouldn't holler and scream."

Kordell's questioning left no doubt in observers' minds about his contempt for the defendants for having left the victim in such a condition. He emphasized that they had clearly caused Vaca's death.

Kordell asked why the physical struggle between Carlin and Vaca had started. Carlin replied, "Well, I mean he almost hit me, he . . . swung and hit her. I mean, it was . . . the man attacked us almost . . ."

Kordell shook his head, disdainfully, looked squarely at Carlin, and asked, "He attacked you in his own house?"

"What else was I supposed to do?" Carlin snapped back.

Turning his back to the defendant, Kordell said, "I don't think I can answer that question for you, sir."

After 13 days of testimony and evidence, the jury delivered verdicts on Thursday, March 24, one week before Richmond's 24th birthday.

James Ray Carlin was found guilty of first-degree murder and Starla Richmond of second-degree murder.

At the sentencing on April 27, 1994, both defense attorneys made impassioned pleas to Superior Court Judge Kenneth E. Conn. Carlin's attorney asserted that the judge should reduce the verdict to involuntary manslaughter. Richmond's defender admitted that she "shouldn't walk way scot-free," but since the "death was accidental," she should serve a much shorter sentence than that mandated for second-degree murder.

During the hearing, Carlin stared intently at the attorneys, while Richmond twitched nervously and turned around frequently to smile and mouth silent messages to relatives who were in the gallery.

Without any editorial comment, the judge denied both motions. He sentenced Carlin to serve from 25 years to life in prison, and Richmond to serve from 15 years to life. They were led away, in chains, to begin many years of a cold, hard existence behind steel bars.

"DIVORCE WAS NOT ENOUGH FOR THE BLONDE BOMBSHELL!"

by Bill G. Cox

It was not until August 1994 that the scandalous drama played to a shocking conclusion in a Dallas courtroom. But the bizarre story began 11 years earlier, on the cool autumn day of Tuesday, October 4, 1983, in a middle-income neighborhood of Richardson, Texas, a Dallas suburb.

Paramedics responded to a 911 call at an address in the 800 block of Loganwood Drive. Inside a bedroom in the home, the ambulance crew and a patrol officer found a gruesome scene. Minutes later, the quiet neighborhood was peaceful no longer.

With sirens wailing and blue-and-red dome lights flashing, police units carrying uniform officers, supervisors, homicide detectives, and crime scene technicians from the Richardson Police Department soon filled the street.

A critically wounded young woman was rushed by ambulance to a hospital. A uniformed officer, who was the first to arrive, explained to detectives that he found the woman—naked and tied facedown on a bed—still alive. She had apparently been shot twice in the back of the head with a small-caliber gun.

As the detective entered the bedroom, they saw that the bloody scene spoke for itself.

Bloodstains were on the sheets and a pillow. What appeared to be two bullet holes were visible in the pillow and some stained facial tissue lay nearby. Pieces of rope were tied to three of the bedposts. The victim had apparently struggled free of the other rope from the bare bedpost. The rope lay on the floor at the side of the bed, near a pool of vomit. A woman's robe was on the bed.

Among the investigators at the crime scene were Patrol Sergeant D.E. Golden (later a captain and deputy chief) and Detective M.R. McGowan (later captain), who was assigned as the lead investigator.

After viewing the bedroom, Golden told news reporters, "This was a cruel crime scene. All this happened with a four-year-old boy in the house. It was really an inhuman act."

The shooting victim was quickly identified by neighbors as 33-year-old Rozanne Gailiunas, a registered nurse.

In the front yard, the sleuths observed that a small boy was crying in the arms of a man who was wearing glasses. The man identified himself as the boy's father. He said he and his wife had been estranged for several weeks.

The father said the young boy had phoned him saying, "Momma is sick. I can't wake her up." The father had called the 911 emergency number and then rushed to the house.

As officers spread over the neighborhood to canvass door-to-door for possible witnesses, another man came to the victim's house, inquiring what had happened. He gave his name as Richmond Finley, and explained he was a friend of the victim's. He said he had been trying to reach Rozanne all afternoon by phone. He was questioned by one of the detectives, but said he knew nothing of Rozanne's activities since talking to her on the phone that morning.

Investigators searching through the neatly kept home found nothing to indicate that there had been a forced entry, nor did they observe any disorder pointing to a burglary. There were no signs of a struggle.

Had the pretty young victim known her attacker and voluntarily admitted him? the sleuths wondered. Or had she been the victim of a random attacker who somehow persuaded her to admit him?

Rozanne Gailiunas underwent extensive surgery for her wounds, but two days after the attack, she died without ever regaining consciousness.

Meanwhile, the victim's young son was unable to shed any light on what happened to his mother. He said he and his mother had eaten lunch at a fast-food restaurant and then she had taken him to a local rink for an ice-skating lesson.

When they returned home, she told her son to take a nap. When he awakened—probably because of the sound of the shots—he went into the living room to play a movie on the VCR but was unable to start it. He went to his mother's room for help and found her tied-up on the bed. Frightened, he phoned his father.

Over the next few days, investigators quizzed relatives and friends of Rozanne Gailiunas and put together some background on the slain woman.

Rozanne and her husband, a doctor whom she had met and married in their native state of Massachusetts, had moved to Texas in 1972. He had taken a job on the faculty of a Dallas medical school, and she went to work as a nurse in a local hospital. Their son was born in 1979. Sometime thereafter, the couple's marriage began to falter.

They continued to live together, however. Rozanne quit her job as a nurse to take better care of their son. Plans were made to build a half-million-dollar home in an exclusive section of Dallas.

The construction was under way at the beginning of 1983, but a short time later, Rozanne told her husband that she wanted to separate and try to sort out her life, perhaps go back to nursing.

But there was more to Rozanne's decision than she revealed, investigators learned. As they continued to dig, the detectives discovered that Rozanne had become romantically involved with the handsome building contractor who was putting up the expensive home, Richard Finley. Finley at the time was separated from his wife, Joy.

It is routine police procedure to check out all of a victim's close relationships. Detectives were able to account for the whereabouts of the victim's estranged husband and her boyfriend, Finley, during the time period the murder was thought to have happened.

Detective McGowan said the homicide sleuths were back at square one, and leaning more to the theory that the slaying had been a random act, perhaps by a killer who had killed before.

In the early 1980s, there was a national focus by law enforcement agencies on serial killers—killers who usually travel extensively and commit the same type of homicides.

An outgrowth of the need to centralize information on crimes of similar pattern had resulted in the FBI's establishment of the national Violent Criminal Apprehension Program (VICAP).

The Richardson detectives contacted the FBI and submitted all details of the Gailiunas murder to the VICAP experts for computerized comparison with other similar murders of women. But as the months passed with no developments, the Richardson investigators feared that their case was doomed to the unsolved file.

On the afternoon of June 14, 1986, an incident occurred in nearby Kaufman County, Texas, that immediately drew the attention of the Richardson detectives who were working the Gailiunas murder.

Richmond Finley, the contractor who had dated Rozanne, reported that someone had tried to assassinate him. Finley was driving to his horse ranch with a friend for some horseback riding when bullets suddenly shattered their vehicle's windows.

Finley received only minor cuts from the broken glass, but his friend was wounded in one wrist. The men sped into town and reported the shooting. In their car mirror, they had glimpsed a man with a raised gun, but they were unable to identify him, they told sheriff's deputies.

The Richardson sleuths contacted the Kaufman County Sheriff's Department to see if any link to the Rozanne Gailiunas case could be uncovered. But they came away with nothing. In fact, the Kaufman County officers said they believed that Finley and his friend had inadvertently come upon a drug deal or poachers who were hunting illegally on the land.

It was two years later, in March 1988, that the Richardson police received a telephone call from a woman who wanted to meet with a detective. The woman sounded scared. She said she knew who had planned the murder of Rozanne Gailiunas. She identified the plotter as Joy Aylor.

The detective who took the call recognized the name. Joy Aylor was the former wife of Richmond Finley, the building contractor who had been having an affair with Rozanne Gailiunas.

The tipster claimed that Joy Aylor was also behind the attempted shooting of Finley on his ranch. The tipster identified herself as Marilyn Andrews and said she was a relative of Aylor's. In subsequent meetings with detectives, Andrews admitted that Aylor involved her in delivering an envelope of money that she now believed to be payment for the Gailiunas killing. Andrews was afraid that the man who received the money intended to kill her, too, because she knew too much.

Andrews told the sleuth that, as instructed, she took the envelope to a designated spot, where it was picked up by a messenger. Later, she received a call from the man for whom the envelope was intended. On the day of the pickup, he told Andrews, he had been watching her from a safe distance. She was pretty, he said; he wanted to meet her.

Andrews and the mysterious man soon became romantically involved.

Andrews told the detectives that the man's name was Robert Cheshire, and that he had admitted his involvement in the slaying. He had also bragged about having done other hit jobs.

Detectives asked Andrews to help them get evidence of Joy Aylor's involvement in the murder conspiracy, promising her police protection for her cooperation. The plan was for Andrews to carry a concealed microphone to record conversations with Aylor.

Andrews met with Aylor two different times in an effort to get some incriminating conversation on tape. Once they met in a restaurant where background noise made it difficult to understand their recorded talk. Then they met in a motel room.

All the while, detectives were outside in a van, with tape recorders and video cameras running.

Though the tapes, when played later, were inaudible in many places—especially the one in the restaurant—enough was understandable to show that Aylor had probably taken out contracts on the lives of both Rozanne Gailiunas and Aylor's ex-husband, Richmond Finley.

The investigators pitched their case to Dallas County assistant district attorney Kevin Chapman. After that session, it was decided to pick up Aylor for questioning.

When brought to the police station and confronted with the tapes, the pretty blonde shrugged off Marilyn Andrews's accusations as those of a mentally disturbed person. The sleuths finally had no alternative but to release Aylor.

But it was the beginning of months of cat-and-mouse detective work, in which the homicide sleuths began to trace the hiring of a contract killer through a chain of sleazy middlemen—all of them passing along the blame for the actual hit onto someone else. Two of the "intermediates" were traced to other states. Detectives traveled to those locations to grill the suspects.

The last man who had been given cash for the contract hit, along with the address and a photograph of Rozanne Gailiunas, was finally identified as an insurance appraiser named Andy Hopper.

Hopper, the detectives learned in their persistent quest, was involved deeply in marijuana trafficking. He had no major criminal record, and he still worked as an appraiser, but it was mostly a front job. Selling marijuana was his major income source.

When detectives located Hopper, he denied any knowledge of the Gailiunas killing. He excused himself to take a phone call and ran out the back door.

In the next few weeks, the sleuths established that Hopper had apparently fled from Richardson. The search for the elusive suspect swung through the Midwest and West, with Hopper managing to stay just ahead of the lawmen.

Detective McGowan met with Assistant DA Chapman and outlined his investigation. The results of the intensive detective work, along with the tape recordings of talks between Joy Aylor and Marilyn Andrews, were presented to a Dallas grand jury. On September 19, 1988, the panel returned indictments against Aylor and five others who were allegedly involved in the murder conspiracy.

An indictment charged Aylor with capital murder and conspiracy to commit capital murder in the death of Rozanne Gailiunas and solicitation to commit capital murder in the attempt on the life of her ex-husband, Richmond Finley.

The other suspects were indicted on conspiracy charges, two of them in the attempted shooting of Finley in 1986. Charged in the attempt on Finley's life were brothers Gary and Buster Matthews.

Joy Aylor was arrested and taken to the Richardson police station. She refused to discuss the case with detectives and was later released on bail.

The intensive hunt for the purported triggerman, Andy Hopper, came to an end in December 1988, when detectives and FBI agents nabbed Hopper after he returned to visit a girlfriend in the Dallas area.

Hopper denied doing the killing. As had the other "go-betweens" the detectives questioned, Hopper also blamed another person for the Gailiunas slaying. He claimed he passed along $1,500 to a drug dealer from Houston, whom he knew only as "Renfro," who said he would do the job.

Hopper had met Renfro during a drug and sex party at a friend's apartment in Dallas. Hopper didn't know his last name, but Renfro later told him he had done the job.

The detectives did not believe Hopper's story, but they knew the only way to disprove it was to find the mysterious Renfro. During questioning of witnesses who had been present at the time Hopper said he met Renfro, one woman recalled that Renfro had mentioned he was once busted on a drug charge in Highland Park.

At the Highland Park Police Department, after an extensive search of the files, the detectives came up with a mugshot of a Renfro Stevenson, who matched the description given by Andy Hopper.

When they showed the mugshot to Hopper and told him that Renfro denied having anything to do with the Gailiunas murder, Hopper broke.

In his statement that was given in writing and taped on video, Hopper related details of that October 4 in Richardson seven years earlier. He had stolen a .25-caliber automatic from a friend's apartment and purchased rope, surgical gloves, and a potted plant before driving to Rozanne Gailiunas's house.

He rang the doorbell and gained entry by posing as a floral deliveryman, proffering the potted plant he had just bought. Brandishing the gun, Hopper ordered Gailiunas to disrobe and life facedown on the bed, where he bound her with rope. When she started to cry, he got some facial tissue and crammed it down her throat. He found a belt, placed it around her neck, and strangled her. Gailiunas began thrashing violently and managed to free one arm. Hopper said he then put a pillow over the victim's head and fired two shots point-blank through the pillow.

The victim's little boy had been asleep in his room at the time.

From their investigation and the statements of the suspects involved in the drawn-out murder-for-hire transactions, it appeared that the killer never knew who ordered the hit.

Hopper was jailed without bond on a charge of capital murder.

Meanwhile, a pretrial hearing for Joy Aylor was set for May 7, 1990, with jury selection for her capital murder trial to follow. But when the blonde defendant failed to appear, prosecutors feared the worst. For one thing, they learned that Aylor had been accumulating a cash supply, making withdrawals from her bank accounts and selling stocks and other holdings.

Lawmen learned that Aylor and 45-year-old Ted Bakersfield, a Dallas attorney who had been arrested on a federal narcotics charge the previous March, had recently been keeping company. Bakersfield, once a competent and respected Dallas County assistant district attorney, had fallen on bad times because of alcohol and cocaine problems.

Detectives learned that Bakersfield and Aylor had met several months earlier when Aylor was considering hiring a new lawyer to represent her in the murder case. She had not employed Bakersfield—in fact, he recommended she stick with her present attorney. But their initial business contact had blossomed into a romantic relationship.

It was after an intensive probe by federal drug agents that Bakersfield was arrested in March on a charge of accepting cocaine. He was freed on a personal recognizance bond, awaiting trial in federal court on the drug charge.

Now there was speculation among prosecutors and officers that Aylor and Bakersfield had fled the country together, possibly to Mexico.

Sleuths obtained federal warrants of unlawful flight to avoid prosecution. Over the next three weeks, the authorities tracked the fugitives through several western states, but Aylor and Bakersfield continued to elude the lawmen who were on their trail.

Investigators quizzed a friend of the couple's who admitted that after he left Dallas with the pair, he dropped them off at a car dealership in Cheyenne. The authorities learned that Bakersfield purchased a 1984 Jeep Wagoneer for $7,800 cash, using his real name in the transaction.

Later, the pair stopped in Cut Bank, Montana, where they registered the Jeep and picked up local license plates. The officers speculated that Bakersfield and Aylor did not want to try to cross an international border with dealer plates on the vehicle. It was believed they were headed for Canada.

Canadian authorities, working closely with U.S. federal officers, next picked up the couple's trail near Vancouver, British Columbia. A man answering Bakersfield's description and a blonde woman registered at a remote hotel as "Mr. and Mrs. John Storms."

However, sleuths learned from the hotel clerk that Storms checked out alone on June 11, and received a partial refund because he had paid through June 14. Immigration officers asked the clerk to notify them if Storms contacted her again for any reason. Only minutes later, Storms did phone and ask if he had received any calls. The hotel employee made up a story that "a woman called" but didn't leave her name. Later, sleuths would learn that Bakersfield had been expecting a call from the departed Aylor.

The hotel clerk told the officers that the man seemed pleased and left the name of the hotel where he was staying in rural Osoyoos, British Columbia.

After being notified, the immigration officers phoned the rural resort hotel and were told that a John Storms was registered there. Within an hour after the confirmation, eight armed officers surrounded the hotel.

One officer phoned Storms's room and told him, "Come out with your hands up!"

Storms, who turned out to be Ted Bakersfield, gave up without any resistance. He agreed to return to the United States voluntarily, and he was later transferred to Spokane, Washington, and then flown to Dallas in custody of a U.S. marshal.

The officers were disappointed that they had not found Joy Aylor with him. Bakersfield told the American officers that she had left him and he did not know where she was.

The attorney said he thought about killing himself, but he had decided to return to Dallas just before he was arrested at the Canadian hotel.

Bakersfield blamed his actions on his cocaine addiction and said he was uncomfortable running from the law. But, an FBI agent said, "He left with Joy because he was in love with Joy. He was trying to protect her."

Checking airline flights at the Vancouver Airport, FBI agents discovered that Aylor had taken a flight to Mexico City on June 7. The investigation moved to that city, but Aylor remained undetected.

The first tangible lead on Aylor's whereabouts surfaced in August 1990 when a woman returned to Dallas from a vacation in Mexico and spotted a newspaper photo of a woman she had known under another name. The photo was of Aylor. It ran in conjunction with a news story about a lawsuit filed by Aylor's ex-husband, Richmond Finley.

The woman contacted the Richardson police. She told them that she had roomed with Aylor, who was going under another name, while both were attending a Spanish-language school in Cuernavaca, Mexico. Following up the lead, officers learned that Aylor had not returned to the school, although she had registered for the next term. Apparently, she was on the move again.

The Richardson officers and FBI sought the help of worldwide law enforcement agencies in their global womanhunt, including Interpol and police in European countries. But the elusive Aylor remained undetected until March 1991.

On Saturday, March 16, Aylor was taken into custody where she had been living a life of leisure in a small villa near a resort city on the French Riviera. On Friday, the day before her arrest, Aylor had been traced to Nice, France.

Officers found out that Aylor had been living in comfort with an American boyfriend identified as Albert Nielsen. She was using the name Elizabeth Sharp. She had rented the villa just outside Nice. The woman gave English lessons to support herself, but kept a low profile, neighbors said.

The live-in boyfriend had fled the area after Aylor was taken into custody. He could not be located.

When arrested, the suspect at first gave the false name, but she soon admitted her true identity. Aylor was transferred to a cell in the local jail. There, she attempted to kill herself by slashing both wrists, but a policeman discovered the attempt, and Aylor was rushed to a hospital. Officials said the wounds were not serious.

Texas authorities began the long and involved legal procedures of extraditing Aylor from France. A big barrier was that France's extradition treaty with the United States contains a provision protecting capital murder suspects from being extradited. France has this law because its own statues do not contain the death penalty.

However, Dallas County prosecutors requested that Aylor be extradited on the charges against her that were not capital cases.

Meanwhile, jury selection began for the trial of Andy Hopper. It took six months to seat a panel and the trial consumed six weeks, one of the longest murder trials in the county's history. The prosecution had hoped to try Joy Aylor first, but the delay in extradition, expected to last several months, changed the plans.

The highlight and clincher of Hopper's trial was the admissibility of the hit man's videotaped confession, a cold recital of the merciless details surrounding the violent death of Rozanne Gailiunas.

One detail that made the jury flinch was Hopper's remark that as Gailiunas lay nude and bound on the bed, he stood over her and masturbated before strangling her with a belt and firing two shots point-blank into her head.

Testimony of two witnesses—a jail inmate and a longtime friend of Hopper's—further sealed the case against the accused. The inmate testified that Hopper admitted the slaying while they were in jail. The friend testified that Hopper wrote a letter to him admitting the murder. He showed no signs of remorse, the witnesses testified.

The defense tried to prove that although Hopper entered the house and assaulted the victim, she had been killed by someone else after he left.

But, as jurors would later tell reporters, it was Hopper's own words in his taped confession that convicted him. The jury found him guilty of capital murder and their verdict mandated that he be put to death by lethal injection. The verdict was appealed to the Texas Court of Criminal Appeals.

Because of all the appeals to various legal panels to prevent it, the extradition of Joy Aylor was not finalized by French court

officials until November 1993. U.S. marshals returned her to
Dallas County to stand trial. It was 11 years after the 1983 slaying.

A far different-looking Joy Aylor was returned to a Texas jail.
As she was escorted through the Dallas-Fort Worth International
Airport, observers noticed that the once-pretty blonde was now
gaunt and drawn, showing the strain of her years of flight.

As jury selection for Aylor's long-awaited trial started in May
1994, Assistant District Attorney Kevin Chapman predicted a
complex legal battle. "She started it," he said. "She's the one
that gave it [the murder] all life. But she's the farthest from the
gun."

The trial got under way on August 1, 1994, before Dallas
County state district judge Pat McDowell. Court TV, a cable
television network, televised the trial live. The tired-looking defendant, shackled at the ankles, entered a not-guilty plea.

Prosecutor Chapman's opening statement to the jury of nine
women and three men included a slide presentation using two
side-by-side projectors. With the courtroom lights dimmed, an
image of Joy Aylor, blonde, beautiful, and suntanned, appeared
on the left screen. On the right screen, photos of people and
places linked to the murder probe flashed by in sequence as the
prosecutor outlined the chain of events.

Chapman also talked about tape recordings of conversations
between Aylor and Marilyn Andrews, which the defense claimed
were inaudible. But Chapman said the jurors could understand
the tapes if they tried.

"You've got to give it time, you've got to work at it. I predict
if you spend some time with the tapes, you'll find that it's pretty
easy to understand," Chapman said.

He also said he would prove that Aylor fled the country because of her fear of being convicted on the murder charge.

Opening state witnesses included those officials who found
Rozanne Gailiunas's body, the doctor who treated her at the hos-
pital, and the medical examiner who performed the autopsy. The
ME said that the victim had died from the gunshots.

The state called to the stand Albert Nielsen, who had been

living with Aylor in France. Nielsen had only recently been arrested on a federal fugitive warrant.

Nielsen testified that Aylor had admitted to him her role in the slaying. He said Aylor wanted her ex-husband's girlfriend dead so she could reclaim him and money that she said he had taken from their joint bank accounts. Nielsen related that Aylor also told him of paying $15,000 in blackmail to Robert Cheshire, who she said had arranged the hit against Rozanne Gailiunas.

Nielsen admitted under cross-examination that he had taken $200,000 belonging to Joy Aylor from banks in Switzerland and Mexico. He claimed he used the money to travel as a fugitive after Aylor's 1991 arrest. According to his testimony, he bought and later sold a $185,000 sailboat.

The defense attacked Nielsen's credibility, alleging he was testifying to please prosecutors as part of a plea bargain on federal charges of passport fraud and concealing a fugitive.

"He's a desperate man," Aylor's defense attorney said. "I'd expect him to say anything."

The state played the tape-recorded conversation between Aylor and Marilyn Andrews—the informant who blew the whistle on the murder scheme—during a meeting at a motel before Aylor's arrest. Jurors were given wireless headphones and a typed transcription of the tape to follow along as it was played in the courtroom.

Although Aylor did not directly admit to involvement in the killing on the tapes, she made remarks that, the state contended, tied her in with other evidence for the murder-for-hire plot.

In the most damning portion of the taped conversation, Andrews says to Aylor, "I got one thing that still bothers me."

"What?" Aylor asks.

"Why didn't you get rid of [Richmond Finley] first?"

"I don't know," Aylor responds. "Stupid, wasn't it? I thought about that, too. It would have been a lot better."

In another comment on the tape, Aylor told Andrews, "I paid for it. Really, I have paid for it, not only monetarily but mentally, I've paid for this."

Next, the prosecutors showed Andy Hopper's videotaped confession to the Gailiunas murder, in which the hit man said he received money for the job from a middleman.

Called as a witness, the middleman told of his part in the plot of giving Hopper money, directions, and a picture of the victim.

Next, the state played the second taped conversation between Aylor and Andrews, the one made as the women sat in a noisy restaurant.

At one point on the tape, Aylor talked about the man she hired to arrange the killing. "He didn't know who I was at the time. He did not know who paid to kill her." The money in an envelope had been given to him by one of the middlemen.

Detective McGowan, whose persistence and relentless investigation were credited by the DA's office with breaking the case, was on the stand for three days. He testified in detail about the probe that eventually went around the world to track down a killer.

The Gailiunas murder had been described by one veteran Dallas officer who worked it, Captain D.E. Golden, as "Dallas's most complicated murder case."

After the state rested their case, the defense, in a surprise move, closed without calling any witnesses. It was a strategic move by the defense, whose reasons would soon become apparent.

Closing arguments of attorneys were scheduled for August 15, but on that day, the prosecutors asked the judge to allow them to reopen testimony in the trial. The state motion asked that one more witness be permitted.

The witness was Ted Bakersfield, the lawyer convicted on federal drug charges. Bakersfield, who had pleaded guilty three years before to the cocaine possession charge, received a 15-year prison sentence. He had been freed in December 1993 after his sentence was reduced to four years.

The state had not called Bakersfield as a witness against Aylor before they rested because they intended to present him as a rebuttal witness after the defense presented witnesses and rested their case.

But by closing rather than resting their case, the defense had blocked Bakersfield's testifying as a rebuttal witness for the state. Thus, prosecutors were forced to move to reopen testimony and to call Bakersfield as a late witness. It was a risky move, but the motion was granted.

Bakersfield described the love affair that started after he first met Joy Aylor in 1988 when she considered hiring him as her attorney. He testified about several conversations in which she admitted her involvement in the murder and her plans to flee to another country.

Bakersfield said he had difficulty in reconciling the woman he had loved with her story of Rozanne Gailiunas's slaying and occasional glimpses of Aylor's coldness.

Recalling one time when they went to a shooting range and he permitted Aylor to test-fire a new 9mm handgun, she had aimed the gun at a mesquite tree and emptied the clip. Handing him the gun, Aylor had smiled and said, "I should've used this on Rozanne."

Aylor had told him, in fact, that she wished she had done the murder herself. Bakersfield testified that Aylor showed no remorse about the killing.

"She said if she had it to do all over again, she'd do it differently," the witness said. "She'd do it herself."

Bakersfield related that Aylor always said that the murder had been necessary, and she felt comfortable with what she had done. He recalled Aylor told him that guilt "was a wasted emotion that could be dealt with under any circumstances and should not be carried around."

Bakersfield said that Aylor had approached him about finding someone to kill Marilyn Andrews, who had tipped off the police. Aylor said she thought the recorded conversations between them might not be admissible as evidence if Andrews was removed.

"The best defense is a good offense," Bakersfield quoted his former lover as saying.

After Bakersfield's damaging testimony, the state again rested their case, as did the defense without calling any witnesses.

In final arguments, the prosecutors rehashed the testimony of

Aylor's two ex-lovers, stressed her around-the-world flight to avoid a trial, and reiterated the contents of the clandestinely recorded surveillance tapes that were so damning.

The defense argued that Aylor never hired anyone to kill anyone but only employed Robert Cheshire to follow and rough up her ex-husband, Richmond Finley. The murder of Gailiunas was the result of an overzealous hired hit man, the defense team told the jury.

But the attorneys for the state reminded the jury that Aylor's comments to several people years after the murder made it plain that she meant for Rozanne Gailiunas to die.

Recalling the recorded comment by Aylor to Marilyn Andrews that "He did not know who paid to kill her," Assistant District Attorney Chapman said: "Does that sound like a woman who ordered eggs and got bacon?"

On August 18, 1994, the jury deliberated for two and a half hours before finding Joy Aylor guilty of capital murder and setting her punishment at life imprisonment. The death penalty was not a consideration because of the agreement that U.S. officials had made with France not to seek the death penalty before Aylor's extradition could be gained. Aylor showed no emotion as the verdict was announced and she was led away to jail.

Meanwhile, Albert Nielsen pleaded guilty to federal charges that he helped to hide Aylor during her years as an international fugitive. He admitted guilt to nine charges, including passport fraud, harboring a fugitive, mail fraud, and using a fraudulent Social Security number. Under a plea agreement with federal prosecutors, he faced a maximum sentence of 50 years in prison. At this writing, the sentence had not been pronounced by a judge.

Buster Matthews and Gary Matthews received sentences of life in prison in the attempted shooting of Richmond Finley.

At this writing, disposition of the charges against the middlemen who allegedly carried money and instructions from Aylor to hit man Andy Hopper had not been made.

The defense said they would appeal Aylor's life sentence. Joy Aylor is serving her time in the Texas Department of Corrections.

"THE SUSAN SMITH CASE: A NATION MOURNS TWO 'SMALL SACRIFICES'"

by Richard Devon

Union County lies in the north central quadrant of South Carolina, in the rolling foothills of the Blue Ridge Mountains. Union, the county seat, is a town of some 10,000 people whose heritage is farming and textile manufacturing, matters that normally keep them from enjoying—or suffering—the glare of the world's attention.

This generally quiet community is no different from any other small Southern town as far as criminal activity is concerned. Crimes that do occur there have never been of much interest outside the county itself. All that changed, however, on the evening of Tuesday, October 25, 1994. For a period of 14 days, Union and its residents were caught up in an event that touched hearts nationwide, and in the end, brought bitterness and grief.

It began with a call to the county's 911 communications system. When the operator responded, she heard the excited voice of a man who stammered, "I'd like to report . . . there's a lady . . . she come up to our door, and she said some guy jumped into a red light [sic] with her car with two kids in it, and he took off and she got out of the car here at our house."

"He's got her kids?" the operator asked.

"Yes, ma'am, and her car. She's real hysterical. I just decided I needed to call the law and get them down here."

"Okay, which direction was he traveling?"

"Uh . . . she's, you know, we can't even get her to figure out which way he was going."

"What kind of car is it? We need to know something."

"We're trying to ask her that." The operator could hear the caller trying to talk to someone else before he said, "A Mazda Protege . . . a burgundy Mazda Protege."

At this point, the 911 operator turned to her colleague and said, "Get 'em going, Pam. They got two kids."

"That's a black guy," the caller said.

"Do you know which way he went?"

"We're trying to get that out of her now."

"Did he have any weapons . . . a gun or anything?"

"Look going towards Chester. Yeah . . . he's got a gun, she says."

"Did you get a tag number out of her?"

"She can't remember. . . . Her pocketbook is still in the car."

"All right, we're sending an officer and we've got Chester [police] going after the car. So if you need to, call me back."

Sheriff Howard Wells was in his 23rd year of law enforcement the night he got the report that someone had stolen an automobile with two little children inside. As he sped through the dark, chilly South Carolina countryside along Highway 49, he could not even imagine the emotional wringer into which he was being thrown.

Over time, as Wells developed his career from wildlife officer to town policeman and now sheriff, he had finished first in his state law enforcement standards class and later first in his FBI Academy class at Quantico, Virginia. He was regarded highly by fellow lawmen, but his schooling didn't necessarily impress the average citizen.

When he ran for sheriff, Wells won by a mere 19 votes, but in the days to come, Union County citizens who hadn't voted for him would likely wish they had. He would, in the coming nine days, conduct himself in such a fashion as to instill pride.

Wells would be at the forefront of a grinding, emotional roller coaster energized by an investigation that stretched to the West Coast and north into Canada.

Arriving at the house of SC 49, Wells was met by Deputy Bobby Hicks and a young man who identified himself as the one who had called 911. Inside, the sheriff found the caller's parents trying to comfort a sobbing young woman. To his surprise he recognized pretty 23-year-old Susan Smith.

Smith's stepfather, a prominent local businessman, was active in Republican politics, and was therefore on the opposite side of the fence during Wells's successful run for sheriff. An even closer connection Wells had with the hysterical young woman was the fact that he was the godfather to one of her young cousins. In time, Wells's connection with Susan Smith's family would heighten the sheriff's awful emotional experience.

Wells set about calming down the young woman, who was in a virtual state of collapse. Eventually, he was able to determine that she had been stopped at the traffic light in the nearby community of Monarch Mills, when out of the darkness a man opened her car's front passenger door, climbed in, pointed a gun at her, and order her to drive.

Doing as she was told, Susan drove an estimated seven miles when the gunman ordered her to stop. When she was forced out of the car, the gunman moved to the driver's side.

"I asked him to let me get my little boys from the backseat, but he said he didn't have time," the sobbing Smith said.

Wells was able to learn that the car in question was a burgundy four-door Mazda Protege, bearing South Carolina license plate GBK 167. He radioed this information to his office, and a "be on the lookout" (BOLO) was immediately broadcast. Later, Wells contacted the State Law Enforcement Division (SLED) and requested assistance, with the result being that the information on the Mazda and its occupants was spread all across the southeastern United States.

Throughout the remainder of the night, Union County authorities searched backroads and major highways looking for the missing vehicle and its occupants. The report of the automobile theft and kidnapping of the children indicated the suspect had left the scene heading toward North Carolina.

The trauma of having seen her sons disappear into the night was more than Susan Smith could bear. Eventually, however, lawmen were able to elicit critical information about the children and the suspect.

The two little boys had been buckled in their children's safety seats in the back, Smith said. The gunman was described as black, 30 to 40 years old, of slender build, 5 feet 9 inches to 6 feet tall and weighing 175 pounds. He was dressed in a plaid shirt, jeans, and was wearing a hat.

Three-year-old Michael, the older of Susan Smith's two sons, was last seen wearing white jogging pants, a green and blue long-sleeved striped shirt, and a light blue outercoat with a teddy bear emblem. His brother, 14-month-old Alex, was dressed in a one-piece white striped playsuit and a blue and red-striped outercoat.

As she was being forced from the car, Smith said, Michael started crying, "I want my mama," he said. "Mama, where are you going?"

"I told him, 'Baby, I've got to go, but you are going to be OK,' " Smith said. "I hollered I loved them, then the guy slammed the door and took off. I just felt such a failure. They need me right now, and I'm not there—and it makes me feel so bad."

The first lead to surface came early Wednesday morning. The kidnapping of the Smith children was aired on a radio newscast that was heard by an employee of a convenience store north of Union. He called to say that between 9:30 and 10 P.M. the night before, a black man fitting the suspect's description purchased $10 worth of gas at the store.

The customer had not acted in a manner that caused the store clerk suspicion at the time, but when he heard the radio broadcast, the clerk felt he should contact authorities. The clerk had not paid a lot of attention at the time, but he remembered that his customer's vehicle appeared to be burgundy. There had been no sign of children in the car, however.

Investigators immediately converged on the store and learned that a surveillance camera had been in operation. Once the film from the camera was studied, lawmen determined that the car wasn't a Mazda, thereby eliminating the driver as a suspect.

On Wednesday morning, the FBI joined the search. Later in the day, Susan Smith helped an SLED agent produce a composite drawing of the suspect. With the composite completed, hundreds of fliers including a photograph of the missing children were produced and distributed.

By Wednesday night, the search for the burgundy car and its occupants began to expand to all points of the compass.

As lawmen gathered at the Union courthouse to evaluate the situation, they agreed that what they were dealing with was not a typical carjacking. Carjackers are usually bent on securing transportation. Kidnapping doesn't usually fit a carjacker's scheme. On top of that, a black man driving around the Carolinas with two white boys in the back would have been unusual enough for someone to have noticed, and so far no one had. A carjacker would not have wanted to be so conspicuous, probers reasoned.

There have been instances, of course, where carjackers have wound up with children in a stolen vehicle, but usually the cars are abandoned a short time later or the children are tossed out as soon as the carjacker finds a means of safely getting rid of their excess baggage.

With this in mind, lawmen fruitlessly searched all along SC 49 in the direction the car was headed when it was last reported seen by Susan Smith.

Soon after daybreak that morning, search teams spread out from the spot where Susan Smith said she was forced from her vehicle. Three helicopters—two from SLED and one from the Coast Guard Auxiliary—began flying low across the countryside. They were joined by two single-engine fixed-wing aircraft. At day's end, the search had turned up nothing to indicate what happened to the car, the suspect, or the children.

The plight of the two helpless youngsters immediately stirred concern among local citizens, many of whom were personally acquainted with the two Smith boys, their parents, and extended families.

Warmhearted Union County residents began to hang yellow ribbons on doors, mailboxes, trees, and anywhere else they could be tied to bring attention to the plight of the two missing boys. Others placed copies of the children's picture in their car windows, in storefronts, and in other places where they would be easily seen.

From the beginning, the carjacking and kidnapping of the two toddlers drew heavy interest from the news media nationwide. Television camera crews, as well as print media teams, began to converge on Union. They all zeroed in on Sheriff Wells, who could offer little information other than that law enforcement agencies were doing everything they could to locate the missing children, the car, and the suspect.

As word of the case spread, South Carolina lawmen began getting calls from all over the nation. These calls numbered in the thousands over the next nine days. People who thought they had either seen the car, the children, or the suspect began to jam phone lines into the Union County Sheriff's Department, SLED and FBI offices in Columbia, as well as other law enforcement agencies and organization that trace mission children. All of these tips had to be checked out, no matter haw farfetched they seemed to be. With the growing number of phone calls, the need for additional help for Sheriff Wells's department became critical. Within the first 24 hours after the reported kidnapping, the number of lawmen involved in the search in that immediate area numbered 100 or more. At the time, no one was keeping count.

At 4:15 A.M. on Thursday, October 27, about 30 hours after the 911 call to the Union County Sheriff's Department, an armed robbery occurred in Salisbury, North Carolina, 100 miles north of Union. The alarm provided information that the gunman was possibly involved with the Union County case.

A clerk in the convenience store called Salisbury police after the holdup. When officers arrived, witnesses confirmed that a black male, fitting the kidnapper's description, had threatened a customer and the clerk with a small-caliber automatic. The pair had been forced to lie facedown on the floor while the robber rifled the cash register.

After the gunman dashed from the store, the two victims got up in time to see him speed away in a burgundy-colored automobile. The witnesses said they weren't sure, but they thought the car had been a Ford Pinto and not a Mazda. However, they were certain the gunman looked like the man depicted in the Union County composite, which both witnesses had seen several times on television.

Lieutenant L.M. Wilhelm, of the Salisbury Police Department, said the robber was described as 5 feet 8 inches and weighing 180 pounds. The man wore a plaid shirt, baggy dark pants, and a dark cap. He had been photographed by a surveillance camera.

After viewing the surveillance tape, Salisbury police turned it over to the FBI. "Our officers on the scene decided the description of the man and the car was enough of a connection," Wilhelm explained.

"All I can tell you is, we've gotten a copy of a surveillance tape, and we're attempting to make a determination if there's any connection to the kidnapping," said Rick Mosquera, assistant special agent in charge of the Charlotte FBI office. "Otherwise, we're running down numerous leads about cars that have been seen fitting the description, or someone who might fit the physical description."

With the robbery in Salisbury, investigative attention had shifted heavily into North Carolina. In the Charlotte area, police received a number of calls concerning a burgundy-colored car reportedly parked at the intersection of Interstates 77 and 85. It proved not to be the missing Smith vehicle.

Charlotte and Mecklenburg County officers also had several other promising calls, including one report of a burgundy Mazda in a grocery store parking lot. However, like all the other calls at that point, the car proved not to be connected to the case.

"We have not received any information that proved there was

an actual sighting of the suspect or the two children," Charlotte Deputy Chief Larry Snider said.

Authorities in several North Carolina jurisdictions were closely following the case, since the suspect was reported heading in that direction, and there had been no reports at that time of sightings south and east of Union.

In Rowan County, the sheriff's department received a call from a person who said he had definitely seen the vehicle, the suspect, and the children, but when this lead was run down, it didn't pan out.

"We're hoping something here will come through," said Captain Rick Thibedeaux, "and we're all looking out for cars that look similar. Sometimes folks get too eager to help."

"When you drive away with kids, that touches everyone," Kannapolis Police Chief Paul Brown said. "Our officers have all been talking about it, and we all want to find these kids. It goes beyond being a police officer."

Meanwhile, back at the crime scene in South Carolina, another careful search of the woods around the home Susan Smith went to after the carjacking-kidnapping failed to produce anything of substance.

A team of divers went to nearby John D. Long Lake, a popular recreation area, and spent several hours probing the murky waters adjacent to an asphalt-and-gravel boat landing.

Later that afternoon, Sheriff Wells faced a growing number of newspeople to report on his frustrating day of investigation.

"Never have I worked a case in which there is so little to work with," the tall lawman said, his face drawn with tension and fatigue. "There is actually no crime scene to investigate. We have a missing automobile and two missing children.

"No suspects have been ruled out—none. We are interviewing family members looking for a revenge motive, but so far, this looks like a random act."

In Washington, Attorney General Janet Reno said finding the children would be a top priority for 200 FBI agents, who were now actively involved in the case. A special FBI unit equipped with a computer to track leads in the case was moved to Union. An FBI spokesman said the computer would speed up the investigators' ability to categorize the tips that were now overloading phone lines. The FBI involvement also provided the investigative team with a brand-new Justice Department manual not yet in general circulation. Designed specifically for guidelines involving kidnapped or missing children, the 220-page manual said that in every missing child case, investigators should respond as if the child is in immediate danger. It also said that parents should be polygraphed as soon as possible.

Historically, the majority of missing children cases involve one or the other parent or other family members, frequently provoked by bitter custody battles, the new Justice Department manual noted.

Lawmen began putting together background information on the missing children's parents. Although the Smiths were separated, as soon as the father was informed about the kidnapping, he left his place of employment and rushed to his distraught wife's side.

Pretty Susan Smith was in such a state of collapse when her estranged husband arrived that she had to be literally carried to a couch, where her husband attempted to comfort her. In spite of their separation, the relationship between the couple was amicable, according to relatives and neighbors. Everyone seemed to agree that neither one would ever harm their children. Still, in order to move forward in such an investigation, the Smith family—particularly the parents—had to be eliminated as suspects.

Susan Smith and her husband had first become acquainted in high school, investigators learned. They began a relationship that broke off after six months.

After high school, Smith went to work at a local supermarket, where he soon became assistant manager. Susan went to work at the same store, as a secretary in the office. It was there that the couple resumed their relationship. When Susan became pregnant, the couple married in March 1991, and seven months later, Michael was born.

Later, Susan quit her job at the store and worked at a manufacturing plant that made tassels for furniture.

Initially, the young couple lived in a house owned by a relative, but after their second son, Alex, was born, the couple moved into a neat bungalow in an upscale neighborhood on the north side of town, where they quickly became popular with their neighbors.

It was not long, however, before the Smiths' marriage began having rough spots, and the young couple separated. They reconciled, but in August 1994, they split up again. In September, Susan filed for divorce, charging her husband with adultery. It was agreed that she would have custody of the two boys, but her husband would retain visiting privileges. The husband made use of his right to be with his boys at every possible time.

"Those young'uns really love their daddy," one neighbor remarked to a television news crew who was cruising the neighborhood. "They'd just come running when they saw their dad show up."

Another neighbor recalled that Michael got a big thrill when his father would sit him on his lap as he operated a riding lawn mower. As far as Susan was concerned, there had never been a more doting mother, the news team was told.

Susan Smith was described by a number of friends and acquaintances as the perfect girl next door. She was described as pretty—but not too pretty—and smart—but not too smart. She was liked by everyone, but was not so popular that she was envied by her peers.

"She was just normal, like everybody else," said a classmate and best friend of Smith's during high school. Susan always seemed happy, the woman said, and despite being popular, hadn't dated much.

At Union High School, the senior class of 1989 voted Susan "most friendly."

There had been one other tragedy in Susan Smith's life. When she was seven years old, her father, a municipal employee of

Union, committed suicide. Over time, Susan's mother married again. Susan's friends said she was particularly close to her step-father.

On Thursday, there days after the boys were reported missing, the Smith couple for the first time faced a battery of cameras and reporters.

"I pled to the guy to please return our children to us safely and unharmed," the children's father said, his swollen blue eyes full of tears.

It was obvious to everyone, as the couple clung to each other at the news conference, that they were now united in their grief and concern for their two sons.

Cable News Network and *America's Most Wanted* did special segments on the case. The result was that people from as far away as New York called in tips on supposed sighting of the burgundy Mazda, the missing children, and the suspect. The Smith story was also featured nightly on all three major televi-sion network news programs.

The most promising lead to surface locally was produced by a call from a woman who said she had seen a man wearing muddy clothing similar to what the carjacker had supposedly worn. She reported seeing the man in the area of the Union Industrial Park. Using bloodhounds and helicopters, searchers immediately returned to make another fruitless search. Some children's clothing was found, but it was determined not to be a size that fit either of the missing children.

Investigators also returned to the vicinity where Susan Smith was forced from her vehicle. Lawmen and citizens in four-wheel-drive vehicles, on foot, and on horseback, searched a four-square-mile area, which again included John D. Long Lake, some seven miles from Union.

By Friday, October 28, there had not been one single con-firmed sighting of the Smith car, the suspect, or the children. "It's just as if they have fallen off the face of the earth," said Hugh Munn, spokesman for SLED, emphasizing the lawmen's frustration.

At a news conference, Sheriff Wells was joined by Robert Stewart, chief of SLED. The two lawmen said the investigation was concentrating outside of the Smith family. Wells said a number of family members had been interviewed in the quest for a motive, but none had been found.

"Looking at family members is a normal part of any investigation," Munn reiterated. "The longer it goes on with no sightings, the more people are likely to say that something else [other that a random act] is up, but we have no indication of that."

However, lawmen were putting two faces on the investigation, one that they were maintaining in the command post, and another that was being offered for public consumption.

Intensifying the frustration resulting from so many false leads was the fact that Susan Smith's recollections of what happened on Tuesday night seemed to be filled with contradictions.

The first thing that struck Sheriff Wells as a problem was her statement that she had been stopped at a red light when no other vehicles were around. Wells knew that the light at that particular intersection would have continued to be constantly green in the direction Smith had been going, unless another vehicle on a cross street had tripped the switch to make the light turn red.

The young mother had also said that she had been on her way to visit a friend, but that friend, when interviewed by lawmen, said he knew nothing about Susan's plans and, in fact, was not even home that evening.

Smith said she went with her two children to a local shopping center, where they spent a lot of time, but after interviewing employees at the major discount store there, investigators could find no one who had seen Susan Smith or her two children.

Except for Susan Smith, the last person to have seen the children was the operator of a day car center, who said Susan had picked up her little boys shortly after 5 P.M. After that, no one could recall having seen Susan or the boys, until she showed up at the house on Highway 49 saying someone had stolen her car with her boys inside.

Also, several people who fit the kidnapper's description were interviewed, but none panned out as a suspect. Indeed, these men seemed to be as worried about the missing children as anyone else.

On Friday, investigators spent several hours interviewing the father of the two missing children, leading the media to press for details. The inquiries produced nothing new, but rumors began to spread that Susan Smith had failed a lie detector test. Sheriff Wells denied this, but he did concede that lawmen had been working to clear up some inconsistencies in her statements. Wells said it was understandable that there might be differences in the hysterical young mother's statements "when you realize she's just been through a carjacking."

Lawmen were actually walking a narrow line between the two faces on the investigation. Smith's grief seemed real enough. Whenever an inconsistency cropped up, Susan had been able to explain it away, but the more seasoned detectives were beginning to get "bad vibes." Adding to the other doubts about the mother was a piece of information developed in an interview with the children's father.

Describing the relationship between the two boys and their mother, he said that Michael had a habit of telling his mother to lock their car doors when they were driving somewhere. If that was the case, and Susan normally locked her car doors, how did the gunman manage to open the door on the passenger side?

Despite these nagging doubts, there was nothing concrete to raise the mother to the level of a suspect.

Then, another promising lead surfaced in North Carolina. A tipster reported that he'd seen a man and two children near the Uwharrie National Forest, east of Charlotte. Civilians and law enforcement personnel conducted a 12-hour search in the area, but again, they turned up nothing.

Again, Sheriff Wells faced the media to explain his disappointment. By now, the lanky sheriff had become a familiar figure to a nationwide television audience eagerly following this unfolding drama. Wells's controlled, professional responses to an eager media were delivered with quiet dignity, but it was obvious that he was deeply grieved by the situation.

Despite the frustrations of false leads that hadn't panned out, and despite the fact that he was getting little sleep, Sheriff Wells continued to insist that he was optimistic about the case. Other than being tired, he said, "I'm just as optimistic we'll solve this case as I was the day it started."

Union County citizens were also in an emotional wringer over the case. Everywhere you looked in Union, there were reminders that two beautiful children were in jeopardy. The children's parents were in seclusion in the depths of the county courthouse part of the time and at the home of relatives the rest of the time, while they awaited word concerning their little boys.

Over the weekend, as sharp-eyed deer hunters spread across the countryside, another promising report surfaced. A hunter told lawmen that he had heard what he thought to be a young child crying in the woods. After several hours, the quest turned up nothing. South Carolina lawmen suspected that the hunter may have mistaken the cry of a bobcat for that of a child, a not uncommon mistake, given the animal's humanlike sound.

On Saturday, special prayer services were held at two local churches, and on Sunday, the children and their families were the subject of special prayers.

In Union that weekend, however, the suspicion grew that Susan Smith had perpetrated a terrible hoax.

"You can't help but wonder," said one woman whose husband worked at the same plant where Susan Smith was employed. "I can't believe she left her kids with that man. I'd die before I gave my kids up."

Some black residents of the town were particularly upset with the situation.

One member of the black community angrily said the sketch of the purported suspect "looked like a handbill advertising for the return of a runaway slave."

"They keep trying to blame it on black people," a local mechanic said. "They can't find the car, they can't find the kids, so why are they just looking for black people? They need to look a lot, lot closer to the mama."

Sheriff Wells, who admitted that Susan Smith's recollections of what happened on Tuesday night were inconsistent, insisted that the media "not read into our [continued] contact with her as laying blame."

A female family member, who had assumed the role of spokesperson for the Smiths, said Susan "is holding up" and hopeful her boys would be returned safely. The relative said she had nothing to say regarding speculation that Susan had lied about the carjacking.

"We're not commenting on rumors," she said firmly.

By now, the number of calls coming into Union County had reached such a volume that five additional lines were installed by deputies who were fielding the calls around the clock. Several calls were from people claiming to be psychics who had visions of where the boys would be found. However, Sheriff Wells told the media that lawmen were trying to stick to what would be termed "hard facts."

Meanwhile, two churches in Union held special prayer vigils on Sunday, while the parents of the two missing boys remained in seclusion. Over the weekend, a newspaper story said Susan Smith had failed a polygraph. Once again, speculation about her possible involvement in the boys' disappearance grew strong.

Lawmen denied that Susan had failed a polygraph. In actuality, the test had been ruled inconclusive, chiefly on Smith's response to a question concerning her knowledge of the boys' whereabouts.

On Monday, October 31, six days after the boys disappeared, lawmen converged on Chester County to the south and east of Union. Sheriff Wells had received a tip that the children had been sighted there. As a result of this tip, investigators searched the banks of a canal off the Broad River, as well as the cold waters of the river itself. Again, there was no sign of the children, the missing car, or the suspect.

With each report of a sighting, hopes for the safe return of the children would soar, only to be dashed by reality.

There was speculation about the young man whom Susan Smith planned to visit the night the children disappeared. But that was squashed when he became the subject of a television interview. Until that time, there had been reports the Smith was romantically involved with the young man, although investigators had denied this.

Although he had attended school with Susan Smith, the textile worker was, in fact, involved with another young woman, who was also friends with Susan. A relative of the young man recalled that the couple came in crying the night the boys disappeared, after they found out about the kidnapping of their friend's children.

On Tuesday, November 1, the Smith family spokesperson read a statement to the media.

"It's a nightmare that seems to have no end," she read. "We can't feed them, we can't wipe away their tears, we can't hold them, we can't hug them. The hardest part of all is not knowing where they are."

Then, seeming to address the missing children, the woman read, "You both have to be brave and hold onto each other, because we are doing everything in our power to get you back home where you belong. We love you."

The family spokesperson said that the parents had decided to communicate in this fashion because they were too upset to speak directly.

Sheriff Wells said he was now advising the Smiths not to speak to reporters who were unfair and overbearing. "I don't know what happened in this case, but I am treating it as a carjacking that happened as it was reported," the sheriff said. For the first time, Wells appeared a little testy with the news media. The sheriff again refused to comment on another report that Susan Smith had failed a second polygraph examination.

Less than 12 hours later, Wells would receive a telephone call that would send his hopes soaring that at least one of the Smith children was alive and safe.

The call, which came at 3 A.M., was from police in Seattle, Washington. Early the next morning, Wells greeted the media with the report that the most promising lead yet had surfaced. He would not elaborate at the time, but his hopes had been buoyed by a call, and it was "going to take some time," he said, to check it out.

In Seattle, a motel clerk had called police to report that a young child, who bore a striking resemblance to the missing 14-month-old Alex Smith, had been left at the motel by a man driving an automobile with South Carolina license plates.

Later that morning, however, Wells's hopes were dashed when Seattle police called to say they had determined the child in the motel was not Alex Smith.

Sean O'Donnel, of the Seattle police, said, "If you look at the comparison photos, you have to look a second time to see if there is a difference between that boy and Alex Smith."

As it turned out, the child in Seattle was from South Carolina and in the custody of his mother. The father had been visiting the child, but no explanation was made as to why he had left the toddler in the motel.

"I am disappointed," Sheriff Wells said. "But this does not lead me to believe this case will not be solved." There was a tome to the statement that led a number of media people to feel that the weary sheriff knew something he was not yet ready to talk about.

Virtually on the heels of that heart-wrenching experience, police in Macon, Georgia, came up with two children who at first were thought to be the missing Smith boys. Momentarily, the thrust of the new information relieved speculation that investigators were onto something in the immediate vicinity that had an important bearing on the case.

However, again, the children spotted in Georgia were not those missing from Union, and there was another round of trying to overcome disappointment.

When questioned again, Sheriff Wells said that investigators were trying to turn up information from people near the crime scene.

"We are looking at everything," Wells said. Asked again if he was looking at the family members as suspects, he said, "I'm not implicating anyone."

After the report from Seattle was cleared up, Susan Smith and her husband agreed to face the media.

Meanwhile, investigators had begun to pursue information that Susan Smith had recently become upset over the breakup of a relationship with a man she'd been dating. An informant said the young man had told Susan in a letter the week before the children disappeared that, among other things, he was not ready to assume responsibility for children, and was, therefore, ending their relationship.

This young man was not immediately identified, but it was later learned that he was the son of the chief executive officer at the company where Susan was employed. Probers were forced to consider the troublesome possibility that the boys may have been in the way of their mother's romance and that only she had a strong enough motive to get rid of them.

SLED Agent Lansing Logan was a constant companion of Susan Smith during the hours and days she waited in the Union County Courthouse basement while the investigation dragged on. His impressions of the young woman would weigh heavily in actions that would take place in two days.

Adding impetus to the continued monitoring of Susan Smith's activities and demeanor was further information concerning the "Dear Jane" letter she had received. A Charlotte attorney contacted Sheriff Wells to say he wanted to give the sheriff a copy of that letter. The young man, employed at the same plant as Susan Smith, had written the letter on a computer, the lawyer said, and it had not been erased.

At his afternoon press conference, Sheriff Wells said, "We're regrouping right now. Nothing has changed. We're still doing the same thing." Wells also said he would urge the parents to make a public plea for the safe return of their boys within a few days.

On Wednesday, November 2, eight days after the toddlers disappeared, police went to Susan Smith's home to conduct a thorough search. Sheriff Wells offered no information concerning what lawmen were looking for, but he said strong consideration was being given to offering a substantial reward for information. It was reported that donors had offered to provide a $50,000 reward.

That same day, at Sheriff Wells's suggestion, Susan Smith made a public plea for her sons' safe return.

"It just seems so unfair for somebody to take two such beautiful children," she said. "I don't understand. I have to put all my trust and faith in the Lord that He is taking care of them and that He will bring them home to us.

"There's not one minute that has gone by that I do not think about the boys. And I pray that whoever has them, that the Lord will let them realize that they are missed and loved more than any children in this world.

"I just know, I just feel in my heart that you're okay, that you guys take care of each other. Your mama and your daddy are going to be right here waiting on you when you get home."

The following morning, both parents appeared on national television to again plead for their children's return. For the first time, Susan Smith acknowledged that she was aware people were saying she had perpetrated a hoax. "It hurts to know I may be accused," she said, "but I do understand why they would do what they are doing."

Soon after that emotional display, Susan Smith was back in the basement of the courthouse, where she was subjected to some probing questions. Later, she was taken from the sheriff's office to a local church where, after spending some time with Sheriff Wells, she agreed to tell him where to find her children.

Once again, Sheriff Wells contacted the State Department of Natural Resources to request a diving team. It fell to two men from that team to go to John D. Long Lake for what would turn out to be the final search for the children.

The depths of the lake had been searched twice before without results, but this time, with information provided by Susan Smith, a sonar was used and the missing car showed up on the screen.

The two divers, armed with powerful lights, entered deep, murky waters and quickly located the missing burgundy Mazda in 18 feet of water. The car lay some 100 feet from the end of a gravel-and-asphalt ramp leading downward to the lake. Previous searches had not been successful because divers had not gone far enough out from the bank to locate the vehicle. The car lay upside down. Hanging strapped in their safety seats in the backseat were the tiny bodies of Michael and Alex Smith.

There was hardly a dry eye among the gathered lawmen who had worked so long and hard, hoping and praying for the safe return of the toddlers, when the vehicle, spewing water from every crack, was hauled into view. After the car was pulled from the lake, the decomposing bodies were taken to the Medical University of South Carolina in Charleston for autopsies. There, a physician determined that the boys had drowned, and since toxicology reports showed no drugs in the bodies, it would be assumed that the children were awake when the car rolled down the ramp and carried them to their lawful deaths.

At 7 P.M. that night, Sheriff Wells stood before a crowd of some 300 grim-faced people and announced that Susan Smith had confessed to sending the car down the boat ramp into the lake with her two sons strapped in their safety seats in the back.

The tragic news shocked the nation. Veteran lawmen, who had spent nine days working and hoping to find the toddlers safe, stood and wept openly as Wells made the announcement.

Violence threatened to erupt in the crowd ringing the area where Wells made his announcement, leading officers to block off the main street in order to control the angry crowd. Cries of "God, no!" could be heard as the grim-faced sheriff told the crowd that Susan Smith would be charged with two counts of murder, and that her car with the two little boys strapped inside had been found in the lake.

After making the announcement, the bone-weary, emotionally drained Wells refused to take questions from the media. Later in the evening, however, he spoke briefly with reporters. "I'm very devastated and disappointed," Wells said. He added that Susan Smith was being held at an undisclosed location and that a bond hearing would be held the following morning in neighboring York County.

Hugh Munn, the spokesman for SLED, said that Smith had been suspected all along, but investigators had feared that if they pushed her too hard on the whereabouts of her children, she might have committed suicide and the mystery of the children might never have been solved.

Although no firm motive was established, one investigator, who spoke on the condition of anonymity, said the children's deaths were a result of pressures Susan Smith had felt over the breakup of her relationship and the responsibility of the children.

The emotional toll on lawmen who had worked long and hard on the case would be articulated later by Sheriff Wells. "I feel like I have aged ten years in ten days," he said. It was a case, he said, that tore down the wall between personal and professional feelings and had affected every member of his department. Lawmen agreed that spouses and colleagues had helped them get through the case that had strained them as never before.

Captain Frank Thomas, chief of the five-man detective unit in the sheriff's department, said everyone had clung to the hope until the last possible second that the little boys would not be in the car when it was pulled from the water.

"We hoped she might have lied and they wouldn't be in there."

Thomas said after the car was removed from the water, he called his wife to have a change of clothes brought down for another overnight stay. He then walked to the intersection near the lake where his wife dropped off his clothes. "That was my chance to get my head screwed back on straight," Thomas said. "By myself, I had some tears.

"I reckon in nineteen years I've sort of built up a wall between my personal feelings and the job," the veteran detective said in an emotional statement. "I've had to. You deal with people's feelings, their hurt. Some things break that wall down. When we found out what happened—when we found those kids—it crumbled that wall."

The following day, what purported to be a portion of Susan Smith's confession was read during a television newscast.

"I wanted to end my life so bad and was in my car, ready to go down that ramp into the water. I did go partway, but I stopped. I went again and I stopped. Then I got out of the car a nervous wreck."

Later, Smith said, she put the car in gear, got out, and watched as it moved slowly down the ramp and out into the lake.

"I took off running and screaming, saying, 'Oh, God—Oh, no, God, what have I done?'"

The shock and heartbreak from the discovery of the bodies came in varying degrees. Aside from the lawmen who had been closest to the tragedy from the outset, it was probably felt most strongly on the street where the victims lived.

On the day after the Mazda was hauled from the lake, a neighbor from across the street sat and stared at the now-deserted Smith house. In the carport, a number of shiny toys were neatly lined against the wall. There were two red Roadmaster wagons, a red, blue and yellow "roaring choo-choo train," a Thomas tank engine with wide, innocent eyes, and a big-nosed and smiling Fred Flintstone, hand raised in a wave.

"I used to stand right here and watch them play," the neighbor said. She then began to cry.

"I just wish somebody would move those toys," she said. "It breaks my heart to see them. I felt like those two children were my own. They were always so playful and happy. I just don't know how she could have done this. She seemed like such a loving mother. Through it all, I stood by her. Now I don't know what to think. I'm just crushed."

Other neighbors, a retired couple, were particularly grief-stricken by the deaths. Their sadness was even harder because they had lost two sons of their own, one at age 27 in a drowning, and the other at age 15 to leukemia.

With tear-filled eyes, the neighbor held her husband's hand as she talked. "We could sit in our living room and watch them playing on the lawn," she said. "They were so sweet. They were so small. They were just little bitty things. They'd get out and play and sprinkle water on each other.

"It's hard to know those kids were alive and in that water just like my son."

The bright yellow ribbons that the couple had placed on their mailbox while the two boys were still missing had now been replaced by blue and white ones. "In memory of those boys," the woman explained.

In their window, they still lit two candles each night, she said. Between them was a copy of the familiar photograph that had been used on missing-person posters during the nine days the children were missing.

Another elderly man who lived on the block said he was like another grandfather to the two boys. Speaking with difficulty, he explained that his daughter was best friends with Susan Smith. "I knew those children real well," he said. "I loved them to death. Everything was special about them. Michael was my little helper. Anything I was into, he was right there."

The announcement of Susan Smith's arrest still came as a surprise to most people.

"I kind of felt from the way she talked that something wasn't right, but I just couldn't bring myself to believe she had done something to her children," said a courthouse employee.

"For that matter, it's hard to comprehend even now. I feel sorry for the father. He obviously had been standing behind her through all this even though she was divorcing him . . . and all the rest of the family, too, on both sides. What a horrible thing to have to go through."

The outpouring of sympathy wasn't limited to Union County and its citizens. By Saturday morning, a steady stream of people were going to the lake where the two youngsters had been drowned, leaving flowers and messages of condolence.

On Friday, November 4, a bond hearing for Susan Smith was held at which she made no personal appearance. Her attorney made no motion for bond. Later that day, Smith was transferred to the Broad River Correctional Facility for women at Columbia, where she was placed under a suicide watch.

Once again, a large crowd gathered at the Union courthouse where Smith was prepared for the trip to Columbia. Manacled with her hands in front of her, the suspect struck a prayerlike pose as she entered the car with SLED agents.

The emotion that affected much of the crowd was expressed by one mother of three who screamed, "Murderer! Murderer! Murderer!" as the car left the parking lot. "They need to burn her," the woman sobbed.

Others were not so vehement. Many offered prayers, not only for the accused, but for her family, as well.

Meanwhile, funeral services for the little boys were scheduled for Sunday, with visitation planned for Saturday night, November 5.

Among those attending the visitation was Sheriff Wells, who stood in line for half an hour before reaching the white casket that held the boys' bodies. The victims' father, overcome with grief and shock, was standing nearby. When Wells reached the casket, he embraced the father, whose knees buckled as he said in a sobbing voice. "Thank you."

The next day, a brief service for the slain children was held. The outpouring of sympathy in the form of flowers reached such a level that it took five tents to display floral arrangements.

In Seattle, best-selling author Ann Rule became aware of the case.

"The minute I heard about it, I had my own feelings of déjà

vu," said the former-policewoman-turned-author. Rule was remembering the case of Diane Downs, a Eugene, Oregon, woman who claimed that a stranger flagged her down one night in May 1983, shot her three children, and wounded her in the arm. Rule spent three years researching and writing her best-seller *Small Sacrifices*, which detailed the investigation that finally resulted in Diane Downs's conviction.

"My first reaction [to the Smith case] was, 'Oh, that poor mother,' " Rule said, "but later on I grew skeptical. Most mothers would die protecting their babies."

Fueling anger against Smith after her arrest was one report that said on the night the car went into the lake, the two boys were asleep until just before the vehicle hit the water. At that point, Smith allegedly said, Michael woke up and began struggling to free himself.

This scenario was vehemently denied by David Bruck, a Columbia attorney representing Smith. The story was being spread to stir ill feelings toward his client, Bruck said.

On Monday, January 16, 1995, a tearful and obviously distraught Susan Smith was arraigned at the Union County Courthouse.

Upon announcing that he was seeking the death penalty, Prosecutor Thomas Pope told reporters, "Some people think I'm extremely callous with the handling of this case. It's not that I'm without sympathy. Sometimes you have to operate and cut out the problem rather than letting it heal over."

"Her mental state was deteriorating," commented Defense Attorney Bruck. "The death penalty is beside the point. Those who worry that Susan will not be punished ought to spend twenty years inside her head. She is lost in an ocean of grief and guilt."

The trial of Susan Smith likely won't take place until the midsummer of 1995. Until the court makes its decision, Susan Smith must be considered innocent of all the charges against her.

Meanwhile, speculation as to why the murders happened will continue to haunt the citizens of Union. The town has a lot healing to do, with ministers and Sheriff Wells working to mend relationships with the town's black community, which feels betrayed by the false tale of a stereotyped black man kidnapping two white children.

Strangers continue to visit John D. Long Lake, bringing flowers and other memorials to Michael and Alex Smith. A week after the funeral, a couple who said they had driven over 400 miles, stood staring at the dark waters that had concealed two little boys for nine terrible days.

"We just had to come here," the man explained as his wife held his hand and tears ran down her cheeks. "We thought if we came, we might get some understanding."

It was a plaintive plea, which the dark waters did not answer.

" 'THELMA & LOUISE' RAN DOWN THEIR GAL PAL OVER & OVER!"

by Charles W. Sasser

It was a case, Oklahoma lawmen said, that from the beginning was almost too weird to believe. While nearby Tulsa had been plagued by a record number of homicides in 1993, the Creek County Sheriff's Department, headquartered in Sapulpa, had worked only three—and for some reason, they had all been bizarre. One was the case of Rose Mary Miller who took her foreign lover to a pond bank and shot him through the head because "she just didn't like men."

And now—someone was speeding around the county, talking about having a corpse in a car trunk.

Creek County sheriff Doug Nichols's office in Sapulpa received its first telephone complaint about the corpse in the trunk at 3:53 A.M. on Monday, March 22, 1993. The caller identified himself as Terry Watts from Mounds, a tiny town about 10 miles south of Sapulpa.

"Some women just telephoned me and said they killed a woman named Robbie and put her in the trunk of their car," Watts began. "They said they killed her because she tried to be a lesbian with them. They don't know what to do with the body, so they're on their way to my house now to show it to me. They said they wanted me to help them dispose of the body and give them money for gas. They sounded drunk. I don't know whether to believe them or not, but they sounded convincing."

Was it a prank call? A hoax?

Police have learned that truth is frequently more astounding than fiction. They can never afford to take any complaint lightly. The dispatcher cast about for a patrol car deputy near enough to Mounds to check out the call.

Creek County, Oklahoma, encompasses a massive territory of roughly 900 square miles, from Keystone Lake, northwest of Tulsa, south for nearly 40 miles. Usually, less than a dozen deputies patrol that vast area at any one time. Before the sheriff's dispatcher could locate a deputy near Mounds, complainant Terry Watts telephoned a second time. Now he sounded frantic.

"Those women with the dead body—they just pulled up in front of my house!" he said frantically. "I'm not going to answer the door."

Apparently, Watts didn't answer the door for lawmen, either. When khaki-uniformed deputies arrived, shortly before 4:30 A.M., they reported finding Watts locked inside his house.

"Did you see the body?" the deputies asked him.

"No," Watts replied. "But they said they had one when they called. They knocked on my door, but I wouldn't answer. So they drove away."

April Fool's Day was only a little more than a week away. Maybe this was someone's idea of a joke. Still, hoax or not, the police could take no chances. The deputies broadcast an APB (All-Points Bulletin) describing the women and their vehicle and asking lawmen in northeastern Oklahoma to keep their eyes peeled.

"Possible corpse in the car trunk," the APB advised.

The vehicle was described as a light-colored, four-door sedan—an older-model Ford, perhaps. It was said to be driven by two "hard-looking" brunettes named "Carol" and "Glenda." Terry Watts did not know where these women lived, and he knew little about their personal lives. He indicated that he had recently met them in a cheap Sapulpa tavern.

Like fish at sea, the pair could easily lose themselves in Creek County. Hundreds of miles of road—including an expressway, a turnpike, and a maze of lesser blacktops and gravel farm-to-market roads—webbed the county, connecting a score of small towns and communities.

As dawn crept into the eastern sky above "Green Country," a tag that the tourist bureau applied to northeastern Oklahoma, lawmen in Creek County and in the Tulsa metropolitan area had still made no progress in finding Carol and Glenda and the alleged corpse in their car trunk. In fact, many officers expressed little faith in the APB report.

"You don't kill somebody and then go around showing off the corpse," was the way one officer put it.

Before Monday ended, however, Undersheriff Mark Ihrig and Creek County Detective Larry Fugate would be tracing a lead in Sapulpa to where Jackson Avenue curved and then ended abruptly in Kelly Lane Park. They were checking out a report that a 19-year-old woman who lived near the park had observed something unusual during the night.

According to her statement to the detectives, she heard some sort of loud noise on the dead-end street near the park shortly after midnight on Sunday. Drawn to her window, the woman peered into the darkness. The street was not well lit.

"I saw the taillights of a car traveling forward," she said. "It went in reverse and came to a stop. Two women got out of the car and put something in the backseat. I saw what looked like a leg sticking up. I shouted to ask them if everything was okay, but they just drove off."

"Can you describe the car?" one of the detectives asked.

"It might have been older and light-colored."

"And the women?"

"They were white, pretty good-sized women."

That was about all the information the young woman could provide. It proved sufficient, however, to help corroborate Terry

Watts's story that Carol and Glenda, whoever they were, just might have a corpse in the trunk of their car. By this time, too, other witnesses were relaying strange stories to Creek County deputies.

As Sunday night seeped into Monday dawn and then into broad daylight, sightings of Carol and Glenda and the locations of these sightings merged into a rather confusing montage. Apparently, the two women were making the rounds of acquaintances, offering to show off the prize in their car trunk.

One of the first reported sightings came early Monday morning in Terlton, a community about 25 miles northwest of Sapulpa, near Keystone Lake. There, the two women unexpectedly appeared at the rural home of a man they knew slightly. According to subsequent accounts of the encounter, the women sought advice on what they should do with their recently deceased traveling companion.

"They told me they had a dead woman in the trunk!" the man later exclaimed. "They acted like they didn't think I believed them. They offered to show me the body to prove it. I told them I didn't see anything and I didn't want to know anything."

So far, no one had actually viewed the reported corpse.

By this time, Carol was being described as a white female in her late 30s or early 40s, about 5 feet 7 inches or so in height, weighing 160 pounds, with long dark hair. She wore glasses and had a prominent nose.

Glenda was described as about 40 years old, slightly shorter than Carol, but heavier—maybe 200 pounds. She wore her light-brown hair relatively short. Her nose appeared slightly pugged.

The macabre saga of Carol and Glenda and the corpse in their trunk continued. The next sighting of the duo reportedly occurred not far from the little Keystone Lake town of Mannford. According to Detective Fugate, Carol and Glenda had apparently been drinking heavily. Carol lost control of her vehicle on a narrow two-lane blacktop and the car slid into a ditch.

Unable to extract the automobile from the ditch, the women walked to a nearby farmhouse, where they telephoned an ex-convict friend named Mel Boggs to come pull the vehicle out. It was about 8 A.M. when Boggs arrived at the scene of the mishap.

Upon questioning the ex-convict later, Detective Fugate learned that Boggs was taken by surprise to discover that the women he'd rescued were hauling a body around Creek County. Boggs related how the pair told him they panicked when they first ran into the ditch and decided to get rid of their victim's remains. They dragged the dead woman out of the trunk and carried her into the woods that lined either side of the road.

This accomplished, they had second thoughts about it. What if the body was found and someone remembered seeing the two women with their car stuck in the ditch?

So Carol and Glenda lumbered back into the woods and lugged the body back to the road and stuffed it once again into the car trunk.

"Do you want to see it?" they reportedly asked Mel Boggs.

"Well, I didn't see it," Boggs told officers. "I didn't want to look at it."

So once again, a witness had not actually viewed the corpse. That meant the deputies might still be chasing about the county on an April Fool's joke.

"But," Boggs recalled, "they said the woman they killed was named Robbie Harris."

Robbie Harris. Finally, the probers had a full name—a name that could be checked out and could be confirmed as an actual person.

Police subsequently disclosed that 34-year-old Robbie Sue Harris, a Sapulpa resident, was a thin sparrow of a woman—5 feet 3 inches and 95 pounds—who had not been seen since sometime during the day on Sunday. A police records check revealed her to be an ex-convict who'd served time for writing bogus checks. A visit to her residence on West 65th Avenue revealed no one home. Robbie Sue Harris was apparently missing.

Her relatives and friends vehemently denied that she would have made any sexual advances toward another woman, as Carol and Glenda had contended was their motive for snuffing her.

"This was totally opposite of Robbie Sue's character!" one of the missing woman's relatives exclaimed. "Robbie Sue has two living children and one that's deceased. Our family totally disputes [that she was a lesbian]."

A woman now married to Robbie Sue's ex-husband agreed that Harris would never even consider homosexuality.

"Robbie Sue has had some rough times, but she was on the way to recovery," the woman said. "She was going to Alcoholics Anonymous and attending church on a regular basis."

So far, said Detective Fugate, the lean, boyish-looking veteran of the sheriff's department who had worked some of its most challenging cases, this investigation was the oddest he had ever conducted. Most probes, he said, began with the finding of a murdered victim. Police worked out the leads and evidence until they isolated a suspect.

This case, on the other hand, had suspects at the beginning—but no concrete proof of an actual victim. The case, what there was of it, seemed to have started where most other investigations ended.

The status of the probe changed dramatically shortly before noon on Monday. At 11:31 A.M., Paul Douglas, from the community of Kellyville, south of Sapulpa, logged in at the sheriff's department with news that he had actually seen a dead woman crammed into a car trunk. And the dead woman's name, he said, was Robbie Sue Harris.

According to Sheriff Nichols, Douglas said that Robbie Sue and he had been out together on Sunday evening at the Wagon Wheel Lounge in Sapulpa. At about 11:30 P.M. Robbie Sue wanted to go see an old friend whom she hadn't seen in several years. She wanted to sell the old friend a TV set.

Robbie Sue and Douglas took off in Robbie Sue's cream-colored Mercury. They drove west out of Sapulpa on State Road 33, then turned south on 245th West Avenue, toward Heyburn Lake. They followed the country gravel road to an isolated "shack" where two women greeted them. The women seemed to have been drinking heavily.

Robbie Sue jumped out of the car and hugged the women.

"They hugged and kissed like long-lost sisters," Douglas said.

The three women and Douglas sat around at the shack drinking, until Robbie Sue apparently became angry at Douglas because he wouldn't give her five dollars with which to buy drugs. The woman hopped into the Mercury and drove Douglas back to where he had left his pickup truck parked at the Wagon Wheel Lounge in Sapulpa. By that time, it was 12:30 A.M. on Monday.

"That was the last I seen of them that night," Douglas said.

Near 10:30 A.M., however, Robbie Sue's Mercury appeared at Douglas's house in Kellyville, driven by Robbie Sue's chums. Robbie Sue was not in the car—at least not visibly so.

"I killed the bitch!" proclaimed the taller woman, whom Douglas knew as Carol Weaver.

Weaver unlocked the car trunk. "Here the bitch is," she said.

Douglas said he looked into the trunk and gasped when he saw Robbie Sue all curled up inside. She was obviously dead.

"They wanted me to help bury her and burn the body," Douglas told the investigators. "I told them to get the hell out of there."

The second woman, Glenda, "said she had nothing to do with the killing," Douglas recalled. "I told her to get away from Carol, but she said she couldn't."

Glenda and Carol left Kellyville with Robbie Sue Harris still in the trunk of her own car, a cream-colored 1984 Mercury. Earlier witnesses had apparently been mistaken about the vehicle being a Ford. Douglas said he immediately sped to Sapulpa to report the encounter to the sheriff.

At least the detectives now had a firm lead on the suspects—Carol's last name—and eyewitness confirmation of a corpse in the trunk. The police Records and Wanteds section isolated the name Carol Ann Weaver. Douglas identified her as the correct suspect. She had been arrested for a number of petty offenses, the police computer indicated, and was an ex-convict for grand larceny.

Apparently, the confused and drunken suspects were having a difficult time deciding what to do with their skinny corpse.

From questioning the night's crop of witnesses, the police concluded that the women had considered burying it, burning it, or dumping it in the woods. Whatever they did with it, they couldn't keep hauling it around forever.

Paul Douglas provided the investigators with directions to Carol Weaver's shack near Heyburn Lake. Deputies Frank Smith, Don Turner and Tim Richison dashed for the rural residence, hoping they might nab the female perps before they could get rid of the body. A corpse in the car trunk was much stronger evidence than a body recovered days or weeks later from somewhere else, or not recovered at all.

Deputies found Carol Weaver's shack deserted. It was shortly after noon on a bright, clear Monday.

The lawmen settled down to wait. Sooner or later, they reasoned, Weaver had to come home, if for no other reason than to pack her bags to leave town.

Less than an hour later, the patient officers spotted a cream-colored sedan barreling along the dusty road toward them. While it was still a good half-mile away, however, the sedan abruptly braked. Apparently, the suspects had spotted the policemen. The car turned around in the middle of the road and started back the same way it had come.

The three deputies in separate patrol cars gave chase. The suspects' car, they saw, was a cream-colored Mercury occupied by two females. It stopped immediately when the pursuing cruisers flashed emergency lights. According to subsequent accounts, Carol Weaver turned to her companions and muttered, "Glenda, this is it. We're through. I'm glad it's over."

Weaver slowly got out of the car as Deputy Turner approached.

"What's going on?" Turner asked her cautiously.

"You know what's going on," Weaver replied. "What you're looking for is in the trunk and the keys are in the ignition."

The deputies opened the trunk and stared at a corpse, in a

fetal position, of a slightly built young woman in whose body rigor mortis had already settled. From the condition of the body, the sleuths estimated that Robbie Sue Harris had been inside the trunk being chauffered all over Creek County since shortly after midnight—a time span of roughly 12 hours. The body was clad in jeans and bra, but the shirt had been partially ripped off.

When Dr. Ronald F. DiStefano, of the State Medical Examiner's Office, autopsied the remains, he reported that the victim, before she died, suffered 10 broken ribs on her left side, along with a damaged liver, injuries to the lower extremities, and blunt trauma to the chest and abdomen.

"I think it's probable," he concluded, "that she was rolled over by the wheels of a car."

The deputies arrested 37-year-old Carol Ann Weaver and 42-year-old Glenda Lois Jones. Like Weaver, Jones was an ex-convict, having been previously convicted of robbery.

By midafternoon, Detective Fugate was videotaping the suspects' confessions. Not only did the women confess, but Weaver also provided graphic demonstrations on film of how the murder was accomplished. The videotape became vital evidence in Creek County DA Lantz McLain's efforts to persuade a jury that the defendants were guilty of first-degree murder.

The defense attorneys immediately took an opposite viewpoint. "I am anticipating that when you hear all the evidence," argued Weaver's attorney, "[you will conclude] that it was a tragic, tragic accident. . . ."

"I didn't beat [Robbie Sue] to death," Carol Weaver insisted. "I was drunk . . . tired . . . I'd been up for days."

In her taped statement to the police and in subsequent testimony, Weaver said she had last slept several days before that fateful Sunday night, and then only for four hours. She claimed that she went on a "final drinking binge" because she was due to check herself into a detoxification unit for alcohol abuse on March 22, the same day she was arrested.

After Robbie Sue joined Glenda Jones and her on Sunday night, Weaver said, the three women ditched Paul Douglas and then went out to celebrate together. Jones and Weaver had not seen Robbie Sue in "five or six—maybe eight—years."

With Robbie Sue driving, the three friends began to look for a "party." While cruising Sapulpa, Weaver said, Robbie suddenly reached over and "she felt my crouch. I said, 'You bitch, don't you ever do that again.' I hit her once and tried to again, but I missed."

Detective Fugate recalled that Weaver denied during questioning that she was prone to violence.

"I'm not really a violent person," she said, "but I don't like anybody touching me like she did."

In her confession, Weaver said she ordered Robbie Sue to stop the car. She then dragged the much-smaller woman out of the car and "kicked her about six times. I jumped on her. I was hitting her, kicking her and stomping on her face. [Robbie Sue] was saying, 'Please, Carol. Please, Carol.' I told her to get back in the car . . . I guess I just tripped out on her . . . 'No, you bitch' I told her. 'I'm driving. Get your ass in the back of the car!' "

Weaver was driving now. Harris was cowering in the backseat. Jones, who was in the front passenger seat, leaned over toward the back and pummeled Robbie Sue some more. She explained to the detectives that she beat the victim because she held a grudge from five years earlier, when Robbie Sue, then in prison, sent Glenda's then-husband a photograph of Robbie dressed only in her bra and panties.

"I didn't even keep [Glenda] off her," Weaver explained in her confession. "I should've, but I didn't. She'd already made me mad."

Weaver said she drove to Kelly Lane Park because "I was going to kick her ass again . . . give her a good old-fashioned ass-whipping."

At the park, Robbie Sue jumped from the car in an attempt to escape.

"Before I knew it," Weaver said, "Glenda said she was out of the car."

Weaver said she threw the car into reverse, hit the gas, and immediately heard two "clunks."

"Carol, you ran over her!" Glenda Jones cried.

The women jumped out and saw Robbie Sue's legs protruding from underneath the car. They dragged the whimpering woman out from under the car and stuffed her into the backseat and took off again.

"Carol—help me! Help me!" the injured woman begged. "I can't breathe."

"I could tell she was crying," Jones confided to Detective Fugate. "Carol said she didn't care."

Instead of rushing the victim to a hospital, the two women continued drinking and looking for a place to buy more beer. About 15 minutes after the episode in the park, Robbie Sue stopped breathing. Carol and Glenda stuffed the body into the car trunk and began their mad odyssey all over Creek County.

"What we needed," Weaver later testified, "[was someone] to tell us something—anybody. We were in shock, drunk, tired, scared. What we needed was someone to sit us down . . . and sober us up."

Prosecutor McLain argued that the two accused women were sober enough and aware enough to drive the car, stop and buy gas, buy more beer, make phone calls to friends telling them what they had done, and drive by friends' houses to show them the body.

When they were stopped by the police, Weaver said, they had finally decided on a method of getting rid of the body. She and Glenda, Weaver said, were en route to her house to pick up a gasoline can, after which they intended to buy gas and take Robbie Sue and her Mercury to the nearby Sunrise Cemetery and set fire to both.

". . . That's the idea I had," Weaver admitted on tape. "If I hadn't been stopped, I don't know that I wouldn't have done it . . . Neither of us wanted to do it."

On Tuesday, March 23, DA McLain filed charges against the two women—first-degree murder, larceny of an automobile, and robbery by force. The women reportedly told the detectives that they took Harris's purse from her, along with several items of jewelry.

Carol Weaver's trial began on September 21, 1993. On September 23, a Creek County jury found the ex-convict guilty of first-degree murder. She was sentenced to serve the remainder of her natural life in the Oklahoma State Penitentiary.

The next month, in October, Glenda Jones pleaded guilty to accessory to murder and received a sentence of 20 years in prison.

Both women are currently serving their sentences.

"DEADLY TEEN LOVERS IN THE MESQUITE FLATS CAMPGROUND"

by Russell P. Kimball

She wanted a better life. Fifty years old and desperately lonely, she wanted to be loved. Instead, she died alone, shot in the back, robbed, and violated after death. The macabre killing, first reported only on the back pages of Phoenix newspapers, eventually captured headlines and proved to Arizona residents that what they thought existed only in the movies could actually happen.

It began late Saturday afternoon, October 19, 1991, when a dispatcher for a power company contacted Arizona's Maricopa County Sheriff's Office. The dispatcher said one of their employees had discovered a body in the back of a pickup at the Mesquite Flats campground beside the Verde River.

The spot is a remote yet idyllic wilderness area about a mile downstream from Horseshoe Dam and approximately 35 miles northeast of Phoenix. This is a land of limestone cliffs and coyotes, gullies choked with Palo Verde trees, and mesquite thickets where wildcats shriek and geckos do push-ups on flat rocks.

Deputies Steve Glennie and Tom Champion, dispatched by the sheriff's office to the high-desert campground, met with the power company employee who found the body. The employee told the deputies that he was directed to the body by two men who had stumbled across it while looking for a place to camp, then led the lawmen to a clearing 30 feet above the river. There, a brown two-tone 1981 Nissan King Cab pickup truck was parked beneath a large mesquite tree.

Deputy Glennie walked cautiously to the truck, careful not to step on anything with potential evidentiary value. He memorized the route so he could follow the same one out, and later show detectives where he'd walked.

The victim was a fair-haired woman who appeared to be in her early 50s. She lay faceup in the bed of the truck, her head lolling to one side. Her brown eyes were open but veiled with the heavy-lidded stare of the dead. Dried blood was smeared across her forehead and streaked the bridge of her nose. Across her chest lay a dingy sheepskin blanket. She was fully clothed, except for shoes and socks, but her black stirrup pants had been pulled down on her hips, revealing pubic hair.

When he lifted the sheepskin, Glennie saw that the victim's shirt was blood-soaked. She had no pulse, was cold to the touch, and showed signs of lividity. Though Glennie could smell the unmistakable stench of decay, the scant decomposition of flesh suggested she had been dead only a day or two.

Glennie radioed headquarters to report that the woman had apparently been murdered and to request homicide detectives.

Meanwhile, Deputy Champion sealed the area with yellow crime scene ribbon and began interviewing a crowd of onlookers. Most were campers lured from their campsites by the commotion of the arriving sheriff's cars and by rumors of murder. Several people in the crowd admitted that they walked up to the truck to gawk at the victim before deputies arrived. No one there, however, knew who she was.

One young man said he had been turned away from a campsite near the Nissan late Friday night. As he drove with his girlfriend toward the area, a Mexican or Indian man leaped from the brush at the side of the dirt road to block their vehicle's path. The dark-clad man claimed that the spaces ahead were reserved, and in no uncertain terms, he suggested that they select another site.

The camper and his girlfriend would later work with a forensic artist to produce a drawing of the man they had encountered.

Dave Carson, 46, told Champion that he arrived at the campground about twilight on Friday, but he hadn't seen the victim or her truck. A gunshot awakened him at 10 o'clock that night. He crawled out of his tent to investigate. Minutes later, he heard voices, then another shot followed by a "rebel yell."

Carson's account got weirder. He rambled on about hearing a cat meowing for two hours after the gunshots. Bragging about being a Vietnam veteran who was well schooled in weaponry, he said he was sure the shots had come from a 9mm pistol.

While Champion was taking Carson's statement, Glennie ran the Nissan's tags and came up with the name of a registered owner: Alice Marie Cameron, of Cave Creek, a cowboy enclave northeast of Phoenix. A driver's license check of Cameron's name produced a physical description that closely matched that of the dead woman.

Within two hours, four homicide detectives and a crime lab technician arrived at the scene. One investigator and a patrol deputy filtered through the campground, sifting for potential witnesses and leads. Three detectives conducted longer interviews with witnesses from the crowd.

The technician snapped photographs of the overall scene and of campers' shoe soles, which might later be compared with any impressions found around the victim's truck.

Detective Douglas Beatty, an eight-year veteran, conducted another interview with Dave Carson. Beatty thought Carson an oddly pathetic character and immediately grew suspicious of him. Carson repeated much the same story he gave Deputy Champion, but Beatty sensed there was more to it. He gently tugged at Carson's memory until the camper had recounted nearly his entire stay at Mesquite Flats.

With the witness's permission, Detective Beatty looked around in Carson's vehicle. He found nothing relevant to the case, but something about Carson was peculiar. Beatty jotted copious notes about the contact. Later, he would pen a lengthy official report about his campground encounter with Dave Carson.

As darkness fell, investigators had been on the scene only long enough to find that the victim had been shot. A quick search produced a brown leather purse near the body. The shoulder straps were missing, and no wallet, money, or identification was found inside.

One salty detective speculated about motive. "Probably a robbery," he grunted to his partners.

The search for more clues was postponed until first light the next day. Guards were posted around the truck where the body lay overnight. Deputies suspected that the dead woman was Alice Marie Cameron—the Nissan's registered owner—but they couldn't be sure.

On Sunday morning, Beatty and Detective Lee Luginbuhl took charge of the scene. They began just inside the secured perimeter and worked in concentric circles toward the truck. A lab technician trailed along, photographing everything the detectives scrutinized, measured, sketched, and marked for collection.

The team turned up only a few tidbits from the slain woman's purse, as well as its broken straps, which was strewn on the ground nearly 20 feet from the truck. Detectives Beatty and Luginbuhl surmised that the purse had been taken from the truck, rifled, then returned.

Also found near the pickup were two spent 9mm shell casings.

Inside the cab, the investigators discovered food, corresponding grocery receipts dated October 18, 1991, women's clothing and camping gear, and an envelope addressed to Alice Cameron. Luginbuhl also found a typed document describing things the author wanted to change about her life:

Fix everything in my life that needs fixing, quickly.

Get me the Right Place, Right Home, Right Occupation now.

Get me wonderful success and abundance within and without.

Get me a wonderful New Age single, healthy unfettered man who will help me in all ways, including loving . . .

Accompanying the prayerlike document was a pulsating "trance" tape, the kind sometimes used to aid meditation.

After placing paper bags over the victim's hands to preserve trace evidence, the investigators inspected the body. She appeared to have been shot twice in the back. One bullet had exited near the left breast. The other had come out under her right arm.

Detective Beatty studied dime-sized punctures in the victim's back and gaping exit wounds in her chest. Then he lined up the ragged holes the slugs had torn through the front of her shirt. Items in the back of the pickup, a blue plastic tumbler and the lens of a black flashlight, also bore telltale signs of being struck by bullets.

Beatty and Luginbuhl did mental geometry, plotting trajectories. Soon they had it figured out. The killer had to have been standing beside the pickup, on the passenger's side near the cab, when the lethal rounds were fired. The decedent must have been sitting up when the slugs ripped into her back.

Sticking with their theory, the two investigators dismantled the pickup's side paneling and recovered one of the projectiles. Though the slugs were badly damaged, there was a remote chance that a firearms identification expert could find enough tool marks to narrow the search for the murder weapon to particular brands or models.

Before having the body taken to the medical examiner's office in Phoenix and leaving the scene, investigators finalized sketches and collected more than 40 pieces of evidence. The crime lab technician took more photographs and cataloged numerous shoe prints discovered in the powdery dirt around the Nissan.

The body was carefully wrapped in a clean, white sheet. Then it was put into a zippered, black vinyl bag and driven to the medical examiner's office. An autopsy would reveal the cause of death and approximately how long the victim had been dead.

The truck was towed to a warehouse in Phoenix where it would be examined with a laser for fingerprints and trace evidence. Oddly, no identifiable foreign prints would be found.

Later that Sunday, using a key found in the victim's purse,

Detective Luginbuhl unlocked Alice Cameron's Cave Creek apartment. Inside, he found photographs of Alice that were identical to the victim. Now he had positive identification.

An address book produced a relative's out-of-state telephone number. Luginbuhl made several calls. Police in a small Missouri town cooperated by notifying the victim's relative about her death.

Luginbuhl and a partner scoured the victim's apartment complex for information about her. They also hoped to retrace the last hours of her life.

Alice Cameron, the detectives quickly learned, was a nice woman. By all accounts, the perky, unemployed legal secretary was a woman who believed in astrological charts, health foods, and visits to psychics and spiritual advisors.

"Alice was not a mainstream person," a neighbor in the complex told investigators. "She was kind of a free spirit, a nudist of sorts, and a leftover from the sixties."

Others characterized Cameron as the "mystery woman" because of her semimonastic lifestyle. Twelve years earlier, after a failed second marriage, the former TWA stewardess had migrated to Phoenix from Missouri. She lived alone, had no suitors or close friends at all, and was estranged from her family.

On a canvass of the apartment complex, sleuths learned from one neighbor that Cameron had been at his apartment about noon on Friday, October 18, 1991, combing the classifieds for a job. She was in good spirits. She had not mentioned a camping trip. That didn't surprise the man, who labeled Cameron "a loner." He claimed she made spontaneous trips into the wilderness alone to study the heavens, hoping to gain insight and new directions for her life. The man confided that Cameron was an optimistic person, but one who believed that she could predict events—even affect them—by charting the stars.

His preliminary inquiries completed, Luginbuhl called for more probers. The team mined Cameron's tight orbit of acquaintances for more information. But the investigators uncovered no one with sufficient motive to kill the slender brunette. Evidently, Alice Cameron had not known the person who murdered her.

Detectives struck out when they checked for credit cards in Cameron's name, and again when they showed her pictures around the grocery store where she bought her food for camping. But they did run across a person who knew the victim and who was probably one of the last to see her alive.

The woman, who was visiting from Colorado, was staying with a mutual acquaintance. She and Alice had talked by phone around midmorning on Friday, October 18. Alice had been chatty and cheerful on the phone. Nothing she said caused the woman to think that something was wrong. And Alice hadn't mentioned intending to go anywhere for the weekend.

Much later that Friday, about four o'clock in the afternoon, the woman even ran into Alice at a North Scottsdale intersection. They didn't speak—the visitor didn't think Alice saw her. But Alice drove away, the woman said, in the general direction of Mesquite Flats. She was alone in her brown Nissan pickup.

The autopsy at the medical examiner's office in Phoenix was completed on Monday. It revealed that Alice Cameron had suffered two fatal gunshot wounds. The bullets had perforated her liver, diaphragm, and pulmonary veins, and had lacerated her spleen. But she hadn't died immediately. A pathologist speculated that Cameron lived for some time after being shot, perhaps an hour or longer while slowly bleeding to death.

During this postmortem examination, the second 9mm slug fortuitously tumbled from the victim's clothing to the stainless-steel operating table. It was in perfect condition for analysis and testing.

Detective Luginbuhl, who viewed the autopsy, was puzzled by the jewelry on Cameron's body. If robbery was the reason for the killing—it seemed to be one of only a few plausible explanations—why hadn't the killer taken the sapphire and silver rings from the victim's fingers or her gold hoop earrings?

Another thing concerned Luginbuhl. Cameron's black stirrup

pants were torn at the waist. Fresh tear patterns in the fiber indicated that the pants had been torn while being pulled down.

Luginbuhl suspected rape. Pubic hair combings and vaginal, rectal, and oral swabs were taken at the detective's request, but a morgue attendant would later misplace them, so it could never be learned whether Alice Cameron was sexually assaulted. At least the state wouldn't be able to prove it.

For Luginbuhl and his eight-member squad, it was back to the streets to pound more pavement in hopes of striking gold in the investigation.

Meanwhile, the August 1991 massacre of nine Buddhists in their temple west of Phoenix was all the town could talk about. While local newspapers were reporting temple case developments with bold front-page headlines, Alice Cameron's killing was relegated to short blurbs on back pages. Nevertheless, detectives busily searched for clues that could unlock the mystery of her death. Within hours, a likely suspect emerged.

Experience had taught the Cameron case detectives that some killers were compelled to insert themselves into investigations. Dave Carson, the man who'd approached deputies at the murder scene with the story about hearing a 9mm being fired in the campground—the man Detective Beatty felt uneasy about—seemed to be doing just that.

Carson was a portrait of torment. A transient, he walked the lunatic fringes of society, his gray hair a trap of snarled knots, his clothes clotted with soil. His piercingly blue eyes orbited in their own private galaxy of mental illness. He suffered from psychiatric disorders that caused profound depression, extreme anxiety, emotional turmoil, fear, and confusion. He blamed it on the Vietnam War.

Carson had served two stints on Okinawa, washing blood and body parts from military vehicles shipped from Southeast Asia for cleanup and decontamination. Viewing the carnage day after day was more than he could take. Something snapped, he claimed.

Carson lived on a disability pension—for a back injury and

his psychiatric problems—and he stayed at Mesquite Flats before or after frequent visits to a Phoenix veteran's hospital.

Dave Carson aroused detectives' undivided suspicions when he came to them with a tale about being acquainted with a woman who bore a strong resemblance to Alice Cameron. He claimed that he occasionally ran into this woman when he camped at Mesquite Flats. He thought it was the dead woman, but he wasn't sure. Finally, he admitted he was talking about Alice Cameron.

"I always felt she was a very independent person," Carson said of the attractive slain woman. "In hindsight, we might have clicked as a team. You never know."

Wary investigators asked Carson about firearms he owned. He brought them a .44-caliber Magnum revolver and claimed it was the only gun he possessed. He allowed them to compare his boot soles with shoe prints found at the scene, but the examination was inconclusive.

Then, on the Tuesday following the murder, Carson presented himself at sheriff's headquarters asking to speak with a Cameron case detective. While speaking to Detective Donald Walsh, Carson's hands shook, he fidgeted and trembled, and he couldn't look Walsh in the eye.

Detective Charles Norton watched from an adjoining room via a closed-circuit camera. He took notes and ran high-tech surveillance equipment the sheriff's office used to record interviews. Soon it became apparent that Dave Carson was a hot suspect, and Norton slipped into the room with Walsh.

Because Carson told several conflicting stories about the events of that Friday night, the impromptu meeting stretched into a 16-hour interrogation. Before long, Walsh read Carson his Miranda Rights, and Carson agreed to continue answering questions.

In one version, Carson claimed he was awakened at 10 o'clock Friday night by loud voices talking about a party. He couldn't go back to sleep, so he decided to go for a walk through the campground. For protection, he carried his 9mm semiautomatic handgun, a gun he allegedly bought in early-October for $225 from a Phoenix coin dealer. Sleuths would find no record of this purchase.

Approaching Alice Cameron's camp, Carson said he heard a commotion near her truck and saw her in the back fighting with a young Mexican male. He rushed to help her fend off the attacker but was overpowered by the man who wrested his gun away. As he and Alice dove for cover, the Mexican shot her in the back, threw the gun in the river, then bolted from the campground.

Detectives Norton and Walsh, however, weren't buying Carson's story. He knew more, and they used finesse and patience to get him to come clean.

"We need to know, Dave. That's what we're here for," Walsh coaxed Carson at one point.

Eventually, Carson admitted that he'd shot Alice Cameron. He claimed it was an accident, that he was firing at the Mexican who was assaulting her, but he had missed and struck Cameron in the back instead. Carson broke down and tearfully gave investigators a vivid account of her death.

He even admitted taking the victim's purse from the pickup, breaking the straps while trying to open it. He acknowledged rummaging through it, perhaps taking her wallet, then putting the purse back where he'd found it.

Sealing his fate, Carson mentioned one last chilling detail.

"Most people cross the street when they see me to avoid me," he began. "She [Cameron] said hi to me twice."

In a voice barely audible, Carson went on to tell sickened detectives that he had kissed and tried to undress her corpse.

Later, Dave Carson drew diagrams of the scene and even went back with detectives to reenact in front of video cameras how he caused Cameron's death and what he did afterwards.

But sleuths sensed that something was fishy. Try as they might, detectives couldn't unearth witnesses or physical evidence to corroborate Carson's account of the slaying. For one thing, they couldn't find the murder weapon. In a bold move, they shut off the flow of the Verde River and searched for the gun in the mucky riverbed without luck. They scratched through pawnshops. Search warrants served on Carson's Chevy Blazer produced similar results. Nothing. Detectives tried tracing Carson's name through Bureau of Alcohol, Tobacco and Firearms files but came up empty. The gun seemed nowhere to be found.

Nothing showed up during several searches of Carson's property that could even remotely be associated with Alice Cameron or her murder. A composite drawing of the Mexican or Indian male who diverted the young couple from the campground the night of the murder—perhaps the same person mentioned by Carson—was published in newspapers and broadcast on television. Nothing developed.

Nevertheless, Dave Carson had confessed to murder. And he provided uncommon knowledge about the scene. Sheriff's detectives were obligated to arrest and book him. The Maricopa County Attorney's Office found that sufficient cause existed to charge Carson with the first-degree murder of Alice Marie Cameron.

Fifteen months later, while prosecutors were putting the finishing touches on their preparations for Carson's trial, the case exploded, and it was Alessandro "Alex" Garcia who dropped the bomb. Garcia, a broodingly handsome high school football player and "ROTC rat," was also a mass murderer. At 16, he was certainly one of the world's youngest.

The soft-spoken, dark-featured Garcia and Jonathan Doody, his 17-year-old confederate, had killed the Buddhists in their temple back in August 1991. Their motive had been robbery. To avoid detection, they executed six monks, a nun, an acolyte, and a visitor, then looted the temple, making off with cash, cameras, and stereo equipment.

They were arrested for the temple murders in late October 1991, after sheriff's deputies uncovered the murder weapons and traced them to the boys. Both confessed.

Doody pled not guilty and demanded a trial.

After losing his suppression hearing, Garcia struck a deal with the state. He agreed to plead guilty and testify against Doody in exchange for escaping a death sentence.

Monday, January 4, 1993, was the day set for Garcia to enter his plea. By eight o'clock that morning, Garcia and his attorney sat in the prosecutor's conference room across the table from major felony Chief K.C. Scull, sheriff's detectives, and a bevy of Maricopa County's best legal eagles.

The work group was studying a carefully crafted plea bargain that would forever protect society from Alex Garcia. It would help convict Doody, too, since the state's case against him was iffy without Garcia's testimony.

And it almost was a wrap. Within the hour, Garcia would plead guilty. The deal had been greased with the court, everything was ready to go. A ravenous media was crammed into a courtroom across the street, waiting for Garcia to appear.

But in the conference room something went dreadfully wrong. Garcia had quit reading and was whispering hoarsely to his lawyer. The plea agreement lay askew on the table.

While he conferred with counsel, Garcia tapped a clause in the document with a meaty finger. His lawyer looked worried, and held up both hands to stave off questions from the puzzled state team. Seconds later, the blood drained from the attorney's face. He bolted upright from his chair, demanding privacy in the room with Garcia.

Hours later, the attorney would tell Chief Scull that Garcia had confessed to a 10th murder. His 11th-hour confession was prompted by a clause in the agreement that required he reveal all criminal activity in which he'd taken part. If he lied, the document said, the deal would be nixed. And Garcia wanted his deal and was intent on saving his own life.

It would be the next day—Tuesday, January 5, 1993—before prosecutors and cops learned Alex Garcia's dark secret: He and Michelle Leslie Hoover, his 14-year-old girlfriend, had robbed and killed Alice Cameron.

By nine o'clock that morning, Garcia was telling a gruesome tale. Though he couldn't explain to Scull and the others why,

Garcia told them how he and Michelle Hoover stalked, then killed Cameron. In matter-of-fact tones, he told a stunned audience how two teenagers had almost gotten away with murder. When Garcia finished, the only sound was the whirring of air through a vent, and his belly chains clanking when he scratched under his chin.

Sheriff's detectives lurched to action. They hit the streets in a sweeping effort to corroborate every detail provided by Garcia. Soon a grisly portrait of a bizarre crime emerged.

Garcia and Hoover had been lovers. They'd met at their high school during the first week of September 1991. Hoover had fallen hard for Garcia. At 14, the rapture of first love consumed Hoover, a frumpy, immature freshman who wasn't—could never be—a local princess. For her, Garcia was a real prize. After meeting him, she behaved in uncharacteristically irresponsible ways. Once a good student, she ignored her studies in favor of spending hours on the phone with Garcia. She neglected chores.

Described later as a sweet slice of American pie, a "Daddy's girl," the acute interest Hoover once had in a relative's hobby of racing cars waned. Sometimes, she'd sneak out at night for a few secret moments with Garcia at one of the burger joints on the far west side of Phoenix where they lived.

But Hoover's real slide from reality began at 11:15 P.M. on Wednesday, October 16, 1991, when she closed the front door of her sprawling custom home carrying two guns that belonged to a family member and a box of bullets to a black Chevy pickup that she commandeered from the driveway.

Initially, Hoover had objected to Garcia's suggestion earlier on the phone that she grab the truck and guns so they could go target shooting. But his soft-spoken challenge had melted her resolve.

"If you love me, you'll do it," Garcia cooed, according to Hoover.

After shooting at cans in the desert near Hoover's sprawling custom home, Hoover and Garcia spent the night in the pickup. The next morning, he suggested they run away.

"Let's just leave," he proposed to the badly smitten Hoover.

Hoover agreed, even suggesting that they go to a cabin she once visited in the mountains near Payson, Arizona. First, Garcia said, they should visit one of his favorite places along the Verde River: Mesquite Flats. It would be on their way.

Garcia drove to his house where he stuffed two army duffel bags with clothing and military camouflage gear, grabbed his .22-caliber rifle, and stole money from a relative before heading out with Hoover in the stolen truck.

Ironically, the duffel bags were the ones Garcia had used to haul loot from the temple. The camouflage gear—Battle Dress Uniforms—were the same clothes Garcia wore when he killed the nine Buddhists with shotgun blasts.

After stopping at a convenience market to stock up on junk food, the young lovers arrived at the Mesquite Flats Campground. For the rest of the day, they camped, talked, explored. By night, they were low on gas and out of food and money.

"We're gonna have to rob somebody," Garcia told Hoover. "We're gonna have to kill them, too. No witnesses. Know what I mean?"

"Okay," was her only whispered response.

The next day, Friday, October 18, 1991, they prowled the campground, looking for a likely victim; preferably, someone who camped alone. It was dusk when they found Alice Cameron.

She was sitting in a lawn chair near her truck, staring into a campfire, when the teens spotted her. As a ruse to check out her camp, they asked to borrow matches. She didn't seem to think anything about Garcia's prying glances around her camp. She answered him affirmatively when he asked if she was alone. She gave the young lovers a book of matches, and they left.

The teens waited until almost midnight. Garcia cinched a web belt across Hoover's chest. He strapped a black canvas holster to the waist belt and tossed her a black Helwan 9mm semiautomatic handgun—one of the guns she'd taken from a family member.

"Do you want me to do it, or do you want to do it?" he casually asked.

Hoover was silent.

Garcia asked the question again.

"Do you want me to do it, or do you want to do it?" This time, Garcia was more intense, almost goading.

Later, Hoover would claim he added, "If you love me, you'll do it, Michelle."

"No, I'll do it," Hoover said softly. *I'll do it for you,* she thought.

Within minutes, it was over. Hoover had pumped two rounds into Cameron's back, while Garcia crouched in bushes nearby.

Even more gruesome, the teenagers waited and watched impatiently while Cameron died. They held her down in the bed of the pickup and Garcia clamped a big hand over her mouth until she stopped pleading for help and asking, "Why? Why are you doing this to me?"

Over an hour later, when Cameron stopped calling for help, Hoover and Garcia stole $1.59, a bank card, and some trinkets from her purse and wiped their fingerprints from the truck and everything they'd touched. They left the purse in the back of the truck, near the victim who was moaning softly and still writhing in pain when the deadly teens finally left.

The couple zipped to the cabin in Payson, and hid out for several days. Acting on a tip from Hoover's relatives, who had reported her as a runaway, police there caught the pair and sent them home to their parents on Tuesday, October 22, 1991.

The love affair between Alex Garcia and Michelle Hoover ended four days later when sheriff's deputies arrested Garcia for killing the Buddhists. No one suspected them of the brutal campground murder.

But killing had changed Hoover. Over the next 15 months, she lived in a world quite apart from the one into which she had been born. At first, Hoover was preoccupied with the need for safety. A Doberman slept on her bed whenever she was in it. Strange sounds sent her into hysterics. Then she grew detached, withdrew behind a shroud of gloom so opaque that smiles and kindness and loving couldn't penetrate.

Hoover's grades plummeted. She snubbed her old friends, took up with a rougher crowd that hung out in the parking lots of fast-food joints and bowling alleys. She started smoking. Most nights, nightmares jolted her awake. Hoover gnashed her teeth, endured night sweats and tremors. She couldn't eat, and she lost weight.

And she was hounded by detectives working the temple case. Since Hoover was Garcia's girlfriend, they dogged her with questions about him. She lied to investigators. She pined for Garcia, and kept their evil secret. Soon she was pregnant by an older man.

After Garcia confessed to the Cameron murder, detectives streaked through Hoover's network of friends, relatives, and acquaintances and took statements from over 100 individuals. On Wednesday, January 6, 1993, they took search warrants to Hoover's home. They found a 9mm handgun in a living-room cabinet. A state firearms expert quickly matched it to the recovered slugs.

Shockingly, Hoover asked the search team leader if he'd seen Garcia recently. When the detective-sergeant replied that he had, Hoover collapsed in tears on his shoulder.

"I still love him," she wailed mournfully.

Michelle Hoover elected to say nothing to detectives about her role in the campground slaying. Following the advice of a relative, she invoked her right to an attorney and sealed her lips.

Hoover was allowed time to have an abortion before she was jailed one week later on Thursday, January 14.

Prosecutors filed charges, but since she was only 14 years old when she shot Alice Cameron, she would never face an executioner because of a high court ruling that declared putting "children" to death was cruel and unusual punishment.

If tried and convicted as a juvenile, she'd spend less than two years behind bars. The state hurried to court to have Hoover remanded to the adult system.

Flashbulbs popped like machine-gun fire and miles of videotape spun at the March 10, 1993, hearing to determine whether Michelle Hoover was to be tried as a juvenile. In the courtroom, she sobbed that she was sorry and argued that she shot Cameron to prove her love for Garcia.

Juvenile Court Judge Linda Scott was unmoved and remanded Hoover to the harsher adult system. Later, Hoover pled guilty and agreed to serve 10 years in prison for her role in the murder.

Public outrage erupted. Some people felt Hoover deserved a ticket to the gas chamber or life in prison. Cops and prosecutors said Michelle Hoover had committed just another insane American robbery. Hers was simply one more alarming but commonplace headline.

Others, especially Hoover's relatives, believed she had been mesmerized to commit murder by Garcia. They said her month-long love affair with Garcia enabled him to control her—enough to get her to commit murder.

"Not of Her Doing," blared headlines in one major newspaper, parroting the sentiments of Hoover's friends and devastated relatives.

For weeks, public debate raged in newspapers and on television. Picketers carrying signs declaring, "Michelle Hoover Must Die," paced courthouse sidewalks while Hoover's friends blitzed newspapers and courts with letters that detailed her virtues, and begged for mercy.

But Judge Ronald Reinstein of Maricopa County Superior Court dashed hopes for anything less than hard time for Hoover. On May 15, 1993, Reinstein cited the need to balance the scales of justice and rejected Hoover's plea agreement as too lenient.

He called Cameron's murder, "cold, calculating, and chilling." He noted that Cameron's "senseless, cruel, and heinous" murder was affecting visitors to the state, as well as residents.

"The killing took place in an area people seek out for peaceful relaxation and recreation," Judge Reinstein told Hoover. "A place where they could put their troubles aside. Now, with this and other murders in such locations, people have a fear of going to campgrounds."

For this reason, the judge said, Hoover deserved 15 to 20 years flat time, more if terms of the plea would have allowed it.

Though Hoover's attorney withdrew her plea and shopped for a more lenient jurist, one could not be found. She made another deal with the state, this one for 15 years.

Alice Cameron's relatives wished only for uncharitable punishment. To them, Michelle Hoover was an unmerciful killer.

"With this single act, any chance of reconciliation with Alice was lost forever," a tearful relative told detectives in court. "I will never be able to tell her how much I loved her."

Another relative said, "Alice was the victim, not Hoover."

Jurisprudence agreed. Superior Court Judge David Roberts bluntly decided Hoover's fate on Thursday, July 15, 1993.

"What she did was totally out of character. It was a bizarre aberration, but it was also murder," the judge said. Then he sentenced her to 15 years in prison, with no chance for parole. This was the maximum sentence he could impose under her new deal.

Michelle Leslie Hoover—"Daddy's girl"—thus became the youngest woman ever sentenced to an Arizona prison. And the system was not prepared to handle her. Because of a state law that prohibits mingling adults with juveniles, Hoover couldn't be put with the general prison population until age 18.

Today, she languishes in solitary confinement, sealed from society in a dingy trailer that squats in the middle of a dusty prison yard.

In July 1994, Judge Gregory Martin, of Maricopa County Superior Court, sentenced Alex Garcia to 10 consecutive life terms. Today he sits in a small isolation cell in a protective custody wing of Arizona State Prison in Florence. Prison officials are certain other inmates would kill Garcia if he were put with the general population, since he has the reputation for being a snitch: he testified against his temple case partner and gave up Michelle Hoover. Garcia's first chance for parole comes up in the year 2265. Obviously, he'll die in prison.

Michelle Leslie Hoover will be 32 years old when she emerges from jail, but her sentence won't end when the iron bars clank open. She still will be confined by the haunting memories of her first love and the night she proved it.

"NEW JERSEY GAL PALS' PREY WAS BAILED OUT & BUMPED OFF!"

by Barry Bowe

Shortly after seven o'clock on a cold winter's morning, two hunters entered the woods of New Jersey's Wharton State Park in Waterford Township, which is about a third of the way between Philadelphia and Atlantic City. It was Monday, December 27, 1993, and the mercury was frozen around the 20-degree mark. Suddenly, from behind them, in the direction of Route 206, the hunters heard what sounded like either a car door or trunk being slammed shut. They turned and spotted a Chevrolet Camaro parked on the shoulder of the road. As they took a few steps toward the vehicle, it lurched forward and sped away. Shrugging, the hunters headed back into the woods.

A few hours later, as the hunters were on their way out of the forest, they passed by the same spot. This time, they saw something that startled them. Near the side of the road, lying in a drainage ditch of an abandoned cranberry bog and partly covered by piles of leaves, was a body wrapped inside a bed sheet. After verifying what they'd seen, the hunters immediately got in touch with the police.

Responding officers from the Waterford Township Police Department arrived in short order, took one look at the body, and contacted the Camden County Prosecutor's Office. The area was part of the state's pine barrens, a vast wilderness and a notorious dumping ground for murder victims—both local and out-of-state victims. Therefore, finding a dead body was not as surprising an event as it might have been somewhere else.

County detectives, evidence technicians and medical examiners were immediately dispatched to the body site in the state forest. Investigator Art Folks of the county's Major Crimes Unit was part of that team. Inside the bed sheet, the probers found a white male lying facedown with a pillowcase over his head. The victim was dressed in a navy-blue sport jacket and gray jogging pants. His hands and feet were bound behind his back with thick brown twine tied to his neck. When the investigators removed the pillowcase, it was obvious that the victim, who appeared to be in his late 20s to early 30s, had been shot in the head more than once.

By the time the victim was pronounced dead and his body was removed from the scene and on its way to the county morgue, the investigators came up with two important clues: a Smith & Wesson .32-caliber revolver found in close proximity to the scene and a yellow slip of paper yielded by the victim's pocket. The gun was believed to be the murder weapon and the yellow paper was a receipt showing that a William Kelly, Jr., had been bailed out of the Camden County Jail, via the Cherry Hill police station, just hours earlier, at 3:41 A.M., according to the notation.

Investigator Folks contacted the Cherry Hill police and got the victim tentatively identified as Kelly. Thus, the probers' first order of business included digging into the victim's background.

What the sleuths soon learned was that William Kelly, Jr., was born on January 25, 1962, meaning that he'd been murdered less than a month shy of his 32nd birthday. He grew up in Pennsauken, a small town nestled between the mean streets of Camden, one of America's poorest cities, and the suburban affluence of Cherry Hill, one of the country's wealthiest communities. Sometime later in life, he'd moved across the Delaware

River into Pennsylvania, for his current driver's license said he lived on Carlisle Street in Philadelphia. His occupation was listed as carpet layer, unemployed.

"I know he's had problems with the law throughout his life," a friend said about Kelly. "He's always been in trouble. He's had about three drunk-driving arrests and I know his overall view of women was kind of low. When he got drunk, he would call them pigs and sluts and bitches—that kind of stuff. And if he perceived someone as being a threat to him, he'd just walk up to that person and slug them."

Investigator Folks learned that Kelly had been arrested three times in New Jersey during the previous five weeks. He'd been arrested twice on November 24—once for simple assault and criminal mischief and once for violating a domestic restraining order—and he'd been arrested on December 19 for aggravated assault. After failing to post 10 percent of his $10,000 bail for the aggravated assault charges, he'd been detained in Camden County Jail ever since.

Granted, the investigator found absolutely nothing in Kelly's background to portray a sympathetic victim, but that didn't change the situation one iota. Someone had killed another human being and—nice guy or not—the law had to be upheld. It was the sleuth's job to get to the bottom of things.

From the Cherry Hill police, Investigator Folks learned that a young white female had come into the Cherry Hill police station sometime after midnight that morning and posted $1,000 in cash to bail Kelly out. The Cherry Hill police had subsequently contacted the county jail, and sheriff's deputies started transferring Kelly to the Cherry Hill police station around 3 A.M. The name of the young woman who'd posted Kelly's bond was Tammy Molewicz.

The investigator checked Kelly's last three arrest reports, but failed to find Molewicz listed on any of the complaints. So who the hell was she?

The investigator soon learned that Tammy Ann Molewicz, 25 years old, dark-haired and attractive, was an unemployed mother.

She had never been Kelly's girlfriend, nor had she ever been married to him. To further muddy the waters, Kelly lived in Pennsylvania and Molewicz lived in New Jersey, in the well-to-do rural town of Medford, in Burlington County, several miles north of where Kelly's body was discovered. Moreover, she drove a red Corvette with Maryland tags. There just didn't seem to be any connection between Kelly and Molewicz. Still, she'd bailed him out of jail for some reason. Investigator Folks needed to know why.

Folks contacted the Medford PD to see if they could locate Tammy Molewicz. Local officers had no trouble finding her and escorting her to the Medford police station. While Medford Chief John Foulk and Investigator Art Folks were listening to what Molewicz had to say for herself, Dr. Robert Segal, the county medical examiner, was performing an autopsy on the victim at the county morgue. The postmortem exam would determine that Kelly had been killed by two .32-caliber gunshots to the head. While all this was going on, something extremely bizarre was happening in a most unlikely setting.

At a TGIFriday's restaurant in Evesham Township, about five miles west of Camden, 32-year-old Peggy Kosmin was meeting a gentleman friend. The dark-haired Kosmin stood a little taller than five feet and was a hairstylist who worked in a nearby hair salon. A single parent with one child, she was also an amateur bodybuilder and an aspiring student of the martial arts. That night, her rendezvous started with drinks around nine o'clock and ended after dinner about an hour later. Her male companion left the restaurant around 10:15 P.M. and she left a short while later. However, she came back inside the restaurant within minutes.

"She was shaking like a leaf," a restaurant employee later recalled. "She said her car had been stolen from the parking lot. I heard her say that her ex-boyfriend had just gotten out of jail and he's the only other person who has access to the car and has another set of keys. I heard her say that he was abusive."

"She had a bruise on her face," another restaurant employee

recalled, "and she was walking with a real bad limp. She told me she had a broken toe. She was wearing cowboy boots and I asked her, 'How did you get into those things?' "

Peggy Kosmin asked the restaurant manager to call 911. While she was waiting for the police to arrive, someone was setting fire to her car in the pine barrens, some 10 miles away from the restaurant.

Corporal Diego Castellanos, of the Evesham Township Police Department, responded to TGIFriday's around 11 P.M. He took Peggy Kosmin outside, into his police car, so that he could fill out a stolen-vehicle report on her 1992 black Pontiac Grand Prix. That was when a once-in-a-lifetime broadcast came over the police radio in Castellanos's car.

"She was calm and didn't panic," Corporal Castellanos recalled. "She heard everything I heard on the radio." What Corporal Castellanos and Kosmin heard on that police broadcast was that Margaret "Peggy" Kosmin was wanted for the murder of William Kelly earlier that morning. The broadcast further described Kosmin as armed and dangerous.

Corporal Castellanos asked Kosmin to step out of the car. He searched her, but he failed to find any dangerous weapons on her person. Then he transported her to the Medford police station. It seems that while Kosmin had been having drinks and dinner at TGIFriday's, Tammy Molewicz had been giving Chief Foulk and Investigator Folks a pretty good idea of how Kelly had been killed.

In what the media would soon begin calling the "Thelma and Louise Killing," named after the movie *Thelma and Louise,* Tammy Molewicz's initial story went basically as follows.

Molewicz and Kosmin had known each other for a few months. In fact, they were neighbors who lived about a block apart: Molewicz in the unit block of Branch Street in Medford and Kosmin in the unit block of Church Street. Two months earlier, in October, Kelly had unexpectedly come back into her friend Kosmin's life—he was an old boyfriend from years ago and the father of Kosmin's child.

Kelly moved in with Kosmin and they started having sex with each other, but he became abusive with her on several occasions and she had him arrested. Nonetheless, Molewicz told the investigators, Kosmin was afraid that when Kelly eventually got out of jail, he'd retaliate against her. So Kosmin engineered a plot to kill him.

Molewicz said that Kosmin gave her $1,000 and told her to drive Kosmin's black Grand Prix to the Cherry Hill police station and bail Kelly out of jail—which she did. Molewicz said she waited for Kelly to be transferred there from the county jail. When he finally arrived, she started to drive Kelly toward Kosmin's home in Medford.

A mile or so from Kosmin's house, Molewicz stopped at a Wawa convenience store so that Kelly could run inside and buy a pack of cigarettes and a soda. While Kelly was in the store, Molewicz lowered the passenger window and got out of the car. She walked around to the rear of the car and unlocked the trunk. Kosmin, who had been concealed inside the trunk the entire time, climbed out and hid nearby. When Kelly came out of the store, he opened the passenger door and sat inside the car. Peggy Kosmin then crept up from behind and shot Kelly through the back of the head—twice.

After Corporal Castellanos delivered Kosmin to the Medford police station, Chief Foulk and Investigator Folks interviewed her for nearly five hours. Her initial story was fairly consistent with what Molewicz had already told the investigators, especially the first part. She added a few of the missing details.

"Where did you get the gun?" one of the investigators asked her.

Kosmin said she'd purchased the Smith & Wesson .32 about a month earlier from someone she knew and had kept it hidden under her bed. On the day before the murder, Sunday, December 26, she'd test-fired the gun in the house, three times. Evidence technicians would subsequently search her home and find three bullet holes, two in the wall and one in the baseboard.

In her account, Kosmin also confused the issue a great deal.

Although she admitted to plotting Kelly's murder, she denied having anything to do with the actual killing. Kosmin declared that it was her friend Molewicz who had shot Kelly.

Around 4 A.M., the Medford police arrested both Molewicz and Kosmin and charged them with Kelly's murder. Bail for each suspect was set at $200,000. From that point on, Ed Borden, the Camden County prosecutor, pretty much took over the investigation. He interviewed both women, then held a press conference the following morning.

"After the shooting," the prosecutor told reporters, "the women drove a short distance to a deserted area, where they put Kelly's body in the trunk of the black Grand Prix. They then supposedly tied up the body and wrapped it up and dumped it just off of Route 206 in the forest and covered it with leaves."

"What about Molewicz?" one reporter asked.

"We are unclear about her involvement," the prosecutor said, hedging a bit, "but we do know she was aware all night long that Kosmin had a gun."

"Do you have a motive?" another reporter inquired.

"It was a premeditated, planned, and carefully executed murder," the prosecutor answered. "She was a victim of domestic violence and wanted to retaliate against him and make sure he didn't do it again. But there are lots of answers [to domestic violence] short of murder.

"Domestic-violence victims don't have to do this. Domestic-violence victims can come to law enforcement and get help. This is a case where the system worked. She went to the police twice and he was arrested both times. He got out only because she let him out.

"This was a homicide that clearly did not have to happen. There are numerous answers where this woman could have sought help. Now we're faced with a clear-cut case of premeditated murder as a result of this woman's continued abuse at the hands of Kelly."

Peggy Kosmin had met Bill Kelly while they were students at Pennsauken High School during the mid-1970s. They started dating, became girlfriend and boyfriend, and she suddenly found herself pregnant at the age of 17. When she became pregnant, Kelly started physically abusing her for the first time. She dropped out of school to have their baby.

After a few years, she broke off her relationship with Kelly and fled to Michigan. Before she left, he warned her that he'd track her down. She stayed in Michigan for a year before returning to New Jersey.

During the mid-1980s, she married someone else and she and her husband eventually bought the home on Church Street in Medford. But that marriage ended in divorce in 1990 and she was subsequently awarded the house as part of the divorce settlement. After the divorce, she started dating and maintained another relationship until right before Kelly reentered her life in October 1993.

Over the years, Kelly had been trying to find Kosmin and she'd known it. Following her flight to Michigan, she'd also moved to Boca Raton, Florida, for three months to avoid him. Once she came back to New Jersey to stay, to be on the safe side, she installed a high-tech security system in her home and two dead-bolt locks on her bedroom door. Still, just as Kelly had promised, he eventually found her, this time living in Medford.

"I told you I'd be back," were among the first words he said to her upon their first meeting in years.

Against her better judgment, Kosmin invited Kelly to move in with her, and things were okay for about a month. Then, on November 24, her old boyfriend tried to phone her. Kelly intercepted the call and his mood immediately deteriorated, unleashing a violent rage.

He cursed Kosmin and threatened to kill her. She locked herself inside the bedroom, but he broke down the door. Once inside, he punched her and he broke her nose before she was able to call the Medford police. Officers responded to the call and arrested Kelly, charging him with simple assault and criminal mischief.

Kosmin immediately obtained a restraining order from Medford Municipal Judge John Dyer, but Kelly was already negotiating his release from jail. That same night, he returned to her house and attacked her again. He was arrested for the second time that day. This time, unable to post bail, he was sent to the Burlington County Prison.

Two days later, Kosmin gave Molewicz $2,000 in cash to bail Kelly out of the county jail and he moved right back in with her.

Four days later, Kosmin appeared before Burlington County Judge John Sweeney and asked him to rescind the restraining order against Kelly. The entire hearing lasted less than two minutes:

"Why do you want to have the restraining order lifted?" Judge Sweeny asked.

"Because he lives with me," Kosmin replied, "and we're getting in bed together and he can't go back into residency with me until the restraint is off."

"Are you going to be safe without this protection order?"

"Yes," she answered in a strong, clear voice. "Yes, I will."

In the weeks that followed, she discovered that she was far from being safe. It was just a matter of time before violence erupted again between Kosmin and Kelly—and it did. For three days, she moved into the Holiday Inn in Cherry Hill to avoid him. Then, on December 19, he found her and a battle broke out, this time in public, at the Woodcrest High-Speed Line train station in Cherry Hill.

Kosmin's complaint to the Cherry Hill police stated that Kelly "beat her with a metal club and dragged her around by the hair." He was arrested and, unable to post bond, he was placed in the Camden County Jail. In regard to the attack itself, there were some differing opinions.

"Without a doubt," one of Kelly's best friends explained, "the dude was an alcoholic. But the dude couldn't hurt anybody anymore. It got to the point where he couldn't even work anymore.

"She threatened him at the High-Speed Line. His face was

cut and his glasses were broken—she hit him and broke his glasses. She started swinging the club first."

One of Kosmin's best friends gave just the opposite slant.

"After the attack, Peggy was shaking like a leaf on a tree," the friend recalled. "Anybody who tries to tell you this guy wasn't a nut is lying. His goal was to make her pay. He was a drug addict and he was a drunk. His ultimate goal was to kill her."

And as it turned out, her ultimate goal was to kill him.

During the first 12 hours after Kosmin's arrest, on Tuesday, December 28, her story started to change somewhat and more information began coming into the prosecutor's office. For one thing, Peggy Kosmin had now confessed to shooting Kelly. For another, a lawyer called and added a new element to the case.

The lawyer told Prosecutor Borden that his client had met Peggy Kosmin in a martial-arts class a few months earlier. On the day when Kelly was murdered, his client met Kosmin and Molewicz between 4 and 5 A.M. At that time, he helped them transfer Kelly's corpse from the trunk of Kosmin's Grand Prix to the trunk of his own car, a Chevrolet Camaro. Afterward, he helped the women dispose of Kelly's body in the pine barrens of Waterford Township.

"He's been very cooperative in the case," the prosecutor told reporters in announcing that another accomplice had been identified in Kelly's murder.

"Is he being charged?" one of the reporters asked.

"That decision has not been made yet," the prosecutor replied, but he did disclose that traces of blood had been found on the carpeting in the trunk of the Camaro and also on its rear bumper.

As news of William Kelly's murder and the women's arrest began spreading throughout the South Jersey communities, conflicting opinions began drifting in about Peggy Kosmin.

"She's energetic and positive," said her boss at the hair salon. "Hyper but good-hearted. Always an 'up-personality' person.

"We just can't believe it. Today, everybody's sulking around in shock."

"She's a sweet single mother who would do anything for her child," said one Medford neighbor, describing Kosmin.

But another neighbor viewed Kosmin quite differently.

"I just do not approve of what went on there," the second neighbor said, voicing her complaints. "Much more than meets the eye. She had parties almost every weekend—wild hot-tub parties in which participants got naked on her back deck.

"We had the police here all the time."

Around half past five o'clock on the afternoon after the arrest, Tuesday, December 28, 1993, another pair of hunters were walking through a portion of Wharton State Park in Shamong Township. They were some three miles from where Kelly's body had been discovered by the other hunters the previous day. When they reached an isolated clearing about a mile from Route 206, they found what was left of a car that had recently been set on fire. They immediately contacted the state police.

State troopers from the Red Lion Barracks responded to the summons and quickly identified the burned remains as Peggy Kosmin's missing Grand Prix. It seemed obvious to the probers that she had conspired with someone to torch the leased vehicle.

The investigators questioned the accomplice who'd helped the women dispose of Kelly's corpse and asked him if he'd had anything to do with torching the car. He swore that he had not, so now it appeared as if a fourth person had been involved in the murder plot. But who?

About a week later, the prosecutor got wind of another interesting twist in the case: Just 10 days before Kelly was murdered, his father had died from natural causes. According to the terms of his father's 1988 will, Kelly's two siblings would each inherit just one dollar, while Kelly himself would receive the balance of the estate. At first estimate, the amount of Kelly's inheritance was gauged to be $120,000.

New questions arose from this latest development: Had Kosmin found out about the inheritance? Had she killed Kelly to get her hands on the $120,000?

"This goes to motive," the prosecutor told the media, "and

we are looking into what part it may play in the investigation. Of course, it doesn't change the evidence of the underlying facts of the case."

"None of this makes any sense," Kosmin's lawyer told reporters, referring to the inheritance angle as the motive for Kelly's killing. "If they were logical, they wouldn't have been caught just hours after it happened. No, Peggy's real fear was, she thought that once he got out of jail, she'd be dead."

In fact, the lawyer told the press, Kelly had called Kosmin from the county jail specifically to inform her of his impending inheritance. The lawyer asserted that Kelly had told Kosmin he was planning to use a portion of the inheritance to bail himself out of jail and get even with her. The fact that Kosmin and Kelly had never legally been married, the defense lawyer pointed out, precluded her from having any legal claim to the inheritance. The lawyer believed that Kosmin's motivation to concoct the murder plan, bail Kelly out of jail, and carry out the plot stemmed from her knowledge that Kelly would have soon been able to bail himself out of jail and come looking for her.

While the early legal maneuverings were taking place, the investigators maintained a steady dialogue with Kosmin, Molewicz, and their attorneys. During those discussions, plea arrangements were being considered, but nothing materialized.

Three months after Kelly's murder, on Wednesday, March 16, 1994, the investigators learned the name of the individual who'd torched Kosmin's Grand Prix. The man they were looking for was alleged to be a 31-year-old resident of Cherry Hill. A surveillance was established to try to find him.

Six days passed.

On Tuesday, March 22, word reached the prosecutor's office that the missing accomplice would be in the vicinity of the High-Speed Line station in Collingswood that afternoon. The prosecutor's office contacted the Collingswood Police Department and county investigators Willie Mahan and Brian DeCosmo were dispatched to begin a joint operation with several Collingswood patrolmen.

That afternoon, the investigators located and arrested the suspect. The criminal complaint lodged against him specified that the suspect met Kosmin in the parking lot of TGIFriday's on the night of December 28, 1993. At that time, Kosmin gave him the keys to her car and a cash sum of $600 to set fire to the Grand Prix. The suspect then drove to a backwoods clearing in Shamong Township and torched the car.

Both the suspect and Kosmin—but not Molewicz—were charged with first-degree arson for hire, a crime that carries a maximum sentence of 20 years in prison and a maximum fine of $100,000.

As the months passed, the prosecutor continued to prepare his case with eyes wide open, looking at it as objectively as possible and considering all of his options. The death penalty was out. In New Jersey, only ironclad first-degree murder cases ever got the maximum penalty, and this case was far from being ironclad. In addition, any time a battered woman was accused of killing the man battering her, there was no telling if a jury would convict the battered woman of anything. Therefore, dropping the charges from murder to aggravated manslaughter might become necessary to guarantee that Kosmin and Molewicz would pay for their crimes.

What made the case for the prosecution even more tenuous was the fact that Peggy Kosmin kept changing her version of what happened. She had gotten around to telling the investigators that she'd been asleep in the front seat of her Grand Prix when Kelly entered the Wawa store and that she was still asleep when Molewicz shot and killed him.

Both women submitted to polygraph testing and both supposedly passed. The plea negotiations therefore continued, but an agreement was not forthcoming because neither woman would admit to pulling the trigger. If an agreement were submitted to a judge under such circumstances, the prosecutor doubted that the judge would accept it.

"In order for a court to accept a guilty plea," Superior Court Judge Rudolph Rossetti explained, "the court has to be satisfied with the factual basis of the confession. In this case, one of them can't be telling the truth."

Still, neither side wanted to go to trial.

The prosecution envisioned a long, expensive trial and feared it might end in a hung jury, with both defendants going free. The defense feared Molewicz and Kosmin could go to jail for the rest of their lives.

"Both attorneys for the defense have been fully cooperative in trading discovery back and forth," an assistant prosecutor reported. "We are still hoping for a resolution of the case."

But no agreement was reached by the beginning of September, so the case was presented to a grand jury. On Wednesday, September 7, the grand jury returned a 12-count indictment against Molewicz and Kosmin, charging both women with first-degree murder, suppressing evidence, and hindering an investigation. If convicted, both faced life sentences with no chance of parole for at least 30 years. In addition, Kosmin was charged with arson and faced an additional 20 years.

In the weeks between the grand jury indictment and the scheduled trial date, the plea negotiations continued. Near the end of October 1994, an agreement was reached. Now what remained to be seen was, would the judge accept that agreement?

On Monday, October 24, 1994, Judge Isaiah Steinberg presided over separate hearings for Molewicz and Kosmin.

Each woman in her own turn made a lengthy statement to the judge. Each confessed to plotting Kelly's death, to dumping his body in Wharton State Park, and to attempting to cover up the crime afterward. Each declared that Peggy Kosmin was a battered woman and that the motive for the killing was self-defense.

One of the statements read into testimony was, "We had already agreed to kill him when he was released from custody."

Near the end of each hearing, it was time for the $64,000 question.

"Who shot him?" the judge asked Molewicz at her hearing.

"Peggy did," Molewicz replied, blotting her eyes with a hanky. She insisted that Kosmin had fired the shots that killed Kelly.

"Although we'd planned it together, I still didn't really believe we'd go through with it. I wasn't certain until Peggy pulled the trigger."

"Who shot him?" the judge asked Kosmin at her hearing.

"Tammy Molewicz did it," Kosmin said with tears in her eyes. "I was drunk and hiding in the trunk of my Grand Prix when she pulled the trigger. Later on, he was shot a second time in my presence."

"I'd like to know the truth," the judge told the media after the hearings, "but you never find out the truth. A jury does the best it can, but only two people can tell you what happened that night, and those two people are not telling."

In the interest of justice, the judge accepted the plea bargains. Peggy Kosmin and Tammy Molewicz agreed to plead guilty to aggravated manslaughter and to receive 20-year sentences, with a minimum of 8 years being served before becoming eligible for parole. In addition, Kosmin agreed to plead guilty to arson charges in exchange for serving an additional five years, this sentence to be served consecutively with the aggravated assault conviction.

"TULSA'S LADY MACBETH COULDN'T WASH AWAY HER CRIME!"

by Charles W. Sasser

Oklahoma frost still crusted windshields when the call came in to the Tulsa County Sheriff's Department about 7:40 A.M. on Monday, November 22, 1993.

"There's a guy in a locked car out behind our building. Maybe he's just sleeping hard, but I think he's dead," the caller said.

In recent years, under the direction of Sheriff Stanley Glanz, a retired city of Tulsa police detective, the sheriff's department has grown into a modern and efficient law enforcement organization of more than 300 deputies and other employees. Minutes after the trouble call arrived at the sheriff's downtown dispatch office, Deputies Gary Ross and Matt Palmer pulled their unmarked car into the parking lot of Bowen's Carpet Center on Charles Page Boulevard. Charles Page is a major artery stretching between Tulsa and Sand Springs. The sheriff's department investigates all crimes committed in the unincorporated areas of Tulsa County.

Next to the carpet center, partly hidden from the street by a storage building, sat a blue 1988 Hyundai four-door sedan. A Caucasian male was slumped on the front passenger seat with his head resting against the window.

A knock on the window failed to arouse the man. He appeared to be in his mid-20s and had light-brown shoulder-length hair. He looked somewhat lanky, about 6 feet tall. His body was partly covered by a blanket, which reached halfway up his chest, leaving exposed his white hooded pullover with the logo "No Fear" printed across the front. All four doors of the vehicle were locked.

The lawmen noted a blood smear, powder burns, and possible bullet holes obscuring the words "No Fear." Detective Ross used a "Slim Jim" tool to get the Hyundai's back door open. That done, he quickly determined that the man inside was lifeless. His body was cold to the touch. Rigor mortis had stiffened the extremities. From his experience, Ross estimated that the man had been dead perhaps 10 to 12 hours, since around ten o'clock or so the previous night.

Two bullet holes were in the victim's chest, one high, near the heart, the other lower, toward the abdomen. The powder burns on the shirt made it clear that the victim had been shot at point-blank range, which would be the distance between two people sitting in the front seat of the car. One of the lethal bullets passed completely through the victim and through the back of the front seat, and dropped onto the back floorboard. The angle of the shot indicated that the victim was behind the steering wheel when the bullets struck him.

The recovered bullet, the sleuths later determined, was a .380-caliber. The other slug still inside the body also proved to be a .380.

"From the looks of things, maybe the 'No Fear' guy should have had a little fear," remarked one of the crime scene specialists and forensics medical experts who were soon crowding the drive and narrow space at the end of the carpet center. They got to work quickly, photographing the body, car, and scene, dusting for fingerprints, and searching for other latent and trace evidence.

"All we know is that when we came in to work this morning, the car was there with him in it," said one of the employees of the carpet outlet. "It hadn't been there Saturday. We don't know about Sunday, since we were closed."

The sleuths recovered two spent .380 cartridge casings ejected by a semiautomatic firearm onto the front floorboard and the seat of the vehicle. Underneath the driver's-side front seat lay a blue-steel Llama .380 semiautomatic pistol.

"Small caliber. Must be the death weapon," a medical investigator surmised. "It looks like a possible suicide?"

Detective Gary Ross had accumulated 15 years of law enforcement experience. A short, stocky man with a pleasant, open face, he had cultivated the habit of carefully studying a crime scene before venturing any guesses as to what had happened. He looked over this scene now and pondered what he saw. A proper "reading" of the items at a scene can tell an investigator a great many things.

"It's not a suicide," Ross finally decided. "It's a homicide. The gun underneath the seat is not the one that killed him. Look, the hammer is cocked. There's no live round in the chamber, as there would have been had the gun been recently fired. Somebody else lit up this guy with a different three-eighty."

The .380 semiautomatic, both lightweight and powerful, has become somewhat a weapon of choice for a lot of street criminals.

As Ross formulated his hypothesis in his field notes, he noted two other facts that supported it. First, there was the position of the front seat. Second, there was the smear of blood on the seat between the body and the steering wheel.

"This guy didn't drive himself here," Ross explained. "He was killed somewhere else and driven here by another person— by a very, very small driver. Probably a woman, but maybe an extremely tiny man. Or even a kid. But I'd bet on a woman."

The victim was a tall man with long legs. Even with his own shorter legs, Ross could not have easily maneuvered himself behind the steering wheel. The seat had been shifted all the way forward to allow a much smaller person to drive.

The smear of blood on the seat surface was consistent with

the bullet hole in the back of the seat: the victim had been behind the steering wheel when he was shot, and then he was pulled over to the passenger side. The shooter then shifted the seat forward to allow for his or her smaller stature and drove the dead or dying man to Charles Page Boulevard. From the looks of it, the killer had carefully, almost tenderly, draped a blanket over the victim before abandoning the dead man and his automobile.

"It is a gesture a stranger wouldn't ordinarily extend to his victim," Detective Ross observed. "The shooter is probably acquainted—and perhaps well acquainted—with the dead guy."

The contents of the wallet found in the dead man's jeans identified him as 24-year-old Donald James Selige, a Tulsan who turned out to have a long police record of narcotics convictions. Police suspected him of being a drug dealer. The wallet contained no money. There was about $3 in change in the car.

The investigators considered what they had so far: a dead dope dealer shot twice, two expended shell casings, two bullets, an unfired pistol, a blanket, no money or drugs in the car, a small-sized killer.

Who knocked off the "No Fear" man? Was the motive robbery? A dope rip-off? Revenge? A jealous lover? A drug-maddened contact?

Drugs, the police concluded, certainly had something to do with the murder.

Papers found inside the car listed Selige's last-known address as an apartment he shared with his common-law wife, Bernice Land, in Tulsa's low-rent, government-subsidized projects in the 6100 block of South Madison Avenue. Since the federal government took over subsidizing the sprawling apartment complexes, crime had risen dramatically in the area. The projects had become hotbeds of narcotics dealing and other assorted misdemeanors and felonies, including drive-by shootings and murder.

To the sleuths, it seemed appropriate that a suspected dope dealer might have been living there. It also supported their theories that Selige's murder had something to do with drugs.

As Detectives Ross and Palmer drove to the South Madison address, they wondered aloud: how big a woman was Bernice Land? It was about 2 P.M. They had completed the crime scene work. Now the footwork would being.

As it turned out, Bernice wasn't home. A member of her family answered the door. She told the investigators that Bernice was out looking for "D.J.," as Donald Selige was commonly called.

"Bernice and D.J. are separated," the woman said. "D.J. has been dating some girl named Nita. Nita called Bernice about six-thirty this morning and asked if Bernice knew where D.J. was. That was real odd. Bernice and Nita don't exactly get along, as you can imagine. This was the first time Nita has ever called here."

Bernice's relative did not know Nita's last name, nor where she lived. When Bernice Land herself returned home, she, too, proved to be of little help when it came to Nita, although one look at her rather bloated figure convinced the sleuths that she, at least, could not have driven D.J.'s Hyundai to where it was found. The woman was seven months pregnant.

"We have 'Caller ID' on our telephone," Bernice told detectives. "I don't know Nita's address, but the 'ID' recorded her phone number the first time she called this morning and no one answered."

The number checked out to an address on West 38th Street North in Osage County, just north of the Tulsa city limits. Detective Ross dialed the number. A man answered and identified himself as Tommy Brown.

"I need to talk to Nita," Ross said.

A woman came on the phone.

"Nita, this is Detective Gary Ross of the sheriff's department. I need to talk to you."

A long, long silence followed. Then the woman said, "I'll meet you at my house." She gave an address in the 7600 block of West 9th Street in a West Tulsa location, Ross noted, coincidentally not far from where Donald Selige ended up dead.

Nita lived there with a couple of family members. The detectives arrived ahead of Nita. One of Nita's relatives, a woman named Candy, was, like Bernice Land, pregnant, so it was unlikely that she would have fit behind the wheel of the abandoned Hyundai. As they interviewed Candy, Ross and Palmer quickly detected a strong, maybe even bitter, rivalry between her and Nita.

"We found D.J. Selige shot to death this morning," Detective Ross informed the two women while he and Palmer waited for Nita.

"That bitch!" Candy blurted out.

"Who are you referring to?" Ross asked.

"Nita! That bitch probably killed him!"

The investigators soon learned that Selige had arrived at the house occupied by the three women around eight o'clock the previous evening—Sunday, November 21. While there, he jubilantly flashed a bankroll of $7,000, all in crisp new hundred-dollar bills. He counted out the money to impress the women.

Nita and Selige, who were lovers, left the house around 10 P.M. in his blue Hyundai, after Selige and one of the relatives did a line of "crank" together. Crank is a powerful synthetic methamphetamine.

"Did Nita have a gun?" one of the detectives asked.

"Yes," Candy answered. Then she seemed to change her mind and went on to say, "Maybe not. Maybe they just had D.J.'s gun. He always carried a blue-steel semiautomatic pistol."

Candy said that Nita returned home at about 5 A.M., apparently in some distress. "I can't believe that SOB did that!" she exclaimed as she walked in. "He left me at the Git 'N Go on Charles Page Boulevard—and I ain't seen the SOB since." Then Nita telephoned a friend, her demeanor suddenly changing from rage to concern.

"Have you seen D.J.?" she asked, speaking into the receiver. "I'm scared. I'm afraid something has happened to D.J."

Candy told the sleuths that Tommy Brown picked up Nita in

his car a short time later. Nita said she was going out to look for Selige. That had been over nine hours ago.

Investigators Palmer and Ross cooled their heels at the West Tulsa address for nearly an hour, interviewing Candy and the other family member before Nita arrived. When Nita finally came, she was accompanied by Tommy Brown, whose phone number Detective Ross had dialed to contact Nita. Nita strode into the house, prompting the waiting lawmen to exchange meaningful glances.

With stringy blond hair and eyes so pale they also appeared to be almost blond, 20-year-old Nita Lynn Carter stood 5 feet tall and looked as though she weighed about 90 pounds. Both sleuths silently observed that she would fit quite comfortably behind the Hyundai's steering wheel. Moreover, like Selige, she had a police "rap sheet' for narcotics violations.

Detective Ross requested that she and Brown come downtown to the sheriff's department CID (Criminal Investigation Division) to give formal statements.

In her first statement, Nita Carter told the sleuths that D.J. Selige had a .380-caliber semiautomatic pistol stuck into his waistband when he and she left her house around 10 P.M. on Sunday. She did not know if he had money or drugs on him, she said, but she herself did not carry a weapon, nor did she own one.

D.J. and she drove straight to nearby Charles Page Boulevard, where he let her out at the Git 'N Go convenience store in the 6600 block of Page. She said he told her that he had to meet "a couple of guys" to transact a "dope deal." Nita said that D.J. was peddling crank.

"That's the last time I seen him," she said finally.

Investigators Ross and Palmer noted Nita's odd demeanor during questioning. She often stared blankly, silently, whenever they asked her certain questions that she seemed not to want to answer. It was as though she had turned off some light behind her eyes. Between turning herself off and responding to the interrogation, she kept sniffing herself, smelling her arms.

Next, the detectives summoned Tommy Brown to the interrogation room. Meanwhile, a female secretary escorted Nita to the rest room. The secretary later described Nita's eyes as looking "possessed."

"I almost expected her head to revolve on her shoulders and green stuff to come out of her mouth," the secretary later commented. "She looked like the Devil Bitch from Hell."

The secretary refused to stay in the same room with Nita. She left the rest room and waited in the hallway.

In his first statement, Tommy Brown asserted that he knew nothing about what happened to D.J. Selige. All he knew was that Nita showed up at his house that Monday morning, saying D.J. was missing.

Outside the interrogation room, Nita suddenly burst into tears and demanded that she be allowed to speak to the detectives again.

"Tommy had nothing to do with it!" she cried out. "I'll tell everything I know." And then, once again, she started sniffing herself. "I can smell blood!" she explained. *"His* blood."

Upon hearing this, the detectives figured they were about to get a confession. Instead, all the young woman did was to elaborate on her earlier statement. She said she had lied about not having seen D.J. after he dropped her off at the Git 'N Go. In fact, she waited at the convenience store for about 30 minutes, then walked to the nearby alley where D.J. was supposed to meet his dope customers.

That was when she found Selige shot twice in the chest and slumped over his steering wheel. Nita said that while she stood there in shock, undecided about what to do next, two men in a car entered the alley with the headlights blazing. Apparently, they were the killers and they had returned to make sure that D.J. was dead. Nita said she dropped flat to the ground to hide until the men checked out their handiwork and left.

"Describe the men and their car," Detective Ross prompted the woman.

But Nita could not describe anything about the pair or their vehicle. It was dark, she said. Besides, she was lying on the ground, trembling from fright, not daring to look up, lest the killers saw her.

After the men left, Nita said, she pulled D.J.'s body to the passenger's side of his vehicle and got behind the wheel herself. She drove about a mile to the carpet center, where she parked the Hyundai at one end behind a storage building.

She told the probers that Selige begged her, "Nita, help me?"

The blonde said she covered him with a blanket and sat there with him until he died.

"Why didn't you drive him to a hospital?" Ross asked.

"I—I don't know . . . I can smell his blood on me . . ."

What she smelled, the sleuths figured, was probably her own conscience. Yet, incredible though her story sounded, the detectives knew that drug abusers often do behave irrationally. In any case, her story now explained the blood smears across the car seat and why the seat was shifted forward to accommodate a small driver.

It *was* possible that she was telling the truth. A $7,000 roll of cash and a load of crank—both missing when police found the body—might well have enticed a pair of rip-off artists, as Nita had described.

"We'll be talking to you again," Detective Ross advised Nita as she left.

But not, apparently, if Nita could help it. The next day, when Ross and Palmer attempted to resume their questioning, one of Nita's relatives said that the blonde had gone off with Tommy Brown and that "she's not going to show up to talk to you."

By this time, December was a week away. The investigators used up the last week of November interrogating relatives and associates of D.J. Selige, Nita Carter, and the other members of that particular crowd. They learned that D.J. reportedly "earned" his $7,000 cash by selling crank, which he and a relative of Nita's had traveled to California to acquire. The sleuths also heard various individuals say that Nita Carter slept around all over town—with D.J., with Tommy Brown, with a man named

Joe Todd, and with many others. The way the investigators came to view the situation, the rivalry between Nita and Candy extended to men—they appeared to be competing over who slept with which men.

One of these men—Tommy Brown—had obviously had second thoughts about his involvement with Nita and Candy. Meanwhile, the police had warned him that he could be implicated in a homicide if he lied to protect his lover. That warning seemingly prompted him to come to Detective Ross with a change of heart. Tommy decided to tell the truth, he said—or at least as much as he knew of the truth.

In his revised statement, Tommy said that Nita Carter telephoned him around 11:30 P.M. on a Sunday, November 21, and asked him to pick her up at a bar called Little Joe's, next door to the Git 'N Go on Charles Page Boulevard, about a mile east of Bowen's Carpet Center.

"I knew she had done something, just not what," Tommy told the investigators. "She had a lot of money and some drugs. . . . When we got to my house, she couldn't take enough showers to get clean. She just kept taking showers."

"Trying to get the smell of blood off," Detective Ross surmised. "I guess it didn't work."

Even that Monday afternoon when the sleuths had questioned her, she kept sniffing herself for the smell of blood.

Tommy Brown went on to explain that he had intended to go deer hunting early on Monday morning with a buddy. When the buddy arrived at Brown's rural home in Osage County on West 38th Street North, Nita inexplicably stepped to the house's back door and fired a .380-caliber semiautomatic pistol into the yard.

"This goddamn gun jammed on me last night!" she exclaimed.

While Brown said he could not explain why he did it—it was just something he "felt" he had to do—he wrapped Nita's .380 in a sock and handed it to his hunting buddy.

"Get rid of this," he instructed the other man.

Running down this unexpected lead, Detectives Palmer and

Ross traced Brown's hunting buddy to a south Tulsa cemetery where he worked as a groundskeeper. The surprised friend immediately took them to little Thieland Lake on Osage Drive and 36th Street North, not far from Brown's residence. There, he threw a stone to show where he had hurled the gun into the lake.

Little by little, the evidence was closing around tiny Nita Carter. It threatened to close even more tightly after a diving team led by Sergeant Bill Bass and consisting of Deputies Joe Masek, John Hanning and L. Coe arrived at the lake to dive to the muck at the bottom of the freezing December water.

Four hours later, the divers surfaced for a final time and triumphantly displayed a gun still wrapped in a sock. By the next afternoon, weapons expert Jim Looney with the Oklahoma State Bureau of Investigation (OSBI) telephoned Detective Ross with the news: he had compared the recovered firearm with the bullets removed from Donald Selige's corpse and his automobile.

The projectiles, Looney said, were definitely fired from the gun that came out of the lake—the same gun Tommy Brown was able to place in Nita Carter's hands on the morning after D.J.'s slaying.

All that the detectives had gathered so far was good circumstantial evidence. It pointed directly to Nita Carter and away from the two unidentified men whom she claimed were responsible for putting deadly fear into her "No Fear" boyfriend's life. Still, Detective Ross remained patient. His cases were so tight when they reached trial that few suspects ever wriggled free from the noose.

In the interim, Nita Carter was nervously skipping about the city, moving from motel to motel. Investigators Ross and Palmer kept tabs on her whereabouts, maintaining surveillance on their now prime suspect while they continued to build a case against her. Her lawyer warned the sleuths that she did not want to answer any more questions. Meanwhile, Ross picked up an interesting tidbit of information that Nita had paid the lawyer a $1,000 retainer—paid it in crisp $100 bills like those D.J. flashed around on the night he died.

At this point, Candy, Nita's pregnant kinswoman, suddenly discovered that she had more to offer to the investigation. Like Nita before her, like her other relative, and like Tommy Brown, she contacted Detective Ross and reportedly said she wanted to add to her previous statement.

While initially saying that Nita did not take a gun with her on the night of D.J.'s murder, Candy now said that Nita not only had a pistol, but that Candy herself also knew where Nita had acquired the weapon. Candy said that November 14, a week before the crime, she drove Nita to the house of a mutual boyfriend named Joe Todd, where Nita obtained a .380-caliber semiautomatic. Nita later practiced shooting the gun while at another friend's house.

Using a metal detector, Sheriff's Detectives Matt Palmer and John Schonholtz scanned Nita's practice range at the friend's house until they found several bullets that she had apparently fired there. OSBI ballistics expert Jim Looney compared these projectiles with the firearm recovered from Thieland Lake. Bullets and gun matched.

The noose tightened even more. Nita and the murderer were becoming a match.

Detective Ross's next step was to locate the owner of the murder weapon—Joe Todd. Todd took a step back in surprise when the detective confronted him. He quickly recovered his composure and said that, yes, he was the owner of the gun. Nita Carter had taken it from his residence on November 14.

"She called me that morning and said she was going on vacation and needed to get some clothes she had left at my house," Todd told the police sleuths. "She came by work and got my house key. When I got home, I found she hadn't bothered to take her clothes after all. What she took was the gun."

Todd said that he had telephoned her immediately and demanded, "Did you take my gun?"

"I need it for protection," she replied. "I'll bring it back after vacation."

Todd hadn't seen it or Nita since then.

November 14 was about the time when D.J. Selige and Nita's relative had allegedly traveled to California to pick up a supply of crank. The detectives wondered: Had Nita started planning as early as that to rob and kill her boyfriend?

Investigators Ross and Palmer, armed with a wealth of additional evidence, took another crack at Nita Carter on Monday, December 13. The previous night, a surveillance team had tailed her to the LaQuinta Inn on I-244 near Sheridan Avenue in Tulsa. When the sleuths confronted her, she instantly requested her attorney. Afterwards, she consented to answer questions in her lawyer's presence.

No, she had never possessed a firearm, she declared.

What about Joe Todd's .380?

Oh, that? Well, she only had it one day before D.J. Selige took it and sold it to get money for dope.

What about the gun she fired outside the back door of Tommy Brown's house on November 22, the day when police found Selige shot to death?

Oh, well . . .

"She kept getting sick and having to go to the bathroom," Detective Ross later recalled. "Finally, her attorney said she was too sick to talk. That terminated the session."

On Monday, December 27, 1993, five weeks after D.J. Selige ended up dead, the authorities turned over the results of their lengthy investigation to Tulsa County district attorney David Moss. He reviewed the impressive array of evidence and filed a charge of second-degree murder against Nita Lynn Carter. The apparent motive for murder, the detectives said, was robbery. Selige's $7,000 cash and his supply of crank was simply too tempting for Nita to resist, boyfriend or not.

The detectives who had tailed Nita for weeks lost her in the city for three days before she surfaced on Thursday, December 30.

"She found out we were looking for her and called us," said Sheriff's Lieutenant Dick Bishop. "She said she was at Fifteenth Street and Columbia Avenue and couldn't find our office."

Upon being arrested for Selige's murder, the young woman immediately professed her innocence. Even when, on Monday, June 13, 1994, she changed her tune and pled guilty to committing the murder, she refused to explain the motive and circumstances of the crime, thus leaving those aspects of the case to linger as a mystery.

Nita Lynn Carter is presently serving a 25-year sentence in the Oklahoma State Penitentiary. The police call her conviction and the murder of Donald James "D.J." Selige, the "No Fear" guy, a "twofer." Her crime took two criminals off the streets—herself and her victim, who was himself an established and often-convicted criminal.

"TWO GREEDY BLONDES BLUDGEONED BILLY"

by John Griggs

William L. "Billy" Woodbridge, 65, the graveyard-shift dispatcher for the Colonial Cab Company in York County, Virginia, sent his last dispatch at 12:31 A.M. on Sunday, November 8, 1992. Cabbies had begun to worry when they didn't hear their dispatcher's voice for several minutes. At first, they thought maybe Billy had gone to the bathroom. But when they couldn't get an answer on their radios or by phone, one of the cabbies swung by the office to find out what was wrong.

The cabbie found Billy in a pool of blood beside his chair. One witness would later say that blood was everywhere—on the desk, on the calendar, and all over the wall.

A 911 call sent Deputy Mike McAllister, of the York County Sheriff's Department, and emergency workers rushing to the scene. They found Billy unconscious and nonresponsive, the apparent victim of a severe, life-threatening head injury.

Emergency workers rushed Billy to Williamsburg Community Hospital, and then to Riverside Regional Medical Center. McAllister radioed his supervisor, Lieutenant Jeff Culler, who in turn, sent Investigator Jim Richardson to the scene.

Richardson arrived at the cab company a few minutes before 2 A.M. Realizing that he had a serious case on his hands, he telephoned his captain, Ron Montgomery, and apprised him of the situation. Montgomery decided to join Richardson at the scene.

Richardson rolled up his sleeves and went to work, photographing, dusting for fingerprints, searching in vain for a murder weapon.

Office employees showed the deputies to the safe, which was hidden in a metal cabinet. The employees explained that they placed their deposits in envelopes and dropped them through a slit in the cabinet counter. Investigator Richardson felt he would never have figured out where the safe was, unless the employees had told him. But evidently the perpetrator of this crime had known just where to go: one of the cabinet's metal doors had been popped open. Because nothing else in the office had been rifled and there were no signs of forced entry, Richardson felt he might be dealing with an inside job.

Apparently, robbery was the motive. Employees said that about $750 was missing from a strongbox in the safe.

The officers were still at the crime scene at about 6 A.M. when they called the hospital to check on Woodbridge's condition and learned that he had died. The autopsy would show that Woodbridge had died of blunt trauma to the head. Pathologists wouldn't be able to narrow down what type of weapon was used; they would only be able to say that it apparently wasn't wood, because no splinters were found in the wounds.

So now, the stakes had been raised. Richardson, assigned by Captain Montgomery to lead the probe, was well-qualified for his task. He'd grown up in the area, and had wanted to be a law enforcement officer since he was a boy. The 32-year-old Richardson had served his department for 14 years, almost five years as a detective. Four other detectives and about 60 deputies work under Sheriff P.S. "Press" Williams in the 85 square miles of scenic York County, serving a population of approximately 45,000 souls. The county averages about two or three slayings a year; about half of those are domestic.

The Woodbridge case promised to be far more difficult to

crack than the typical domestic killing. Richardson looked into the victim's background, hoping his research might point him to the killer.

Billy Woodbridge, the sleuth learned, was a gentle, childlike man much loved among folks in the area who knew him. The son of a former dean at the College of William and Mary Law School in nearby Williamsburg, Woodbridge had a learning disability that had held him back in school. He loved to ride his bike sporting his trademark red knit cap. He'd worked as a telegram courier on his bicycle during World War II. He'd held the dispatcher job for the last decade.

Without an obvious enemy in Woodbridge's background, Investigator Richardson turned his attention back to the facts at hand. The detectives knew that the killer had struck sometime between 12:31 A.M., when Woodbridge was last heard on the company radio, and 1 A.M., when his body was discovered. The detectives asked employees if they remembered anything unusual about that time, or if they'd seen anyone hanging around the office earlier in the evening.

Cabbies told the detectives that a woman who used to drive with them, 23-year-old Carolyn Marie Dean, a heavyset blonde, had been hanging out at the office late Saturday night. They remembered that she had parked her battered blue Toyota beside their external vacuum cleaner, which they used to clean their cars.

Investigator Richardson decided to find the woman to see what she knew. But by 8 A.M. on Sunday, he was dog-tired. He went home and hit the sack.

Returning to headquarters on Sunday afternoon, Richardson and his fellow sleuths set out to find Carolyn Dean. Through motor vehicle records, they got a solid description of her car: a light-blue 1978 Toyota two-door with a damaged front end and bearing Virginia license-plate number KIW 673. The detectives circulated the description of Dean and her car throughout their department.

About 10 o'clock Sunday night, Richardson and a fellow officer were riding around, looking for the car, when they spotted one matching its description parked across busy Route 60 from a Williamsburg motel. The license plate number on the parked car confirmed that it was Dean's.

Richardson and his fellow officer stopped and talked to the occupants of the car. Dean wasn't among them.

The driver, Kenny Britt, told Richardson that he had borrowed the car from Carolyn Dean to go to the store and pick up some cigarettes and sodas for her. Dean was staying in the motel across the street, Britt said.

Richardson, realizing he'd need some help, radioed Captain Montgomery and Sergeant W.V. Moore. The superiors quickly arrived. Getting Dean's room number from the motel clerk, Moore and Montgomery set out for the room. Richardson asked Britt if he'd mind getting out of Dean's car and having a talk with him in Richardson's car. Britt agreed.

Area law enforcement officers were familiar with Britt, who'd had his share of drug problems. Richardson asked him if he knew anything about Billy Woodbridge's murder. Britt said he didn't know a thing. And so the conversation went, until finally Richardson laid it flat out for Britt: they were talking about a capital murder case here, the most serious crime in Virginia, the only one a felon could get the death penalty for.

Britt began to talk a little more. He said he wasn't getting in trouble for anybody, but all he said was that Dean had been trying to borrow money from him on Saturday, during the day.

And where had he been that Saturday night? Richardson asked Britt.

Britt said he spent the night with a woman in Williamsburg. He gave Richardson the woman's name and phone number. Right then and there, before Britt could confer with the woman, the sleuth dialed the number on his car phone. The woman answered and confirmed that Britt had in fact been with her the night before.

So it wasn't the most productive interview in the world. Investigator Richardson would soon learn that his colleagues Moore and Montgomery weren't having much better luck.

After knocking on Carolyn Dean's motel room door and identifying themselves as law enforcement officers, Dean let them in. The officers told Dean they were investigating the slaying of Billy Woodbridge the night before at Colonial Cab. Was she aware of it?

No, Dean said, she wasn't.

Had she been there the night before? the sleuths asked.

Dean said she had. Both she and her friend, 31-year-old Pamela Sue Sayre, who was also in the room, had gone by the cab company. They got there about 11:30 P.M., Dean said, and left about an hour later, at 12:30 A.M. on Sunday. She went inside, Dean said, and Sayre waited outside.

The detectives kept their mouths shut, but they knew that Woodbridge had last been heard from at 12:31 on Sunday morning. Either Dean was one of the killers and had just made a big mistake, or somebody else had slipped into the office and killed Woodbridge scant seconds after Dean and her friend left.

To a point, Dean's story did not contradict the known facts. Her arrival time jibed with what the other cabbies had said earlier. She even said that she'd parked by the vacuum cleaner outside, just as the cabbies had reported. She also remembered that while she was in the office, one of the drivers had called in to say that he had hit a deer. The sleuths later found out that that conversation had, in fact, taken place.

To explain why, as a former employee, she was in the office in the first place, Dean said she often went there because she hoped to get her old job back. Another peculiarity in her story concerned a detail she said she noticed as she and Sayre were leaving the office. A few hundred yards from the office, Dean said, they saw a man with a long dark coat walking toward the cab company. He held his head down so they couldn't see his face. Trying to give her the benefit of the doubt, detectives looked into the angle, but they never found any evidence to support the mystery man's existence.

Montgomery and Moore asked Dean why she and Sayre were staying in a motel in town and not at the home they shared in nearby James City County.

Sayre had had a fight with her boyfriend, Dean explained, and Dean and Sayre were afraid he would become violent.

Moore and Montgomery asked Dean how much money she and Sayre had. Dean said they had about $100 that they'd borrowed from friends on Saturday. The detectives eventually learned that the rooms went for $85 a night. That would have left the women with about $15. But the sleuths felt the women might have more money than that, since there were several empty pizza delivery boxes lying around the room and they'd sent Kenny Britt out with money to buy them the cigarettes and soda. Yet, earlier Saturday, they'd been trying to borrow money from Britt.

Had the women come upon a deadly windfall? If they had, they weren't saying.

Montgomery looked Carolyn Dean right in the face and said, "The reason I'm here is, Billy Woodbridge didn't die right away."

Dean didn't flinch. Her expression seemed to say, What are you telling me for?

Montgomery snuck looks at Dean's shoes, finding no signs of blood on them.

Moore and Montgomery ended the interview and left the room. The sleuths talked to the motel clerk, who said neither Dean nor Sayre had appeared nervous or upset when they checked in about thee o'clock that morning.

Both Dean and Sayre were unemployed. A computer records check on them turned up nothing on Sayre, and only one arrest for a bad check on Dean. Of course, prior records are sometimes no indications of one's potential for violence. And the women *had* been the last to see Woodbridge alive . . .

The next day, Monday, November 9, the detectives persuaded Dean and Sayre to come down to headquarters for interviews. Richardson interviewed Sayre, who seemed almost perky, in one room; Montgomery interviewed Dean in another. The women's stories basically meshed. And both were saying they had nothing to do with the slaying. There was only one possible weak point: Dean denied asking Britt for money on Saturday.

The sleuths persuaded the women to take polygraph tests. The detectives set up an appointment for Dean on Wednesday with Captain Danny Diggs, a polygraph operator at the nearby Gloucester County Sheriff's Department.

Polygraph test results, while inadmissible in U.S. courts, often play vital roles in helping detectives feel their way in cases. Many a suspect, cowed by the seriousness of the test itself, has broken during the exam.

The two key questions for Sayre and Dean were: Did you help in or plan the robbery or murder? Do you know for sure who robbed or murdered Billy Woodbridge?

Dean, who'd said she had a cold, started coughing in the middle of her exam, rendering its results inconclusive. The sleuths felt her coughing fit was intentional. Diggs told the sleuths that his gut feeling was that Dean was not being truthful on the key questions.

Sayre had her appointment with Captain Diggs the next day.

Sayre didn't have a coughing fit, but her test results were also inconclusive: They didn't indicate that she was lying, but neither did they indicate that she was telling the truth.

As the days since the slaying stretched into weeks, the women acted as if they had nothing to hide. They let the detectives take photos and fingerprints, and they repeatedly called to check on the progress of the probe.

Dean allowed Richardson to search her car. He found a white towel with a light stain on it. Wondering if the stain might be blood, he decided to have forensic scientists analyze it. The lab was backlogged with other cases, so it would be several weeks before Richardson would know the results of that test.

One day, weeks after the slaying, Richardson got a call from Sayre. She told the sleuth that she and Dean were tired of all the talk linking them with the killing and wanted to know if they could leave the area for a while.

Richardson explained to Sayre that they weren't under arrest and were, in fact, free to go. He did tell her that he'd like to know where they would be.

Sayre said they were headed to a relative's in Wheeling, West Virginia, where Sayre was originally from, and gave the sleuth the relative's address and phone number.

Richardson and his fellow sleuths continued working the probe as 1992 surrendered to 1993. But all leads kept coming to dead ends.

One potential witness told detectives that a certain woman had said she heard Sayre talk about committing the crime. Richardson tracked down the woman, who denied hearing any such conversation.

Still, Richardson kept returning to the fact that Dean and Sayre had been the last to see Billy Woodbridge alive, and the fact that only about a minute passed between the time they said they left and Woodbridge was last heard on the air. That left very little time for another killer to slip in.

As far as physical evidence, the detectives had found no prints inside the safe—the only place prints would have been of any real value. Even if they'd found Dean's prints inside the office, the woman had been there by her own admission.

Detectives still suspected that Kenny Britt, the man who'd been driving Dean's car, was involved in the crime somehow, despite his girlfriend's voucher that he was with her on the night of the slaying.

The case bugged Richardson. It occupied most of his waking thoughts, even as he worked other cases. Once, he thought about asking *America's Most Wanted* to air a segment on it. The TV show had profiled another of his cases.

Almost two months after the slaying, Richardson got back the results of the forensic analysis of the stained towel found in Dean's car. The scientists had determined that the stains were, in fact, blood—human blood—but there wasn't enough of it on the towel to determine the type.

While the evaluation wasn't the best news in the world, informant Oscar Hines soon came forward with something more valuable. Hines told the sleuths that Dean tried to solicit his help in the slaying. He said Dean had come by his house late that Saturday night. She said it would be easy to kill Woodbridge: The old man, Dean said, worked at the office at night by himself, so one person could easily lure him away from the radio, and the other person could beat him.

Hines declined to help.

Richardson talked the case over with fellow detectives. He decided to press charges of capital murder and robbery against Dean alone for now. She was the only one he could positively place inside the victim's office. Later, Richardson hoped, he could make a case against Sayre. He swore out the charges against Dean in early February 1993.

The case was circumstantial, but the evidence had depth. As a previous employee of the cab company, Dean knew the location of the safe. Witnesses said she'd never really cared for Billy Woodbridge, and the night she was in there, she kept asking about another cabbie she'd never really cared for, either. Thus, her reason for being at the cab company in the first place was suspicious. It was unusual for her to come by, witnesses said.

Witnesses also said that Dean had been desperately trying to borrow money before Woodbridge ended up dead, yet after his dead, she had money for a motel room and plenty of pizza.

Most important of all, there was the informant's story.

Captain Montgomery called Sayre's relative in Wheeling. Sayre lived at another Wheeling address, the relative said. Montgomery said he just wanted to check on a couple of points of the case with her and told the relative to have Sayre call them.

Sayre soon called back. Not knowing that the sleuths had secured a warrant for Dean's arrest, she gave the captain her address. Montgomery told Sayre to keep in touch, then hung up.

On Sunday, February 14, Richardson and Sergeant Moore set

out on the eight-and-a-half-hour drive from York County to Wheeling, slowly climbing up into the mountains and increasing cold. The skies threatened snow. They checked into a Wheeling motel that night.

Richardson was ready but apprehensive. While the case was strong circumstantially, it wasn't yet the best one to take to court, not without a confession from Sayre or Dean. The minutes after Dean's arrest would be crucial: Richardson's one and only shot at getting either woman to confess.

On Monday morning, Dean and Moore met with Wheeling police lieutenant Joseph Davis, the head of the department's detective unit, who assigned Detectives Lawrence Manning and Thomas Williams and Patrol Officer Gary Gaus to assist the Virginia sleuths. The time was 9 A.M. as they drove off to make the arrest.

Snow that had fallen the night before carpeted the ground. Richardson was dressed in a sports coat and slacks, his 9mm in a waist holster underneath his coat as they approached the door of the house where Sayre and Dean were staying with Sayre's boyfriend. Although Wheeling police had checked and found no record of the women causing any trouble in their town, the officers realized that caution is always the best policy.

The boyfriend, Lyle Trump, answered the sleuths' knock. Upon learning the detectives' business, Trump soon awakened both women and had Dean at the door.

"Do you remember me, Carolyn?" Detective Richardson asked Dean.

She said she did. The sleuth said, "I have felony warrants for your arrest for the capital murder of Billy Woodbridge."

Dean's mouth dropped open, but she said nothing. Richardson read her her Miranda Rights, handcuffed her, and led her to a car for transport to the Wheeling Police Department.

Now, Richardson turned to Sayre. He told her she wasn't under arrest. But he urged her to help them. Sayre's boyfriend became an unexpected ally, telling his girlfriend she better talk if she knew something. Sayre agreed to do so.

It was like shooting ducks in a barrel. Unbelievably easy. Richardson and Moore, trading quick looks, contained their excitement. Richardson read the woman her Miranda Rights.

Sayre said she understood and was willing to talk. She said Dean had told her that if she went down for the crime, Sayre was going down with her.

The story was simple: Dean beat Woodbridge to death with a hammer so she could steal the money in the safe's strongbox.

Richardson told Sayre he'd like to get a taped statement from her. Would she come down to Wheeling police headquarters with them? Sayre worried about how she'd get back to her house. If she wasn't involved in the slaying, Richardson told her, he'd drive her back. She agreed to go.

By 9:50 A.M., Richardson and Sayre were alone in an interview room at Wheeling police headquarters. Richardson advised the woman of her Miranda Rights once more. A tape recorder was rolling as she began to talk.

Sayre explained that Dean had done the crime because they owed Kenny Britt, the man who'd been driving Dean's car the day after the slaying, $260 for crack cocaine that they both used. She talked about how Dean did the crime with a steel-shanked hammer. She said she went into the office with Dean after everyone left and stood by as Dean committed the slaying.

Afterwards, Sayre said, they threw the hammer over the Chickahominy River Bridge, near York County. The money was in a box, Sayre said, and they threw that box and some of their bloody clothing into a Dempsey Dumpster.

Dean called herself and Sayre "Thelma and Louise" after the two women in the movie of the same name. In the movie, one of the women kills a man, and they flee law enforcement officers across the country, sticking together the whole way. Sayre said Dean had said it was like that with them: all for one and one for all. They'd done the crime on their own, she said, and Kenny Britt was not involved.

Sayre said she'd seen *Thelma and Louise*. Coincidentally, Investigator Richardson had just rented the film and watched it, as well.

At one point, when she'd thought they had gotten away with the killing, Sayre thanked God and swore to Him that she'd never smoke crack again. She said Dean had dragged her into the crime, and she felt so bad about Woodbridge that she'd come close to confessing to Richardson before, or at least giving him hints about the crime. Sayre cried, saying she was sorry for the victim and his family.

As the interview drew to a close after about an hour, Sayre asked Richardson if he could keep her out of jail. He said he couldn't do that. Sayre said she would kill herself to keep from going to jail. Richardson would later make sure that officers kept a close watch on her.

The investigator ducked out of the interview room and made a fast call to Captain Montgomery in Virginia. Up to the time Sayre broke, the sleuths had continued to believe that Kenny Britt was involved in the slaying, despite his tight alibi.

Richardson told Montgomery that he wasn't going to believe it, but the two women acted alone. Briefly, he described his interview with Sayre.

Montgomery wanted to know what Dean had to say.

Richardson said he hadn't talked to her yet; he was getting ready to now. But he needed warrants secured against Pamela Sayre for first-degree murder and armed robbery.

Right after Montgomery hung up, he went before a magistrate, secured the warrants, and faxed them. They were in Wheeling within minutes, and Richardson served them on Sayre.

Moore joined Richardson in an interview room with Dean. They read her her Miranda Rights and went to work. As they began to question Dean about Woodbridge's death, she said, with a surprised look on her face, that she didn't know what they were talking about.

The sleuths told Dean they knew what happened, that Woodbridge had been beaten to death, and that the weapon had been tossed into the river. She shouldn't lie to them, they said. It was going to be hard for her, they said, but all they wanted was the truth.

Dean dropped her head. The detectives knew they had her. She then raised her head, a tear in one eye.

"Well, here it goes," she said. "I was smoked up on crack when I did it."

The sleuths read the suspect her Miranda Rights once more. Then they turned on the tape recorder.

Carolyn Dean confessed to killing Billy Woodbridge with Sayre's help. Just as Sayre had said, Dean said they'd acted alone. But Dean's statement was more vague than Sayre's, and she tried to pin some of the blows on Sayre.

Dean said that as she began striking Woodbridge, he cried, "What are you doing! What are you doing!"

Dean said she struck Woodbridge with the handle of the hammer. That would be consistent with the pathologist's findings. Dean never explained why she choose to use the handle rather than the head.

After Woodbridge fell to the floor, Dean said, Sayre, who had been standing in a corner, took the hammer and struck the victim.

That part didn't make sense to Detective Richardson. He would see one perp pushing the murder weapon on the second, but not one actually grabbing out for the murder weapon.

In contrast with the emotional Sayre, Richardson found Dean cold enough to "send chills up your spine." The only emotion she showed during the whole interview was the one tear she shed when she broke at the beginning.

At the end of the interview, Dean said she wished she could tell Woodbridge that she was sorry. Her wish didn't strike Richardson as being particularly sincere.

The sleuths charged Dean with capital murder and armed robbery.

Both women were eventually extradited to Virginia, where they were held in jail as they awaited trial. Commonwealth's

Attorney James H. Smith would be pursuing the death penalty against them.

No women have been executed in Virginia since the early part of the century, so it promised to be a landmark case.

For their part, Richardson and his fellow officers kept working. They had Virginia State Police divers search the deep, murky water near the Chickahominy River Bridge numerous times for the murder weapon, but their efforts were all in vain. They were also unable to recover the money, strongbox, or bloody clothing.

In the end, Sayre and Dean escaped the threat of the death penalty by pleading guilty in York County Circuit Court. In July 1993, Sayre pled guilty to first-degree murder and armed robbery. The following November, she was sentenced to 60 years in prison.

In late September 1993, Dean pled guilty to capital murder and armed robbery. Judge John M. Folkes sentenced her to two life terms in prison.

The victim's relatives approved the plea agreements, telling a reporter that the relatively quick resolution was preferable to a death sentence and the subsequent appeals process that could drag on for years.

After sentencing Dean, Judge Folkes said the slaying might not have occurred save for cocaine.

"There are so many victims in this case as a result of this drug," he said.

"TEXAS'S MURDER BY 'PROPHET' "

by Turk Ryder

"It makes no sense," said the South Texas detective who was standing in front of the yellow ribbon barricade stretched around the suburban home's driveway. Not the victim, not the place— none of it made any sense at all.

A few minutes earlier, just before seven o'clock on Wednesday, March 3, 1993, in Rancho Viejo, near Brownsville, Texas, Albert Joey Fischer was standing in the driveway washing his car, which he then planned to drive to school.

As the handsome teen with the toothy smile held the garden hose in one hand and sponged down the rear chrome bumper with the other, a dark sedan turned the corner and crept along Cortez Avenue.

The two men in the car did not know the upper-middle-class neighborhood in which they found themselves so early in the morning. It was far removed from the grinding poverty of the Mexican barrio where they grew up.

Inching along, they saw the 18-year-old honor student in the driveway.

"That's him," the passenger said. "We're in luck."

Joey Fischer's back was turned as the sedan lurched to the curb.

One of the men in the sedan—the passenger, probably—stuck a .38-caliber revolver out the window, took hurried aim, and fired three times. The sedan then roared away.

That's how one of the most bizarre criminal cases in South Texas history had its bloody beginning.

The shooting was reported to Rancho Viejo police at 7:06 A.M. The dispatcher taking down the information was so floored by what she was hearing that she wondered if she got it down right. Shootings just aren't that common in towns like Rancho Viejo.

Patrol officers arriving on the scene found Joey Fischer sprawled in the driveway, his head wreathed in a pool of blood. The 18-year-old had been shot twice in the head and once in the chest. He was dead when patrol officers rushed to his side to check for a pulse.

Word of the shooting reached the Cameron County Sheriff's Office. A homicide team headed by Lieutenant Ernesto Flores, with Abel Perez, Jr., as chief investigator, hurried to the scene.

Police and sheriff's cruisers lined both sides of Cortez Avenue, and lawmen were busy keeping shocked neighbors behind a yellow ribbon barricade.

In the driveway, a bloodstained sheet covered the body of Joey Fischer. Investigator Perez lifted one corner and looked at the oddly peaceful face of the dead teenager.

After the brief examination, investigators questioned the victim's family, who were stunned and shocked by the early-morning shooting.

They told detectives that Joey had finished eating breakfast and was washing his car when they heard shots. They ran outside and, to their horror, saw their son sprawled on the cement driveway, the water hose still in his hand. It took a moment to realize that he had been shot. They had no idea why anyone would want to hurt their son.

Neighbors were questioned about what they had seen and heard. One said that she was inside her house making pancakes for breakfast when she heard the fatal discharge of the pistol.

"My husband saw the body lying in the driveway," she told detectives. "He said, 'My God, somebody has been shot!' "

Another neighbor a few houses away heard gunshots and went to the front door in time to see a dark sedan hurtling past the house. He described it as a late-model American sedan with two men inside. He didn't recognize the car or the passengers.

Rancho Viejo is not the sort of place where people are shot in their driveways by hit men in dark sedans. It is, rather, a middle-class landscape where skateboard accidents, not drive-by shootings, are the chief worry.

The motive for the shooting was puzzling. Joey was an honor student at St. Joseph Academy, and something of an all-American kid—not exactly the profile of a drive-by shooting victim.

Hoping they might learn more about the victim and perhaps come up with a motive, detectives went to the teen's private Catholic school.

Teachers and three counselors were busy consoling the victim's shocked and stunned classmates.

Fischer, detectives learned, was 11th in his graduating class. A creative writing teacher called the victim "a brain" and one of the most gifted and talented students he had ever taught.

"A few of the seniors who were very close to him have gotten permission to leave the class and talk to a counselor," the school principal said. "Everybody is in a daze. That is understandable. Joey was just such a nice kid."

"Nice kid . . . top student . . . well-liked . . . brain . . . creative"—all words describing Joey Fischer. They were words that belonged in a high school yearbook, not in the notebook of a homicide investigator. They spoke of a great tragedy and human loss but did not begin to clear up the central mystery—why had Joey Fischer been gunned down?

The autopsy was scheduled for that evening with the preliminary report made available the next morning. The single-spaced, four-page document revealed that the 18-year-old honor student had been shot once in the back and twice in the head. "He died almost instantly," the pathologist noted. "It is possible he did not know what hit him."

The slugs had been fired from a .38-caliber weapon, a large handgun as popular in Brownsville as it is in most parts of the Lone Star State.

Detectives still had not determined why those bullets were pumped into the young man. But that did not mean that the case had stalled.

Searching the street in front of the Fischer home, investigators had found a fresh bullet casing that had been ejected from the murder weapon. Ballistic technicians would be able to match markings on the shell to the murder weapon, if it was ever found.

But of greater importance was a crumpled card found during a search of Cortez Avenue. The card was creased but appeared new. A seven-digit number was written on the back. It appeared to be a telephone number. The prefix, however, was not a local number.

It took a few calls before detectives put a name to the number: Daniel Garza, 43, of San Antonio. Garza, however, was not home.

Who was Daniel Garza?

No one in the Fischer family had heard of the San Antonio man. And no one on the block had heard of him, either.

A computer crime check did not turn up anything noteworthy. San Antonio police hadn't heard of him, either. Garza, according to records, was just another upstanding citizen, with no police record, and no warrants. The only thing that made him different was that his telephone number was found at the scene of a murder.

Meanwhile, calls about the case flooded the Cameron County Sheriff's Office. Some were of the type that police usually receive in such high-profile cases. Others came from well-intentioned citizens who believed they had information that might help find the killer.

One tip led police to a Chevy sedan that had been abandoned near the border. The car had been reported stolen earlier from

South Padre Island. Detectives determined that it could not have been the car used in the shooting of Joey Fischer.

Other tips took detectives to the Brownsville Jail, and across the border. One rumor had it that Fischer had been killed by a hired gunman who had shot the wrong person by mistake.

Detectives checked out the rumor and questioned the man who had allegedly been the intended victim.

Weeks passed. On March 31, detectives located Daniel Garza. The San Antonio resident said he had been traveling and had just gotten back into town.

Detectives told him that they were investigating the murder of Joey Fischer. Garza acknowledged the statement with a nod. "It is too bad," he admitted. "But what has this to do with me?"

Detectives told Garza about the card found in front of the Fischer home. Garza said he had no idea what the card was doing there.

As the interrogation continued, police noted that Garza appeared increasingly ill at ease. His forehead broke out in a sweat, and his hands shook uncontrollably.

Detectives asked if he had ever driven through Rancho Viejo or perhaps along Cortez Avenue.

Suddenly, in a burst of candor, Garza said, "I thought they were going to beat him up. I didn't know they were going to kill him."

Garza then began a lengthy statement. When he was through, detectives had the motive for the killing of Joey Fischer. It was also about as bizarre a statement as the detectives had ever heard.

Garza said it began when his marriage began to unravel. He had been married for 22 years and had two daughters and a son. His son had muscular dystrophy.

"He was getting worse," Garza said. "He needed care. My wife got to the point where she wanted to end her life."

Out of his mind with grief, Garza sought help from a Brownsville fortune-teller.

"From who?" a nonplussed detective asked.

"My fortune-teller," Garza replied. He explained that she was a folk healer and he had been consulting her for years. "I needed to know from her why all these bad things were happening in my life."

He said he believed that his wife's mother and aunts had worked through a *curandera*—another fortune-teller—in San Antonio to put a bad spell on his wife to make her leave him.

"My mother-in-law never liked me," Garza confessed. "Nobody on that side of the family liked me."

Garza said he visited the fortune-teller in June 1992, hoping that she might be able to lift the spell that had turned his life upside down. He said she scattered Mexican fortune-telling cards on the table and told him that she suspected the bad spell had come from his wife's relatives. She said she could remove the spell but that it would not be easy.

Or cheap. Garza said he gave her $300 for telling his fortune.

After that visit, he kept calling her and meeting her about once a month. He said he didn't remember how much he spent, but it was a lot.

In December, Garza went to visit the fortune-teller again, when she made a surprising offer: she would pay him $3,500 if he would do "something" for her.

Garza said he nearly jumped out of his cowhide boots. "She said she needed someone beaten up, and asked if I knew anyone who would do it," he told detectives. It seemed like a strange request from an elderly woman who made her living reading tarot cards and selling folk remedies. Garza said he was not exactly sure that he heard her correctly.

But the fortune-teller insisted he heard her correctly: She needed the services of a man who would administer the lumps to someone. She said if such a man could be found, her client was prepared to pay as much as $3,500.

"She said they had to be trustworthy," Garza told police, wincing as he recalled the fateful conversation. "She said if I could do this favor for her that she would use all her resources to help me with my broken marriage."

Garza believed the fortune-teller, "I know it sounds crazy. It even sounds crazy to me. But she gave me hope. I was desperate. I would have done anything."

The fortune-teller never told Garza who the client was. She was also tight-lipped about the identity of the victim.

Garza said he would see what he could do. But what could he do? "I didn't know the first thing about hiring such people," he told detectives. "I had no connections to the underworld."

But after Christmas, Garza said his wife announced that their marriage was over and kicked him out of the house.

He returned to his fortune-teller to ask what went wrong. During their chat, she asked if he had found anyone or gotten anyone to do the "job" they had discussed.

"She guaranteed me that my luck would change if I helped her," Garza said. "I should have known better, but I was stupid. I told her I would do my best to help her out."

A few weeks later, Garza found himself in a nightclub in Grand Prairie, Texas. It was one of those rough kind of places where the topless dancers had more tattoos than the truck drivers and ex-convicts who watched them.

Garza said he was still licking his wounds over the dissolution of his marriage when he overheard two men next to him talk about a shooting in Brownsville.

"One of the guys said he had shot a guy and thrown his body in the Rio Grande," Garza recalled. "He acted like it was no big deal."

Garza said he introduced himself and told the stranger he might have a business opportunity for him. The stranger, who introduced himself only as Israel, said he and his buddy were interested.

"I told them about the money and that made them *real* interested," Garza said.

They kept in touch and later met at a motel in Brownsville. Garza passed along a snapshot of the victim that the fortune-teller had given him and gave the two men directions to the boy's house.

"They were supposed to beat him up and then I was to pay them the money," Garza said.

The day Joey Fischer was shot, Garza saw a snapshot of the victim flash across the television screen. He immediately recognized the young man as the one in the photo given him by the fortune-teller. Garza was stunned.

He met the two men at the motel two hours after the killing. "The one called Israel said it was done, that he wanted his money."

Garza gave it to him and they left. He hadn't seen them since.

"I wish it never happened," Garza said. "I thought they were only supposed to beat him up. I didn't know about the guns until I saw the television."

Garza blamed the fortune-teller for his misfortune. "She took advantage of me because I was weak," he said. "She said my marriage would get better if I did this favor for her. But nothing happened. My wife divorced me. The fortune-teller lied."

Garza's information led detectives to Maria Martinez, 71, who owned The Hummingbird, a dingy little storefront stocked with exotic herbs, unnamed potions, and amulets guaranteeing cures for a variety of ills.

A native of San Luis Potosí, Mexico, Martinez could write neither English nor Spanish. But her purported ability to make errant husbands return to their spouses and a host of other special talents had given the fortune-teller a steady, profitable business.

But what, detectives wondered, had prompted the grandmotherly fortune-teller to branch out into the dirty, violent business of contract hits?

The detectives decided to find out.

On April 5, police officers with weapons drawn burst into Martinez's modest Brownsville home and found her sitting on her bed, dressed in a nightgown.

"What is this? Who are you?" the septuagenarian gasped.

Martinez was handcuffed. She was informed of her Miranda Rights. Then she was told to sit while deputies searched her small home. A second search was conducted of her store.

"What is this all about?" Martinez asked in Spanish.

Detectives told her they were investigating a homicide. They asked her if she wanted to make a statement. The elderly woman said she didn't know about making a statement because she was a simple fortune-teller who knew nothing about any murder.

At the police station, Martinez was given another opportunity to make a statement. When she said she did not read English or Spanish, Lieutenant Perez verbally gave her the Miranda Rights and explained what they were.

"It is very late," she said. "I am tired."

The fortune-teller's future, however, didn't look good. Detectives told Martinez they knew she had acted as the "middleman" in the contract hit on Joey Fischer. If she didn't want to talk, that was her right. But detectives assured her that they could make no deals unless she decided to cooperate.

"We heard that you were doing this as a favor," one detective said. "If that is true, then you have nothing to worry about."

"I don't know anything," Martinez insisted. But suddenly, Martinez was singing like a canary. It was a story even more bizarre than the one Daniel Garza told—if that was possible.

It began in the fall of 1992 when a Dora Cisneros, a 55-year-old mother of five and a longtime client of Maria Martinez, came to the small fortune-telling shop and explained that she was having a personal problem.

Joey Fischer, Cisneros said, had been dating one of her daughters. They started dating in March, and a month later, Fischer gave her daughter his class ring to wear. Then in June, Fischer broke up with her daughter.

Cisneros was greatly upset by Fischer's behavior. Why had he done this to her daughter? She asked Martinez if the breakup was permanent. Martinez read the tarot cards and said they indicated that Fischer looked to be very far away from her.

"Señora Cisneros was very unhappy," Martinez said. "She was a little bit angry."

She said Cisneros paid the five-dollar fee and left.

Several days later, Cisneros returned with a specific request in mind. She wanted Martinez to put an evil spell on Joey Fischer so that something bad could happen to him.

Martinez said she refused to help; she was not in the evil-spell-making business.

Then around Halloween, Cisneros returned to the quaint little shop and asked Martinez if she could find somebody to do a little job.

"I thought she wanted yardwork or working around the house," Martinez said. "You know, a little job, like cutting the lawn or painting a fence."

Cisneros was a very good client, and Martinez told her she would see what she could do.

It was about this time that Daniel Garza came in for assistance with his marital problems. Martinez saw that he was hurting and asked him if he was interested in doing the "little job."

"Señor Garza said he was interested," Martinez told the detectives.

She told Cisneros that she had found a man to do the work for her.

Cisneros stopped by a few days later and dropped off a sealed envelope. When Garza arrived for his appointment to have his fortune read, Martinez passed him the envelope. He opened it, revealing some papers and a photograph of a young man wearing a bow tie. He left, saying he'd take care of the guy.

Martinez said she did not learn what Garza had been paid for until a few days later when Cisneros called and divulged that the "little job" was actually a contract hit.

"She said she wanted the young man good and dead," Martinez said, barely able to contain the excitement in her voice. "She also said for me to keep my mouth shut."

Martinez said she was terribly shocked. "Cisneros is a very honorable woman. That she wanted this boy murdered was terribly upsetting. But what could I do? I had already given Mr. Garza the photo. He had his instructions and the picture of the boy. How could I stop him?"

When Garza called, Martinez relayed Cisneros's explicit instructions. "I told him to kill him," Martinez said. "Those were the instructions of Señora Cisneros."

Sheriff Perez was informed of the surprising developments in the Fischer murder case. The veteran lawman was stunned by what he heard. Dora Cisneros was the wife of a prominent Brownsville surgeon. She was the mother of five children and was prominent with several medical associations and local charities.

In short, Dora Cisneros was a pillar of Brownsville society. But if the fortune-teller was telling the truth, Cisneros was the author of one of Brownsville's most shocking murders.

But how to prove it?

Detectives concocted a plan. On the morning of April 6, the fortune-teller contacted Cisneros and said they had to talk. Cisneros swung by and picked her up. As they drove through downtown Brownsville, Martinez, wearing a hidden microphone and followed by an unmarked sheriff's car, discussed the Fischer shooting.

During the drive, Cisneros said on tape, "There isn't any evidence that I did anything" in regard to the shooting. Then prompted by the fortune-teller, she passed along $500 extra payment for the hit men.

After money changed hands, deputies moved in and stopped the car. Cisneros was taken from one side of the car, Martinez from the other.

Cisneros appeared shocked when she was told she was being arrested for the Joey Fischer murder. She was taken to the sheriff's office where she was asked if she wanted to make a statement. She declined and said she did not want to say anything without an attorney present.

After a brief appearance before Justice of the Peace Tony Torres, Cisneros was taken to the Cameron County Jail. "Are you guilty of the charges?" reporters asked as the solemn 55-year-old pillar of the community was taken to jail, where she was joined by Daniel Garza and Maria Martinez.

"A tragic mistake has been made," Cisneros's attorney told reporters. "This charge is absolutely fallacious."

Sheriff Perez said that while the case was so bizarre as to be almost unbelievable, there was no doubt in his mind that the right suspects were in jail.

Although the alleged "brain" behind the Fischer hit was behind bars, detectives had not yet found the two men paid to carry out the hit.

Garza said he'd met them at a Grand Prairie bar and that the name of one of the men was Israel. Poring through old criminal records and with the help of Mexican authorities, detectives were able to identify the gunmen. They were small-time crooks who made a living stealing and transporting cars from Texas into Mexico.

Warrants were issued for their arrest.

At her arraignment, Dora Cisneros pled not guilty to first-degree murder. She was promptly released on $300,000 bail. Daniel Garza and Maria Martinez were also charged, Garza with murder and Martinez with conspiracy to commit murder. They remained in jail, unable to make bail.

The trial, which attracted media attention from around the country and was one of the most closely watched in Brownsville history, began in February 1994, 11 months after Joey Fischer was gunned down in his driveway.

Dora Cisneros sat primly in a black dress, a portrait of quiet dignity, as District Attorney Luis Saenz described her as an obsessed woman who had killed a young boy because he had spurned her daughter.

"Time goes on, Joey Fischer moves on," he told the packed courtroom on February 25. "But one person the evidence will show cannot, does not, and will not forget that Joey Fischer walked out on her daughter."

Cisneros, through her attorney, argued that the evidence was not strong enough to convict her. "They are trying to kill my client because her daughter happened to date that boy," the defense argued.

But it was the jury, not well-schooled attorneys, who had the final say. And they had no trouble determining the verdict. On March 9, after just two and a half hours of deliberation, they found Dora Cisneros guilty of capital murder for arranging the death of Joey Fischer. Cisneros showed little emotion as the verdict was read. A marshal removed her jewelry and took her into custody.

Daniel Garza was also found guilty on identical charges.

The victim's mother said she was pleased with the jury's swift vote, but she noted that nothing was going to bring back her son.

On April 18, Dora Cisneros was sentenced to life in state prison. By law, she must serve at least 35 years before she is eligible for parole.

Attorneys for the 55-year-old convicted killer said they will appeal.

Daniel Garza also drew a life sentence. He probably wouldn't mind an appeal but is realistic about his chances of having the verdicts overturned. "I'll never leave here," Garza said. "I pray that [God] will give me the patience to live with all that I am going through. What else can I do?"

Maria Martinez pled guilty to conspiracy to commit murder and was sentenced to 20 years in prison. Because she cooperated with authorities, however, she is expected to be released in just two years.

The two men who actually shot Joey Fischer were arrested in Reynosa, Mexico, on auto theft charges. One of the men known as Israel claimed he never killed anyone and knew nothing about the murder-for-hire scheme.

"I steal cars," he said proudly during a jailhouse interview. "I no kill no one."

Efforts have begun to have the car thief returned to the United States to stand trial.

His partner was also jailed for car theft but has since escaped. He is currently believed to be hiding somewhere in Mexico.

"FLORIDA'S NOTORIOUS COUCH POTATO CASE: WAS IT MURDER OR SUICIDE?"

by Julie Malear

The Florida night was the sort of humid-hot that sizzles brains, boils tempers, and makes people do things they know they shouldn't do. High above the resort city of Boynton Beach, an ocean breeze swept clouds across a lemon moon, its pale nocturnal glow casting eerie shadows underneath the earthbound palms.

By 3:10 A.M. that sultry August 9, 1990, most of the town's residents were asleep. In a small section of middle-class homes nestled just north of Old Boynton Beach Boulevard, the lights of one neat corner house suddenly burned brightly. Tragedy had struck. After dialing 911, a frantic wife and three teenagers waited impatiently for help.

Across town, Detective Bob Bayerl (pronounced the way a Southerner pronounces "barrel") forced himself awake to answer his home phone. A Burt Reynolds look-alike with dark brown hair and mustache, Bayerl was "on call" for the Boynton Beach Police Department. This meant he would respond if a shooting occurred.

And there *was* a shooting, the dispatcher told the detective. A suicide. She gave him the address.

Arriving at the two-bedroom residence on NW 8 Court around

3:35 A.M., Detective Bayerl noted that it was a small quarter-style stucco, not very well kept but comfortable. There was nothing extravagant about the place. The family, the detective learned, had lived in it about two years.

In addition to three uniformed officers, five people were waiting inside the house: the victim's wife, Mary Grieco; their 15-year-old daughter, Ann; 18-year-old Melvin Steele, who lived there temporarily because of family problems at home; Sally Denver, a schoolmate friend of Ann's who was merely spending the night; and John O'Malley, a former priest and friend of the family. The latter, who lived close by, had been there earlier that night and had come back when Mary Grieco called him after the shooting.

As soon as he entered, Detective Bayerl met with Officer Richard Root and Sergeant Mike Kerman, two of the three uniformed officers who had responded to the 911 call. The deceased, the men told him, was in the southeast bedroom where the other officer, Donald Bateson, was guarding the scene. They went at once to the bedroom.

The victim was lying faceup on the left side of the bed, as naked as a newborn babe. He was a middle-aged man about 5 feet 11 inches, with a somewhat heavy build—around 200 pounds. There were three patches on his body where the paramedics had tried to revive him in vain. Blood was everywhere. The deceased man lay with his head on a pillow, his right arm extended in an upward position almost touching the wall.

Sergeant Kerman filled Detective Bayerl in on the circumstances: Joseph Grieco, the victim, had apparently committed suicide "with a self-inflicted wound to his head." The information the trio had gotten from headquarters was that he'd killed himself while lying beside his wife, Mary Grieco. She was sleeping at the time of the gunshot and turned the light on to find her husband bleeding from the head.

The officers had already questioned Mary Grieco. She told them that she'd been awakened about three o'clock by what she thought was "a firecracker." At that point, reaching over to nudge her husband awake, she felt something wet. She then immediately notified other family members and called 911. The Boynton Beach paramedics responded at once. Assuming Grieco was alive, they turned him over and tried to revive him. At last, finding no vital signs, they left. He had been bleeding since then.

As soon as Officer Bateson saw the gun, he'd taken it out of the victim's left hand. Not knowing whether Grieco was dead or alive, he "was afraid the man might pull the trigger again," he told Detective Bayerl. Bateson kept the gun in his own pocket until crime scene officers arrived, then turned it over to them. He also removed the magazine of the .32-caliber automatic handgun, taking it for evidence.

While crime scene investigated the bedroom, the victim's family and friends stayed in the kitchen with Officer Root. Ann, the teenage daughter, was sobbing.

Ar around 4:45 A.M., Detective Bayerl conducted the first interview. Speaking with the wife, Mary, a slightly graying blonde of 48, the sleuth learned that the victim had gone to bed "around nine-thirty at night." She told him their friend, John O'Malley, had been there to have dinner. They'd all watched TV, then her husband had gotten up without saying anything and left the room. This was not unusual for him, Mary said. "He was a very quiet individual, and . . . anything he did, he didn't ordinarily explain."

After John O'Malley left, Mary continued, she went to bed herself around 11 P.M. and found Joseph awake. She then, as usual, watched news and weather until 11:20. There was no conversation between the couple until she switched channels. At that point Grieco asked, "Are you going to leave that on all night?" Mary replied that she wasn't, turned over, and went to sleep. Mary had no idea, she said, whether her husband went to sleep or tossed and turned. She did not open her eyes again until the sound of the "firecracker" awakened her around 3 A.M.

During the interview, Detective Bayerl could see how upset Mary Grieco was. She was also apparently quite angry at what her husband had done to her and the rest of the family. The sleuth asked her about Joseph's physical health, which, as far as she knew, was okay. He hadn't been to the doctor for several years and that was to stitch up an injury he'd gotten on his job. He'd never spoken to her about any medical problem. But then, with Joseph so quiet, Mary told Bayerl, he never discussed *any* problems with the family.

Mary described her husband as a "man who expects things to be done when he wants them to be done." As an example, Mary mentioned that one day the week before, he asked her to go out and buy a box of bullets. She asked him for a reason, since they didn't have a gun.

"Don't worry about the gun," Joseph had told her. "Just go out and get the bullets like I asked you to!"

Mary complied, taking with her a magazine he gave her so the clerk could give her the correct size of bullets for the gun.

But Mary swore to Detective Bayerl that the first time she saw the gun was when she woke up and saw it in his hand two hours earlier. She had no idea whether he'd recently purchased the weapon or whether he'd had it since they were married 27 years before. Mary added that between his first marriage and hers they had a total of six children, all girls ranging from 15— Ann, who lived with them—to 30.

The detective ferreted out that the couple had had some financial problems, although not recently. In fact, they had just caught up on their house payments.

Delving into their occupations, Bayerl learned that Joseph and Mary, as well as John O'Malley and Melvin Steele, were all employed at the same private ocean club a few miles to the south. Joseph was chief maintenance engineer; Mary was executive housekeeper; John O'Malley was chief comptroller; and teenager Melvin Steele was a waiter. Daughter Ann attended school.

Even though the scene had all the obvious earmarks of a suicide, Detective Bayerl had phoned his supervisor, Sergeant Sam Carrion, who had arrived around 4 A.M. with Sergeant Harry Ostaszewski and crime scene technician Terry Deighan.

Crime scene investigation revealed a definite entrance wound just above the victim's left ear in his hair. At first, they could see no powder residue at the wound site, its gray color so closely matching that of the victim's hair. Next, the body was changed back to its position when first seen by Officer Bateson. Before the paramedics moved the victim for life-saving attempts, the victim was lying almost on his stomach, slightly tilted on his right side with his head lying so that his face, on the pillow, was tilted to the left. His right arm was extended in an upward position underneath the pillow. He was rearranged with the gun returned to his hand as Bateson recalled it.

When Detective Bayerl had a moment to speak with Sergeant Carrion, he observed that there were several things unusual for a suicide. He felt that there was either something wrong with that deduction or else the victim was "a very cold, uncaring person to go ahead and kill himself right next to his wife in bed." As they spoke further, Bayerl added, "Jeeze, he must have hated her an awful lot, if that's what he actually did." The two sleuths had never seen anyone who'd gone through with suicide in the presence of another person. They agreed that "normally, when someone kills himself they go off, usually in a corner of a garage and wait till they're alone. They're not going to do it right there."

And then there was the matter of the time element. Bayerl mentioned to his sergeant how unusual it would be "if he'd gone to bed around nine-thirty at night and laid there six hours before he decided to kill himself." He then added, "and if he didn't lay there, why would he go to sleep and then decide to wake up and kill himself?" What's more, there was no note.

Bayerl next spoke with John O'Malley, whom Mary Grieco had described as her husband's best and "possibly only friend." O'Malley said they had indeed been friends for a long time. He, too, described Grieco as "quiet." He said the victim was a macho sort of person who had to be in "control of any type of situation." He told the detective that on numerous occasions when they were together he would discuss problems at work, indicating his disgust over certain events and people in the workplace. If his wife walked in while they were talking this way, Joseph would stop talking about the problems.

"He was of an extremely pessimistic personality," O'Malley said. He rarely found any humor in anything and would rarely see the positive side of any incident. O'Malley said that about one week earlier, he and Mary Grieco both noted that Joseph seemed much lighter in his approach to things. Perhaps the victim felt that way because "he'd decided to take his own life," O'Malley mused. That was strictly his own opinion, he told the sleuth, based on his previous experience as a Roman Catholic priest.

The three teenagers, Bayerl learned, had been asleep at the time of the suicide, but as far as the kids knew, there'd been no arguing or yelling before the gun went off.

The lawmen gave Mary Grieco a routine test for gunpowder residue to see if she'd recently fired a weapon. She had no problem with the request. Swabs of her fingers were sent to the Federal Department of Law Enforcement (FDLE) for processing with negative results. The Boynton investigators left the house around 6 A.M.

Since they'd found no ownership papers on the gun in the house and Mary Grieco claimed no knowledge of it, Detective Bayerl first tracked down its type then contacted the Agency for Tobacco and Firearms (AFT) to check it out and run its history. Agent Edgar Dominch worked on this.

Several days passed. The funeral for Joseph Grieco was held. The body was sent north for burial.

Results of an autopsy revealed that the gun had been fired approximately two inches away from the victim's head, consistent with a suicide. Grieco's hands had been bagged, but because the ME no longer did the atomic absorption kit test at autopsies, no examination had been made to see if the victim had, indeed, fired the gun. So Grieco's death was officially labeled a "suicide."

On August 14, Bayerl received a call from a Miami Beach woman who identified herself as a "very close friend of the victim." She told the sleuth that Joseph would never have killed himself. Asked to explain, she said that in all the years she'd known him, he had never owned a gun and had told her he'd "never allow one in the house."

In addition, Joseph was planning, with the rest of the family, to take a trip to Massachusetts and New Hampshire the week of August 13 through August 20. The woman said that he'd told her when they'd spoken together the previous week that he was "looking forward to going up there and seeing his daughter and new grandson." The woman was sure that Joseph wouldn't have taken his life knowing he was getting ready to go up north.

Detective Bayerl noted that the woman based her belief on her longtime friendship with the victim and not on any specific factual reasons. At her request, the sleuth made an appointment to meet with her and talk further on Saturday afternoon, August 18. She would make a taped statement, she told Bayerl.

The detective had scarcely hung up from the Miami Beach woman when a close relative of the victim's called from Massachusetts. The relative said he didn't believe the suicide story, and he gave the same reasons as the friend: Joseph wasn't "the sort of person to take his own life," he said, adding that he'd "never had a gun." Besides that, Joseph had planned the trip north at this time specifically to see some members of his family, namely his father who was being treated for cancer and was not expected to live. "I don't feel he would have done something so drastic without first going to see the family," the relative said, although admitting that he hadn't talked with the victim in a number of years and had no actual evidence to counteract the suicide theory.

The relative added that he'd learned that Joseph was seeing a "girlfriend" whom he believed to be the Miami Beach woman. The relative met her at the funeral service, and they discussed the impossibility of Joseph killing himself. Today, the relative said, Mary and Ann Grieco were on their way to Massachusetts for a few days to attend a memorial service for Joseph.

After the two phone calls, Detective Bayerl met with Sergeant Carrion to discuss those aspects that didn't seem consistent with a suicide. "The position of the body," they both agreed. "On his stomach with his hand and arm under the pillow—more like a sleeping position than a position of somebody ready to shoot himself." And the location of the gun? "If a person would have shot himself in that position," Bayerl said, "the gun would have immediately dropped from his hand . . . rather than staying in the victim's hand and then having the hand move in a position up away from the body."

The sleuths discussed again how unusual it was for a person contemplating suicide to lay in bed for six or more hours only to wake in the middle of the night and shoot himself, and how strange it seemed for a person to shoot himself while lying next to his wife.

The fourth point they considered strange was the gun itself. Everyone said Joseph Grieco didn't have one, but this gun was old and tarnished with rust. It didn't look as though it had been newly purchased in a pawnshop. Although it could have been a war souvenir, it wasn't likely that his wife of 27 years wouldn't have known it existed.

The lawmen set out to interview Grieco's co-workers to see if he'd obtained the weapon from someone at the club where they worked. They began to investigate secrets in the victim's life—health problems, other women, or anything else that would have caused the victim to commit suicide. Because Grieco's hands had not been checked, the lawmen also decided to test-fire the gun to see if it caused blow back or residue on the firer's hand. The detectives also began investigating more deeply the backgrounds of everyone present at the house that night, including Ann Grieco's friend, Sally Denver.

Reinterviewing John O'Malley, Detective Bayerl noted the former priest's reasons that the victim may have committed suicide. Grieco was "an extremely insecure type of personality," O'Malley said. He was a nonconformist who would rarely wear a tie, a very strong type of person who was "completely in control" of his house.

What's more, Grieco had experienced some recent tragedies—his sister was killed the past 4th of July by a drunk driver out West and his father was dying of cancer. O'Malley wondered if Grieco hadn't killed himself over his own medical problems. The victim had experienced a few chest pains less than a month before. He may have awakened in the middle of the night, thought he was having a heart attack, and, afraid of becoming paralyzed or incapacitated, got the gun and killed himself.

Describing Grieco further, O'Malley said the victim got a lot of enjoyment out of just lying around watching TV—primarily programs like *National Geographic*. The victim had not been a person who cared for people, chitchat, or friends. In fact, if the family did make friends with someone, Joseph's coarseness usually drove a wedge between them right away, said O'Malley.

That same day, the sleuths had a setback regarding the gun. The ATF agent told the Boynton lawmen that there was no way to trace the weapon, that there was no record of it having been brought into the U.S.A., and that it was probably a memento of some soldier who'd served his country overseas.

Next to be reinterviewed was 18-year-old Melvin Steele. Medium-built, with shoulder-length brown hair and hazel eyes, Melvin was caretaking the Grieco house while Mary and Ann Grieco were in New England for the victim's burial.

Melvin told Detective Bayerl that before the suicide, he'd been living at the house for several weeks. The family opened their doors on a number of occasions to different people in the area, the teen said. These were usually juveniles who'd been having problems at home and didn't have a place to live. Since the time he'd moved in, there'd been several other kids sleeping on the couch in the living room. Two of them had the same first name— Danny Datson and Danny Moore. He said that Danny Datson was back living with his mother in nearby Delray Beach.

Melvin told the detective that he was certain that Joseph Grieco had been asleep after midnight because he heard him snore. He'd heard Joseph snore before, he explained, but had never heard Mary Grieco do so. Therefore, he was sure that the victim had been asleep when he went to his own bed around 1:45 A.M. Until Ann and her friend Sally Denver decided to go to sleep around 1 A.M., Melvin had been watching a movie with them in Ann's bedroom, which was painted completely black and had heavy-metal posters on the walls.

When Melvin was awakened by the gunshot and went toward the master bedroom, Mary came into the hall momentarily and asked him to "go stay with the girls for a couple of minutes." That's when he realized that Joseph had been shot.

Probing to see how Melvin Steele felt about Joseph Grieco, Detective Bayerl asked the youth how they got along. Melvin answered, "Pretty good." He said they used to discuss cars when he'd be outside working on his. Inside, the older man was quiet, he said.

Melvin mentioned that Ann did not get along too well with her father and that there was scarcely any conversation between the two. Ann's dad had never physically abused her, so he didn't know why she disliked the man so much.

Melvin recalled that Joseph had told him about his war experiences, mentioning that he'd been involved in killings while he was overseas on secret missions. Melvin said Joseph had told the other boys about those times, too.

That was strange, thought Detective Bayerl, for Mrs. Grieco had specifically stated that she'd never heard her husband talk about his war experiences. He had only talked to her about it once, then he refused to do so again.

Melvin Steele told the detective he was taking care of the house until the family returned on Sunday, August 26.

When Detective Bayerl sought the fifth person who was present at Joseph Grieco's death, he ran into problems. Sally Denver's home was vacant with a "for sale" sign in the front yard and a padlock on the front door. Possibly it was being repossessed, he thought. The neighbors didn't know where she'd gone.

Then on August 22, a new development arose. Sergeant Carrion notified Detective Bayerl that a woman had come to the police department with information on the case. Bayerl hurried down to the station and met with Mrs. Datson, mother of Danny

Datson, one of the teenagers who'd stayed for a while at the Grieco's.

"On Monday night," she told Bayerl, "Danny told me he had information about Mr. Grieco." Detective Bayerl quickly pulled up a chair and urged the woman to continue. Danny, she told the detective, had been a good friend of Melvin Steele's for approximately two years.

"On Monday," Mrs. Datson said, "he informed me that Mel had confided to him that he was responsible for the death of the victim, Joseph Grieco." The woman went on to state that according to her son, Melvin had told him that the gun was his and that he was wearing a pair of gloves when he shot the victim.

This revelation, of course, confirmed the detectives' suspicions of homicide. Bayerl urged Mrs. Datson to continue.

Ann Grieco, the woman told him, was originally supposed to shoot her father. However, she changed her mind at the last minute and Melvin Steele took the gun from her and did the shooting himself.

Prior to the shooting when Melvin first got the gun, he had tried to file off its serial numbers so it couldn't be traced.

Mrs. Datson went on to say that she hadn't been able to sleep since Danny told her what happened. She'd tried to get him to come with her to the police, but he'd been afraid of retribution from Melvin's and Ann's friends at school if they found out he'd ratted on Melvin. Her son had also said that he was sure the police would figure out it wasn't a suicide because Melvin had told him there was no gunpowder residue left on the victim's hand.

Mrs. Datson told the sleuth that her son Danny had drifted away from Melvin a couple of months before because he didn't approve of Melvin's lifestyle. Besides that, Melvin began to date Danny's ex-girlfriend, the sister of the other Danny—Danny Moore. The two Dannys were still good friends.

Danny Moore had told Danny Datson that Melvin Steele gave him a box of .22-caliber bullets, which he'd purchased to use in the shooting but which turned out to be the wrong size.

Mrs. Datson further recalled a time in June or July when Ann

Grieco had come to her house to visit Danny. The girl turned to her that evening and said, "I wish my father was dead. I wish someone would shoot him." The statement had shocked Mrs. Datson and she asked her why. "I hate him because of the way he treats me!"

Knowing they would need to speak with Danny Datson, Detective Bayerl tried to set up an appointment. The teen's mother said that when she brought Danny home from work at the record shop that night, she would tell him the police were going to be there at 10. She felt he would cooperate once they were there. Later that afternoon, the woman had to call and postpone the appointment until the next day because Danny was going to a concert that night.

According to the agreement, Detective Bayerl went to the Datson home at 2 P.M. on August 23, where he met with Danny and his mother. The teenager was very cooperative. He told Bayerl how much his conscience had been bothering him because of his knowledge but how afraid he was of Melvin's friends getting even if he ratted on Melvin.

After he started talking, however, Danny told the sleuth countless details he couldn't have known unless he were there, or had been informed by someone who was. "Mel personally told me that he had shot the victim one time in the head because of the fact that nobody else in the family would do it." Danny Datson told so much that Bayerl asked him to come down to the Boynton Beach Police Station and make a "taped statement."

Once on tape, Danny told even more. He and another boy had been staying with the Griecos until two weeks before the shooting, Danny said. During that time there had been "numerous talk" among the family about wanting to have Joseph Grieco killed.

When Danny first heard them, Melvin, Ann, and Mary were whispering about it in the kitchen and they became silent. "It made me feel uncomfortable," he said, explaining that sometimes "Mary would say, 'I hate that bastard,' and Mel talked about hurting and killing—mainly Joseph." Melvin also kidded about getting Joe's red car.

Asked where the victim was as they discussed his death, Danny said, "Sleeping or at work."

The other teen moved out a few days later, and Danny soon did, too. After that, although he didn't hang out much with Melvin Steele, they continued to be friends.

When Detective Bayerl asked him when he'd first heard of the shooting, he said he was at Danny Moore's house.

"Mel and Ann pulled up in Joe's red car. They'd first stopped at my house and my mother told them where I was."

Speaking again of how he learned about the murder, Danny said, "I got in the car and sat in the backseat. Ann and Mel were laughing hysterically. I wondered what they were laughing about, and I laughed, too. They said, still laughing, 'Joe's dead.' I was in shock and very uncomfortable. We went to a car shop. I asked what happened and only got laughs. At first they said it was a heart attack. Then they said he'd shot himself. I believed them. I didn't want to know the truth."

Danny Datson heard the complete story when he went to Danny Moore's home and Melvin Steele came by soon afterward. When he and Melvin found themselves alone for a few minutes, he told Melvin he found it difficult to believe that Joseph would commit suicide, especially since he'd heard the talk among the people in the house of how they "wanted him dead." Danny also reminded Melvin that he knew all about the other attempts on the victim's life. "What really happened?" Danny asked.

Melvin then told Danny that on the night of the murder, he himself had walked into the bedroom with Ann Grieco and that Ann had a gun in her hand and was packing back and forth and wanted to kill her father. Melvin stated that Ann was unable to pull the trigger, so he took the gun out of her hand and said, "I'll do it." When he opened the bedroom door, Melvin continued, Joseph was snoring and as Melvin stood by the side of the bed next to where the victim was, he "leaned over and shot him one time in the head." Immediately following the shooting, Melvin hid the gloves or destroyed them before Mary called the police.

Danny then told Detective Bayerl that Melvin had told him that he, Ann, and Mary had planned on killed the victim two nights earlier but changed their minds when John O'Malley came over and stayed much later than usual. Melvin told Danny, too, that when he went out to buy bullets, he'd gotten the wrong size, but knowing that Danny Moore did target shooting, he gave the box to him. Mary then purchased the correct bullets for the gun which, Melvin said, came from a guy whose name he wasn't sure of.

After repeating Melvin's tale to the law officers, Danny cooperated thoroughly, even offering to be "wired." That way, he could again get Melvin to admit what happened on tape so the police would have enough evidence to arrest him.

After Detective Bayerl conferred with Sergeant Carrion, Lieutenant John Hollihan, and Captain Carl Dixon, they decided to have Danny Datson wired with a Unitel and go to the residence where Melvin Steele was currently residing and get into a conversation that could be recorded. The lawmen had Danny make a phone call from the police department to the residence on NW 8th Court. Melvin wasn't there. Danny rang Danny Moore's house. Melvin was there.

"Hi, what are you guys doing?" Danny Datson asked. He then told them that he was coming over.

Since the "suicide" had now become a homicide, Detective Bayerl contacted Paul Moyle at the state attorney's office. The chief prosecutor for homicide in the county okayed the Unitel plan but wanted a release from Mrs. Datson regarding the wiring as well as an agreement from Danny that he wouldn't talk to Melvin after the taping prior to the arrest.

At around 5 P.M., Sergeant Chip Kuss of the Vice Unit fit Danny Datson with a Unitel. Detectives Bayerl and Roger Cash went in one car. Sergeant Kuss and Detectives Carrion and James Mahoney took Danny with them to the Datson house in Delray where they had the teen practice taping. Although they were anxious to get the confession recorded, the men took their time with him. Then they obtained the releases and left with Danny, leaving only Detective Mahoney behind with Danny's mother so she could be kept informed about what was happening. Monitors in the apartment and both cars were tuned to the transmission.

"Don't be nervous," the men told Danny. The youth had watched a lot of *Miami Vice* episodes, so he knew to do exactly what the police told him. But he couldn't help being nervous.

By 5:30 P.M, the tall brown-haired teen was out of the police car, walking toward Danny Moore's residence, stating his name so the Unitel on his back would pick it up. He went behind the house and found the boys working on a boat. The three teens talked in an ordinary manner until Danny Datson said, "I wanted to talk to Mel for a few minutes." At that, Danny Moore went in the other room, seeming to understand.

Danny Datson told Melvin that "the police came up to me asking about you." Melvin didn't seem surprised. As the two went inside, Danny again said, "Tell me what happened that night."

Melvin said, "This is what we told the police. After we shot Joe, the cops came over and questioned us about Joe. I said I'd fallen asleep on the couch. We heard a bang and we called the police. Sally Denver was in the room with Ann the whole time, we told the police. A friend visited, left about eleven. Ann and Mary were pacing. I was on the couch. Mary went in Joe's room." Melvin Steele was repeating the same story he'd first told Danny Datson.

Danny said, "Come on, dude, tell me what *really* happened. Come on, dude, 'cause I *knew* he didn't really kill himself."

Melvin said, "Nobody would do it, so I decided I was going to do it. I finally said, 'Ann, put these gloves on me.' Then I went in and took the gun from Mary. Afterwards, I gave it back to her and walked out. Mary was lying beside Joe."

As he talked, Melvin used Danny Moore's bed to show Danny Datson how he killed Joe Grieco. "I leaned over the left side of the bed—over Mary," Melvin told Danny. "I looked at the angles, ducked down, went over, squatted down, leaned over Mary, and shot him.

"I was worried Sally might say something. So I went in and laid down with her and made out. Sally said, 'What happened?' I said, 'I shot him. I shot him.'" Melvin Steele laughed coldly as he told the story to Danny. He added that if Ann should go to the police and say that he—Melvin—did it, they wouldn't believe her, since she was only 15.

Hardly had Melvin Steele finished his story than a worried Mrs. Datson phoned and asked for her son telling the other Danny, when he answered, that she'd "brought shrimp" and wanted him home to eat. When her son picked up the phone she told him tensely, "Come home *now. Get out of there!*"

Danny Datson left immediately. He walked out to Germantown Road where he was picked up by Sergeants Kuss and Carrion, taken to his house, and praised for his performance.

After speaking further with Danny Datson, Detective Bayerl realized that the teen also knew very well that Mary and Ann wanted the father dead. It wasn't unusual for them to sit around discussing how nice their life would be without Joseph around.

Assured that they were now dealing with not only a homicide but a conspiracy, Detective Bayerl and Sergeant Carrion decided not to proceed with Melvin Steele until his accomplices in the murder returned from New England. If they arrested Steele now, he could inform the women not to come back.

After the sleuths presented the tape to the state attorney's office and asked that they hold off on the arrest, they went to Melvin Steele and asked him to come in for a taped interview on Monday, August 27. Mary and Ann Grieco would have arrived the day before, so they could come in, too. Suspecting nothing, Melvin was very cooperative.

On Monday, Ann was not ready to go when the officers came to pick up the trio. Bayerl took Melvin; Mary came later when her daughter was dressed. Once at the station, Melvin was Mirandized and questioned again about what happened on the fateful night.

At first, the teen repeated what he'd told police before. But then Detective Bayerl mentioned that police had found problem after problem with the suicide theory, including ones posed by the newly received test results on the victim's hands.

"And he didn't fire a gun?" Melvin asked.

No, Bayerl said, adding that they'd also gotten tests back on Mary's hands. "She didn't fire the gun, either."

"So what about, like, gloves or something?"

"That's what we thought—gloves," the detective told Melvin. "Think she'd wear a pair of gloves to do that?"

"She's got a pair of gloves," Melvin replied.

"I talked to Mary," Detective Bayerl said. "I really didn't think she did it. . . . And you woke up right away, and nobody was coming from the hallway. And Ann was sleeping. So what we've really come to decide now is that you shot him."

"What! How do you figure?" Melvin's eyes were wide with shock. The sleuth told him they'd figured it out.

"What are you talking about?" Melvin asked, his nerves apparently fraying.

This was it—confession time. Bayerl told Melvin to listen closely. "You shot him. . . . No question that you shot him. You went out, bought the bullets, you got the wrong kind of bullets, got the wrong size. We found out where you went. Mary went out and got another box of bullets. Those were the ones that were used. Mary, her idea is to get the insurance money. The situation there was intolerable according to them, according to everybody I talked to. They hated him . . . but they couldn't bring themselves to kill him. . . ."

"Now listen," Melvin spoke fast, "I've been in a lot of trouble before. I've been in jail and everything. Huh, that's the last thing I would do. I didn't do it!"

"It's over now. You did it. I've already got a warrant for you," Bayerl said.

"I didn't do it!" Melvin protested.

"Yes, you did. . . . Listen to the way I have the ducks in a row, and you're going to know I have all the information. . . ."

Melvin Steele protested but Detective Bayerl continued, telling him that he lay down with Sally Denver, telling him he'd told Sally he shot Joseph.

"Uh-uh, wrong answer!" Melvin countered.

The sleuth continued to reveal what the police knew, to let Melvin understand that he had no secrets left. Desperately, Melvin asked him to talk to Mary. He continued to say he didn't do anything.

"Joe didn't shoot himself," Detective Bayerl said in an even tone.

"He didn't shoot himself," Melvin finally admitted.

In answer to Bayerl's question on what he'd gain from the death, Melvin said, "Talk to Mary. . . . I'm not getting anything out of it. Mary's getting the money out of it. Ann's getting some peace of mind in a little different environment to live, to finish getting raised under. Hey, they lived under a situation. . . . Poor Joe, nobody like him, but by the same token, that's not the way you handle it.

"Oh," Melvin went on, "he's helped me with my car. He helped me, like, every day. I didn't hate him!"

The lawman asked about the bullets, then told him they were at Danny Moore's after Melvin lied about them. Gradually, Detective Bayerl introduced the subject of Danny Datson, repeating back to Melvin some of the statements he'd made on Danny's tape. "You told me, 'I shot him,' " he said.

"No, I didn't," Melvin replied.

"Yes, you did . . . 'cause I got it on tape," Bayerl said. After echoing what Melvin said to Sally Denver, Bayerl asked him to remember the previous Thursday night.

"Hey, dude, what happened?" the sleuth said, imitating Datson. "Tell me what happened, dude. 'Well, this is what I told the police, I was in the bedroom with Ann . . .' "

Finally, faced with the monitored conversation that Danny Datson had taped, Melvin said he was only trying to impress

Danny—that he had not, in fact, shot Joseph Grieco. "I told them I did it, 'cause I thought it might, you know, might look good and that. But I didn't pull the trigger. Talk to Mary. I didn't pull the trigger!"

"No? Well, how did he get shot?"

"By Mary." The teen wiped his brow.

Bayerl continued his interrogation, asking to hear Melvin's side. At last the suspect said, "She told me and everything . . . 'cause I knew they were planning it anyway, like you said before, and . . . she went ahead and . . . See, all the girls and everybody thought that I would do it and everything, and so I went to the bedroom with Mary and everything, but I didn't do it. We walked out and I walked back in there to make it, you know, to look— and I said to them that I did do it, 'cause I didn't want Ann thinking that her own mom, you know, did that thing. I didn't! I did not pull the trigger! *Mary* did. Believe it or not."

Melvin Steele described how Mary had knelt in bed to shoot Joseph. He'd gone in, Melvin said. He had the gun in his hand, but he told Mary he couldn't do it. He gave her the gloves, she put them on (Ann, he said, burned them later), and killed Joseph. Melvin then told about the gun they'd procured about two weeks before. He said Ann kept it under her mattress.

Melvin told the sleuth that Sally Denver was only at the house to make it look less suspicious. The girl was not in on the conspiracy. She spent most of the evening in Ann's bedroom. He claimed he told her afterward that he'd shot Grieco, a statement Sally denied when Bayerl finally found her at her dad's home.

By the time the detectives terminated the interview with Melvin Steele, the two other suspects had arrived at the police station. Without having a chance to brief Sergeant Carrion, the detective escorted Mary Grieco into the interview room while his sergeant went in another room to question Ann Grieco.

Detective Bayerl found Mary extremely talkative. Not realizing how much Melvin Steele had told, the woman continued to act as though the case was a suicide.

The detective explained to Mary some of the inconsistencies

the police had found, adding that they no longer believed the death was suicide. The snoring Melvin had heard, for example, proved the victim had been asleep, which someone contemplating suicide would probably not have been.

Trying to explain, Mary said, "He snores when he's awake. . . . H-h-he can lay on the sofa . . . with one of his programs on TV . . . and his eyes are closed, and he's snoring and you yell at him to wake up and he says he's awake."

"Well, I say that all the time," the sleuth said lightly.

"Yes, but you ask him what just happened on TV, and he'll tell you." Answering the detective's question about arguments that night, Mary said, "We never fought. He didn't fight. And I'd get mad at him, you know. [We'd] have our arguments and that, but last year . . . I wanted a divorce. I wanted out from twenty-seven years of being dominated. I wanted out. And he wouldn't . . ."

After a few more questions, Mary Grieco added, "I couldn't see calling the police to get him out of the house, which is the way I'd have had to do it. As much as I hated the guy, I loved the guy. You know it's a love/hate relationship, you know. But when I really wanted something, if, uh, he thought it was right, he'd give it to me. If he knew it was wrong, he would not, no matter what kind of temper tantrums or anything else I pulled. And I always went by what he said, because he's always been right. In twenty-seven years of trying to prove a guy wrong and you can't prove him wrong, you know—you learn to do as he says."

Detective Bayerl asked Mary if Joseph had ever abused her. She answered "Mentally," saying that she'd been hospitalized in 1982 for acute depression after she had a "nervous breakdown." After that, Mary said, she and Joe had a long talk and decided they could work things out. "It was not a bad relationship. It's just that, you know . . ."

Still talking suicide, Mary said her daughters had told her to put it all behind her and not worry about "why he did it." She said Joe never showed affection. "When the kids, up until they were about two years old, he was . . . you know, he'd play with them. After that, close it off, lock the wall up again, you know? I mean he was good to them. He never really abused any of them, but it was just that—no emotion. That's it, you know? Blank wall. And that's hard to live with."

Bayerl brought up Ann. Mary agreed it was hard for the girl. "At her age, too, teenagers hate their mothers, hate their fathers. She was beginning to hate him, because he was getting so strict with her. She'd been in with the wrong crowd of kids. You know, she's been to this police station, I don't know how many times. . . ."

Mary rationalized that Joe knew he was making Ann miserable; that he knew, too, he might follow in his father's footsteps by having emphysema. "He just waved and gave out, you know?" As if she were justifying the "suicide" by predicting how bad Joe's health might have been had he lived, Mary said, "I think Joe did it for us and for himself, that he just didn't want to put up with it anymore."

After that, the sleuth began listing reasons the police didn't believe it was a suicide. For each point, Mary had an answer. Finally, Bayerl grew serious. He hammered the facts about the lack of gunpowder on Joseph's hands, his position in bed, the position of the gun—the impossibility of suicide. "We were considering the fact that maybe *you* were responsible."

"Maybe *I* did it?" Mary replied, stunned. "I would do myself first before I'd do him."

Then Bayerl told Mary Grieco everything Melvin Steele had admitted. "I know it must have been a lot of torture. . . . I'm not second-guessing you. I'm not passing judgment, but there had to be a better way. A divorce. Walking out. You had a pair of gloves on, and you shot him. Ann has, in the meantime, taken the gloves and burned them. Am I right, Mary? Can I get you some water, Mary? Mary, listen to me, come here, give me your hand. Mary. Take a deep breath. . . . Oh, were things that bad!"

Detective Bayerl talked to her, trying to calm her.

"Mary, look at me. Everything I said, is that accurate?"

The woman nodded yes.

"Yes?" Bayerl prompted.

Mary, unable to speak, nodded yes again.

"You don't know how bad I feel about this," Bayerl said. "I really wish you weren't doing this right now. It's probably the most unusual case I've ever worked."

"What will happen to him?" Mary asked through tears about Melvin, then asked about Ann. "She didn't know, though. She didn't really know."

"But she was gonna do it," Bayerl said. "She would have done it herself, but she couldn't."

Mary denied Bayerl's words. Finally, the woman was able to continue the interview. She told about the gun, then, identified it. She said she was kneeling when she pulled the trigger. She didn't remember if Melvin was in the room or not.

"I should have gone with my instincts the first time and let it go—getting rid of the gun," Mary told the sleuth. Then, looking wistful, she added, "I wanted—I wanted to do it, but I didn't want to do it. Like I said, he was a miserable bastard, but he had his good points, too."

When Mary Grieco's interview was over, Sergeant Carrion had just finished with Ann Grieco. He told Detective Bayerl that Ann had told everything, and that it was Melvin Steele who had pulled the trigger. Shaking his head, Bayerl told his sergeant what Melvin had explained and that Mary had confessed to actually pulling the trigger, although, of course, they were all in it together and were all being arrested.

The two lawmen reviewed the startling case. The tape Carrion made of Ann, an eighth-grader just the year before, revealed that she was in it as much as the others—perhaps, even, was the motivating force, although the lawmen decided she really never believed it would happen.

At the start of the sergeant's interrogation, Ann had summed up her feelings regarding the whole affair. "Everything was fine until around 1984, [when] my parents started becoming in debt, and they were having a lot of pressure on all of us, and we were always yelling at each other and whatnot, and things just progressed to get worse and worse. . . . I kept moving back and forth from my relative's house in New Hampshire to here, trying to get away from my family—get away from my dad, basically, because I couldn't handle what he was putting himself, my mom, and I through. And things weren't working out at my relative's, so I came back here, and I can no longer go back up there. And so I had to put up with my dad's stuff, my dad's bull, whatever you want to call it, the way he was acting. . . . He was always yelling and never had anything good to say, and he's—he was—miserable. He'd come home from work and all he'd do was either lay on the couch and watch TV or—that's *all* he did. He just, like, he never did *anything* . . . I couldn't stand being there. . . . And then Mel moved in . . . and then Danny." She said she'd talked in front of them—even Danny—about how she hated her father.

Squaring her shoulders, Ann Grieco continued, "I had talked to my mom many times about divorcing him, and she—her answer was always that she didn't have money, which she didn't. So the idea came up of, what if he was dead? And we just kept going on with that idea, and eventually got a gun, and the result is, he's dead." Ann mentioned how both she and her mom had tried to shoot him a few days before, but neither could do it. Then on the murder night, according to Ann, Melvin decided that "it's gonna be done."

After the gunshot, Ann said her mom got "completely hysterical. She couldn't believe it happened." She and Melvin heard the story her mother told the police; they told the same story. She told Sergeant Carrion about the gun, which had been found through a school friend of hers who talked to a teenager who'd recently stolen a gun. She and Melvin and Mary drove to a meeting spot and picked up the teen. Mary went in to a check cashing store to get the money so they could pay him. Ann told of burning the gloves she thought Mel had worn. She told of test-firing the gun into a pillow a few days before the murder and having a guy she knew dig out the bullet fragment. Ann said Joe never physically or sexually abused her, in spite of what some relatives thought.

The prior attempts on her dad's life, Ann explained, were made
by putting cocaine (procured by Melvin) into his drink and later
acid (procured by Danny Moore) into a stuffed chicken Mary
had cooked. Although the idea was to induce a heart attack—
make it "more of a natural death"—neither the coke nor the
huge LSD dose worked.

Ann admitted that she, Melvin, and her mom did drugs themselves but not on the murder night. She added that they'd all
discussed the LSD and other methods before lacing Joseph's
food with acid. "He had all the signs of going into a trip, but
he thought he . . . was having another heart attack," Ann recalled. "Although . . . he was laughing a lot more, was laughing
with me, you know, and my mom, and he was just all around
acting a lot better . . ."

"Do you feel you did the right thing?" Detective Bayerl asked.

"I did the right thing because it put him out of his misery,"
Ann replied, "and because my mom and I now will be, you
know, won't have him always pushing us and making us so miserable. . . . I'm glad that he's gone now because it put everyone
out of misery. But I wish he were still here, though."

Bayerl, summing up his feelings on the strange case, dubbed
"the couch potato murder" by the press, later said, "I think the
actual motivation was the fact that he never did become part of
the family. He came home and he was tired. His primary enjoyment in life was in turning on the TV and watching something
like *Wild Kingdom* or some of these nature programs. He didn't
run around, drink, have any bad habits. He just liked to come
home and rest. I'm sure there's lots of husbands guilty of the same
thing.

"I think the motivational factor was that they were just tired
of the situation," Bayerl continued. "They wanted him gone."

The three conspirators accomplished their goal. Joseph no
longer bothered them. The result, however, wasn't exactly what
they'd pictured. After the detectives, working with Prosecutor
Dale Buckner of the state attorney's office, tied up the loose
ends, the cases came to three separate trials for conspiracy and

murder. Ann Grieco pled guilty and received 20 years. Mary Grieco received life plus 25 years. As for Melvin Steele, it took the last jury only 90 minutes to decide his guilt. He, too, received life imprisonment.

"NORTH CAROLINA HOMICIDE PUZZLE: DID A BLACK WIDOW CLAIM THREE LIVES?"

by Chris Kelly

In the small town of Kinston, North Carolina, 59-year-old Billy Carlyle White was a well-known and respected figure, a successful businessman, civic leader, community volunteer, loving husband, and caring father. When his wife, 55-year-old Sylvia White, contacted the Kinston Police Department shortly after dawn on the morning of Wednesday, January 22, 1992, saying that she wanted to file a missing-person report, law enforcement officers were quick to respond.

The worried woman reported that she had not seen her husband since he'd left for a business meeting the previous night. Billy, a leading salesman for the Jefferson-Pilot Insurance Company, was to meet a potential client near the town of Trenton, just across the adjacent county line. The client said he'd just purchased some land and was eager to buy an insurance policy. Sylvia said he had given her the necessary directions, which she then passed on to her hardworking husband.

Billy usually telephoned if he was going to be delayed, so Sylvia remained by the phone all night, but he never called. She was worried. Something had to be wrong. Was he ill? Perhaps he had suffered a heart attack or had an automobile accident? Or maybe he'd been mugged or had his burgundy Chevrolet van carjacked? Sylvia was imagining all sorts of terrible things that could have happened to her husband during the past 12 hours.

Since Billy White was a familiar face around the King Street police building and in the halls of the Lenoir County Sheriff's Department down the street, word of his disappearance spread quickly, and soon Sheriff Billy Smith and his deputies joined the search for the missing insurance agent.

As the search intensified, the Whites' children joined Sylvia as they waited for some news, taking what comfort they could from each other.

A Kinston Police Department plane was sent up to search the Lenoir-Jones County area where Billy was to meet his new client. The plane flew low over that sparsely populated section and along the Trent River. With a small body of water as its source, the Trent meanders through heavily wooded land, widening at the town of New Bern, where it flows into the larger Neuse River, which empties into Pamlico Sound and the Atlantic Ocean.

Eight hours after Billy White was reported missing, the search plane, flying close to the tops of scrub pines and hardwood trees, spotted his Chevrolet Lumina minivan near a remote logging road. About 4 P.M., officers converged on the van and found Billy White's body lying facedown next to his vehicle. From what they could see, he had been shot twice.

Even as White's family was being informed that their worst fears had come true, other officers began arriving at the crime scene, joined by State Bureau of Investigation (SBI) agents and their mobile crime lab, to get the murder probe into gear.

The site, miles from any homes or businesses, seemed to be a rather strange spot for a business meeting, but an excellent setting for a murder. The probers checked White's body and discovered that his wallet, checkbook, and jewelry were missing.

This discovery led them to wonder whether the slaying was the result of a robbery gone bad.

The investigators began combing the area for clues. It is believed that all perpetrators bring something to a crime scene and take something with them when they leave. It might be as minuscule as a hair, fabric strands from clothing or from the carpeting of a vehicle, or fingerprints—all of which can link a suspect to the crime.

SBI Agent Eric Smith took impressions of all the tire tracks he found in the soft dirt. Meanwhile, the body was transported to the state medical examiner's officer in nearby Jacksonville.

Almost everyone knew White, or knew of him, and all offered their condolences to his grieving widow.

As the probers routinely checked into Billy White's background, they learned that he began his successful career as an insurance salesman in the early 1960s, knocking on doors and collecting weekly insurance payments from people who became more than just clients—they liked the affable salesman and became his friends. Billy was so successful that in 1990 he was named the insurance company's salesman of the year.

The six-foot-two gray-haired grandfather was a friendly man, blessed with the gift of gab, and even though he appeared to be a workaholic, he also devoted many hours to civic work. He was a member of the Kinston Chamber of Commerce and the United Way, and he served on the board of a domestic violence shelter. Billy was also one of the founders of The Exchange, a service group providing scholarships for deserving students, and served on the local Crimestoppers board. He was known as the "first to volunteer for anything," with his goal being to make his hometown a better place in which to live.

Every Christmas, Billy White could be seen standing outside the mall, acting out his version of Santa Claus. Dressed in a three-piece business suit, he would hand out dollar bills to children as they walked by and would find happiness in their smiles.

Billy also found time for another love—politics. His office walls were covered with photographs of local and national Republican politicians, including President Ronald Reagan and North Carolina senator Jesse Helms. Indeed, on the very day Billy's body was found, Helms's office staff phoned the White home to offer condolences. Flowers sent by Helms's staff were placed in the center of the kitchen table by the widow to show visitors that her husband had been an important man.

The investigators learned that this tragedy was not the first the Whites had endured over the years. When they were married on December 3, 1971, both Billy and Sylvia brought with them unhappy memories from previous marriages.

Billy White's first marriage was dogged by illness; his wife suffered a nervous breakdown and was frequently in and out of institutions. When the up-and-coming insurance man moved his growing family to a larger home in Kinston, their new neighbor, Sylvia Ipock, seemed to be "heaven-sent." The energetic widow not only took care of her own three children, but she was also often at the White home, helping with their four youngsters.

Sylvia knew what it was like to be motherless—her own mother had died when she was only five. When Sylvia was only 17, she got married, but her young husband walked out on her and their baby after only 16 months.

Sylvia remarried and had two more children. Leslie Ipock, a truck driver, seemed to be a devoted husband and father, but Sylvia said he had become depressed over health problems. Leslie complained of a numbness in his fingers and legs and wound up being hospitalized. Then, one morning shortly after their eighth wedding anniversary, Sylvia awoke to find Leslie's bedroom door locked. She enlisted the aid of a neighbor and they forced the door open. Inside they found 32-year-old Leslie Ipock dead, a pistol by his lifeless hand, a bullet in his head. Sylvia buried her young husband, reserving a spot for herself next to his grave with the granite tombstone.

Four and a half years later, when Sylvia married her third husband, Billy White, it seemed to be much more than a marriage of convenience. Billy, already ambitious, was nudged up the ladder of success by his new wife. His career took off as

Sylvia did her part, attending dinners with him and serving as a volunteer.

Sylvia White's energies seemed unlimited. She was an immaculate housekeeper, a veritable "cleanaholic." She turned the rooms virtually inside out, taking down the curtains and even taking the beds apart to vacuum the box springs. What most housekeepers think of as "spring cleaning," Sylvia did as part of her everyday cleaning.

Always elegantly dressed, she accompanied Billy to the seemingly endless functions connected with his charity work or civic organizations, and she did her part in entertaining clients and friends. Hers was a familiar face at Lenoir Memorial Hospital, where she performed volunteer work, visiting patients, and helped out with fund-raising activities. For three years she served as a "house parent," working with the mentally retarded, helping youths feed themselves, teaching them to take care of their basic needs. When she described her experiences with the youngsters to her friends, she said she felt sorry for them and wished she could take all of them home with her.

"She was just so loving," one friend said about Sylvia White.

Then, the investigators learned, tragedy struck again. "Little Bill," Sylvia's four-year-old stepson, died suddenly on June 21, 1973. As he was playing at home, he apparently choked on a plastic dry-cleaning bag. Sylvia rushed the child to the hospital, but it was too late. He was pronounced dead on arrival. It was three months before the coroner signed the death certificate, ruling it an accidental death.

Billy senior was devastated by the death of his beautiful blond-haired, hazel-eyed son. As the small casket was lowered into the ground, Sylvia stood stoically at her husband's side.

In public, the Whites presented a perfect picture of togetherness as a distinguished and successful couple, but at home, the investigators began to discover, things were not so rosy.

Billy, after having entertained clients and friends at the country club for years, developed a drinking problem, and Sylvia threatened to leave him. She would pack her clothes and load them into her car, only to end up unloading them again as Billy lay down in front of the vehicle so that she could not drive away. For a few days after each episode, husband and wife would give each other the silent treatment. Then things would become "normal" again, with the fighting resuming in full force. Friends told the probers that Sylvia was quick-tempered and "jumped down Billy's throat" at the slightest provocation, even though Billy seemed to be trying very hard to please her.

In 1991, after the six remaining children had moved out on their own, Billy and Sylvia moved one last time. On a corner lot just a few blocks from Billy's insurance office they built a beautiful spacious two-story brick home. The large lots in that quiet and exclusive neighborhood were professionally landscaped, far from the slums of the town. The Whites moved into their "dream house" just before Christmas and celebrated by throwing a large party for family and friends.

Now, just a few weeks later, Billy White was dead. He would never get to enjoy his splendid new home. Family members and friends sat with the grieving widow, offering sympathy, hoping their expressions of love would help, reassuring her and each other that time would get them through the pain, unaware that events were about to take an even more ominous turn.

The murder of one of its most revered citizens alarmed the citizens of Kinston. Named for King George of England, Kinston is located on a bluff above the Neuse River, at the intersection of a major north-south, east-west highway. It sits midway between Raleigh, the state capital, and the Atlantic Ocean. The wealth of the area is derived from tobacco, which was introduced there in the early 1700s. In recent years, however, other cash crops, manufacturing companies and industries have begun edging out tobacco as the money king.

After Billy White's tragic murder made the news, the police received a startling telephone call.

"Oh, my God! Lynwood Taylor has done it!" the individual on the line exclaimed to the investigators.

The informant said that while he'd been in a local bar during the summer of 1991, a drinking buddy of his had shown him a photograph of a wealthy man. The buddy told him that a certain self-employed Kinston carpenter, Lynwood Taylor, had asked if he was interested in helping with a contract killing. The tipster said that the man he saw in the photograph was Billy White, and that Taylor said he'd been offered $20,000 and a vehicle to get rid of a woman's husband for her.

On Tuesday, February 11, 1992, officers picked up Lynwood Taylor for questioning. The 39-year-old down-and-out carpenter was well known to the police as a drug dealer and informer. Taylor wore his dark hair in a ponytail and was often seen riding around town on a Harley-Davidson motorcycle, but his tough-guy stance didn't hold up long under the detectives' intense questioning. Not only did Taylor confess to being involved in White's murder, but he also began pointing the finger of blame at several other individuals, including the grieving and seemingly inconsolable widow White.

Now SBI agents made yet another visit to the White home. During previous interviews, Sylvia White had told them that Billy had no enemies—everyone loved and respected him. Why, the entire town held him in the highest regard! She gave them all the information she had about the mysterious client and the location of the property for which he wanted to purchase insurance immediately.

When SBI Agent Smith began to question the widow about Lynwood Taylor, she denied knowing anyone by that name, or anyone who fit his description.

Back at police headquarters, the investigators had Taylor telephone Sylvia while they taped the conversation. When Taylor told Sylvia that the police were questioning him, he asked her how they had gotten his name. She quickly replied, "I didn't tell the police anything."

Lynwood Taylor was the first to be placed under arrest. Then, during the wee hours of February 13, 1992, a team of officers again went to the White home and took Sylvia White downtown to be charged with Billy's murder.

The next day, as White and Taylor appeared in the Jones County District Court in Trenton for their arraignment, Taylor's 39-year-old uncle, Ernest Basden, was sitting nearby in the courtroom. After the hearing, Basden sought out some officers and confessed that he, too, had taken part in the murder.

Basden, also a Kinston native, was a tall, slender man with a ruddy complexion, brown hair thinning on top, and a scruffy brown mustache. He was an auto mechanic. His meek manner belied the gruesome, coldhearted confession he gave to the investigators.

From Taylor and Basden, the crimefighters heard a story of drugs and greed, of killers with ice water in their veins, and of a woman who seemed driven to get rid of her husband.

Taylor told the detectives that he met the insurance agent's wife through a family member during the summer of 1991 and was hired as a construction worker on the building of the Whites' mansion. He said that Sylvia White approached him immediately and told him that she was looking for a hit man.

She said she wanted to get rid of her husband because he beat her and "made her do bad things in sex." The price she placed on her husband's head was $20,000, with his Chevy minivan thrown in for good measure.

Sylvia White's loyal and devoted manner was deceiving. Taylor soon learned that she was having an affair. Moreover, she didn't want to give up her lover or her new house or the $200,000 her husband's insurance would pay upon his death.

Taylor said that at first he told Mrs. White what she really needed was professional help, that she was crazy, but she continued to pester him. She was determined to have her husband's blood spilled. Taylor said he even approached his uncle, Ernest Basden, about helping him, but Basden dismissed the whole idea as being absurd. Then, sometime around New Year's, Basden reconsidered, saying he would do it because he was "strapped for cash."

Taylor told the probers that Sylvia White masterminded the plot and met with him several times to work out the scenario. She told him to use a made-up name and lure her husband to a desolate spot on the pretext of buying insurance. She even helped him check out the logging road just over the Jones County line. When Taylor argued that Billy would refuse to meet him at such an odd, out-of-the-way place, Sylvia disagreed, saying that her husband was so greedy, he would do anything to sell a policy. She even drew a map to the logging road to insure that her husband did not get lost on his way to his rendezvous with death.

After eight o'clock on the night of January 21, Billy White, Sr., drove his minivan up the dirt road where Lynwood Taylor was waiting. After introducing himself and shaking his intended victim's hand, Taylor excused himself, saying he needed to urinate, and walked towards the tall bushes and trees surrounding the field.

That was Ernest Basden's cue. He picked up a shotgun lying beside the car he and Taylor had driven there, pointed its barrel at the kindly insurance agent, and pulled the trigger. Surprisingly, nothing happened. The gun failed to fire because the hit man had neglected to cock it. Meanwhile, Billy made no attempt to flee, possibly because he was in shock. He just stood there. Basden cocked the shotgun and pulled the trigger again. This time, the weapon fired, the blast catching White in the stomach. After White fell to the ground, Basden reloaded and shot him again.

The second blast hit the victim's chest. The coroner later said that the blood vessels around White's heart were nearly severed. Billy probably lived for some time after being shot, suffering considerable pain before he died.

The two hit men then drove to Taylor's home and reported to Sylvia White that she was now a widow. When she heard that they had not taken her husband's personal items, though, Sylvia demanded that they return to the crime scene and make it look like a robbery. The two men went back in a different car and took the dead man's wallet, checkbook, a ring, and the map.

To get rid of any evidence that could link them to the murder, Taylor and Basden burned the wallet, the map, the clothes they had worn, and even the shotgun shells from the murder weapon. They sawed the shotgun barrel into five pieces and placed them inside a bucket filled with concrete, which they then dumped into the Neuse River.

Several days later, the "grieving" widow made her first "contract" payment of $1,500 for a job well done, promising to turn over the van and the remaining $18,500 after she received her husband's insurance benefits. Then Taylor paid Basden $300 for his part in carrying out the hit.

During his confession, Lynwood Taylor told SBI Agent Smith that the tire impressions the sleuth had taken at the crime scene should match the tires on Taylor's vehicles. Smith swore out an affidavit and obtained a warrant to seize the two cars—a 1969 Chevrolet Camaro and a 1986 Oldsmobile Cutlass.

Meanwhile, police scuba divers began searching the Neuse River and soon found the bucket of concrete containing the embedded pieces of the murder weapon.

Friends of Ernest Basden questioned by the probers described him as always being glum-looking. The sleuths learned that he had been a marijuana user for 15 years, drank heavily, and suffered from kidney stones and arthritis.

Basden apparently thought of his nephew, Taylor, as his best friend, but a defense psychologist would later describe their relationship as something other than friendship, saying that Taylor controlled his uncle and was his chief drug supplier. The probe revealed that before going to the planned murder site that night, Basden had doped himself up—smoking pot, snorting cocaine, gulping down Valium pills, and drinking moonshine whiskey. Later, Basden claimed to have felt nothing when he did the killing, experiencing what psychologists call "dissociation" as he pulled the trigger. It is described as a feeling that one can see his or her own hands move and act without any control by their owner.

Later, the two men would blame each other for insisting on carrying out the contract killing: Taylor said that his uncle needed money; Basden said that it wasn't just the money—he did it to help out his best friend.

Sylvia White, Lynwood Taylor, and Ernest Basden were arrested and charged with first-degree murder and conspiracy to commit murder. All three were incarcerated in the Trenton jail and were denied release on bond.

Taylor's confession provided the investigators with yet another story that would soon shock the citizens of Kinston even more. He said that as he and Sylvia White drove around, scouting for a deserted spot to kill her husband, he told her he didn't want to go through with the murder. He said he told her, "There's no way I can take a man's life." And that, he said, was when Sylvia blurted out, "It's not that hard to do! I had a stepchild—I put a bag over its head until it stopped breathing—and it was better off!"

After hearing this confession, the crimefighters immediately began an intensive investigation into the tragic death of "Little Bill" White, who had choked to death on a large, wadded-up plastic bag.

Six months later, on Thursday, July 16, 1992, Billy White senior's old friend, Sheriff Billy Smith of Lenoir County, announced that Billy junior's little body would be exhumed and transported to the chief medical examiner's office in Chapel Hill.

Billy White, Sr.'s, family was very supportive of Sheriff Smith's investigation into the youngster's untimely death, and old, nagging suspicions kept hidden for 20 years finally surfaced.

When Billy senior married Sylvia, his youngest son was only two years old—an active, energetic, inquisitive toddler who couldn't help messing up his fanatic stepmom's squeaky-clean, orderly house from time to time.

One member of the family remembered taking care of the adorable, blond-haired tot when his parents were out of town. "That little boy was scared to death," the relative said. "If he knocked over something, or spilled some water, he'd go to cryin' and hollerin', 'Don't tell my mama! Don't tell my mama!' He was going to get a whuppin' if she found out!"

The investigators soon learned that Billy senior's kin had quietly harbored a disturbing belief that maybe Little Bill had not died accidentally. They had always wondered whether it had been more than a freak accident. Just a few weeks before his death, young Billy had been burned on his arms. Sylvia told everyone that it happened when the adventurous four-year-old tried to light their outdoor grill by himself.

At the day-care center where Little Bill was taken each day, workers recalled that the child often arrived looking unkempt and dirty, with his clothes wrinkled and his hair uncombed. They never saw him being shown any affection by his stepmother, because someone else always dropped off the tot and picked him up.

On the day Little Bill died, Sylvia White was the only person in the house with him. After the funeral services, several people heard conflicting stories about what actually took place.

One person questioned by the detectives remembered Sylvia saying that she had gone outside to the garage and left Little Bill playing under a table. When Sylvia returned, she heard the boy making odd noises. Realizing that he was choking, she reached into his throat and felt the plastic, but she said she was unable to pull it out.

Another person told the sheriff's detectives that Sylvia said the child had been eating, that she left the room for a moment and when she returned, she found him with his head on the table. She rushed the limp little boy to Lenoir Memorial Hospital, where he was officially pronounced dead.

Even though the tragic incident happened almost 20 years earlier, two emergency room nurses who were there vividly recalled that day. As the wadded plastic was being pulled from the dead child's throat, one nurse said she had thought, "The anatomy of it just didn't make sense. I don't see how in the world anyone could have swallowed it, much less a four-year-old child." She added, "Ever since it happened, I never forgot it."

The second nurse remembered the tragic incident because it had been the first child's death she had experienced during her emergency room service. She recalled the manner of the death as having been "so unusual."

The youngster's death had an adverse effect on the entire White family, eventually leading to conflicts that resulted in some of the children leaving home, but Billy senior steadfastly continued to believe in his wife. When the coroner pronounced the death as accidental, the elder White seemed satisfied and would allow no one to express any suspicions over Sylvia's actions that sad day.

Now, the pathologist's report on August 20, 1992, disagreed with the coroner's 1973 findings about little Billy's death. Dr. John Butts, Chief Medical Examiner, wrote, "I do not believe a child of this age could unintentionally force a plastic bag . . . deep into the airway." He added that there was sufficient reason to suspect a homicide. His report also stated that the child had suffered other abuses in addition to having been badly burned in the weeks just prior to his death. When the small skeleton was X-rayed, an extensive skull fracture, four inches long, was discovered. Any blow that could have caused that large a fracture would have been extremely painful and would probably have knocked the toddler unconscious, leaving him with a very large swelling.

A Lenoir County grand jury met on September 29, 1992, and indicted Sylvia White for a second crime—the 1973 murder of her stepson. One of her coconspirators had testified, "She told me she didn't like that child and wanted that child to die, and she put the bag over the head of that child" until it was dead.

On Monday, March 15, 1993, Ernest Basden was the first of the three defendants to stand trial for Billy White, Sr.'s, murder. The trial was moved from Trenton to Kenansville, more than 40 miles away, because of pretrial publicity. It was held in the Duplin County Courthouse, with Superior Court Judge Henry Stevens III presiding. Prosecutors for the state were District Attorney William "Bill" H. Andrews, whose office covers Jones, Duplin, Sampson and Onslow Counties, and Assistant DA Greg Butler.

Basden's original defense attorney, Tim Merrit, withdrew from the case because of illness and died 11 days before the trial began. The defendant's new court-appointed attorneys were William E. Craft and Chris Henderson.

It took more than two weeks for a 12-person jury with three alternates to be seated.

Standing accused of firing the two fatal shots that killed Billy White, Sr., Ernest Basden pled "not guilty by reason of diminished capacity." His lawyers argued that because of their client's heavy drinking, drug use, chronic pain and depression, he was mentally impaired, which left him incapable of forming the "intent" needed to be found guilty of first-degree murder. Instead, they asked the jury to find Basden guilty of second-degree murder, and not guilty of the conspiracy charge, because he had never met the widow and had no part in planning the crime.

Basden admitted in court that he fired the shotgun, but he claimed that his nephew had talked him into it, promising him half of the $20,000 bounty.

On Monday, April 5, three weeks after the trial began, a seven-man, five-woman jury took only one hour and 15 minutes to decide that the defendant knew what he was doing when he waited on that logging road for the victim to arrive, and that it was his finger that pulled the trigger of that shotgun.

The jury, agreeing with DA Andrews that Ernest Basden "did it for as cold-blooded a reason as you can commit for murder ... for money," found Basden guilty on both charges.

Two days later, after hearing all the aggravating and mitigating circumstances in the case, the jury was again sequestered, this time for the penalty phase. After nine hours of deliberation over a two-day span, the panel agreed that Basden had been under his nephew's spell and that he suffered from emotional distress and other problems, but they decided that none of this excused the fact that he had killed another human being. Their verdict was the death penalty.

As the jury sentenced the convicted man to die, he showed no emotions, a demeanor he had displayed throughout the trial.

Three days later, petite Sylvia White, often described as the "mild-mannered granny," sat in another courtroom, accused of killing her stepson by placing a plastic bag over his head until he suffocated, and then wadding up the bag and stuffing it down his throat.

Because of the extensive publicity, the trial was moved more than 50 miles away from Kinston to the Martin County Courthouse in the town of Williamston. Superior Court Judge William C. Griffin presided, with District Attorney Donald Jacobs and Assistant DA Imelda Pate handling the prosecution.

The prosecution's chief hurdle would be to prove that Little Bill's death, once ruled an accident, had instead been a homicide. DA Jacobs told the jury, "This case is going to turn on physical evidence [the exhumed body] and a confession [the stepmother's confession to her hired gun]."

On Monday, April 12, 1993, most of the potential jurors who were questioned said that they had read stories about the case, but they had formed no opinions as to Sylvia White's guilt or innocence. One juror, a respiratory therapist, was accepted by both sides because of her knowledge about children's tracheas (windpipes). It took only one day to select a panel.

During what proved to be a one-week trial, Sylvia White sat primly between her two attorneys, Robert Whitley and Eugene Jenkins of Kinston; she wore simple but elegant dresses with almost no adornments. Her pale face appeared devoid of makeup, her short brown hair was simply curled, and she wore huge glasses that dwarfed her small face.

A former chief medical examiner for the state testified that, in her opinion, "the bag had been forced into the [child's] throat," and that it was possible that the child had been suffocated beforehand.

The defense lawyers attacked the credibility of the prosecution's star witness, Lynwood Taylor, arguing that he was only testifying in an attempt to avoid the same punishment his uncle had received for murdering Billy White, Sr.

With his ponytail gone and dressed in a three-piece suit, Lynwood Taylor raised his voice, pointed at the defendant from where he sat on the witness stand, and declared, "That woman right there is responsible for me being here today, for my uncle being on death row! I told that woman to get professional help! Tell 'em, Mrs. White! . . . She told me she killed that boy!"

Ernest Basden was brought from death row to testify so that the jury would hear his nephew's story corroborated.

During closing statements, Assistant Prosecutor Imelda Pate told the jury why Little Bill had been murdered. It "was a planned killing by someone who wanted to get rid of an annoying child," she said.

In his turn, Prosecutor Jacobs contended that if the coroner had done his job in 1973, the suspicious circumstances of the tot's death would have been recognized 20 years earlier. Jacobs said about the coroner, "He comes in, gets the plastic out of the boy's throat, he leaves and doesn't do his paperwork!"

On Friday morning, April 16, after less than two hours of deliberation, the jury found Sylvia White guilty of murdering her stepson. She was subsequently sentenced to life in prison. The death penalty was not an option because North Carolina did not have capital punishment in 1973, when the murder was committed.

Sylvia White was led out of the courtroom without handcuffs to wait in Sheriff George Ayers's office for her prison paperwork to be completed. There, she slipped unnoticed into a rest room and locked the bathroom door. When a prison matron called to her and received no response, sheriff's deputies had to break down the door. They discovered that Sylvia had attempted suicide by trying to swallow a plastic bag containing several white pills. Sheriff Ayers pulled the blood-covered bag out of the woman's throat and had her taken to a local hospital by ambulance.

After being examined, White was handcuffed. Sheriff Ayers wasn't taking any more chances on another suicide attempt. He had the prisoner's handcuffs shackled to a leather belt fastened around her waist.

As she left the hospital, White told reporters that her unsuccessful suicide attempt was further proof that she was not guilty of murder. But others saw it differently, saying it was indisputable proof that a four-year-old child could not have stuffed a large plastic bag down his own throat.

Lynwood Taylor was the second defendant to be tried for the murder of Billy White, Sr. His trial, too, was moved from Trenton in Jones County because of pretrial publicity. Jury selection began on Monday, November 8, 1993, in the Sampson County Courthouse, with Superior Court Judge Henry Stevens presiding. On Friday, November 19, after almost two weeks, 12 jurors and three alternates were finally chosen.

Taylor's defense attorneys, Rivers Johnson and Louis Foy, Jr., had filed a pretrial motion to suppress the statement Taylor had given to lawmen in February 1992, when he was arrested. Judge Stevens did not rule on that matter until after the jurors were seated. He finally denied the defense motion, ruling that Taylor's confession about taking part in the murder plot could be part of the prosecution's evidence.

When the trial reconvened on the following Monday, November 22, the defense attorneys had a surprise for the court: they withdrew their client's not guilty plea, saying that Taylor now wished to plead guilty.

Taylor's sentencing has been postponed until after he testifies against the woman he says hired him to kill her husband. The confessed killer may face the death penalty or life in prison and a maximum of 30 years on the conspiracy charge.

Sylvia White's trial on the murder charge and masterminding the conspiracy to kill Bill White, Sr., has not been scheduled at the time this issue went to press. Law enforcement officials suggest that it may be sometime later in 1994 or 1995.

Meanwhile, Sylvia Howard Taylor Ipock White is currently serving a life sentence in Raleigh's Women's Prison; Ernest West Basden sits on North Carolina's death row; and James Lynwood Taylor is in jail, awaiting Sylvia's second trial and his own sentencing.

Billy Carlyle White, Sr., Bill II, and Leslie Elton Ipock,

Sylvia's second husband, are all buried in Kinston's Pinelawn Cemetery, just a stone's throw away from each other.

UPDATE:

Sylvia Ipock White was found guilty of second degree-murder in the death of her husband, Billy Carlyle White. She was sentenced to a term of life plus 50 years, to be served on the expiration of her life sentence for the murder of her stepson.

APPENDIX

"Sexy Bride's Honeymoon Of Horrors" *True Detective*, January 1994

"Tina Killed Mom To Wine, Dine, and Get Back Her Ex-Beau!" *Front Page Detective*, August 1994

"Surgeon Caught A Bullet Between His Eyes!" *Master Detective*, May 1994

"Kissing Cousins Killed For Kinky Thrills!" *Master Detective*, November 1993

"Twisted Trio's Rx For Murder: Witchcraft" *Master Detective*, November 1994

"Bloody Welcome For The Returning Sailor" *True Detective*, December 1992

"He Gave Them A Lift—They Slit His Throat!" *Inside Detective*, September 1994

"Spurned Seductress Snuffed The Three-Timing Romeo!" *Inside Detective*, May 1994

"Ruthless Lovers' Bloody Valentine To Elvie" *Master Detective*, May 1994

"Drugstore Cowboys Throttled The Runaway" *Master Detective*, May 1994

"Pizza Man Became A Human Jigsaw Puzzle!" *Front Page Detective*, November 1994

"Tulsa's Man-Hating Teen Left Her Date Floating In A Pond!" *Inside Detective*, April 1994

"Lethal Lesbians' Matricide Plot" *Official Detective*, April 1994

"Who Hacked Charlie's Head Off?" *Front Page Detective*, June 1993

"Pregnant Came The Teen Slasher!" *Master Detective*, December 1993

"California's Greedy Couple Scared Their Victim To Death!" *Official Detective*, December 1994

"Divorce Was Not Enough For The Blonde Bombshell!" *Master Detective*, April 1995

"The Susan Smith Case: A Nation Mourns Two 'Small Sacrifices' " *Master Detective*, May 1995

" 'Thelma & Louise' Ran Down Their Gal Pal Over & Over!" *Front Page Detective*, August 1994

"Deadly Teen Lovers In The Mesquite Flats Campground" *Official Detective*, April 1995

"New Jersey Gal Pal's Prey Was Bailed Out & Bumped Off!" *Inside Detective*, May 1995

"Tulsa's Lady Macbeth Couldn't Wash Away Her Crime!" *Crime Inside Detective*, February 1995

"Two Greedy Blondes Bludgeoned Billy" *True Detective*, August 1994

"Texas's Murder By 'Prophet' " *Master Detective*, February 1995

"Florida's Notorious Couch Potato Case: Was It Murder Or Suicide?" *True Detective*, December 1992

"North Carolina Homicide Puzzle: Did A Black Widow Claim Three Lives?" *Inside* Detective, February 1995

HORRIFYING TRUE CRIME
FROM PINNACLE BOOKS